Matthew Dunn. Bestselling author of the 'Spycatcher 'and
'Ben Sign 'series. Former MI6 Intelligence Officer.

'David Bickford has used his inside knowledge and experience of
Britain's Security & Intelligence Agencies to write an immensely
readable modern thriller. Placed against a background of
contemporary international politics and intrigue, it is a fast
moving read which is both compelling and frightening.'
Richard Taylor-Norton. The Guardian

'A tightly wound plot of intrigue, corruption and the terrible
dilemmas involved in fighting the war on terror. Bickford uses
his inside knowledge of intelligence to crackling effect.'
Anne McElvoy . Evening Standard.

'A page-turning story with a sophisticated plot not to be missed.'
Elizabeth Rindskopf-Parker. Former General Counsel, CIA

'Katya combines just enough professionally informed realism
with great plot and character development to hold a former
intelligence officer's attention-a great read as only the Brits can
do it.'
Paul Redmond. Chief, CIA Counterintelligence, Retired.

ALSO BY DAVID BICKFORD

KATYA

KATYA - The Informer

The Face of Tomorrow

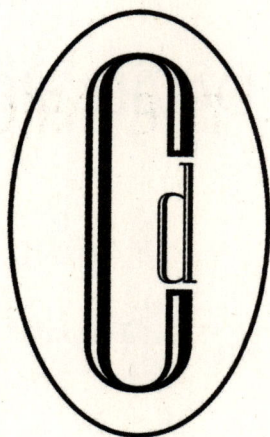

www.coinkydink.co.uk

KATYA

KATYA – THE INFORMER

DAVID BICKFORD

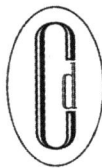

For my beautiful wife Cary, brilliant co-writer and conspirator–
so much more than a diamond.

THE AUTHOR

Under Secretary of State and Legal Director to the British Intelligence Agencies, MI5 & MI6. David spent his working life diving into the cold murky seas of terrorism, espionage and organised crime. At the forefront of the battle against international terrorism he was among the first to predict its onslaught. David is recognised, both in the Agencies where he was made Companion Order of the Bath for his work, and in the business he now runs, for his ground-breaking solutions to defeat the terrorists and international organised criminals who threaten us.

A NOTE FROM THE AUTHOR

Although I worked in the Intelligence and Security Agencies, the characters and plot in Katya are entirely a work of my and Cary's imagination. That is not to say that I would not like to write about those who work in intelligence. As their legal director, I have nothing but admiration for the officers who do this work. Working closely with them, in the tunnels of secrecy, fighting terrorists and corruption he saw their dangers and trials and their courage and imagination as they overcame them. The qualities and sacrifices that lie behind this extraordinary work.

I really hope you enjoyed this book and thank you for supporting me on my journey from the Intelligence community to the world of writing.

ONE

As soon as she burst through the open gates of the Russian military airfield, Katya knew she was in trouble. The only aircraft standing on the concrete apron was an ancient Russian Polikarpov, smoke billowing from exhausts that had seen service on the front in World War Two. She turned to look at her pursuers–three balaclava'd Federal Security men, followed by two of the gate guards. They were not more than two hundred meters behind her, weapons readied. If they caught her she'd be interrogated and the Federal Security Service methods were designed to be especially brutal for women. After that. . . after that. . .

She raced to the aircraft, two men in white overalls emerged from behind the stubby engine cowl, shouting, waving their arms. Without stopping she barged into them, leapt onto the cantilevered wing, slid into the cockpit. Feverishly she looked over the controls. Yoke, throttle, rudder pedals. She looked forward, over the engine cowling, through the spinning propeller. Was horrified she couldn't see the ground in front of her. One of the men in overalls started to climb onto the wing. Frantically, she engaged the throttle, the propeller thrusting the aircraft forward. He flailed his arms and slid away. Leaning out of the cockpit she could just see in front of her. The FSB men had nearly caught up and were rushing to cut her off. Working the throttle, yoke and rudder she accelerated down a concrete taxiway.

The old fighter-plane was fast but clumsy. What was the take-off speed? Suddenly she saw the taxiway ended at a low maintenance shed. She pulled back the yoke slightly as a test. The plane yawed, stuck wilfully to the ground. The shed seemed to grow larger. Gritting her teeth against rising fear, she pulled the yoke again. Lurching to the right the aircraft lumbered off the taxiway. She fought the urge to grip the yoke tight, gently used the controls to start a slow turn over the airfield to follow the river Neva and out to sea. Below her she saw the faces of the FSB goons–shouting. She laughed in relief. Looked ahead. She was heading straight for the Troitskiy bridge.

She had no option. The aircraft was too low to pull up over the looming steel structure. Keeping the throttle open she pushed hard on the right pedal and swung the aircraft to face a gap between the huge upright pylons. She felt the controls turn to lead, fighting stability as the plane slumped down towards the black water. With seconds before an inevitable crash she forced the stick forward. The aircraft lurched, straightened, made it through the gap and under the bridge.

The plane would survive but her future as an intelligence agent would be finished before it had even started.

TWO

It was a tense moment in the conference room of the G8 Intelligence Agency Headquarters. The issue being discussed by the Directors was vitally important. Was the new recruit, Katya Petrovna, ready to be sent on her first operation as a G8 agent–to infiltrate and break open a suspected Russian *mafiya* operating near the Black Sea.

The large square room contained a state-of-the-art steel conference table and the latest desk top computers. Two large wall mounted plasma screens showed pictures of Katya Petrovna. Her violet-blue eyes and long, sweeping auburn hair seemed to radiate from the screens, intensifying an indefinable electric energy in her.

John Hammond, the Agency's Director General, looked at the pictures as if they could provide an answer to the enigma that was Katya.

He turned to Lev Leviatski, the Russian Director, who was sitting opposite him–an indestructible ex-KGB officer. 'Do you think she's ready, Lev? This is a Russian *mafiya* we're talking about, she makes a rash move and she's dead.'

Lev had known Katya since she was a child growing up in Moscow. He was fiercely protective of her. 'She's dynamite,' he said simply. Then, as if to emphasise his words, he drew on one of the Abdullah 7 cigarettes he always smoked. 'She has great courage and a natural charm. But, I've found that on training operations, if driven to it, she can be highly manipulative. Extremely persuasive. Certainly dangerous.'

Walt Sable, his American counterpart sitting beside him, immediately became difficult, his Yale accent as sharp as cut glass. He leaned across the conference table towards John to enforce his point. 'Those are certainly the makings for a G8 agent. But Katya's not qualified to take on any operation as important as this until she's had more training. She's undisciplined–look at that stunt in St Petersburg when she flew that Polikarpov under the Troitskiy bridge . . .'

John Hammond's strength was his icy self-control and to him either Katya was sufficiently trained and capable of doing the job or she wasn't. 'She will certainly be enthusiastic. But if you're really saying she's undisciplined, Walt, then my concern is that these failings might literally prove lethal for her– '

Lev cut across him, smoke from his cigarette gushing from his mouth, propelled by his disagreement. 'Walt, that aircraft stunt was in 2001–a year ago–when she was training with the Russian Federal Security Service. Anyway, don't you forget FSB training is tough. She came out top of her year. Of course, she's ready.'

Walt's shaven head crinkled into a frown, which it did most often when office banter softened the dangers of the agents' work– his standards were high. 'She rushes her fences,' he said sharply. 'She doesn't calculate risk.'

'Katya Petrovna can do it.' Lev insisted. 'She's Russian and she's finished her training . . . I kept in touch personally with her FSB trainer, Andrei Savin, and he classified her outstanding. No surprise there–we're talking about a woman who survived running with the street kids in Moscow when she was a teenager.' Lev had endless informative connections, perhaps necessary to a man who'd survived years of existence in the maze that was KGB politics. 'I say we send her to Russia to find out what's going on,' he said decidedly.

'The FSB relegated her to the Federal Immigration Service

because she's headstrong and impulsive,' Walt replied sarcastically, then added a telling point, 'Russia needs every worker and tourist they can get into the country, they aren't refusing anyone entry at the moment–her *only* job was to rubber stamp visa applications. So, what sort of responsibility did she have?'

Lev was true Russian and, with his combination of magnetism and doggedness, he wasn't letting go. He jammed his cigarette end into the ashtray in front of him. 'You're forgetting her father was a KGB Colonel who'd been disowned by them. It was she who paid the price for that.' He saw Walt open his mouth; interrupted him. 'Have you seen her handle a large sailboat in a force ten gale on the Black Sea? Well I have. Her father used to force her out alone in all weathers to toughen her up–teach her to survive. He was a two-time bastard, but he had guts and determination and, I tell you, she's inherited them. She's strong, determined, fearless. If anyone has the guts to take on a Russian *mafiya* and find out all we want to know about it, she has.'

There was a silence as both men sat back, as if to determine the effect of their salvoes on each other.

John Hammond thought about the two hundred highly trained G8 agents who worked in the huge steel-framed warehouse that housed G8's Headquarters in the heart of Basingstoke, England or who worked in the field all over the world. Their job was planning and executing the destruction of vicious organised international criminals and terrorists. Fighting an underworld whose deadly trade netted trillions of dollars a year and was threatening the economic stability and, even, the existence of democracy. These were the people Katya would be sent to deal with–dangerous, lethal. Lev and Walt had highlighted the difficulties Katya would face but they'd left the problem of whether she was ready to become operational still unresolved.

He took a moment to study each of his fellow Directors. They had all been together for two years since the G8 nations had set up the Agency in 2000 when the effects of the end of the Cold War were beginning to be felt. The running down of intelligence and law enforcement activity in the afterglow of peace had encouraged organised criminals and terrorists to the point where they were devastating and threatening their countries' existence. He relied on these two men to help him guide G8's fight against them.

Lev, at 50 with grey hair above a creased face was the eldest of the G8 Directors. Whatever the crisis, John found Lev's humour never far distant. Yet he was the most duplicitous and calculating man he'd encountered. Walt, on the other hand was 35, had majored in politics and law out of Yale. Precise and cautious he'd made his mark as a staffer in Washington then as an FBI Assistant Director. Together they made a formidable duo.

John knew he could side with either of these men and they would have accepted his decision. He knew they trusted his judgment. But the question before them at this moment was too critical for anything other than a unanimous vote. Was Katya Petrovna *really* ready to be sent on this particularly dangerous operation?

He made up his mind, broke in on the silence. 'Let's have her up here and talk to her.' He pressed a button on his console which connected him to the Tac Room and spoke into the mic, 'Is that Ami?' He paused. 'Good. Would you find Katya and ask her to come to the directors' conference room, right away. Thanks.'

THREE

Ami Orello–a watchful and careful G8 agent, a fine analyst–was slightly nervous of Katya. They were both in their mid-twenties and had joined G8 on the same day in 2002. They were good friends, played tennis together, often meeting up for a drink after a long day's work. She admired Katya's untiring vivacity and drive, but she found Katya's love of extreme danger disturbing. Everyone knew about the FSB Board of Inquiry into Katya's stunt–when she'd flown her aircraft under a bridge in St Petersburg–and now there was a rumour she'd been flashed by the Traffic Police last night doing 150 mph down the M3 motorway from London to Basingstoke.

As Ami walked through the Tac Room towards Katya's workstation, these thoughts were pushed aside while she took in the nerve centre of the organisation. It never ceased to thrill her even after six months of working here.

The Tactical Operations Room was the biggest space inside the warehouse that was G8HQ. It housed the highly trained multilingual agents, who fought transnational terrorism and organised crime. Here they planned operations to destroy major criminals, terrorists, people traffickers, narcotics cartels and moneylaunderers who dealt in murder, kidnapping, extortion, pornography, prostitution.

Most of the Tac Room floor space was filled with work stations which faced eight huge plasma screens fixed onto the front wall which was forty feet high. The rear wall consisted of three balconies where yet more stations faced the screens. To one side of the massive room was a bank of three Paternoster lifts, their open platforms constantly revolving to enable a stream of agents to travel between floors quickly and efficiently.

The atmosphere was charged as the agents collected, analyzed and collated intelligence reports from informants and electronic surveillance around the world– operating clandestinely amongst the most vicious, terrifying criminals. *Mafiyas*, *Tongs*, *Cartels*. Carrying out G8'sole objective–to bring their targets to justice. They attacked corrupt bankers, lawyers, journalists, judges and, even, governments who colluded with the criminals–whose trade netted trillions of dollars each year and was threatening global economic stability and, even, the existence of stable government.

The plasma screens remorselessly showed the operational results in a maze of coloured lines and patterns which constantly flashed and changed as the agents fed in vital information and intelligence from their personal computers which ultimately connected the criminals to their crimes.

Katya's work station was at the far end of a row and she was intensely studying one of the plasma screens which displayed a shifting body of intelligence tracking her target. She fed in some new information on her computer. It was immediately analysed by the G8 central control computers. She watched the result come up on the plasma screen–a red coloured line flashed across the screen to connect to a blue square with a name printed below.

Ami hurried over to her. 'Katya, you're wanted in the directors' conference room.'

Katya kept her eyes on the screen. 'Thanks, Ami.' She typed a command on her console keypad.

'Right away,' Ami blurted.

Katya frowned slightly.

'Katya, the DG said right away.'

Katya swore lightly in Russian. 'I've just cracked how Obolov laundered the proceeds from his fraud on those pensioners. You know he had the nerve to filter that cash through eight separate banks–a classic starburst. The money ended up in a cousin's family trust in the Isle of Man.'

Tearing her eyes away from the screen, Katya jumped up. 'Thanks Ami I'll go straight away–let's have a coffee later!' she added. Her long stride took her past the rows of agents at their work stations as she headed for the paternoster that would carry her up to the third floor and the Conference Room.

Ami watched her go. She rather hoped she'd been sent to find Katya about her speeding offence and not a plan to send them both out on a joint operation. She valued her life and, however much she and the other agents admired her, this dynamic, irrepressible woman had no regard for danger.

FOUR

Katya stepped off the paternoster and walked across a dimly lit hall towards an unpainted steel door marked "Conference Room." She stopped there, feeling uncertain.

When she had been recruited by G8 she had immediately noticed that the Agency demanded a lot more discipline of its agents than she'd experienced while training with the FSB–well, not discipline precisely but self-control, responsibility for one's actions. In the FSB that sort of discipline, in a hangover from the days of the KGB, was ignored in favour of taking any opportunity possible to advance one's career or line one's pockets. So, her speeding offence would have been of little moment unless it could have been used by someone to their advantage. She was sure that that was not the case in the eyes of the G8 Directors and, if her offence had come to their ears, she could be in trouble.

The thought decided her–she must tackle the problem head on. Appear confident. She smoothed back her hair with one hand, straightened her loose-fitting white top, tucking it quickly into the waistband of her black Whistles jeans. A neat appearance was the first requirement of a bold approach.

She didn't knock but opened the door and marched purposefully into the room. She briefly took in the long conference table and the Russian and American Directors facing her. She then focussed on the Director General sitting at the head of the table, looking down at a document lying in front of him. He looked up to face her, his sandy coloured hair catching the light from the overhead neon lighting. She saw he was still wearing a chunky cardigan and open neck shirt, the same get-up he'd worn when he'd taken the lead in her final interview. She'd thought then that he was young, early 30s. And from the experience of her training with the FSB, she'd put him down as laid-back, someone she could manipulate. She'd quickly learned that that was a façade, hiding a dominant and powerful personality. Now, seeing him in the formality of a Directors' meeting she was struck by an aura, a magnetism about him and there seemed to be unlimited energy behind those deep grey eyes.

She gathered herself, took a breath. 'Good morning. Katya Petrovna reporting as you requested.'

Lev immediately encouraged his protégé. 'Thank you for coming so promptly, Katya. You needn't be so formal with us.'

She felt reassured. Lev had always supported her. He'd known her family ever since her turbulent childhood days.

Walt wasn't going to let Lev take the lead. He nodded curtly in her direction. 'Ms Petrovna.'

John told her to sit down next to him. He then said evenly. 'Thank you for coming, Katya. We have been discussing your future. . .'

Katya didn't hear the rest of what he was saying. His words hit her like boiling water. Oh god they *were* treating this speeding on the motorway seriously. She was being fired. Instinctively, she knew she mustn't show fear. She looked at Lev. 'I wasn't familiar with that vehicle, I had no idea what . . .'

John raised his hand to stop her. 'We're not talking about your training reports, Katya. You're here to answer a question we have.' He paused to see her response.

Katya stayed silent. Her life at her home in Moscow with a

harsh father and a dilettante mother had taught her never to ask a question if it wasn't necessary.

'The background is this,' John said. 'We've had a report from Customs at Heathrow airport this morning concerning a Russian woman on a flight from Kropse–'

'I know Kropse,' burst in Katya. 'It's a port town on the Black Sea in Russia. I used to sail there.'

'We're aware of that,' Walt said, dryly.' Not, in my opinion, that it helps much.'

John continued as if the interruption hadn't occurred. 'The woman was carrying an Attaché case stuffed with a quarter of a million dollars.'

'All in hundreds or in various denominations?' Katya asked.

'Good question.' Lev thoughtfully lit another Abdullah. 'I told you, Walt, Katya knows the *mafiya's* trademarks. And a quarter of a million dollars cash coming into London from a Russian casino looks like *mafiya* to me.'

John looked sharply at him. 'What you're really telling us is that a new *mafiya* could be trying to open up a base in the UK? If so, that spells imminent danger.'

Lev laid it out. 'Cross border crime–murder for hire, arms, prostitution, child trafficking, drugs, moneylaundering. You name it.'

'Spreading here, to London.'

'Spreading everywhere.'

'Then we've got to stop them–immediately.' John set the objective.

Walt put forward a suggestion which he hoped would avoid tasking Katya as operational. 'Make a search on the Web. We can find out who we're dealing with.'

'Our tech team tried that. There's nothing,' John replied. 'I spoke to them and they're as frustrated as I am. These search engines look good but they've only been going since the mid 90s and they're not programmed for this sort of information. Not much help.'

Walt looked thoughtful. 'Satellite surveillance?'

'Tried that too. But Tech say it's still too unreliable to cover Kropse. And they're right. Look what happened to our agent in Columbia when that satellite reported back the wrong coordinates . . . They said give it a few more years and it will be invaluable but not now.'

'So, it's boots on the ground,' Walt said disapprovingly. He was wedded to tech.

John continued calmly, his grey eyes studying Katya intently, 'From what the woman told customs at the airport, the money was given to her by someone in a casino in Kropse. She was to have been met at Heathrow. She didn't know who by.'

'There are two ways to follow up this information,' Lev added. 'Either from enquiries at Heathrow or from Kropse.' He pointed his cigarette at Katya. 'Which would you choose?'

'Only if you were operational,' Walt clarified.

They watched her as she thought about it. 'There would be no helpful lead at Heathrow,' she said. 'I mean, who would we be looking for. If this woman is being truthful there's no lead. And she knows if she does tell us she's dead–the *mafiya,* whichever one it is, will hunt her down.'

John nodded. 'You're right. We've placed the woman in witness protection.'

Katya looked straight at Walt's face. 'So, the answer's in Kropse.' She rushed on. 'Whatever you say, Sir, I am ready. I'm Russian, I know the area and I can handle *mafiya.*'

'I must emphasize that Katya is ideal for the job of infiltrating this casino if it is run by *mafiya.* She mixed with the *mafiya* in their Moscow cellar nightclubs in her teens.' Lev fixed his eyes on her. 'Didn't you.'

'Well, I knew a number of them, knew how they operated, but I wouldn't say I mixed with them exactly.'

'That's an honest answer.' John interjected. 'Being honest with us is vital if you are to become operational.'

Katya jumped at his words. 'You want me to become operational?' She heard the excitement rising in her voice, 'I can't wait.'

'No. This is what we're discussing, Ms Petrovna, not what we want, or at least not what *I* want. I don't think you're ready,' Walt said sharply, cutting her down to size. 'What is your cover, if you do go?' His mouth was turned down to emphasise his doubt that she'd even thought of this before charging in with her offer.

'We had gambling in the beer cellars when I was in Moscow. I couldn't bet much because I didn't have the money but I watched. From what I saw I don't have the experience to go for a job. Croupiers and hosts and stuff need experience.'

'There you are then, you don't have a cover.' Walt waved his hand in satisfied dismissal.

'You don't need experience to bet.' Everyone looked at Lev. 'She's the daughter of a KGB Colonel. Dead, maybe, but well known. It's common knowledge KGB senior officers made a lot of money on the side–' He stopped as he saw everyone look away. 'No. I was not one of them–I came here instead.'

'No-one thinks that, Lev,' said Walt forcefully. 'You're just playing the sympathy card. You needn't. I've watched Katya here, seen how she behaves . . . and,' he crumbled, 'yes, you're right, she might be ready to be operational.' Still not quite certain, he looked across at John a question in his eyes.

'I never had any doubt, Walt, but I've seen her training here and you haven't.' John turned to Katya. 'You will go as a punter. Your task is to find out if the casino is passing on criminal cash and if it is who is behind it and how it is being done. Nothing more, understand? This is your first operation and the danger you'll be in will be more than in doing the job, it will be in your going too far, pushing the boundaries. Something you have a reputation for.'

Katya stayed silent, knowing that any protest could make the Director General, or DG as John Hammond was known, change his mind. And, as the question of her speeding at 150mph hadn't come up there was no point in prolonging this interview. 'Thank you,' she said, meekly. 'I will get started straight away if that is alright with you?'

He nodded and she stood up, walked towards the door.

'See Guy Leeming in Tech,' Lev called out after her. 'He's into tracking gambling cash, he'll be able to give you good advice.'

FIVE

Katya climbed on the paternoster. She was so deep in thought she failed to notice the lift was passing the Tac Room floor. It was too late to jump out without getting caught between the floors. She felt foolish as she had to wait while the mechanism took her two floors down before winding around and bringing her back up to the Tac Room. This gave her time to remember Lev's support and, then, Walt's obvious opposition to her going operational and finally John Hammond's cool warning, telling her she was headstrong. She felt her temper rising as she got off at the Tac Room floor. There was no way she was going to be pushed around by the G8 Directors doubting her ability. She may only have been a visa clerk in the FSB but not getting a promotion had been entirely the fault of her father. He'd stupidly disobeyed the KGB's orders during the Chechen war and had tried to negotiate a ceasefire with a Chechen leader whose idea of negotiation was to publicly execute him. As his daughter, she'd personally paid the penalty for that.

Head-hunted by G8, she'd romped through her G8 training, coming out top in her year, and now it was time the Directors realised they had a fully qualified operational agent on their hands.

Guy Leeming, one of the specialists in the Information Technology Team felt these vibes radiating from Katya as she jumped off the paternoster and strode towards him. He'd heard about her mercurial approach both to life and to work and she made him feel uneasy. In his late twenties, he was a reserved man, an honours graduate in science, used to hiding behind algorithms and computer programs. Handling people was not his forte.

Katya saw the anxious expression on Guy's face and his instinctive step backwards as she came up to him. She burst out laughing. 'Oh god, am I as bad as that? I'm sorry.'

He grinned, sheepishly. 'Yes. But no need to apologise. We all get bad days here.' The soft burr of his West Indian accent didn't disguise his sense of concern. 'Tea?'

Like most Russians she took jam instead of sugar with her tea. Her determined chin went up as she anticipated yet another jibe about what was seen by most of her colleagues as a strange habit.

'No, no,' he said urgently. 'I only meant would you like–'

Katya interrupted, cut across him. 'And to think I came to you for some help!' She smiled at him and he watched her violet-blue eyes crease at the corners as she said, 'I'll have tea later. Can we start again?'

"Mercurial" was right, he thought. She was tall and beautiful too, but more important she could relate to people. She had that essential essence which made communication easy. *"Simpatico"* as the Spanish and Italians called it. Although, he laughed to himself, the same word in the original Greek meant *"suffering together."*

'Lev sent me to see you,' she continued. 'He– '

'Yes, he's just told me. You want some information on gambling–casinos and that sort of thing.'

'No, I know about that.' She shook her head, a strand of auburn hair falling across her eyes. She put up her hand, brushed it away impatiently. 'Could you come up with some betting system I can use, that's what I want to know. Something I can break the bank with– you know–get noticed.'

'Why?'

She was disconcerted by his terseness. Lev had obviously briefed him so he must know the aim of her operation.

Guy looked amused. 'Lev told me the owner or owners are probably *mafiya*.'

'Yes, I know.' She saw a hint of a sceptical smile on his face. 'I can handle them.'

'Tell me which *mafiya* casino has had its bank broken?'

She stared at him, searching for an answer.

He didn't wait. 'If you really think you can handle them, you should know that.'

She mentally kicked herself. It was exactly as the DG had said, she had charged in thoughtlessly, underestimated Guy–seen him simply as a maths analyst. A means to her getting a viable gambling system. She hadn't considered that he might know about the Russian *mafiya* casinos.

'None of them,' he said. 'No *mafiya* casino will ever allow its bank to be broken. The odds are fixed to prevent that happening. And if a punter starts making too much money, a casino host either distracts them or the fix goes in.' He took off his black horn-rimmed spectacles and rubbed the lenses absent-mindedly on his shirt sleeve. 'No, you'll not get to the owner that way,' he told her firmly.

'So, what do I do?' The question sounded horribly plaintive to her ears.

'Just play the tables. You're a novice so you'll lose eventually and– '

'I can't do that, I'll be using G8 money.'

He ran his hand through his tight curly black hair. She was extraordinary–perfectly willing to risk her neck taking on a Russian *mafiya* but cavilled at losing a chunk of G8 cash.

'Best thing you can do though. If they spot you as a beginner they might be tempted to fleece you. And if that leads you into debt you might find a way of paying them back which involves casino work.'

'Sex, you mean?'

To his surprise Guy saw her eyes flash angrily in the bright light.

'No. I don't do that. I use my wits. Well, if you won't give me a system I'll have to make it up as I go along.'

He watched her go as he'd watched other overconfident rookie agents go off on their first op. He took in her long stride, the determined tilt of her head, the sheer vitality of her. She'd learn, and fast, he thought.

The space where G8 agents went to relax was known simply as the Bag Room. The name was of unknown origin but was taken to explain that the tea and coffee served there came in bags only– the DG kept G8's budget for operations not frills. The room was painted in light sky blue and soft peach colours. HR had decided that pastel shades and cool lighting would give the agents a chance to unwind. There was a central area where groups of people could relax–but not for too long–on chairs and sofas. On one side of the space there was a café area and along the other walls were bench seats and tables for eating. Three doors led to the Tac Room and other working areas. It was the only space in the warehouse where the walls and furniture were not steel or painted grey.

Ami was sitting on one of the sofas, her legs curled beneath her. She got up as she saw Katya coming towards her–the coloured beads in her plaited jet-black hair rattling a little as she did so. 'Over here!' she called. 'And I've ordered you some tea and that disgusting jam you like to put in it. Ugg . . . How you can drink that stuff is quite beyond me!'

There was laughter in Katya's eyes as she came up to her saying, 'It's very Russian– you don't know what you're missing!'

As they both sat down a waiter came over with the tea. Katya put her mobile on the low table in front of them. Ami poured out the tea, handed Katya a cup. She looked wistful as she said, 'I'd love to go to Russia. I hear its really cool now, great night clubs and chic boutiques. When my father went to Moscow from Ghana, as a student, he said it was very Communist, very grey and very dull.'

Katya stirred the jam into her tea saying, 'Hmm. Yes, things are changing. I remember it in the 90s in my teens–life with the street kids–there was western jazz in the cellar cafes, knock off designer clothes, all colour and excitement and expectation in the air, none of the gloom your father went through. Mine too,' she added reflectively. She took a sip of the tea and put the cup down. 'But then there were also the *mafiyas*. You had to be on your guard and wide awake to cope with them.'

'Did you operate against them when you were in the FSB?' Ami asked.

'No,' was Katya's short answer.

Ami was surprised at the abrupt reply. She was about to probe further when she caught the expression in Katya's eyes, dark violet, stormy blue. She hastily changed the subject. 'Have you been–' she looked mischievous, 'On the carpet for that speeding on the M3 last night?'

Katya relaxed as she laughingly replied, 'What for doing 150 mph in the middle of the night on an empty motorway? You're kidding.'

'You're not in St Petersburg now, Katya,' Ami said with mock severity. 'You need to watch out or you'll lose your licence.'

Katya looked at her, still with the laugh in her eyes. 'You're a great friend but don't worry, I won't get caught again. No. It's more exciting than that. I've been made operational. I'm– '

She got no further. Lev had arrived silently at her shoulder. 'Katya. A quick word.'

Ami got up, mumbled something about the Tac Room and hastily left.

As Lev sat down Katya saw his eyes go to the mobile in front of her.

He coughed out a cloud of cigarette smoke. 'What's that?' he rasped.

'My mobile. I'm going to set up a secure messaging system.' She picked it up and tapped the keypad. 'It's simple. I type my message in messages then press the star key rather than send. The message will automatically be encrypted and squirted to G8. For incoming messages a sun sign will come up on my screen. I press the hash key to download the message.'

Lev waved away a stream of smoke. 'Throw it away. They don't allow mobiles on the gaming floor in casinos–to stop card counting and math calculations. It'll be taken from you as you go onto the gaming floor. These people are *mafiya* so they'll check it electronically. They'll find the gimmick and you'll be in trouble.' He sniffed loudly as she was about to interrupt. 'And no, if you're gambling you'll have to leave it where you are staying and they'll check it there. Just throw it away. Now.'

'So, I'll be completely my own?'

'No. We'll communicate the old way. The *mafiya* believe all our surveillance and communication are electronic these days–bugs, satellites. So we'll use DLBs.'

"Dead letter boxes? Wow! That takes me back to my first sessions with the FSB trainers.' Katya laughed, her eyes lighting up. 'I hope I'll remember how to do it.'

'One of your many problems, Katya, are your dealings with authority. I get complaints all the time– ' He described an arc with the cigarette in his hand. 'Don't interrupt. I was going to say that I personally count that as a quality. Question, question, always question.' He switched abruptly to another topic. 'I hear Guy doesn't rate you much as a gambler.'

'It can't be that difficult going to a casino and gambling.'

'As long as you always keep in your mind who you are dealing with. Now, your cover. We've arranged with FSB in St Petersburg for them to be on the look-out for any queries about you from Kropse. They have made arrangements for the Immigration Department records to show that you are on leave from your old job as a visa clerk. The story is that, following your father's death, the probate for his estate has taken you away to deal with his affairs. As far as the casino visit is concerned you have decided to take a holiday, visit your old haunt where you sailed with him on the Black Sea. You are spending your inheritance. But, don't forget, if you catch their attention, the casino will check you out. So be careful not to give away any background that they can check and find suspicious.'

Katya's mind raced to keep up with him. This was the way Lev operated–fast talking, straight to the point. 'Where will I stay? How long for?' she asked.

'We've hired a *dacha* just outside Kropse. You'll be there two weeks. If you haven't got a name by then we'll walk away. The budget is limited and has to be used to get results. You'll take fifty thousand dollars cash with you.'

'Gambling money?'

'No. That's for clothes, accessories–living expenses. You'll use a separate MasterCard to buy gambling chips. It's the most common card and you'll have a credit limit on it of fifty thousand dollars. You must fit in with a crowd that has money. Can you do that?'

An image of her mother came to Katya's mind. Tatiana Petrovna had been a Principal dancer with the Bolshoi Ballet in Moscow–always elegant, beautifully dressed, always at home with the more sophisticated Muscovites. A mother she remembered as exciting but remote–a shadow life she'd glimpsed, a glamour she'd desperately yearned for in her early years. 'Oh yes,' Katya replied. 'I can do that.'

'Good. You'll travel from Heathrow to St Petersburg under an alias. The name on your false passport will be Inessa Golubeva. When you arrive in St Petersburg you will stay the night there. The next day you will go on to Kropse as Katya Petrovna. That way it won't be possible for anyone to trace you back to here. The details on your own passport and driving licence will show that you live in St Petersburg.' He stood up. 'Well, I'll leave you. Remember to take care and to stay focussed.' He put a hand on her shoulder for a moment, then walked away.

Watching him leave, Katya felt as alone as she had during those grim days in Moscow. Days where she had been allowed no friends, no free time by her authoritarian father. The loneliness she'd experienced . . . Not to mention the cruelty . . . She got up, shrugged, threw the mobile into a nearby waste bin and left.

SIX

A day later, having shopped and packed, Katya boarded a plane at Heathrow. She arrived in St Petersburg at four in the afternoon where she would spend the night before flying on to Kropse. In contrast to the bright September sun outside Polkovo airport, the lights inside shone dimly as if to mourn the government neglect that had seen passenger use decline by half in the years since the break-up of the Soviet Union. She'd heard there had been promises from the St Petersburg authorities of a new airport, but, so far, not even a draft design had materialised.

None of these thoughts dampened Katya's excitement at being back in the city where she had been to university and had spent her subsequent training days in the FSB. Excited, certainly, but some memories brought back by the airport's surroundings were not happy. Her seduction by a cynical, long gone university lecturer–being ostracised by her FSB colleagues after her father's fatal mistake were amongst them. It was strange, she thought, that this operation seemed so often to bring back these memories of her past. She was still thinking about this as she handed her passport over to the Immigration Officer sitting behind a glass screen at one of the desks.

The woman glanced at the pages briefly. 'You are Inessa Golubeva?' She inked the visa stamp and raised it above the relevant page.

'Yes.' Katya kept her reply brief, not wanting to invite further questions about her alias.

'Staying in St Petersburg?' The officer asked, as if by rote.

'No. I'm going on to Kropse.' Katya couldn't believe she'd said that. How could she have been so stupid? She'd just blown her alias. After an overnight stay in the FSB housing quarters, she was to travel to Kropse on a passport naming her as Katya Petrovna, residence St Petersburg, occupation visa clerk. This woman now knew she had come from England as Inessa Golubeva and was on her way to the Black Sea port. She was in a prime position to feed this information to those who paid for it. People like the *mafiyas* who, if they wanted to check, would find that no-one of that name had arrived in Kropse.

Wordlessly she took her stamped passport and, as if to hide, hurried to the baggage hall. Mentally she castigated herself every step of the way. And when she got to baggage reclaim she suspected she was already under some sort of surveillance. A woman in a headscarf had fallen in next to her and was looking intently at Katya's baggage as Katya hefted it off the carousel. The two bags were un-labelled, a black leather suitcase and a Simpson's Classic Attaché case. She'd bought them in London to support her cover of a wealthy woman. They would not normally have attracted attention, but this woman seemed to be overly interested in them. Katya knew that enquiries would confirm that in St Petersburg airport they belonged to Inessa Golubeva, but a check in Kropse would reveal the same bags belonged to Katya Petrovna. What a stupid mistake she'd made. When she got to her room in the FSB quarters she'd have to ditch her baggage and buy more. That is if she could shake off this woman who was now following her at a discreet distance to the Customs Hall.

Rapidly Katya thought of various places where she could hide until the woman went away. Restrooms were useless unless one was ready with a disguise to wear on exiting. Bookstores and cafes had no rear exit for someone with baggage. She could dump the baggage and run for it, but where to? The idea triggered a solution. Not brilliant, but workable.

She arrived at the Customs inspection area and, instead of walking through the green channel she stopped in front of one of the customs officers in the red channel who was standing behind a long metal table.

'Can you help me?' she asked with a beaming smile as she put her cases on it and started opening her black suitcase.

She saw the woman who had been following her hesitate, then walk on by, lengthening her stride. She disappeared around the corner leading to the exit.

Katya rummaged around inside her suitcase and produced a bottle of Picasso scent, another expensive purchase she'd made on G8's cover budget. She opened her eyes wide and looked directly into the officer's. 'Do I have to pay duty on this?' she asked, innocently.

He took the bottle from her and put it back in the case, pulled the lid down and snapped the locks shut. *'Ne vy, mem.'* There were ways of saying "Not you, ma'am" and the meaning behind his expression was explicit. She took her cases and sauntered away, briefly looking back to give him a dazzling smile.

She discreetly searched for her pursuer in the Arrivals Hall, trying not to appear conspicuous as she wove her way among the milling passengers. The woman wasn't there. Nor was she anywhere to be seen as Katya walked through the swing doors leading out of the terminal and found the taxi rank.

The driver of the taxi that pulled up had obviously seen her Attaché case and marked her down as a business passenger. He waited sullenly in his seat, shoulders hunched, coat collar pulled up, as she opened the trunk and put her bags inside it. No tip for him, she vowed as she slammed the lid shut, and climbed into the back seat. 'Gorokhovaya Ulitsa 198,' she told him abruptly and settled back to look out of the window at the city.

St Petersburg was where her father had sent her to university. His primary objective hadn't been to educate her, but to make sure she was taken into the FSB, the successor to his alma mater the KGB. She had hardly known him as a father and what she did know brought back painful memories of a home life marked by harsh discipline. He'd even hired a female ex-army drill sergeant to make sure his merciless regime prepared her to follow in his footsteps. The sergeant did her job well, reporting news of her misdemeanours, however trivial, to her employer which often resulted in brutal punishment. No wonder, Katya thought, she had crept unseen out of the house at night and fled to join the street life of Moscow in order to get away from the loneliness and terror of life at home. And where was her mother in all this . . .

Katya suddenly realised that, in all this deep reflection, she had lost track of where the taxi was going and was now in an unfamiliar part of the city. Certainly, she wasn't on the right route from the airport to the FSB quarters.

'Where are you going?' she called out to the driver. He didn't reply. She repeated herself, more loudly this time. He silently rubbed his woollen hat as if to relieve an itchy scalp. She was alarmed now. She'd dismissed the woman at the airport as not presenting a danger. That had been a mistake. Automatically she looked out of the rear window to see if she was being followed. The frame was filled with the shape of a black Mercedes closely tailing them. Its windows were deeply tinted. She peered out of the side window of the taxi. They were travelling past some sort of park. It was wholly unfamiliar to her. She began to panic. 'Stop this cab immediately,' she shouted. The cab driver slammed the taxi to a halt.

'Certainly, Katya.' Lev turned in the driver's seat and looked at her. 'Not a very successful start, would you say?'

Katya was dumbstruck. She struggled to make sense of it.

'I remember your G8 training session on false identities,' Lev said in an even tone, 'I told you all that when you travel on two passports you are two different people. One entirely divorced from the other. Why weren't you listening?'

'The Immigration Officer,' stuttered Katya. 'She . . . she . . .'

'She was FSB, on the lookout for you. I thought she handled you very well. She told me you had a faraway look on your face as you approached her. Probably thinking about your past life here, she said.'

'She was right,' Katya said bitterly.

'As John says, Katya, you are honest. I doubt you will make the same mistake again.'

Katya pulled at her long hair, twisting it round her fingers, inwardly cursing her stupidity. 'Am I to be sent back to HQ?'

'Well, that would be a waste of a considerable amount of money. By the way, you weren't all bad–you handled our tail very well . . . And the Customs Officer couldn't stop talking about you. Very smitten he was.'

'That's sexist, Lev.' Katya rallied, feeling she could use his first name to soften the accusation.

'I'm an old KGB hand, Katya, that sort of complaint cuts no ice with me. I think, if our relationship is to continue, you should know that.' He paused. 'And, yes, you can call me Lev. You have done what many agents do on their first op–made a mistake–and you'll make more. But you had the wit and nerve to recover and shake off that tail and that kind of determination makes for the best agents. Now I'll take you to your quarters.'

He put his foot down on the accelerator. 'You'll need a good night's sleep if you're going to outwit the *mafiya* in that casino tomorrow.'

SEVEN

The following day Katya caught an early afternoon flight to Kropse. She'd been very careful with her counter-surveillance and was pretty sure she hadn't been followed to Kropse. She was relieved her gaffe at St Petersburg airport hadn't compromised her.

The *dacha* that G8 had hired for her on the outskirts of the small port town of Kropse surprised her. She hadn't had time to look at any pictures of it before she'd left the G8HQ. She'd been expecting the sort of traditional wooden fishing shack that her father had hired when they'd visited the town for two weeks every summer when she was a girl to go sailing. But, as she climbed out of the taxi that had brought her from the airport, she saw that her accommodation was luxurious–a modern steel A-frame house with large windows overlooking the Black Sea. Beyond the *dacha* she saw evergreen trees clinging to the bare grey rock of the distant Caucasus mountains which were already darkening dramatically as the sun set. She thought It could have been one of the North American lakeside cabins she'd often saw in glossy magazines. It was just the sort of place a well-heeled Russian tourist would choose for a holiday.

'Bring my bags, will you,' she told the driver as she got out. No-one staying in this place would carry their own luggage.

She walked up a short stone paved pathway towards the front door. The brown, yellow and grey colours of the Caucasus stone was so like the path to the old wooden fishing shack of her childhood that she caught her breath. Into her mind flashed a picture of her father walking down a similar path with her as a young girl, forcing her to sail out alone in fearsome storms.

She erased these thoughts, switched back to the present. She wasn't about to make the same mistake she'd made at the airport where she'd compromised her alias by letting her mind wander.

Briskly she unlocked and opened the front door.

'Put the bags down there, please—just inside the door,' she said to the driver. She took out a wallet from her jeans pocket and saw him take in the new shiny black leather with its green and red Gucci stripe and, satisfied she'd made exactly the right impression, added a large tip. Word of a new rich tourist in Kropse would soon get around.

With a nod and a large toothy grin, he turned and left.

Katya shut the door behind her and looked around. She was in a large,

Open–plan sitting room painted soft white with a kitchen and dining area to one side. There were two dark blue doors which presumably led to a cloakroom and utility room. Brown and grey furniture completed the Caucasus colour scheme. Looking up, she saw a vaulted ceiling stretching up to the rafters, the full-length front window flooded the stone floor and pale-yellow sofa and chairs with light.

She looked at her watch. It was already past six p.m. There was just time to unpack, have a shower and review her cover before she went to the casino. She picked up her bags and hefted them up the flight of open stairs that led to a mezzanine area. Two doors faced her. She opened them and found each led to a well-furnished en suite bedroom.

Katya stood thinking for a moment, then went into the left-hand room. French windows overlooked a balcony and a silver birch tree which almost touched it. She opened the windows and studied the scene. There was a small garden below enclosed by a low wall, beyond which there were some scrubby bushes leading towards the foothills of the mountains. If she needed one, the tree would make an excellent escape route through the garden and over the wall. The tree also provided for an easy illegal entry. But if she was in the bedroom she could counter that. If she wasn't, the open staircase and atrium would offer little or no cover to an intruder. Satisfied, she left the French windows open and began to unpack.

An hour later, having settled in, she was on her way in a taxi to the Sea Dragon Casino. She was dressed in an off-one-shoulder black top, high waisted white trousers and a wide white belt with a gold buckle. She was also wearing her mother's gold necklace—she was never without it—complemented by discreet fine gold earrings, bracelet and pale gold T-bar shoes. With her gleaming auburn hair swept to one side and held back with a gold clasp she felt as sophisticated as she remembered her mother always used to be. Her MasterCard and driving licence were safely in her small black clutch bag.

Kropse had developed from the fishing village she had known into a tourist spot and seemed to have been built around the Sea Dragon Casino. It was the only casino in the town and as the taxi drew up in front of it Katya saw it looked like a Tsar's summer palace, with its greened copper domes, red tiled minarets and ornate 18th century windows.

She climbed out of the taxi and walked slowly up the red carpeted steps, flanked on each side by flames from lighted torches.

She was fired up but suddenly felt a rush of nervousness as an obvious *mafiya* heavy came towards her—a tall man, menacing, dressed in black. She took in a breath.

He wasted no time in pleasantries. 'You wish to enter?' he said as he looked her up and down.

Katya automatically reacted to this intimidation. 'Can you think of another reason I'd be climbing these steps?' she said curtly in the rough Moscow street accent she sometimes used to intimidate people.

He was caught unawares. His usual approach to beautiful women was to scare them and then approach them later with a proposition they couldn't refuse. This woman was different, he thought. Her accent told him she had street cred. She was obviously not a hooker and not a business woman–she had that definable air of being trust fund moneyed. She could be trouble. He shrugged, stood aside–there were plenty of other women, he reflected. 'Show some ID when you see the floor manager,' he grunted.

She ignored this and swept past him through the gilded doors into a huge marble pillared hallway.

The floor manager was more discerning. He came towards her saying, 'Good evening. My name is Anatoly, I'm the floor manager for your evening. I must ask you for identification. An impertinence, of course, but also a duty.'

Katya took the driving licence she'd been given at G8HQ out of her bag and handed it to him.

He studied it. 'Thank you. You are new here, I think.'

Katya nodded, waiting for what was to come next.

'I must apologise,' he said with a small bow as he handed it back to her. 'But I have to ask you to give your handbag to this lady for inspection.' He pointed to a slim blonde woman who gave Katya a beaming heavily red lip-sticked smile. She was dressed in a matching red jumpsuit with black shoulder flashes spelling "*Security.*"

'I'm not a terrorist.' Katya laughed, gauging just the right amount of pushback that would seem natural from a wealthy woman used to having all doors opened to her.

'No,' Anatoly replied. 'But as a newcomer you perhaps wouldn't know the rule that you may not bring a mobile phone into the casino.'

'That I do know,' Katya said. She watched the woman rummage in her bag. 'By the way, is there a maximum stake at the tables?'

Like the bouncer on the entrance steps, Anatoly was uncertain how to deal with Katya. He thought at first, he was dealing with an ingénue but obviously this confident young woman knew her way around and, probably, more than around casinos. And she was on her own, no escort. He felt a tinge of curiosity.

'No limit, madam, provided the cashier is satisfied with your credit references,' Anatoly said.

Katya took her bag from the security woman. 'I must meet the cashier then.'

Anatoly was eager all of a sudden. Rich punters equalled large tips. 'He's available now– '

'No. I want to see how the floor plays first.'

He couldn't believe he'd been so wrong about her. His curiosity was now fully whetted. He wanted to take the conversation further, but she'd gone–walking with a long, purposeful stride onto the casino floor, the gold in her hair catching the light from the chandeliers.

EIGHT

Katya could see at once that no effort had been spared to extract the maximum amount of cash possible from the punters. She was faced with four long rows of garish coloured electronic slot machines, flickering their wares in a pandemonium of heavy metal music competing with the shrill thump of levers desperately wrenched down time after time. The crowds of people added to the cacophony giving yells of triumph or groans of anguish. She looked up and saw a plain ceiling dotted with video cameras that were surely recording every moment and every movement. She thought it was all very disappointing. The elegance of the outside façade had prepared her for something more sophisticated.

'If you will follow me, Ms Petrovna . . .'

She looked down. A Chinese girl, she couldn't have been more than fourteen, touched her elbow. 'This is not what you are looking for, I think. I have been asked to direct you to the inner floor.'

Katya took in the green cheongsam which matched the girl's eyes. Green eyes were a rarity in China, she thought. She must come from Liqian. Katya spotted blonde streaks in her dark hair and was then certain of it. What was she doing here in Russia, wasn't Liqian way up in North China by the Gobi Desert? Katya decided to probe. 'You are a long way from home.'

The girl giggled. 'You know where my home is?'

'Yes. Liqian.'

'You are very clever. No-one has ever asked me. I was brought from–' She broke off quickly as a tall, heavily-built woman dressed in a tailored blue business suit, her chestnut coloured hair scraped sharply back from her face, appeared from behind a slot machine. The woman looked directly at the girl, raised her chin. The girl looked scared, Katya noticed.

'Eu Meh, you know better than to chatter to the guests. Go to your post–at once.' Without waiting the woman continued, 'Ms Petrovna. I apologise. We're still training her.'

The girl was now walking so fast she was almost running– towards a group of men clustered around a slot machine.

'It's no problem,' Katya replied. 'She's very young.'

'She's twenty and should know better. Now, my name is Taban. I'm your floor host and I'm delighted to meet you. New clients are always welcome to the Sea Dragon.'

Katya recognised Taban's name. Mongolian. She made a quick search of the woman's face, from the high cheek bones to the faint heaviness around the cold, hazel coloured eyes. This woman probably hadn't lived more than a day's distance from Liqian. Was there a connection? Taban had lied about Eu Meh's age and obviously controlled the child. She decided Taban would be worth cultivating.

'I was really interested in the architecture of your casino. So reminiscent of the Tsarist period. It must be very old.'

Taban bowed slightly, eager to put this nosy woman in her place.

'A lot of people think it's Tsarist, but, of course, gambling wasn't permitted in Russia until 1989. There were a lot of casinos built after that and the Sea Dragon was one of the first. A group of ex-KGB officers,' she almost spat out the words, 'invested their cash in it. Being KGB, they naturally modelled it on the high rolling casinos they spent their time in during their postings in Europe. Later they sold it.'

Katya was keen to learn more. This was the first intelligence about the casino she had unearthed. And she was on the point of asking who the buyer had been when she remembered the point of her question was architecture. It was Taban's obvious hatred of the KGB that had led her to tell the story of the casino's origins. So she backed off–there would be another opportunity to follow up with Taban later. 'Thank you so much, that's really interesting– the building had me fooled. If it's alright with you, I'd very much like to start at the roulette table.'

'First, I will show you the tables then we will visit the cashiers. Then your evening is your own–unless of course you have any questions?' Taban forced a smile. How she despised these trust fund women. She'd grown up in a one room apartment in a poor neighbourhood with no heat in the cold winters and often going without food. Yes, she hated them–their certainty that the world owed them a living. She'd had to fight her own way out of poverty. At seventeen she'd been abused by a KGB lout and had fled with no money, hiding on a train going to Moscow. On arriving at the station tired and exhausted she'd been approached and picked up on the station by a member of the *mafiya*. Rising through the ranks she had made it to where she was now.

Katya wondered whether Taban's remark about whether she had any questions was loaded–had Taban overheard her talking with Eu Meh? She dismissed the thought. The noise of the machines would have drowned out any conversation. Unless– Katya looked up again at the video cameras in the ceiling. She would have to be more careful in future. Taban led her away from the machines towards the end of the room and down some wide white marble steps flanked by waterfalls. The noise of the tumbling water increased as they descended until it finally drowned out the clatter of the slot machines. Clever, thought Katya–concealed microphones enhanced the sound and threw it out of hidden speakers. What other sounds did they throw out and where to, she wondered.

The scene at the bottom of the stairs was a revelation. It was the gaming floor, a square at least a hectare big. A wide aisle in its centre led directly across the room from the foot of the steps to a long bar with high-back stools. In front of the bar were tables, intimately and discreetly lit. On either side of the aisle, spaced well apart were the gaming tables—roulette, blackjack, chemin de fer, poker. This was nothing like the dingy illegal cellar casinos Katya had seen in Moscow. Here the walls were of gleaming white marble, hung with exquisite 18th century tapestries and illuminated by gold filigree French wall lights. The floor was covered in thick Aubusson carpets which muffled the conversations between the croupiers and gamesters, leaving the impression of a low hum. Hanging from the plaster ceiling, between frescoes, were long Bohemian crystal chandeliers with at least twenty branches each. The room was simply breath taking. Katya recognised a beautiful exaggeration of an early French or Italian casino. She also knew that KGB cash may have built this place but the only identifiable link she could see to that organisation was the cunning in the hidden microphones.

The contrast between the "clients" on this floor and the punters on the slot machine floor was as stark as the contrast in atmosphere between the two rooms. The crowd she'd seen by the fruit machines were mostly dressed in casual jeans and T-shirts—exuberant, pummelling the machines, sweating with the effort and anticipation of a stream of coins pouring into their hands. Here, at the gaming tables, the clients were elegantly dressed and either watching the play or softly strolling and quietly chatting. The women were all in evening dress, showing off French and English couture, often splashed with Russians' favourite colour—red. Their necks and arms were decorated with exquisitely fine jewellery, mostly diamonds–a few emeralds–which flashed or twinkled under the candelabra lights. The men wore bespoke black or white dinner jackets–no other colours–and seemed to be competing as to who wore the largest gold finger rings. There was an air of calm. It was as if winning or losing was a matter of indifference to the players. It wasn't, she knew, but she grasped the amount of wealth it took to enable such sangfroid. Her fifty thousand dollars suddenly seemed a very small bank roll.

Taban was speaking. 'You come from St Petersburg I'm told. I have never been there but I wish I could go and see the Hermitage Museum–the paintings, the sculpture.' She stopped, inviting a reply.

Katya looked at Taban and wondered how the woman had found out she was from St Petersburg. The only other person who knew was the floor manager, Anatoly, who'd inspected her driving licence at the front door. For the first time, she noticed an earpiece nestled behind Taban's hair. Information was passed around here faster than a village grapevine. The thought was followed by a sense of alarm. Finding the owner of this place and what was going on relied on her getting into conversation and, possibly, covert searching. How was she going to accomplish that in the face of this barrage of surveillance? She saw that Taban was watching her with an expectant expression. How long had she been waiting for an answer? Katya took a second longer to choose her reply. She could be smart and reveal her knowledge of this bush telegraph or she could feign ignorance. Her mission was to get information and provocation was a good weapon for securing it.

'Anatoly told you about me, did he? I didn't expect so much interest, but I suppose I'm new and you must check me out.'

'Oh. I've offended you, I'm so sorry. Please accept it's nothing to do with checking you out. We just like to know our clients so that we can serve them the best we can.'

Taban's answer was smooth and flawless, a lie which highlighted the sophistication of this enterprise. Katya thought back to the woman picked up at Heathrow airport for carrying cash–the one that John Hammond had briefed her about. She'd guessed then that the woman had kept her mouth shut for fear of revealing a *mafiya* connection. Taban's answer seemed to confirm the woman had been wise. But further probing might be suspicious. Katya drew back. 'That's a kind thought. I've been used to St Petersburg manners so forgive my bluntness.'

'Then perhaps I won't visit St Petersburg after all.' The woman gave a brittle laugh. 'Let me take you to the cashier.'

She led Katya across the room, between the gaming tables, and past one table where two men were sitting gazing intently from behind their piles of chips as they played *vingt-et-un*. Katya noticed the croupier lift his eyes fractionally to give her the once over. Katya ignored him. Arriving with Taban at the cashiers' desk she took her Gucci wallet out of her bag. No cage protection for the cashier she observed–they must be confident of their security staff. She reached for her MasterCard and pushed it across the maple wood desk to the cashier.

'Welcome, Ms Petrovna.' The young, wiry, crew cut man wore a black dinner jacket and white shirt and looked like an accountant. 'What can the Sea Dragon do for you?'

Take me for fifty thousand without blinking, thought Katya. Instead she said, 'Five thousand dollars, please.'

'How would you like your chips?'

Katya was stumped. She'd not thought about this. She was acting the know-it-all punter but she had no clue how to handle her bets or what chips she'd need. So far she'd created just the right amount of attention and she didn't want to spoil it. 'In five hundred's', please.'

The cashier took in the beauty of her–couldn't help breaching protocol and trying for a conversation with this stunning, young and obviously wealthy woman. He leant towards her. 'That gives you only ten bets.' He smiled at her invitingly.

'Why do I need ten?' she joked, laughing provocatively, drawing him in. 'One bet should be enough to support me for the evening.'

He caught Taban's eye and straightened up. His smile vanished and he quickly counted out ten purple chips, each one with a picture of a dragon rising out of the sea. He handed them to Katya. 'Have a good evening.'

Taban led her to a free chair at a roulette table that was, unusually, covered in white baize rather than the traditional green.

Katya looked at it and then at Taban with a question in her eyes.

Taban replied, as smooth as silk. 'This is the table we introduce our virgin guests to.' She paused before elaborating. 'It is more welcoming than the dark green, don't you think? Less intimidating.'

Lamb to the slaughter, was the expression that came to Katya's mind. 'Another thoughtful touch,' Katya replied. 'Thank you.'

Taban exchanged a look with the croupier Katya noticed. It was no doubt the one Katya thought he would recognise as "we're unsure of this one–treat her gently."

Hoping she looked suitably unconcerned, Katya shook Taban's hand in dismissal and sat down.

Before she could even look around at her fellow players, the croupier called "*Faites vos jeux.*"

Katya lined up her ten purple chips in front of her and deliberately put one of them on number sixteen.

NINE

The roulette wheel was spinning, expertly flicked into action by the croupier after he'd tidied Katya's bet with his stick.

Katya didn't watch the ball rattling on the wheel. Her gaze drifted to the bar. It looked like a scene from a Manet painting with its tall mahogany wood counter and wooden stools facing a mirrored wall lined with various labelled bottles of alcohol. A middle-aged man sat at one end, moodily swirling the drink in his glass. In contrast, a group of young people were laughing at a shared story.

She caught a bartender's eye. He nodded to where her chips lay on the table and raised his eyebrows as if to ask why she wasn't watching her bet. She shrugged– rich woman bored.

'*Numero seize*.' The words hardly registered at first, then she turned to face the croupier took in the formality of his black jacket, white shirt, black waistcoat and bow tie. '*Numero seize*,' he was telling her. He reached out his stick and flicked thirty-five purple chips towards her, folding them together into a pile. Seventeen thousand dollars she thought to herself.

She felt exhilarated then caught herself. She must remember her cover. What was that sum of money to a woman of her supposed wealth? A good dinner with ten friends. She put up her chin, tossed a purple chip to the croupier–whose blank expression didn't change–got up from her chair and walked over to the cashier with the crew cut. 'Cash me in, will you please.'

He was amazed. 'Aren't you going to ride your luck?'

She looked back at the white table. 'I've had the perfect ride thank you.'

He took her MasterCard and put it in the machine on the counter in front of her. She punched in her PIN number and took back the card.

'We'll see you again?' he said hopefully. But she had already turned away and was walking across the floor to the bar.

Katya took a seat near the bartender she had exchanged glances with.

He came up to her and made eye contact. 'First time at the tables?'

'No.'

'Didn't think so. You knew when to stop. What made you put your money on sixteen? Habit?'

Bartenders, she thought, the perfect fact finders. But this was the friendly approach and she might be able to turn him, get the information she wanted. She gave him a crumb. 'No. It was my flight number from St Petersburg–zero zero one six.' They– whoever they were–could find out that fact quite easily, so she'd given nothing but had shown she was happy to talk.

'Takes all sorts.' He smiled. 'Champagne?' He picked up a bottle of champagne from an ice bucket on the shelf behind him. Then, grinning, he lifted an eyebrow and said, 'Or is champagne too upmarket for a Moscovite?'

These people are smart, she told herself, word had got around. No good denying she was born and bred in Moscow. 'Yes. No. And no, you don't get my life history.'

'Pity,' he said, his eyes glinting. 'It would be interesting. I can tell.'

She looked around the room. 'I used to sail here in Kropse as a child. Stormy weather. Not like this place, all peace and quiet.'

'Glad to be back?'

'I never came into the casino. Too young.' She paused. 'I suppose they don't have boats here that clients can hire?'

'I don't think so.'

'I presume the owner doesn't sail.'

'The owners– '

'Hello, Katya. I can call you Katya can't I, after that winning play you made.' Katya turned. It was Taban.

Taban waved the bartender away, adding, 'Why didn't you continue to bet.

One win usually precedes another, even a winning streak.'

Katya swallowed her annoyance at this unwanted interruption. The bartender had been about to talk. 'I was just meeting the challenge your cashier set me when he suggested I would run through all my chips. Following instructions, I suppose.'

'Instructions?'

'Well, I assume he's not just a cashier. An accountant would be my guess. And putting temptation in a client's way is as good a way to snare a profit as any other, wouldn't you say?'

It was some time after Katya had left the casino and returned to the *dacha* that the casino manager, Daniil Morosov, held his end of play wash-up with his senior employees in his office at the top of the casino. The room was painted a blinding white and was bare of furniture save for a single desk where he sat facing an open laptop. There were no windows to light the place, simply a naked ceiling bulb next to which a meat hook had been screwed into a hidden beam. A loop of piano wire hung from it.

Morosov counted on the starkness of this room to unbalance his most troublesome visitors. They were mainly clients who had forgotten the basic rule– play and pay. Even the most hardened welsher left terrified after ten minutes there with Morosov. Some didn't leave at all until a body bag was brought to the room for their disposal. Morosov's only weakness was vodka and this appeared in his cunning, pudgy face almost hiding his cold blue bloodshot eyes. An explosive, violent temper also counted as an indication of his alcoholism. His hand trembled slightly as he slid it over his thinning dark brown hair while he studied the spreadsheet of figures on his open laptop.

The day's profits had been calculated. Two bad debtors had been scheduled for a meeting and Katya Petrovna's name had come up.

It was, of course, Taban who had raised the query about Katya. She was puzzled. The woman couldn't reconcile the feistiness Katya had shown with her obvious unfamiliarity with casino etiquette. Gamblers didn't ask personal questions of anyone, let alone staff. Also, she had fifty thousand dollars in her bank–trust the cashier to have prised that out of her MasterCard details–yet she was happy to go home with $17,000 when another bet was the obvious next move for any un-seasoned punter. The card held fifty thousand but Morosov was sure that was just the tip of the iceberg. . . a bankroll for gaming. His guess was there would be a lot more cash to come if they could get to grips with her. The bouncer and Anatoly had both mentioned Katya's assumed use of a Moscow street accent. That didn't sit with her being born into wealth. What made Katya Petrovna even more intriguing to Morosov were her conversations with both Eu Meh and the bartender, all recorded on the overhead video cameras. She had been able to get them to the verge of divulging important information, despite his rule that staff must say nothing about the casino or who ran it. That showed real talent. She was a mystery. Seasoned punter or novice? One to watch or one to milk?

It was agreed that investigations would be made in St Petersburg. And the friendly cashier was tasked with taking her sailing for an hour or two–find out everything he could about her.

TEN

Katya spent a restless night in the *dacha*. She had arrived back from the casino in an optimistic mood. She was pleased that she'd resisted the temptation to chase her win and felt reassured that Guy–back in the G8 Tech Room–had misjudged her when he had predicted she would win a couple of times and then lose. On top of that she had made contact with two people–Eu Meh and the bartender–who'd been about to tell her something when they were interrupted.

Now, lying in bed, listening to the waves slapping onto the shore and the wind whistling through the trees, she began to question herself. What impression had she made on Taban? She'd been pretty rude to the woman. Had she appeared defensive? Put Taban on her mettle? She needed her onside; not as an enemy. And how friendly or useful was the bartender, really? Like her, his job was probably to give a little information in order to get some in return. And Eu Meh . . . Well, she was just a child. Or–could there be a story to get out of her? Above all, she mustn't forget she was almost certainly dealing with a *mafiya*, not some half honest gaming casino. Andrei Savin in one of his training sessions had warned her that her need to drive forward made her overconfident. She must remember that.

Then, because she was young and tired, sleep overtook her and she didn't wake until she heard the front door opening.

She sat bolt upright, for a moment not realising where she was. Then, swiftly, she jumped out of bed, grabbed a bathrobe, wrenched the bedroom door open and raced down the stairs. The sun was blazing through the hall window and for a moment she didn't see the figure in the shadow.

'Who are you? What are you doing here?' she shouted, thoroughly alarmed.

'Good morning, *bab.la*.' A woman's voice. She was about fifty-five years old, short in height with curly brown hair. Light blue eyes looked out at Katya from a round, heavily lined, but kindly face.

'Did I disturb you? My apologies.'

Katya was confused–*bab.la* was used as a term of respect, like ma'am in England. But she couldn't be a servant, they were not common in Russia. Besides Lev had said nothing about a cleaner in his briefing about the *dacha*. She put the question again, 'Who are you?'

'Ludmilla, *bab.la*. Come to do the cleaning.'

'I don't have a maid,' Katya said crisply. 'So, again, who are you?'

'The *dacha* owner employs me. Please, I'm only here to help.'

Katya knew that if she went on protesting, it would look suspicious. Anyone in Russia would be only too pleased to have a maid during their vacation. Something had to be off. She decided to wait and see what it was. 'Ludmilla, I'm sorry. I wasn't expecting you.' She forced a smile. 'How delightful you are here.' She didn't shake hands, that would be too friendly.

'I'll make some tea.' Ludmilla walked towards the kitchen.

'Thank you. With strawberry jam if there's some in the kitchen.'

Ludmilla turned and nodded. 'I brought some with me.' A gleam of respect crept into her eyes. 'The foreigners never have it, do they?'

Ludmilla turned out to be invaluable. After a shower and a

change into faded blue jeans and an old but favourite red T-shirt, Katya went downstairs to find she'd rustled up blinis for breakfast. And not only was there strawberry jam to stir into her tea but there were fresh strawberries to put on the blinis. Katya was very pleased but the cynical thought remained that this treatment was more than standard for the *dacha*. Was Ludmilla a gift from the casino reporting to a *mafiya*? Katya suddenly felt more alone and less certain of her ability to get anywhere near her target.

'Have you been to the beach?' Ludmilla asked as she cleared the table.

The idea cheered up Katya immediately. Of course, she could go to the old boatyard where she'd sailed from as a child. It would give her a chance to reminisce with the fishermen–if they were still there–and innocently slide in some questions about the casino. 'No, but that's a good idea. Thank you,' she replied.

She put on a pair of blue boat shoes, left the *dacha,* and walked down the path towards the beach. The sun was shining and she felt a slight breeze on her back. She looked around, things had changed since she was last in Kropse. She saw that the beach front road was now tarmac'd rather than the sandy strip it had been in her day. To her left there was a new cantilever concrete café boldly painted red and white. A couple were sitting at an outside table under a Cinzano umbrella. The sea in front of her was just as she remembered it, calm and serene, no tides to disturb its endless tranquillity–until a storm came and then all hell let loose. She pushed the recollections aside as she made her way down the road to where the black outlines of boat sheds and fishing vessels told her she'd find old comrades.

She passed some wood and tar fishing shacks that were there in those days but most had now been torn down and replaced by modern wood or concrete *dachas,* gaily painted and with plenty of glass to capture the view. She smiled. In her early years, the last thing one wanted were glass windows overlooking the sea. Storms would fling the sand off the beach and the rain would stick it to the wet glass making cleaning a chore. These new buildings probably had self-cleaning glass and a wonderful view as a result . . . She was getting nostalgic again. She *must* be on her guard against that.

The fishing wharf a few yards further on hadn't changed a bit. Even a couple of old Taka boats were there still, with their high prows and lateen rigs, painted in the bright reds and yellows she used to delight in. Larger, less well-kept steel hull trawlers were moored, ready to sail. She picked her way through them and around the usual orderly collection of nets, ropes and fish trays. 'Hello,' she called. 'Hello.'

A grizzled man with a Stalin moustache stepped out from between two of the boats. He peered at her, his old faded blue eyes almost completely hidden in the deep creases around them. He rubbed his oily hands down his brown woollen trousers and took out a pipe and some loose matches from a pocket. Katya thought for a moment she recognised him but she wasn't sure. She waited as he scratched the match on the hull of a trawler he stood next to and fired up the tobacco in his pipe. Blue smoke drifted in the light breeze and she was reminded of Lev and his Abdullah No 7s.

Unperturbed, he slowly nodded at her. 'Hello, *Malyshka.*'

"Little girl" The name the fisherman, Viktor, had called her all those years ago—even into her teens. She could hardly believe that the only adult friend she'd had as a child here in Kropse was still alive. She'd thought he was ninety then.

'Viktor! It's you! How wonderful.'

His broad grin spread across his face in the kind of welcome Russians give to their special friends. 'I hoped you'd come back before I hopped my twig. You look . . . well not like the scrawny child I last saw throwing that Taka around the sea as if she was attached to you. . . d'you still sail?' He ended abruptly.

'Not for a while. No. You haven't changed Viktor.'

'That's not what your face told me when you saw me just now. What're you doing these days?'

She was used to his abrupt questions, used to his curt orders, as well. But she wasn't quite prepared to lie to him–he was too honest. But she knew she had to. 'I'm a visa clerk,' she told him.'

He sucked on his pipe, studied her, the creases around his eyes tightening into a look of disbelief. 'If you say so–but that's not the *Malyshka* I knew.'

'Things happen, Viktor . . . Father . . . Mother . . . You know.'

'He was a damn fool getting himself killed like that–a bully too. I. . .' He tailed off. She knew what he meant–the cruelty of her father, forcing her to sail alone in the big seas the sudden storms threw up.

She shrugged. 'It's all over now. Well he's still there. . . in my mind. . . but not so often.' She paused. 'Did I ever thank you for saving me?'

'At sea? I don't recall you ever needing that– '

'You know what I mean, I felt safe with you.'

The lines on his face softened, 'You were worth better than a visa clerk. . . still are.'

'Well, I'm spending my father's money now, his estate. He was rich, you know.'

'What KGB colonels weren't?' He spat.

'It's funny, I won a large sum of money at the Sea Dragon last night. I wonder what he would have said about that.'

Suddenly his mood changed. 'You want to keep away from that place,' he said sharply, his eyes narrowing.

She picked up more than the thought in this humble man that gambling was unchristian. 'Why? What's wrong with it?' she queried.

'Spend that bastard's money–but not up there, you hear?'

She was *Malyshka* again, she realised.

His eyes softened. 'I wouldn't tell you if I didn't care.' He then bent to pick up a coil of rope. 'Now, I've got work to do.' He straightened up, moved away–an old man who'd missed her.

ELEVEN

That same morning, Taban had been busy. She had just spoken on her mobile to Vasili Oborin, her boss's ex-KGB contact in St Petersburg to see what she could find out about this Katya. Even though the KGB had been disbanded over twelve years earlier, most of its retired members were still the best source of underground information useful to the criminal fraternity.

Taban was shocked to hear Vasili literally spit when he heard the name Katya Petrovna.

'That bastard father of hers,' he shouted. 'Attempted to do a deal with the Chechens. Got himself killed and a damn good thing too.'

Taban had tried to make sense of his outburst. 'You mean his family is *PNG*?'

'Persona non-grata? Oh! No. They had nothing to do with the Chechen thing.' He abruptly changed the subject. 'He was a right thug, treated the mother and daughter appallingly.'

'So, if the daughter's here, she's clean? Nothing for us to worry about?' Taban asked.

'*Tak, tak, tak* . . . I remember he was fanatical about the daughter following in his footsteps–almost trained her for it–brutal. I remember meeting a terrifying woman at his apartment, too. An army drill sergeant . . . what was her name . . . no, it's gone . . . Anyway, rumour was she kept the girl chained up– '

'My god. So, the daughter is what now? FSB–Federal Security

Service?' Taban had only wanted to know if Katya had money to burn in the casino, now it seemed there was good reason to worry about her approaches to Eu Meh and the bartender.

'Too good looking for FSB. . . No, no, no I'm joking. I know the bastard forced her to join FSB from university–the one in St Petersburg . . . she did extremely well there, got a red diploma– '

"Yes, yes.' Taban was getting impatient. 'So, she *is* FSB?'

'Hmm?'

'I said, she is FSB?'

'Oh. No, not at all. She did the training course all right but then her father disobeyed orders and was offed by the Chechens. As I said the daughter wasn't *PNG*'d but FSB weren't sure they could trust her–thought she was too independent, too like her father. You know she flew a 1/72 Polikarkov under the Troitskiy bridge– '

'Vasili, just tell me if she's FSB or not.'

'You don't realise what a gutsy thing that was to do . . . the 1/72 was in the Aero Club as a relic . . . it had an appalling safety record, killed pilots . . . she took it and . . . well the FSB held a Board of Inquiry and what with their worries about her trustworthiness–she was quickly shunted out and sent to the Federal Migration Service–kept in her place as a visa clerk– '

'There's no money in that job,' Taban said stating the obvious. 'So how can she have fifty thousand dollars in her MasterCard account?'

'No surprise there. The father had access to millions of dollars in the KGB operations funds, he must have squirrelled away a good fortune. I mean he was one of us, we all

did . . .' He tailed off as if he'd said too much–abruptly changed the subject. 'What's she said about it?'

'Do you think we'd ask her? It's why I'm asking you.'

'Well don't worry about her. If she's having a good time on

her father's cash let her. Poor kid had a rotten enough time of it.' He laughed suddenly. 'But she's very bright, so make sure she doesn't break your bank.'

Taban wasn't amused. 'Goodbye, Vasili.' She cut the call–tapped Morosov's speed dial on her mobile.

Katya was unaware of any of this when she visited the casino that evening. As she climbed the carpeted steps to the front entrance, she noticed a difference to her previous visit. The bouncer eagerly ushered her to the front door and wished her good fortune. A good omen, she thought, which she traded up by thanking him and, handing him a hundred-dollar bill as she asked him his name.

'Luka, *bab.la*,' he said with a small bow as he slid the note into his back pocket.

'Well, Luka,' she said solemnly, 'if I want a friend I'll know where to come.'

For the first-time ever in all his dealings with beautiful, rich women he had no smart reply at the ready.

Katya walked on through the main doors and found Anatoly, the floor manager, waiting for her. He first noted her pale-yellow silk blouse tucked into black tapered silk trousers. The thin green belt at her waist matched a square emerald brooch pinned just below her left shoulder, where it shimmered under the lights. High heeled, black strappy shoes made her seem taller. She truly was out of the ordinary, he thought and must be treated as such–Morosov had told him there was money to be mined here.

Katya held out her black purse-bag, teasing him as she nodded to the security guard. 'Anatoly, for your inspection.'

Anatoly looked her up and down and, bowing, waved away the proffered bag. 'Katya Petrovna you are most welcome as our guest.'

'No longer a client, Anatoly? I wonder what my promotion has in store for me?'

He ignored this. 'Taban will show you to your gaming table,' he said as Taban walked up.

Katya caught the quick eye contact between them and then looked away, down past the fruit machines, towards the gaming room. 'Not yet, Taban, thank you. I want to move around for a bit. I didn't have a chance yesterday. I want to see more of your magnificent décor.' She nodded at them and drifted off, leaving a whiff of Picasso scent behind her as she walked through the ranks of crashing slot machines and the pack of yowling punters.

She stopped at the top of the steps leading down to the gaming tables. For a moment she watched the clients, or were some of them "guests" like her? Most of them were seated, others stood around intently watching the play or walked about, fetching drinks, smoking or idly and quietly chatting. There was no real pattern—just the moneyed doing what they always do in a casino—enjoying themselves, either perspiring on a last bet—opening champagne on a lucky break—or . . . what was the "or"? Something niggled at the back of her mind. She searched for it. She was sure there was an "or".

She looked around again. Her eyes alighted on a short man, weaving his way slowly around the baccarat table. Abruptly, he slid through a group standing by the bar. His gait stirred an image lurking in her memory. Something to do with a man she'd half noticed the night before but hadn't picked up on. Something unusual . . . This time she studied the man's slight build, bland facial features, his dressed down clothes. The sort of man G8 would welcome as a surveillance officer with that innate ability to move around un-noticed. She continued to watch him as he unobtrusively made his way to the cashiers' desk, timing his arrival to the exact moment when a cashier was free. In two swift, covert movements he handed in a pile of chips and the cashier, without counting them, passed him a wad of dollars. The man was obviously at home in the casino so it may have been an innocent swap of chips for cash. Or it may have been a personal transaction between them. Or it may have been the practised moneylaundering of illegal cash through the casino cashier. In which case the casino turned a blind eye or was part of the transaction.

Taban had silently approached Katya from behind. She'd marked Katya's head following the punter, Roman, as he moneylaundered his first tranche of chips to receive a clean $10,000 cash from the cashier. She wondered if, earlier, Katya had also seen Roman pay the cashier $10,000 to receive the same chips. But, she dismissed the thought. That was foolish, Katya had only been there a few moments. It was unlikely she'd realised what was going on. It was worth checking it out though. 'Hello, Katya. You seem absorbed. Anything interesting?'

Katya mistrusted Taban. She'd met this sort of woman in the cellars of Moscow as a young teenager–the kind who minded the prostitutes. The kind who'd bullied her to go on the game and got nasty when she'd refused. Who knew the tricks of laundering money. Taban would almost certainly have noticed her watching that man with the cashier. Katya rapidly analysed how she was going to reply. Any answer she gave Taban that hinted at her knowledge of any of those possibilities could be dangerous, fatal.

She turned, swiftly, as if disturbed from a reverie. 'It's the people, isn't it? Who *are* the people who love casino life? Look at me, for instance, I love the décor and how people relate to it. The fruit machine crowd are always noisy, even when they're feeding in their last dollar. Then there are the guests on this floor, mostly hiding their excitement or addiction or overdrawn bank accounts. I mean take that man just leaving.' She pointed to Roman. 'There was no way he wanted anyone to know he'd won. I wonder why not? Divorced and doesn't want his wife to know? Got creditors he wants to avoid? Fascinating. And it must be fascinating for you, working here. You must see all kinds– ' She broke off, leaving a question.

'I'm used to it, I don't notice any more.' Taban shrugged. 'You aren't used to casino life are you, Katya? You know enough to give the impression you are a regular gamester, but hardened gamblers only notice people for what they can get out of them, never simply for mere interest's sake.'

Katya turned her mouth down. 'So, you noticed,' she said innocently.

'Trust fund money?'

'No. No. Just holiday money. I save up because I like to come to Kropse.'

Taban ignored the obvious lie. It wasn't likely Katya would reveal the source of her capital. But it was useful to let her know that the casino thought she was moneyed and would treat her as an honoured guest. 'Well, whatever. You are most welcome. Now, would you like to go to your table?'

'No, I'll have a drink first, Taban, thank you. There's plenty of time.'

Taban took her down to the bar and left her there. As Katya sat down, she was aware of admiring glances from both the men and the women who were seated alongside her. She swept her eyes over them and they suddenly became interested in their drinks or canapes. Except one heavily set man with slicked back dark curly hair who was sitting next to her.

'May I get you a drink?' His eyes held hers–The words an invitation to more than that.

'Why?'

'That's not polite– '

Another voice broke in. 'Good evening, Katya Petrovna.

What can I get you, champagne, glass of wine?' The bartender she'd met the night before had cut him short. The man grimaced; walked further down the bar in search of better luck.

Katya noticed a new, distinct coolness in the bartender. She remembered Taban interrupting him as he was about to open up about the casino and the casino's owner. She'd probably reminded him to keep his mouth shut. But that wasn't a problem. Katya knew the best way to lure a man was to be short with him to the point of ignoring him. 'Yorsh,' she ordered and turned away to study the room. She'd told Taban that people watching was her hobby so she may as well get on with it. She felt rather pleased with herself that she'd set up this simple excuse for studying exactly how the casino worked.

The bartender put her drink on the bar. 'One part vodka to four parts beer,' he said.

It wasn't necessary for him to say this. The mix was standard. She wondered whether he was signalling an apology. Even if he was, it was unlikely he'd open himself up to conversation so quickly. Without turning around, she kept up her freeze. 'You drink it weak here. Make mine three to one.'

'That's street strength. Not your background—or is it?'

The question made it obvious he was fishing and she guessed then that he must have been reprimanded for his lapse the previous night and told to fish for information. She wasn't going to get anything out of him. 'Just get me my drink,' she said coldly.

Katya looked around the room. Nothing seemed to be out of order. The roulette wheels clicked, croupiers softly announced the winning spin or shuffled cards and dealt them with deft flicks of the wrist and fingers—the speed of their dexterity almost at odds with the stony concentration of the punters. Chips rattled as high and low stakes found their way onto the blackjack table. She'd learnt that each blackjack table won casinos a guaranteed 7% of the play. Roulette punters were luckier, they only handed over 5% of their hard-won money. Winning, Katya remembered Guy telling her back at G8, was the name of the game for every casino. And that also meant for the bartender and for Taban and for Eu Meh.

Katya suddenly realised she hadn't seen Eu Meh since their first meeting. Probably her night off she thought. Although she had seemed scared when Taban saw her off the previous night.

It was the mental image of Eu Meh's Chinese nationality that prompted Katya to have another look at a blackjack table below one of the ornate chandeliers. It was slightly to one side of the floor, almost private. She wondered if it was for chosen players, rather like the private poker rooms that she'd heard talked about in Moscow. What had attracted her attention were the three Chinese women evenly interspersed among three Caucasian males. The men all had the round faces, broad noses and fair skin of Russians. Sub-consciously Katya realised she had been watching the betting patterns. The Russians had won and lost in a random fashion. But the Chinese hadn't won a single bet. Katya was sure of it. She picked up the fresh Yorsh the bartender had put on the bar, shifted herself slightly on her stool and, sipping her drink, pretended to look away as she kept her eyes on the table.

A few moments later, she turned back, put her drink on the bar. 'I'm trying blackjack,' she told the bartender and began to get down.

A shade of alarm crossed his face. 'Don't try that table,' he warned.

But she'd already gone, striding across the deep pile carpet; edging past a well-lit punter trying to pick her up.

The croupier at the blackjack table looked up, startled, as Katya took the empty seventh chair. No-one else paid her any attention.

She tossed him her MasterCard. 'Ten thousand please.'

'You get your chips from the cashier,' he said, apologetically.

'I want to be in on this deal. If I leave now, I'll miss it. It's my luck I'm trusting. I'll trust you to deduct my stakes as I place them.'

'It's unusual– '

'But acceptable.' She waved her hand, gesturing to the other players who were impatiently rattling their chips. 'Come on, my friends here want to play.'

He sniffed. 'Place your bets.'

'Four thousand dollars,' Katya said. She watched the other players shovel their chips forward. The Russians bet small. The Chinese bet at least ten thousand dollars each. And this was just their ante.

The dealer smoothed the cards out of the shoe and slid them across the baize to each player.

Katya looked at the four of hearts she'd been dealt. Not a bad card. The next card she received was better–the three of clubs. That gave her a good chance of reaching the twenty-one or near it to win. Should she go for it and double her stake? The shoe held eight decks of cards. That's as far as her calculations got. She wished she'd asked Guy back in the Tac Room at G8 how she worked out the odds of being dealt the right cards. 'Double down,' she said quietly, 'eight thousand.'

The dealer flicked her a card. Eagerly, she looked at it. A Queen, making her total seventeen. It could hardly be worse. Then suddenly she realised she wasn't here to win but to see what the other players and the croupier were up to. Was this game legit or was it, as she suspected, a moneylaundering set up? She hadn't taken in what the other punters had done. She swore to herself. Russian words picked up in an earlier life.

Suddenly the croupier was shovelling chips to two of the

Russians. They must have won. He then drew the bets of the Chinese women towards him. Each bet must have been forty or fifty thousand dollars in one thousand dollar chips. He looked at Katya. 'Eight thousand from your MasterCard,' he told her. She looked at him, surprised. She'd been so busy cursing herself she hadn't noticed whether she'd won or lost.

'Dealer made nineteen,' he intoned.

She'd lost eight thousand in two minutes. What the hell would Lev say. Then suddenly she realised what she'd seen. The Chinese women had consistently lost. And in the only game Katya had been in they'd lost at least a hundred thousand dollars between them–and there had been no reaction in their expressionless faces.

She felt exhilarated. She had to get to Lev. She had enough information for him and the Directors. They'd been right in G8– this casino was laundering money. And laundering big. And somewhere in the mix she'd discovered a Chinese connection.

TWELVE

Katya left the Sea Dragon immediately. It was dark, beginning to rain, and as she went down the steps Luka held up an umbrella for her. He started to chat but she couldn't wait to get back to the *dacha* and make arrangements to see Lev in G8. She hurriedly thanked Luka and climbed into one of the waiting taxis at the bottom of the casino steps.

Outside the *dacha* she paid off the cab and ran up the pathway, oblivious of the puddles splashing her shoes and legs. She opened the front door, turned on the lights and went straight to the telephone on the side table by the sofa. She'd already discarded the idea of using the dead letter box to set up the meeting with Lev. The procedure was too slow, too cumbersome. She needed to brief him urgently, tomorrow at the latest. She dialled the number for Aeroflot and, as she held the receiver to her ear listening to the interminable ringing tone, she thought how ridiculous it was not to have a mobile phone. She made the decision to tell Lev so when she saw him. A voice at Aeroflot finally answered and she booked a seat on the first flight to St Petersburg the next morning.

She was buzzing with excitement. She'd only been in Kropse two days and she'd cracked her case already. And wouldn't John Hammond be pleased she'd found the Chinese connection. G8 had close dealings with the Chinese and they could hand over the case to them—they would be glad to sort out their end. Elated she punched the air with her fist. It was a win win.

Suddenly, she heard the door-bell ring. Her first reaction was to ignore it. Then caution took over. The lights were on and even through the streaks of rain she may have been seen from outside through that massive A-frame window. It might seem odd if she didn't answer the door. Anyway, it would be interesting to find out who wanted to see her so late in the evening.

She crossed the room and opened the door. Standing there under the porch light, leaning an umbrella against the door post, was the cashier from the casino. He was still dressed in his dinner jacket and black tie. Katya sighed inwardly, she was too busy to cope with what was obviously an attempt to chat her up.

He must have read her face. His opening words were not what she was expecting.

'Hello, Katya Petrovna.' He made a small bow. 'I brought you this.' He held out his hand.

She looked at the piece of plastic in it. Recognised it as her MasterCard! How could she have forgotten to collect it from the croupier? That was careless. She was about to say so and send him on his way when abruptly she realised this might give her an opportunity to talk to him—to find out more about the casino. She gave the idea life as she took the card. 'That is so kind of you. Come in, do. I owe you a drink for bringing it to me.'

Yuri needed no encouragement. Taban had asked him why the croupier had Katya's card and why, after losing that almost urgent bet, she'd left so abruptly. It was odd, Taban had said, and needed looking into . . .

In the typical Russian way, he made firm direct eye contact with Katya. 'You are very impulsive, aren't you? Shouldn't you know my name first?' Before she could reply he said, 'It's Yuri.'

'That's always been a fault of mine. I can't believe I left my card behind. I think it must have been losing that bet . . . I mean I won all that money last night and I was convinced the next deal on that table had my name on it.' She turned and moved into the open-plan sitting room.

He laughed as, shutting the front door behind him, he followed her. 'The croupier couldn't believe you gave him your MasterCard–it's against all the rules and he was even more amazed he agreed to let you bet.' He looked into her eyes again, admiringly. 'I can see why though.'

'I'll take that as a compliment. Thank him for me, will you? Now, what do you drink Yuri? My favourite's Yorsh.'

'That's good with me.'

He looked around the room as she moved away to the dining area and fiddled with the bottles on a sideboard. 'A beautiful place you have here, the nicest area in Kropse. I wish I could have a place of my own like it.'

She poured vodka and beer into a small mug. 'It's rented. Do you live on the casino premises?'

'Yes. All the employees do.'

She walked over to him, handed him the mug. 'Everyone?' She wasn't sure this was unusual or not, but it seemed so. 'That's unusual, isn't it?'

'They like to have us on the premises, you know. Some gamblers have their favourite staff so that way we're always on tap.'

'I would have thought the owners would have lived elsewhere.'

'No. There's a penthouse and apartments above the casino. They . . .' He stopped abruptly. He was happy to talk to this stunning woman, but Taban had asked him to question her, it was not for her to question him. He began to think Taban had a point about Katya–she asked too many indirect questions–on the other hand he knew Morosov didn't agree with Taban's almost paranoid suspicion of Katya. Morosovs' view was informed by that old KGB lag Vasili who thought Katya was a wash-out, simply having a good time on her father's cash. But Taban couldn't tie this in with

Katya's obvious interest in the players on the gaming floor. She'd insisted that if Katya was there to have a good time, she'd be punting for all she was worth and drinking and looking for a man. And she wasn't. So Taban, the inquisitor, had her own way and Morosov had agreed that Katya should be probed further.

Yuri was suddenly frightened, felt he'd gone too far, given Katya information about the owners she didn't need to know. And the owners . . . He swallowed a mouthful of Yorsh–fought for breath in a violent fit of coughing. He heaved air into his lungs. 'What the hell is this?' he spluttered.

'Yorsh,' replied Katya, drinking from her own mug.

'Not this strong.' He coughed. 'There's something else in it.'

'Nonsense, it's only two to one–my party drink. I thought you'd like it.'

'Not if I'm driving back to the Sea Dragon. Taban doesn't tolerate over the limit driving.' More information he didn't need to give, he thought. 'I must be off.' He laughed, handed her the mug, saying, 'I won't say thanks for the drink!' He headed for the door.

Katya had noticed how Yuri had stopped himself part way through talking about the owners. She thought of delaying him to probe further but he might take that as an invitation of another sort.

'I'm sorry. I wouldn't want to get you in trouble.' As they walked towards the front door, she threw out a different lure. 'I didn't think Taban was a hard person.'

Remembering Taban's instructions, he said, 'I understand you used to sail around here. I'm free this weekend if you'd like to come out with me.'

Katya was pleased. So, there was more to come from this man. The thought was swiftly followed by another. She'd be back at G8 over the weekend, wouldn't be here again to take advantage of another meeting with him. Her operation here was over. She was about to tell him she couldn't make it when she realised he didn't need to know. 'Thanks. Let me know where and when.'

She shut the door behind him. A pity—if she had needed to continue her op he would have been ideal to cultivate as an informer.

THIRTEEN

After a sound night's sleep Katya packed, called a taxi and left Kropse for the airport. She took a plane to St Petersburg arriving just before mid-day on the early Aeroflot flight. She had travelled as Katya Petrovna and had taken her baggage with her. She was aware that, although she wouldn't be returning to Kropse, the casino *mafiya* might track her movements if they were suspicious of her sudden absence. Any indication that she had flown to London might spoil the chances of G8 rounding them up. Her plan, therefore, was to travel straight on to London from St Petersburg in her *alias persona*, Inessa Golubeva, on the teatime BA flight. But she could not take her baggage with her as this would pinpoint her as Katya Petrovna.

As soon as she exited St Petersburg airport, she took a taxi to the Ladozhsky Railway Station. She would leave her luggage there. G8 would then arrange to have it sent on to London at a later date.

The interior of the station took her by surprise. It had only been finished that year and she'd been expecting more of the heavy-handed stonework of the Moscova Rail Station. But here it was like being in a medieval cathedral. Curved steel girders replicated slim arches soaring to the ceiling. And, at the top, instead of intricate stonework there was glass - as if to tell the traveller that not just the world but the whole universe lay before them.

The attendant at the left luggage area was welcoming and, after Katya had taken a couple of items out of her suitcase, stowed her baggage away.

Katya went on to the restroom. There was no-one there. She took a dark blue beret out of one of her jacket pockets and fitted it over her swept up hair, tucking in the loose strands. She then took a pair of severe plain-glass spectacles with heavy brown rims out of the other pocket and slid them on. She looked at her reflection in the mirror over one of the wash basins and was happy to see Inessa Golubeva staring back at her. She thought for a moment, did she need to do anything else? She remembered Andrei Savin, her FSB training officer, saying, "*Less is more.*" She looked in the mirror once more and, satisfied, she left the restroom and went to catch a taxi back to the airport.

The journey was uneventful. As was the flight to London Heathrow. No-one had followed her and the only hold up was at the immigration desk when a fresh faced female officer challenged her.

'You travelled to St Petersburg only three days ago. Why the sudden return?' she asked.

'I found my boyfriend had cheated on me. There was nothing to stay for,' Katya said sorrowfully.

She obviously hit a nerve. 'They're all bastards,' the woman snarled as she slapped the passport on the automatic reader.

'Good reply,' Katya said with a smile and with no time for chitchat, she nodded and swept through the green customs channel and out to the taxi rank. 'Basingstoke Station,' she told the driver as she jumped into the cab.

England hadn't changed in the three days she'd been away, she thought, as the cab sloshed its way through the usual downpour drowning the M3. Still, it wasn't going to depress her spirits. She was on tenterhooks to see the Directors' faces when she told them her news. And to think they'd actually had difficulty in deciding whether to send her to Kropse. Things would be different for her now. There was a real career ahead of her. No stamping visas like that poor female at the airport, no interminable training. Well, except flying. She loved that above all. She remembered the day in St Petersburg when she'd been given her pilots licence–the independence, the freedom it gave her.

Her thoughts were interrupted by the taxi driver who was telling her they'd arrived at the station. She paid him off, walked onto the platform and found the restroom. She went in; found a free cubicle and, inside it, took off the blue beret and the severe spectacles and shook out her hair. Once more she was Katya Petrovna.

Another taxi took her to G8HQ. Seeing the vast grey warehouse that was her base, she felt like embracing it–the most permanent refuge she'd known. This was home and the security guards at the main door seemed to sense this as they welcomed her. She was popular with them–always gave them one of her devastatingly attractive smiles and was feisty enough to trade backchat.

As she walked out of the security area, there, in front of her, was John Hammond. She quickly walked towards him, her face alight with success.

He looked thunderstruck. 'Why are you here Katya? What's wrong?'

It wasn't the response she was expecting from him, but then she had surprised him by turning up unannounced, which was good. It meant her cover had held and she'd made no mistakes on the return journey from Kropse. She felt even better about herself. 'I've got important intelligence to report– '

'Why didn't you use the DLB to make your report?' His voice was severe.

'Well, I've finished the op I've got everything we need.'

Katya saw the expression of surprise on his face now deepen into astonishment.

'Right,' he said. 'Come up to the conference room in thirty

minutes. I want Lev and Walt to hear this.' He turned and walked away down the corridor.

She almost hugged herself. She had known that she would bowl him over with her success and now the American chief, Walt, who'd objected to her doing this op because she wasn't ready would have to eat his words.

She headed for the Bag Room. Various agents and personnel were sitting around talking and drinking coffee. She nodded or waved to the ones she knew as she looked around to see if Ami was there.

Katya saw her sitting on a sofa by herself, her head down tapping on her mobile phone. Katya hurried across the room to join her. She was bursting to tell her about Kropse but knew the only people who would ever know about her part in investigating the casino would be John, Lev, Walt and Guy. Need to know–the rule never to be broken. She noticed Ami had combed her hair out and had it straightened.

'Hi Ami, love the hairdo, it looks good on you.'

Ami looked up. 'Hi Katya! Thanks! What are you doing here? I thought you were on an op.'

Katya felt she could answer this without falling foul of the rules. 'I finished it.'

'Wow! That was quick. Good for you.'

Katya shrugged–modest. 'I'm just going to debrief the DG.'

'The DG? Himself? That's impressive–you must have done well.'

'Tell me what've you been up to while I've been away?' Katya deftly changed the subject.

'Oh, more training. Informant handling.'

Katya thought of Yuri–almost disappointed she hadn't had the chance to cultivate him further as an informer. Now, he'd be scooped up in a G8 raid on the casino and put away in some prison–she found herself hoping it wouldn't be the notorious Butyrka prison in Moscow. He wasn't tough enough to survive the brutality in there.

She realised Ami was talking. 'If you've got time on your hands now, what about a game of tennis this weekend? The weather's going to be fine–and there's this tennis pro I've seen there . . .'

'Ami! What happened to that squash player in the last two days–what was his name?'

'Jim–he's toast. Don't know what I saw in him. Anyway, are you coming?' She saw Katya hesitate. 'The pro's bound to have a friend,' she added enthusiastically.

The idea jarred with Katya. She was still recovering from an affair she'd had at university in St Petersburg. Learning that lecturers made promises of love and commitment they didn't keep. She remembered the words of the immigration officer at Heathrow– *"They're all bastards."* How right she was. 'I'm not interested,' Katya told Ami, bitterly.

Ami looked at her curiously. So, Katya had been burned in a relationship–she hadn't suspected that. Her friend was always so confident around men.

Katya glanced at her watch. 'Got to go. See you for tennis.'

She slipped away and got on the Paternoster. The memory Ami had stirred up had slightly damped her spirits. But she was not one to dwell on bad experiences and, by the time she had got to the third floor and reached the conference room, she was bubbling to tell her story about Kropse.

She found John there, seated at a console facing the large plasma screens on the steel wall in front of him. One screen showed Lev looking incredulous and Walt, on the other screen, looking cynical.

'Katya, thank you for coming.' John gestured to Walt and

Lev. 'As you can see, this is a video conference. Now we'd all be grateful if you'll debrief us.'

'I've cracked it,' Katya began.

'Perhaps you'll start by telling us why you didn't report through the DLB procedure.' Walt made each word an accusation.

'It's as I said, I've cracked it. I don't need to be in Kropse anymore, so the DLB was a waste of time.'

Lev screwed up his eyes, peering at her through a cigarette haze. 'Sorry. I don't understand, Katya. What do you mean you've cracked it? What exactly have you cracked?'

'I know for sure the casino launders money. I saw it happening–twice.'

Silence.

Katya went on enthusiastically. 'On one occasion a man changed a pile of chips for dollars and the cashier didn't count the chips in or the dollars out. The other time I sat at a blackjack table where three Chinese women bet big and didn't win a single hand.'

'I see,' John murmured, unconvinced. 'And who were these people?'

'Well, punters, of course.' Katya thought he should be able to catch on more quickly.

'Laundering for themselves or the casino?' Lev was as bad as John. What was wrong with them? Didn't they realise what had happened.

'The casino, of course.' She tried not to sound exasperated.

'They told you, did they?' Walt asked brusquely.

He'd soon be apologising, she decided. 'No. Of course not. It was obvious. The women who lost were all Chinese, the men were Russian and they won, well two of them did.'

'What's the relevance to the casino being involved in moneylaundering that these women were Chinese?' John, being obtuse again.

'There was no reason for them to be there. China's thousands of miles from the Black Sea.'

'St Petersburg is nearly two thousand miles from it–yet you were there, so what's so special?' Lev, talking like an atlas.

'There was a Chinese girl, Eu Meh there. It ties in with the Chinese punters.'

'OK. What else have you got for us?'

John had changed the subject–he'd obviously accepted she was right. Pleased, she pushed on. 'Taban, the floor host, asked me a lot of questions. She was suspicious, protective of the casino. She'd clearly been tasked by the owners to suss me out.'

'What sort of questions? Your job? Your family? Where you lived?' Lev, the ex KGB interrogator–on the attack again.

'No. She asked where my stake came from–was I a trust fund babe. Why I was so interested in watching the punters, that sort of thing. And the cashier asked me to go sailing with him, he was so interested in getting me to talk–that's typical *mafiya* tactics.'

'And *were* you interested in the punters?' Walt, totally ignoring her earlier report about them.

'I've already said so. Of course I was interested in them–Oh! And the owners live in penthouses above the casino–the cashier told me that by mistake. I know they're *mafiya* and I've got enough information on them for us to go in and get them.'

'So you disobeyed instructions and risked coming came all the way here instead of sending a DLB message just to tell us what we already knew from the woman picked up at Heathrow?' Walt, scornful.

Katya couldn't believe what he was saying. She opened her mouth to protest.

Lev saw her, cut in, protecting his protégé. 'Walt, we didn't know about the Chinese. That's new.'

'Katya, Walt's right.' John said softly.

She hardly heard him. Her heart was thumping. These men didn't believe her. Didn't recognise what she'd achieved.

John sensed her reaction. She needed an explanation. She really had believed she'd done a good job. Walt must stop blaming her and Lev must stop protecting her. Her G8 training officer had said she was brilliant. She mustn't have her confidence destroyed on her first op. What she'd done wasn't uncommon with new agents–getting overconfident and exaggerating their achievements.

He turned and looked straight at her. 'Walt is right. You've given us very little. We already suspected the casino was moneylaundering. What you've done is to tell us you saw a few people acting suspiciously. You didn't follow that up with more visits and covert surveillance. Had you done that you might have confirmed exactly who are these people– who housed them. You should have got their details, seen if they had any relationship to the people running the casino. Estimated how much cash was being laundered each evening. Have you tried to find out who the manager is–who these owners are who live in the penthouses? Have you tried to search them, find out if there's any incriminating information there–any safes?'

'Where is the casino safe, anyway? There must be one. You've actually found out nothing.' Walt was scathing; biting into her.

'No need to bully her, Walt.' Lev sounded protective again. 'I've been on ops like this. One can get over-enthusiastic–interpret things the way we want to see them rather than how they are.'

For the first time Katya was seeing things the way they really were. Lev was right. She'd built everything up in her mind; the big picture in her imagination hid the detail she should have found out. She'd ignored the essential elements needed to create a successful operation. She'd failed miserably. She suddenly felt sick.

'What you need is a Yorsh,' Lev suggested, kindly. He raised a bushy eyebrow in John's direction.

'Katya doesn't need a Yorsh,' interjected Walt, 'she needs more training. Remember, I said so at the very beginning of this debacle.'

John ignored him. 'Lev's right. Go to the Bag Room, Katya and get yourself a Yorsh. We'll have another session tomorrow and put things right.'

Katya fought down a sense of panic. They were going to pull her off the op. She wanted to plead with them not to, but she felt breathless—no words came.

Lev knew instinctively what she was going through. It wasn't just the shattering knowledge that she'd been too cocksure that was making her beat herself up. It went back to the merciless tyranny of her father, who'd shouted at her, abusing her emotionally for every little mistake that she made. And Katya was Russian and felt these things more than most. He would make sure that this experience didn't destroy her. 'We must send you back to Kropse Katya. You can build on what you have found out so far. Correct Walt? John?'

FOURTEEN

Dense fog had blanketed the Black Sea when Katya arrived back in Kropse the day after her disastrous visit to G8HQ. It had descended from the Caucasus Mountains and rolled onto the Black Sea whilst she was being grilled in far-away Basingstoke.

She had felt hammered in that G8 conference room. Only Lev had really supported her. Walt had been harshly dismissive and John only held the ring so as to agree she should continue her op. But, she acknowledged to herself, the fact was they were right. She knew she deserved Walt's frustration and John's barely concealed unease. She'd rushed her fences and totally failed to step back and coldly analyse the information she had for them. It was as if she'd been in this fog, only hers had been one of self-delusion. She wouldn't make that mistake again, that was for sure. And to help her on the way to that goal, she had to get to the fishing wharf and see Viktor right away. She needed a favour.

First though she made her way to the *dacha*. Once there she had a long hot shower which revived her spirits and changed into a pair of dark blue jeans and a comfy, oversized red jumper. She grabbed her jacket and was now on the beach, picking her way along the darkly indistinct sea edge–the nearby *dachas* were each an amorphous blur, only slightly greyer than the fog. Not a ripple disturbed the dark water to distinguish it from the sand. The danger filled boom of a ship's bass foghorn or the nervy shrill whistle of a motor boat coming out of the gloom gave an eerie sound to the sense of foreboding. Black Sea it was and it echoed her own bleak feelings.

But Katya's was not a character to remain subdued or defeated for long. A throwback to her mother, she thought, who'd continually hung on to her dazzling life as the means to dull the abuse hurled at her by her domineering, controlling husband. Despite the debacle at G8HQ, Katya remained sure that, if she'd been able to report to G8 without having to delay by using a dead letter box she wouldn't have been in so much trouble. That meant having a mobile phone, something Lev had forbidden. It being, in his opinion, a security risk. She was now sure Lev had been wrong and she'd paid the price for that by racing back to London and making a fool of herself. Well, that wasn't going to happen again.

On her way through St Petersburg she'd bought a burner at Ladozhsky Railway Station. It was in her pocket now. If she was going to complete this op, and she'd vowed to herself that she would, this mobile would be a lifeline–an untraceable lifeline unless it was found on her. That meant she must find a secure hiding place, well away from the prying eyes of the *mafiya* and–she felt no twinge of conscience about deceiving him–Lev.

She wrinkled her nose at that thought. Then prayed that Viktor hadn't decided to stay at home and out of the fog.

She could see nothing of the wharf until she carefully climbed the steps onto it. She stopped there, knowing the area was strewn with fishing gear. She pulled her jacket tightly around her, shook out her wringing wet hair and shivered as fog molecules streaked down her neck. The silence was broken by another ghostly boom from a ship's siren.

Viktor wasn't there. The wharf appeared to be deserted. She decided it was too risky to walk around it. She could break an ankle or worse, tripping over some unseen rope or anchor. She began to leave.

Just then the fog shimmered suddenly, as if pushed away, revealing a shape picking its way towards her.

The figure came closer. She felt a surge of relief as she recognised Viktor.

'I heard you'd left Kropse,' he said accusingly, as if she owed him an explanation for not telling him of her plans.

She wondered how he knew she'd been away. Word from the casino? Hardly–he'd warned her against going there. Who else might have been interested enough in her to note her absence? Of course, it had to be the maid, Ludmilla–gossip between locals. She relaxed. She was getting paranoid.

'Only for a visit to St Petersburg,' she told him, evenly, still hating that she had to lie to him. 'I had to sign some papers about my father's estate.' She peered around the dock. The usual sounds of fishermen working on engines or shifting nautical gear were missing. The dim outline of boats, hazed amidst the fog blanket, seemed almost forlorn.

'Are you alone?' she asked him.

'Weather's unpredictable,' he replied without answering her question. 'The mullet don't like fog,' he added inconsequentially.

He hadn't changed since her teenage years when he'd helped her with the finer points of sailing a two-master boat. He'd been so phlegmatic back then that she'd itched to shake him awake at times. But he'd never let her down, always allowing her to make her mistakes and then taking the wheel or the rope or the sail and showing her how. Always in slow time.

'I wondered if there is someone here I could see about hiring a sailboat–when this fog lifts.'

'You don't want to hire a boat from here.' He pursed his lips, thoughtfully . . . 'Well, I suppose there's that old schooner you and I used but she's not been out for a year at least– her hull will probably need some caulking.' He scratched his cheek. 'I'm alone,' he said slowly. 'If you want to tell me why you want to know.'

'I need a favour, Viktor.'

He looked away as if seeing something through the fog. 'That's new. You never asked before . . . and you had plenty of reason to as I recall.'

'You know I had to take care of myself. If I hadn't . . .'

'Your father would have drowned you for a weakling . . . I knew that. Didn't make it easy for me though.' He took his pipe, a tobacco pouch and some matches out of a pocket in his oil stained brown overalls.

She'd seen this gesture a thousand times before. He always lit his pipe before giving up his knowledge of seamanship. This time she knew he would be giving something different. She waited.

He didn't speak until the flame from the match he'd struck had died down on the tobacco in his pipe. He drew on the pipe stem and watched the blue, sweet smelling smoke drift away. 'I heard you've been to that casino,' he began, stopping her from interrupting him by showing her the flat of his gnarled hand. 'You always listened to me so I knew you wouldn't have gone unless you had to . . . 'Or–he pointed the stem of his pipe at her–you were ordered to. So, who are you? Someone who's changed or someone who's working for FSB?'

'No–'

'Katya, I'm old but I know you and I know your father was desperate for you to follow him into the KGB.' He drew on his pipe again and the words came out with a stream of tobacco smoke. 'But they were disbanded and the only successor was FSB.'

The gesture reminded her so much of Lev. Would every man who looked after her interests be a smoker? 'Do you think I'd tell you, old friend, if it was true that I'm an agent? What danger would it put you in? No, I simply want a favour.'

'Tell me.'

She pulled the burner out of her pocket. 'Keep this for me. They don't allow them in the casino.'

He took it, turned it over in his hand. 'Why do you go there if not to spy on them?'

She shook her head and smiled at him. 'Oh Viktor, the man who knows

everything . . . My father left me a bundle of dirty KGB cash and I'm spending the damn lot. I don't want a rouble of it.'

FIFTEEN

Viktor wasn't the only one who was put out that Katya had left Kropse without a word. Back at the *dacha* she found Ludmilla there, furiously hoovering. When she saw Katya, she switched the machine off with a sharp snap muttering something about her not telling her she would be away and about Moscow manners.

'No, I was in St Petersburg.' Katya laughed.

'That's not where you come from with that accent–I can tell,' she muttered darkly.

Katya left it at that. She wasn't about to discuss her birthplace or anything else with her maid, or was she the *mafiya's* maid? Katya felt it was just as well she'd managed to get her mobile into Viktor's hands before Ludmilla had arrived. She didn't want a word to get back to the casino that she kept a mobile at the *dacha*. On that point Lev had been right.

Katya picked up the pencil and notepad that lay by the telephone in the hall and walked towards the dining room table and sat down. It was time for her to sort out the system she'd been thinking about to beat the odds at roulette.

She'd played quite a lot of *Nardy* during her days in Moscow. The game only needed two players, it was like backgammon using two dice and was popular in Moscow street life. She had enjoyed doing something else other than just listening to the songs in the jazz cellars. She'd found it easy to listen to the music and, at the same time, remember all the moves that had been made during the game. This had often surprised opponents who thought her mind was on the current pop group and not on their strategy. It hadn't taken her long to learn that the most frequent number to come up after a roll of the dice was 7. She'd also taken the trouble to find out that this probability was supported by mathematical theory and that the next most common numbers to come up were 4 and 10.

She remembered this and wrote these numbers down on the paper–7,4,10. Looking at them, she realised she had no idea why these numbers would be relevant to roulette. How could the roll of two dice be linked to a small ball rolling around in a roulette wheel? She twisted her long hair with one hand, racking her brains as she thought about it.

Ludmilla surreptitiously looked over Katya's shoulder as she put a steaming cup of hot tea down in front of her. She stabbed her finger on the paper. 'You need the 1 and 13,' she said.

Katya's first reaction was to tell her not to interfere. Her next was to realise that 1,4,7,10,13 was the sequence starting a down line on a roulette layout. This maid knew the game and must know she was working on a system. If Ludmilla was *mafiya* she would tell the casino and that would go in Katya's favour. It was no secret that gamblers who had systems were wedded to casinos–they had little time for anything else. Taban and Yuri might then accept that she really was there to gamble and stop prying into her background. Then she would have a better chance of finding out more about the place.

'Oh well done, Ludmilla. Of course, you're right.' She wrote 1 above the 4 and 13 below the 10.

She studied them for a moment. As she'd thought before, there was no basis for a roulette betting system there. 7,4 and 10 might come up most frequently in a dice game but there were no dice in roulette. Another bright idea, she laughed to herself. Then she remembered how dismissive of systems Guy had been back in the Tac Room. Well, if that was the case then one system was as good as another. Anyway 7 was a lucky number in Russia and the number 4 was lucky in England. People did sometimes win with their systems. She wrote the main figures down again. 4,7,10. Why not? If she stuck to these, one or other must eventually come up. She could even break the bank.

Katya arrived at the casino later that evening wearing a stunning short emerald green, sequined sheath dress teamed with her gold T-bar shoes. She'd arranged her hair to fall in waves down her back. She thought she looked pretty good and she felt optimistic as she walked in, her head held high.

She wasn't sure whether to be pleased or suspicious when Taban met her on the gaming floor and didn't mention her absence. Taban simply welcomed her and asked what her preferred table would be that night. She then accompanied Katya to the cashiers' desk and had made no comment when she heard Yuri enthusiastically mention the next day's sailing trip. This didn't seem to add up to Katya. Employees were not meant to fraternise with the guests and Taban had been tough with Eu Meh when she had done so. Yet for some reason Taban approved of Yuri's invitation. She seemed to want Yuri to get alongside Katya.

Katya felt that this was possibly her first breakthrough. She could handle Yuri easily and if she handled him right, she could turn him—make him an informer. So, she told him she was looking forward to their meeting on the Saturday morning and cashed $30,000 into $1000 chips. She noted that neither he nor Taban made a comment. Obviously to cash that amount was not remarkable, which indicated the sort of wagers this place was used to dealing with. She smiled to herself— all the more to win when she took their roulette table to the cleaners.

She decided to avoid the virgin table and to spend her evening at the roulette gaming table nearest the bar. When she got there she almost changed her mind. The green baize with its red and black squares and numbers and signs seemed dark and, somehow, foreboding. She told herself not to be so Russian and stood beside the table watching the play.

Sitting there was a dark-haired oriental looking woman of about thirty, wearing a black cocktail dress and a glittering diamond choker necklace. She was losing badly, plunging steeply. Katya watched her play the red and black areas in sequence. The woman was becoming increasingly irate as she lost three times in a row. She'd bet $10,000 dollars a time and she had only two chips left. Katya saw her turn to the dark-haired man sitting on her left –almost certainly Russian–and asked him what she should do. He leant over and took one of her chips and placed it on the area for even numbers, the jewelled gold ring on his index finger glinting in the light from one of the chandeliers, as if to herald good luck.

The wheel spun. The ball clicked onto 17.

'Come on, I'll buy you a drink,' the man said to her as he stood up.

The woman got up immediately, picked up her chips, handed them to the croupier, saying, 'Keep these for me.'

As she turned and saw Katya looking at her, she grinned. 'I hope you have better luck.' She looked at the man who was now standing at her elbow. 'Come on, whatever your name is, you owe me a drink.'

Katya watched them go. So, she and her man friend were strangers to each other– and the woman was clearly Chinese. Was it significant she'd lost just like the others?

The croupier looked at Katya and at the vacant seat, inviting her to take it. Katya knew it was now or never and with a sudden rush of adrenalin she sat down. She had thirty thousand dollars in chips and three numbers to use from the system she'd worked out. She couldn't lose. All she needed to decide was whether to go all in or to spread it over ten bets. She wanted a good return so it would probably be best, she reasoned to herself, to spread the bets. Her 4,7 or 10 numbers must surely come up in five spins of the wheel according to her theory. If she won on just one of them she'd have nearly seventy thousand dollars to play with, even more if her system really paid off.

Confident, she leaned over and placed two chips on each of her numbers.

The croupier adjusted his bow tie, spun the wheel, intoned, "*Rien ne va plus*" and propelled the ball around the top of the wheel. Fascinated, Katya watched as the ball slowed down and hit one of the compartments. It bounced, bounced a few more times and then settled.

'Seventeen,' the croupier announced. Interesting, Katya thought. It was the same number that had come up when the Chinese woman had lost. Were they going to make sure Katya lost too? She smiled confidently to herself. There was no chance of that with her system.

She waited until the croupier had cleared the table and then put two chips each on the same 4,7 and 10 squares on the baize cloth.

She wasn't dismayed when number 26 was called. She still had three bets left and she knew with her spread bet plan she must win.

Her next two bets went swiftly. The numbers 32 and 0 came up. Still no sign of her 4,7 or 10. Katya felt a tinge of alarm. She looked down at her last six chips. Was it prudent to lower the stakes to a thousand dollars each to give her two plays or stick to the plan and risk all on one bet? She picked up the discs and slid them through her fingers, looked over at the roulette wheel as if trying to read what it had in store for her. She heard the croupier say, "*Rien ne va plus.*" She fixed her eyes on him as if to influence his spin of the wheel–shoved all six discs forward onto her chosen numbers. She kept her gaze on him, willing the clicking ball to fall into one of her numbers.

"*Eleven*" she heard the croupier call. She didn't hear the rest of his spiel. She'd just run through thirty thousand dollars of G8's budget and her grand scheme of breaking the bank and attracting the attention of the casino owners lay in tatters. She was no further forward in her investigation than when she'd been roasted by the Directors at G8HQ.

Feeling beaten, she got up from the table. The croupier caught her eye–waiting for his gratuity. She had nothing to give him except a brief smile.

She was about to walk away when she saw him raise his chin and point it towards the table. The green baize was clear of chips except three that still lay on the First 12 Box area. Katya shrugged.

He used his rake to sweep the chips towards her. 'Your winnings.'

Without thinking she said, 'No I didn't bet on the First 12 Box.'

'One thousand you placed there. I don't make mistakes. Take it, otherwise I will be in trouble.'

She pictured herself placing the bet, her eyes willing on the croupier–of course, one of her chips must have rolled onto the First 12 Box by mistake. It was incredible. She had won three thousand dollars. She tossed one of the chips she'd won to the croupier.

'You're lucky for me.' She laughed.

'No, I think I was lucky for you.' The Chinese woman wearing the diamond choker had returned, alone, and was sitting down beside her.

That was almost the last thing Katya remembered clearly about the evening.

In the mist that descended she could just make out the vague shape of Yuri cashing her MasterCard into chips, then later his excitement as he'd called Taban over. Katya dimly remembered being given papers of credit to sign; memories of feeling hot and cold as she'd watched the croupier's rake folding in chips; of utter disbelief that she was losing; of Taban giving her ever more credit papers to sign – the compulsion, 4,7,10 . . . Unshakeable,

Dizzying . . . the obsession 4,7,10–4,7,10 over and over again. She must win. She must.

Then of Taban leaning menacingly over her, saying, 'No more credit Katya. Your limit has been reached–you owe fifty thousand dollars.'

SIXTEEN

K atya's first sensation when she woke up in her bedroom the next morning was one of cold fear. She couldn't believe what had happened at the casino the night before. How could she have been so arrogant, so stupid as to think she could have won with her system. How could she have lost over a hundred thousand dollars.

There was no way she could go back to G8 and confess what she'd done. It wasn't the loss of the cash that made her shiver. G8 could afford that. No, it was her total loss of control that John and Lev and Walt would not understand. They'd mark her down as unstable under operational conditions and her career would quite simply be over. She began to try and unravel what had happened and then realised how useless that exercise was for her. There was no excuse, getting caught up in a gambler's reckless certainty that luck would change was as foolhardy as accepting a drugged drink. What on earth had she been thinking . . .

As she turned over she shifted her pillows, as if the action would somehow change the situation, make it better. But, she knew, from bitter experience that she could expect nothing and no-one to help make things right. She'd fended for herself from childhood, when she'd waited in vain for her mother to come home. She'd gone from the lonely days and nights on the Moscow streets to being cold shouldered by her FSB colleagues when they'd learnt of her father's perfidy. But this was worse–she could see no viable future for herself–and she cursed herself for being such a fool.

These thoughts were abruptly interrupted by the shrill ring of the front doorbell. She pulled the pillows over her head and waited for Ludmilla to answer the door, hoping whoever it was would go away. The doorbell rang again, an urgent tone to it. Swearing under her breath she pushed the pillows aside and sat up. Of course, it was Saturday and Ludmilla had the weekend off.

Surely it couldn't be someone from the casino wanting their money? She'd have to fob them off. Jumping out of bed she flung on a pair of jeans and a T-shirt and raced down the stairs, running her hands through her hair to straighten it. She opened the front door.

'Katya.' Yuri looked her up and down, his eyes focussed on her bare feet. 'You are still in bed?'

'No, no Yuri.' The last thing Katya wanted was to give him any hope in that direction, 'I was exercising, doing my morning yoga.'

'Ah!' He looked at her. 'Are you still sailing with me?'

She really didn't feel up to a day with him or with anyone, she was exhausted and her mind was racing on how she could sort out the disaster of last night. She started to put him off. 'Really? Now? I thought–I thought it was tomorrow.'

'The wind is getting up tomorrow . . . you should know how quickly it strengthens here . . .' He let the words hang.

He didn't need to remind her. Her father had never cared how strong the wind was when he'd sent her out. "*Overcome adversity*" he'd shouted as he'd pushed her sailboat out into the white capped waves. She heard the echo of those words. "*Overcome adver*sity."She shrugged. 'Come in and sit down. I'll go and get my shoes.'

She went quickly up the stairs and into her bedroom. Going over to the cupboard, she pulled out a pair of boat shoes and grabbed a heavy knit sweater. Thinking furiously, she put them on. If she got Yuri on side she might be able to put off repaying her debt to the casino at least long enough to use him to find out who owned the place. If she could do that, a hundred-thousand-dollar loss might not look so bad on the G8 balance sheet. And if she could get Yuri to go so far, there were other things he could do for her–such as give her a look at the casino books or at least tell her about them.

'That was quick,' he remarked as she came down the stairs. 'You didn't give me time to join you.'

Katya did an abrupt *volte face*–some encouragement for him was going to be necessary if she wanted to turn him. She looked at him and laughed, saying, 'Too early Yuri –and we don't want to be too late do we . . . I mean, with the wind getting up?'

She shut the front door behind them and followed him down the path towards the beach road.

Yuri felt satisfied. She hadn't said no. And the exhilaration of a fast, heeling sail would probably get her to say yes later. 'All the gear's on the boat. I keep it there.'

'Aren't you afraid it will get stolen?'

'*My* stuff? Get *stolen*? You're joking.'

There was something in the way he said it that caught Katya's attention–the emphasis on "*my*" the way he expressed the impossibility of the idea. She probed, subtly.

'Oh. Does the boat belong to the casino?' she asked casually.

He was stung by the implication that he wasn't the owner–couldn't afford a sailboat. 'Of course it belongs to me. But the casino looks after me–us. Everyone knows that.'

In Moscow or St Petersburg when someone said something of that sort to her, it meant *mafiya*–keep out. She pretended she hadn't sussed the implication. 'They're good employers then? The owners?'

'They're alright.' He pointed to a yellow beach buggy with outsize wheels parked by the kerb.

Katya went towards it saying, 'That looks like fun.'

'Hop in.'

Yuri took the vehicle off road immediately and onto the sand. 'The beach is best,' he shouted over the noise of the high-pitched engine. 'And a lot faster than the road!'

Katya began to revise her opinion of this man–she'd marked him down as a number crunching accountant. She had thought that flattery and a little excitement might lead him astray. The flattery would definitely work–his reaction to being told he couldn't afford a boat had told her that. What worried her was that she didn't think a little excitement was going to influence him much. He may be a tougher proposition to recruit as an informer than she had bargained for.

They drove into a small marina sandwiched between a dull, steel-caged, plate-glass- windowed hotel, and a smaller hotel which, with its pale blue painted Trezzini exterior, was obviously a high-end boutique "residence". In complete contrast, the marina was classic late communist, concrete and more concrete. Built to last, but Katya saw the tell-tale rust marks of corrosion, probably caused, she thought, by a mix of sea water during construction– typically corrupt building methods.

She looked around and was surprised at how few boats were moored there. Was this indicative of a limited membership of the marina? And, if so, was it *mafiya* membership? She caught herself–she was jumping to conclusions again. Yuri pointed out his boat and Katya immediately recognised it as a neat Antila Elba 27 sloop. The vertical prow and sloping stern made for a fair bit of speed and the broad beam provided good stability. She had only sailed one once and had found it an exhilarating boat with its open cockpit and tiller steering.

They came to an abrupt stop and got out of the buggy opposite the sloop.

'Climb aboard and I'll show you around,' Yuri said.

Katya clambered over the boats safety rail and waited while he opened the hatch to the cabin. It wasn't locked, she noted.

He led her down the steps of the short companionway saying, 'Here is the saloon– table, benches–there's the head.' He pointed to a small door to the rear.

'Mmm. I know,' Katya replied.

He sounded surprised. 'You've sailed one of these before?'

She smiled. 'Once.'

He opened another door in the rear bulkhead revealing a double bed. 'So you'll know about this then?'

'No, Yuri. It was a short get-to-know the boat sail, not a get-to-know-the man.'

He raised his eyebrows. 'We've got all day . . .'

She sighed. 'Yuri, are we here to sail or am I going to have to wrestle you away from me all day? Sail–I'll stay. Wrestle–I'll go.'

He grinned. 'Sail,' he promised.

'Good. Let's go.' She turned and climbed back up the companion steps. 'It's very small this marina. Must be difficult to get in and out. But I suppose with only those few boats the membership is pretty exclusive.'

'Yes. I'm lucky. The casino owns it and only the owners and life members get to park their boats here.

Her first thought was how strange it was that casino owners would sail such small boats. The second thought sent her pulse racing. If she watched this place she could identify those people who came to sail. She knew it had been the right thing to do to cultivate Yuri.

He started the outboard engine and manoeuvred the boat out of the marina. They raised the mainsail and jib; the Antila caught the wind and, with Yuri at the helm, swept out across the whitecaps.

Katya sat on the gunwale and pulled on the jib sheet to

tighten the sail and add a little extra speed. She looked back at Yuri. 'You sail her well, but you're a bit cautious, aren't you? You could bring the mainsail in a couple of notches.'

'She's stable but not that stable–and this wind's gusty.'

'I thought you said we're going for a sail? This is just pottering about. Come on, give me the helm.'

The last thing he wanted was to have her in charge of the boat in this unpredictable weather. He'd seen how reckless she could be. Last night she'd gone wild at the roulette table, punters had crowded around cheering her on as she'd placed bet after bet. Utterly calm as she'd lost and lost. But he needed her on side. Morosov wanted to know more about her. She was into the casino for fifty thousand dollars and he wanted to know how much more he could squeeze out of her. She may be more willing to talk if she got a fright– and she would be frightened if one of the sudden squall's hit; the boat was stable but there were limits.

He moved over, handed her the tiller. 'Go on then.'

Immediately, she tightened the mainsail and told him to do the same with the jib. The boat heeled over, gathering speed rapidly, sea water bubbling along the coaming. The wind noise heightened and the leaches of the sails shimmered under the strain.

Katya threw back her head and laughed, her eyes shining. 'Yes. This is sailing.' She looked sideways at him. 'Like last night– right out on the edge.'

Yuri held on to the jib sheet, leaning back to balance himself against the steep heel of the deck. 'You lost a hundred thousand dollars and thought it was on the edge? Right over the cliff more like.'

'Why? There's plenty more cash where that came from. I just need some time to get it out of my trust fund account.'

'They don't give people time, you should know that.'

She adjusted the tiller to meet a steep wave. 'Who's they?'

'The owners. Well Morosov really–' He suddenly noticed a patch of roughened sea rushing towards them. 'Watch out,' he yelled. 'Squall coming. Let out the main.' He started to loosen the jib sheet.

'Don't you dare do that,' she shouted at him. 'This is my boat now.' She narrowed her eyes; watched the seething area of water as the wind suddenly howled and beat against the sails. Water now creaming over the gunwale along the deck. The speed increased and the boat heeled over further–Katya's arm taut as she held the tiller, making small adjustments as the boat tore through the water.

Yuri was terrified. He'd sailed these waters for years but had never been in a boat so near to capsize. He clutched the jib sheet, gritting his teeth. If he let go of it now the boat could go out of control. He clung on, eyes tight shut.

The wind suddenly lessened–the squall rapidly disappearing.

'Oh! That was brilliant.' Katya stood up, handed Yuri the tiller. 'Now you know what your boat can do.'

He took it, his hand shaking. 'Shit that was a crazy thing to do. You could have drowned us.'

She took hold of the jib sheet. 'Rubbish, Yuri. You're chicken that's all. If you'd lost that amount last night you'd have run away by now.'

He was furious. Furious with himself for having shown her his fear and furious she had none. Well, he would show her what real fear was. 'You can't run from them. Ever.'

At last, she thought. The first hint of who these casino owners really were–*mafiya*. If she said the word out loud she'd have to implicate Yuri and if she identified him as *mafiya* he would report it to the owners. So it meant that Taban was definitely one of them. But what about the Chinese women, they wouldn't be part of a Russian *mafiya* gang. She never heard of *mafiya* mixing with

Chinese Triad gangs. She would have to think about that later. Now she must play up to Yuri. 'I'm glad I won't have to find out. I thought you told me your bosses were nice people, that they looked after you. Well, if they're going to be difficult about waiting for me to get more funds you can give me your help.'

Yuri knew there was no way he could help her. Morosov wouldn't wait. He only waited when he knew the punter's background. Yuri stalled. 'You really think I'd do that after you nearly drowned me? Anyway, I'm a cashier, I haven't that sort of influence.'

'Then I'll speak to this Morosov you mentioned. He'd have influence.'

Yuri became alarmed. Why had he mentioned Morosov's name? The man would be furious he'd been identified—and Katya was just the sort of person to go and see him. The only way out was to get to Morosov before Katya. 'Well, I can mention you want to see him. That may make it easier.' He paused. 'But only if you can convince me you have the cash to pay off the debt.'

Katya knew she would have to give some information if she was to stall this Morosov. 'My father was KGB. He was killed recently and I'm his only beneficiary.'

Yuri knew that "*beneficiary*" meant there was a Will. Wills went through a probate procedure, and that meant there'd be records. It should be easy for Morosov to get at those records and to the details of Katya's inheritance. This was valuable information and Morosov would be pleased with him for getting it. 'Time to go back,' he said. 'I don't like the look of that weather on the horizon.'

'Well, you wouldn't, would you.' Katya shrugged. 'OK, let's go back.

'Ready about,' he called, and moved the tiller.

Katya let go of the jib sheet, took hold of the other jib sheet and, as the boat swung around, pulled it, bringing the sail taught.

The boat steadied on the new course heading for the Marina in the distance.

'Who was that Chinese woman next to me last night?'

'Xiao Cheng? Oh, she's always at the tables. I'm sorry she kept pushing you to bet more last night. It was obvious you were on a losing streak. But she loves spending other people's money.'

'People like whoever bought that diamond choker for her–'

'She isn't a . . .' Yuri stopped himself. This woman was dangerous. She led him into saying too much.

Katya took advantage of Yuri's confusion. 'I'm not a fool, Yuri. She was with a man last night that she didn't know, yet was happy for him to lay a bet for her and to go off with him. She's a hooker isn't she–high class?' She narrowed her eyes; suddenly shouted, 'Watch out for that buoy!'

He violently pulled on the rudder. The boat narrowly missed the channel buoy for the marina. He steadied the helm.

'It wouldn't be wise for you to say that about Xiao Cheng on the gaming floor,' he muttered.

Katya lifted up a white plastic fender from the deck and put it over the side of the boat as they approached the jetty. 'Is that a threat? What sort of a place is Morosov running there, Yuri?'

He held the end of a mooring rope out to her, sought her eyes with his. As she took the rope he said, 'Your father was KGB, Katya. You want to be careful. Morosov has no love for the KGB.' He looked away and then sideways at her. 'You ask too many questions.'

SEVENTEEN

Yuri took Katya back to the *dacha* and left her there. She'd looked surprised when he just drove off. No doubt she'd been expecting him to make a pass at her, he'd thought. But he couldn't wait to see Morosov and report what he'd learned. He'd made the excuse that he had to get back to the Sea Dragon and cash up for his shift.

Dumping his beach buggy outside the casino, he ran up the steps, brushed past Anatoly, the floor manager, and raced up the stairs to Morosov's office.

He burst through the door and stopped dead. Lying directly in front of him on the floor was a punter, a man called Jensen, his face blotched deep red, his tongue protruding below bulging eyes. He wasn't breathing.

Luka was bent over Jenson, cutting away the wire that dug deep into Jensen's neck. Luka didn't stop to give Yuri a welcome and Yuri, himself, was disinterested. He'd seen these executions of welshers before. He stepped over the body and went on into the main part of the office. It was more important to speak to Morosov—who was sitting at his desk.

Morosov didn't look up. He was typing on his laptop keypad and watching the results on the screen in front of him. After a moment, he drew in a breath between his teeth and, looking up, glared at Yuri as if what he'd seen on the screen had been the cashier's fault. 'The shit! Didn't even pay the interest.' He glanced indifferently at Jenson's body. 'A dead loss of eighty-five thousand dollars. And I gave the sod an extra two days to pay. I tell you that's the last time I do that. If word gets around that I'm soft. . .' He let the rest of the thought go unspoken, as if not worth mentioning. 'So, what the hell's up with you barging in here?'

'It's about Katya Petrovna. We need to talk.' Yuri jerked his head at Luka.

Morosov tightened his lips. 'Get out Luka. You can finish that later.'

Luka put the wire cutters on the desk. He wondered what that little bastard Yuri wanted to tell Morosov. But that didn't stop him walking straight out through the door. He had a soft spot for Katya. She was his kind–a street kid. But that wasn't a good enough reason to tangle with someone like Morosov.

Yuri watched him go; turned back to see Morosov taking a bottle of vodka and two glasses out of a drawer in the desk.

'Thanks.' He kept any sign of relief out of his voice. He hadn't been worried when he'd seen Jensen's body because the decision to give the man leeway to pay had been Morosov's not his. But Yuri knew his position was only secure for as long as he provided information on the punters and he had found nothing to suggest that Jensen was broke. Morosov might have blamed him for that.

Morosov filled the glasses with vodka shots; handed one to Yuri, saying, 'So, what do you know about the Petrovna woman? Apart from the fact she's into us for fifty thousand dollars?'

'I took her sailing today and she opened up about herself. Her father was KGB, got killed and she's his beneficiary. That means we can ask our Moscow contacts to get into the Probate file at the Registry and find out how much cash she has access to.' He tossed the vodka back. A gesture of satisfaction.

Morosov drank his vodka, put the empty glass on the desk and poured another shot. 'You know, Yuri, you are beginning to concern me.'

Yuri felt his stomach churn. His palms were sweating. 'But, why? This is good information.' He tried to keep his voice steady, fear gripping him.

'Like the stuff you didn't get on that piece of meat there?' Morosov pointed at the body on the floor with his glass, vodka slopping on the desk. 'Shit.' He wiped the small puddle off with his hand. 'I know about her father, Yuri. What do you think I do here—just knock off punters? She's broke. That's what you should be telling me. She blew her father's cash on that blackjack table and she's taken us—you—for fifty thousand dollars.'

'But. . . but how d'you know?' As soon as he'd uttered them Yuri knew the words were lame. He felt his breathing go shallow. This was trouble—deep trouble. While he'd been trying to get the woman into bed, Morosov had obviously been checking up on her—doing the work he, Yuri, should have been doing. Rapidly he searched his mind for an excuse. He could find none. His natural cunning took over. If there was no excuse, find a diversion, a credible diversion. 'I realise it was my job to find that out but I got involved in a different angle. Look, she's different to normal punters. Haven't you found that? That's she's different?'

Morosov didn't disagree with him. Taban had said much the same thing. The interest Katya had taken in the punters and what they were doing—the strange behaviour at the blackjack table, trying to get Eu Meh into conversation, the friendliness with Luka, a bouncer for god's sake. 'Go on,' he said sharply.

'Who started this place? The casino? The link with China?' It was a rhetorical question. 'The KGB—well, not *the* KGB but ex KGB officers . . .'

Morosov squinted at him. 'And her father was KGB, is that what you're saying?'

'Exactly.'

'But why? They're finished.'

'The organisation is–but the men aren't.' Yuri paused. 'Nor are their children.'

'Shit! You're not telling me there's some conspiracy of grown up KGB children to take this place back? That's out of Planet X,' Morosov said scornfully.

Yuri began to believe the idea himself. 'Why not? It's been fifteen or so years since the KGB was disbanded. The money they made from this place is probably gone. Why not try and get it back? With the Chinese end we earn not short of three quarters of a billion dollars a year.'

Morosov gestured to Yuri to hold his glass out and picking up the vodka bottle he refilled it. 'And you think she's an advance reconnoitre for these KGB grown up children?'

'I do.' Yuri left it at that. The proposition was too much of a conspiracy theory to stand much immediate probing but it seemed to have caught Morosov's attention which is what he wanted.

Morosov's mouth turned down. 'Then we need to ask her.'

Yuri put his glass on the desk. He looked over at the remains of the man on the floor. 'I'll get Luka to clean up this mess.'

Morosov shook his head. 'No. Leave it. He can clear up both bodies after I've finished with Katya Petrovna.'

EIGHTEEN

Katya had been surprised but relieved when Yuri left her at the front door of the *dacha*. She'd fully expected him to come in and pester her to sleep with him. She did wonder, though, whether she'd gone too far in showing him up as fainthearted during the squall. She knew she'd let her joy of sailing dangerously get the better of her. She should have backed off, let him take the helm and reef in—played to his ego. It was the weakness her training officers constantly put on their reports—*"reckless"* they called it, and inwardly she cursed her father for having instilled in her a constant demand for courage.

Then, she thought, there was nothing she could do about it and, having said goodbye to Yuri, she went up the stairs, stripped off and went into the shower. As the warm water beat down on her she started to run over the information she'd been able to glean from Yuri. Most important was the knowledge that the marina was owned by a Russian

mafiya . . .

She was interrupted by the ringing of the doorbell.

Yuri must have come back. There was no way of knowing how things would develop if she met him wearing just a towel. He'd have to wait. She turned off the taps and towelled herself down; pulled on a tracksuit, found some flat shoes, tied back her hair and went down to open the door.

'Viktor!' Katya looked around to see if anyone else was nearby.

He smiled and held up a string of three red fish.

'Oh! Red mullet,' she exclaimed, loudly in case anyone was listening. 'That's so kind of you. Come in, do.'

'Thank you, *Malyshka*.' He gave a small bow and walked in, looking around. 'I'll put these in the kitchen.'

She went ahead of him saying, 'Follow me. I haven't had fresh fish since I've been here, Viktor. Thank you so much.'

They went to the back of the sitting room into the spacious kitchen area. She showed him a large sink in the middle of the central island–switched on the cold-water tap saying, 'Put them in here–I'll clean them later.'

'That is what you did as a girl.' He laughed, then coughed. 'Not now you are grown up. I will clean them for you.' He put his hand in his coat pocket. 'Oh, and I have this for you.' He pulled something out, hidden in his large blue-veined hand.

She looked mystified.

He opened his fingers–there, in his palm, was her mobile phone.

She reacted immediately. 'Viktor, I don't want that here. I told you– '

'Someone phoned.'

She was incredulous. 'Phoned? Me? On the burner? They couldn't have. No-one knows I have a phone–only you.' The last words were said with a hint of accusation.

'It was a man's voice and he asked for you, *Malyshka*. He said, "*Can I speak to Katya.*" I told him you weren't there. He didn't give his name, just told me to ask you to phone him back straight away.' Viktor sounded confused. 'Did I do something wrong?'

She realised she'd hurt him. He would never mislead her. She put her hand on his arm. 'I'm sorry, I just didn't expect it that's all.' She took the phone out of his hand and put it on the island. 'I need some tea–I expect you could do with a cup as well.'

While he cleaned the fish, she made the tea, black and strong as she knew he liked it. 'How much jam would you like?' she asked over her shoulder.

'What is it?' He looked across at the jar in her hand. 'Cherry? Ah! Good, two spoons please.'

He took his mug and the spoon from her–dug the spoon deep into the jam jar.

'Viktor!' Katya laughed.

He grinned, put the jam from the spoon into his mouth and drank the tea through it. 'Cherry is always best.' He put his free hand on her shoulder. 'Now you need to phone whoever it is who wants you.'

'Thanks Viktor and I'll see you soon.'

He nodded, handed her his mug, turned, walked through the sitting room and left the *dacha*.

Katya picked up the phone from the island, tapped in her password. There was one number in the Recents list. She didn't recognise it–pressed redial and waited for an answer.

'Katya.'

With a start, she recognised Lev's voice. How the hell did he know she had a phone? She clamped her jaw shut, as if that would spare her from having to answer. This was real trouble.

'Katya? Are you there?'

She remembered her mother's words to her after one of the frequent vicious rows she'd had with her father. "*I envy you Katya. You are always happy even if you're in trouble.*"

She made the effort saying lightly, 'Lev. How great to hear you. I was about to call you.'

Lev's reply was sheer ice. 'Really? On a burner you hid from me? Something I had forbidden as it was too risky–You were trained to do better than that.'

This was even worse than she had anticipated. Lev had always been her friend. . . well not a friend but a staunch ally, someone who had always supported her. Perhaps an apology would go down well, plus a bit of flattery. 'Yes. I'm sorry, Lev, but I need a mobile– anyway how did you find out, I thought I'd covered it up completely.'

'That's a stupid question–I'm talking to you, aren't I?' He changed the subject abruptly. 'Why is the casino checking up on you in the Moscow Probate Registry?'

His cold anger bit into her. She felt sweat reach down her back. What did he mean? She knew the casino would check up on her but not that they'd go this far. If they got into the Registry in Moscow they'd find out she had no more cash. She wouldn't be able to bluff them long enough to get her op finished. And Lev knew. How did he know? Of course– through his old KGB network.

Lev's voice came through, relentless, 'They'd only check-up if you were in debt to them, so what's going on?'

What could she say? Tell him she'd burned through a hundred thousand dollars? No way.

'Who gave you authority to punt on tick?' Lev's Russian was more colloquial than she'd ever heard it–a sign he'd nearly lost patience with her.

She rushed the fence, saying hurriedly, 'I lost a hundred thousand dollars and I'm into them for fifty–but I've got a lead–' she broke off so as to get his interest.

Silence.

She hurried on. 'There's this cashier, Yuri, who I went sailing with and he's definitely *mafiya* and he's part of a *mafiya* group that runs a marina where the casino bosses park their sailing boats and if I can carry out a discreet surveillance on it, I can identify them. That's what we want isn't it?' She stopped. Adding detail would only give more for Lev to attack.

Silence.

'Lev, are you there? Lev?'

Silence.

She realised she'd lost him. He must have cut the call. She took in a deep breath. Where to go now?

'No more . . .'

Katya expelled the breath in a rush. Lev was back. What had he said? 'Sorry I didn't hear that.'

'I said "*no more money*". I can't get it out of the budget.'

'But I need to cover that fifty thousand dollars otherwise I'm in trouble–they must know I can't pay it back as things stand.'

'Listen to me Katya. If I tell John and Walt about this conversation you will be on the first plane back to the UK and out of G8. For good. Do you understand.'

'But if they know I'm near a breakthrough, surely–'

He cut across her. 'If you think I'm going to let the other Directors know how reckless you've been, and have you kicked out when it was me who supported you and recommended you for this op you are very much mistaken. There will be no more money.' His tone was final.

Katya's mind reeled as it gave voice to the future Lev had created for her– "*What do you think this mafiya will do to you now they've found that the money in your father's estate has been spent, the well is dry?*"

She shoved the thought aside–refused to let Lev hear her fear. 'Then I'll make this breakthrough by myself.'

Lev made no compromise. 'If you choose to stay and stick it out, you'll have to do the thing alone.'

That said, he thought to himself, she was Russian, like him– often difficult to understand, sometimes too eager–made mistakes but had that courage and resolution that always saw them through the hard times.

Katya heard the click as he ended the call.

NINETEEN

Katya knew she had to hide the burner. She found a bag of instant coffee at the back of one of the kitchen cupboards, emptied some of it out and pushed the mobile down into the bag. Ludmilla only drank tea so Katya was satisfied she wouldn't discover it.

Pouring herself a Yorsh, Katya took it onto the terrace and sat down in one of the long chairs, stretching out her legs. The sun was setting over the sea, its reddish glow casting faint tinges of colour onto the rippling waves. Her thoughts were on what she had learned in her conversation with Lev. He wasn't interested in how she might exploit the information she had gleaned from Yuri. He had made it clear there were only two outcomes now the casino knew she was broke–the end of the op or the end of her. Either way she was finished. There seemed to be no way out.

She had never experienced a time when she had come to a full stop. There had always been some way out–climbing out of her bedroom window at night as a young teenager to avoid the oppression of her home; running errands for street corner *mafiya* to avoid their violence. She had developed evasion as one of her survival tools. So why was she finding it so difficult to find a third option other than the two Lev had predicted for her?

She half watched the orange sun sink slowly into the sea; the evening shadows were lengthening over the water. She shivered slightly. From the sudden chill in the air? Or was it the chill inside her? She sipped her Yorsh and, as if the mix would somehow provide the answer, ran over the reason for the mess she was in. It was simple–the casino would find out from the Probate Registry that there was no more money in her father's estate. She took another sip of the Yorsh. But was it so simple? They may have found out in the Probate Registry documents that he was KGB. She took the thought further. KGB officers always had secret funds–well, almost always. They were totally corrupt and not even the President had any idea how much cash had been secreted away by them from the Central Office Funds and spread across the globe. The *mafiya* running the casino would know this, added to that they were greedy. She began to see some light. Could a well told story about waiting for cash hidden by her father in some tax haven buy her the time she needed? They might believe her–at least for as long as she needed to have a good look at the marina and see who went there. If she was convincing enough, there was a good chance she could fool them.

She now had a plan–and she knew the sooner she got to the casino the better. She must give no indication that she was trying to avoid them. She must look positive, totally in charge–which meant wearing her highly sophisticated red scoop necked dress. It was fitted to the waist and then slightly flared out to a midi length. Her matching red handbag and high heeled black sandals would be perfect.

She went up to her bedroom to change. Finally, she added her gold chain necklace and clasped her wide gold bracelet onto her wrist. The jewellery would contrast strongly with the red of the dress and make the finished look dramatic. She carefully made up her face, putting on an extra layer of green glitter eyeshadow and applying the expensive red Dior lipstick she'd saved for when she wore this dress. Lastly, she gave herself a generous spray of Picasso. Almost ready. She took a hundred dollars from the roll she'd kept back for emergencies and put it in her bag.

She knew she had made the right decision with the outfit when Luka almost ran down the Sea Dragon's front steps to greet her with a wide admiring smile.

'Katya Petrovna. Good to see you. We thought you might have been too upset to come back today after your bad luck yesterday.'

'Thank you, Luka,' she said, pressing a fifty-dollar bill into his hand.

Anatoly was also pleased to see her.

Taban wasn't.

She met Katya at the top the stairs leading down to the gaming floor.

'You can't go down there,' she said sharply. 'I need to see you repay last night's debt before I let you play the tables again.' Her lips were pursed and hardly moved as she obviously enjoyed saying the words.

Katya went into her act, saying airily, 'I don't understand, Taban. Of course, I have the money to repay the debt but It's going to take a few days to get it here. I'm sure you can accept that.'

'*You* may be sure of the money,' Taban said rudely, 'but I'm not. No more credit–I want that fifty thousand dollars repaid now.'

'And I said you'll get the cash when I've received my funds. So let me pass.'

'My job is to– '

Katya saw that they were attracting the attention of the gamesters on the floor. She looked at Taban. 'I'll see Morosov,'

Taban was taken aback. How did Katya know Morosov?

Katya noticed her hesitation, pressed her advantage. 'Take me to him now. And when I see him I shall report your unhelpfulness.'

Taban felt more uneasy. Had Vasili got it wrong? Was the old

KGB warhorse out of touch? Was there some cache of dollars that Katya's father had told her about and she hadn't declared to the Probate authorities? Morosov would soon find out. 'Very well. If that's what you want I'll take you to him.'

Katya followed her up the stairs to the door of Morosov's office. Taban knocked, opened it a crack, leaned her head through the space. 'Katya Petrovna to see you.'

Morosov had seen and heard the interchange between Taban and Katya on the ceiling monitor. The Katya woman had sounded very positive that she had the funds. Had she got some offshore account somewhere? It had been standard KGB practice for its officers to set them up. So, if there was more cash to be squeezed out of this Katya he'd better not send her the same way as that punter, Jensen. He made up his mind. 'Take her to my apartment Taban. I'll be there in a minute.'

Taban hesitated, feeling a tinge of jealousy as she knew Morosov only saw women in his apartment for one purpose–to seduce them.

She heard Morosov's muffled voice. 'What are you waiting for?'

Turning to Katya she said, 'Come this way.' Her jealousy faded a bit. Morosov could be violent if he didn't get his own way. Serve this bitch right.

Katya followed Taban along a marble floored, wall lit corridor to a bank of lifts. They took one to the top floor.

When Taban opened the door into Morosov's apartment Katya saw it was furnished on the same lines as the casino. No doubt from the expensive stock of some KGB officer's furniture warehouse. A bit of undisclosed private enterprise.

The sitting room was large enough to host a tennis tournament. There was room for three immense chandeliers and three separate seating areas where pale grey sofas and chairs were spread around to allow for easy conversation. Bureaus and drinks cabinets lined the walls beneath modern paintings. There were eleven pictures she could see–the cost must have been near two hundred million dollars and there must be more in other rooms.

The man Katya suddenly saw standing in the doorway opposite her was studying her. He was not more than five feet tall; heavily built. He was dressed in a sharp tailored grey suit, dark maroon tie and a black shirt with dark maroon buttons. There was a gold Rolex watch on his wrist and various large flashy gold rings on his pudgy fingers. His flabby body was topped by a fleshy face and wisps of thinning brown hair were combed over his head. His dull colourless eyes were crawling up and down her body and in them she saw the lifelessness of the truly cruel.

He started speaking, his voice a whine. 'Katya Petrovna.' He twitched his head at Taban. She left without a word, shutting the door behind her.

He walked over to a drinks cabinet near one of the richly draped windows. 'Vodka?'

'Yes, Yorsh, please.' Katya decided to lead the conversation. 'Thank you for understanding about my temporary lack of funds.'

'Of course.' His mouth curled into a smile. But his eyes–cold, expressionless–said different. He gave her a mug of Yorsh and signalled to her to sit on a sofa.

She expected him to sit next to her. He didn't–instead he chose a chair opposite and raised his glass to her. *'Zdorovya.'*

'Zdorovya.' The taste of beer was overpowered by the strength of the vodka. She'd had this trick played on her many times before. She held out her mug. 'Fill it with beer, please.'

Wordlessly he took it, did as she'd asked and handed it back. 'You're as smart as you look.'

She ignored him, looked around at the paintings. 'I love your art.' She pointed to a painting of various multi-coloured elongated human figures in gymnastic poses. 'You must have been lucky to find that early Warhol.'

'Don't talk to me about art, I know nothing about it. You'll have to ask the punters who gave them to me–us.'

She was puzzled.

Morosov saw confusion on her face. Explained. 'Payment for gambling debts.'

She knew immediately what was coming next and wondered how many other innocents had walked into the same trap. She mentally kicked herself for mentioning the word art. Making it so simple for him to ask her what her intentions for paying off her debt were. In the most civilised way, of course.

She was right.

'And how do you propose to pay your debt, Katya Petrovna?' He made her name sound like a whore's alias.

She gritted her teeth. 'Like I said, my funds are temporarily held up but I will settle up as soon as they arrive in my bank. As you know my father was KGB . . .' She let the sentence trail off.

'Good. Good. Yes, I know about him.'

She inwardly sighed with relief. She'd known deep down that these people wouldn't just rely on the Probate Registry for information. Lev had been wrong about that. He'd had her really worried for no reason. She raised her glass to Morosov. 'I can tell you. He left me very well off.'

'Well, let's not waste any more time. Come with me. There's something in my office I'd like to show you.

TWENTY

As Morosov hadn't made a pass at her in the penthouse sitting room Katya expected him to make a move in the small confines of the lift. He didn't. Instead he pressed the lift button, saying, 'I thought your father would have funds offshore–which place did he favour, Virgin Islands, Antilles?'

Katya was totally unprepared for this question. She'd led him to believe she'd be getting cash and she hadn't prepared herself for this question. She knew any hesitation in naming a place would be suspicious. But, if she did name an offshore tax haven, Morosov would ask questions about which bank or fund was there. If she identified one he'd almost certainly have a contact who would check up. If she didn't, he'd be even more suspicious. She'd been careless again. What to do? Evasion. Play for time.

Hoping she sounded off-hand, she said, 'I've just met you and I've only been here twice. I hope you don't think me rude if I keep that information to myself.'

'No, not rude at all. Foolish perhaps, seeing as you owe me–us, and you're asking for time to pay.'

It was too late to turn back. Katya pressed on. 'Well, I agree I would be foolish if I didn't have the money.'

Morosov gave a short, humourless laugh. 'True.'

The lift stopped and the doors opened. 'Come. You are going to be really interested in what I have to show you.' He walked along the corridor, opened his office door and held it as Katya went in. He let the door go and walked straight to his desk. He stood behind it and looked at her, his hooded eyes giving nothing away.

Katya heard rather than saw someone slam the door shut behind her. She turned to see Luka there, locking it.

She swung around to face Morosov, trying to keep the alarm from her voice as she demanded, 'What's going on?'

Morosov stayed standing, his mouth working, 'You think you are so smart don't you. The beautiful Katya Petrovna. Dressed in your power red clothes, wearing your sexy scent.' He mimicked her. "I've got money offshore–oh I couldn't tell you where, I don't know you." Who the fuck do you think I am–who *we* are?'

Katya was shocked into silence. She felt a tremor slash right through her. It took all her strength not to stagger. She'd been sure this man had believed her. He was talking again–snarling–his fleshy face reddening with anger, 'You *will* tell me where this money is.'

She summoned all the contempt she felt for this *mafiya* bully– no different from those she'd met on the Moscow streets. 'Don't you try and bully me. I've got friends. My father's friends.'

Taban had come in and joined Morosov at his desk. She looked past Katya's shoulder. 'This is wasting time. She's bluffing. Let's get it over with.'

Katya followed Taban's eyes and suddenly saw Jensen's body in the far corner of the room, the wire in his neck glinting in the naked overhead light bulb. She felt the blood rush up to her head, darkening the room. She fought for breath, stupidly remembering Lev's words, "*You are alone*"

'Are you going to tell me?'

Was Morosov giving her a last chance. But a last chance to do what? The darkness cleared but no ideas came to her. She watched as Taban nodded to Luka who was still standing by the locked door. He moved away from it and came to stand behind Katya. He was so close she could feel his breath on her neck. Katya turned rapidly to fight him off– stopped in her tracks as she saw him holding a loop of piano wire fixed to a meat hook in the ceiling. So, this would be how it ended. She could fight or plead. But she knew Luka was too strong for her–and Morosov was too disinterested. She decided to plead.

She swung back to Morosov. 'I can be helpful to you.'

He laughed. 'How? Sell your body? You wouldn't last a month here, less in Da–' He stopped abruptly as Taban nudged him. 'I know your sort,' he finished lamely.

'Get on with it, Luka. I've got guests waiting for me downstairs.' Taban, impatient.

Her words conjured up for Katya an image of the punters quietly going about their business–or their bankruptcy–ably assisted by Taban and the Chinese woman and Eu Meh– and who else?

'I can be a floor host.' Katya rushed out the words.

'What do you know about being a host?' Taban said, her voice scathing.

'I'm attractive.' Katya looked at Morosov–remembered the blackjack table, the Chinese women, their huge losses–took a blind thrust into the dark. 'Maybe not strong enough to be pimped but I know enough to steer punters to the right table.'

Taban and Morosov exchanged looks and Katya knew she'd struck home.

'And how would you do– ' Morosov started to say.

Taban cut in, her voice coming from deep in the back of her throat, like an attack

dog. 'This is ridiculous. I'm not having this welsher anywhere near the tables–I don't trust her.'

Katya dived into the split between them. She looked directly at Morosov, cutting Taban out of her line of sight. 'You told me I'm smart, dressed in my power clothes, wearing sexy scent. I impressed you so I can impress high end punters–women as well as men.'

Morosov narrowed his eyes as they travelled over her again and he remembered Yuri's warning about a conspiracy of KGB offspring aiming to take back the casino their parents had founded. Preposterous–but was it? If this woman was dead he'd not find out– alive, he would. He waved Taban away as she leaned over him to say something.

Katya, seeing the hesitation, crashed through the gap. 'And I can persuade the punters to use my system. They'll lose millions.'

There was a stunned silence. Then Morosov burst out laughing, a rasping sound. He thumped his fist on the table. 'Fuck, that beats all. Oh, shit, you're fucking unique.' He rolled his eyes. 'Your system– ' He turned to Taban. 'Take her downstairs and put her to work. Floor host only. Nothing else. Right?'

Taban glared at Katya. 'You'll regret this, believe me.'

She pushed her out through the door past an expressionless Luka. Katya wondered how long she had before she was in this room again.

TWENTY-ONE

As they walked down the stairs to the gaming floor Taban made her position quite clear to Katya. 'You screw up once, you cow, and Luka will finish the job of getting rid of you. You may have Morosov on a leash now but when that money still hasn't arrived he'll cut you loose quick enough.'

Katya ignored her–left her standing on the bottom step as she spotted a tall, elegant, middle-aged woman dressed in a long dark green evening dress. Its severity lightened by a glittering gold necklace; the white, rose and gold colours of her Russian wedding ring glinting in the overhead lighting.

'You seem a little lost.' Katya smiled as she went up to her and held out her hand. 'Katya Petrovna. Can I help?'

The woman took the outstretched hand in her long fingers and held it. 'Hello, Katya. I'm Svetlana Ivanov and yes I do need some assistance,' she said gratefully. 'I don't really know what to do. This is my first time in a casino. My late husband's oil shares paid a big dividend yesterday and I'm celebrating.' She looked around. 'I'm not sure where to buy some chips or which table to go to.'

'Of course, Svetlana. If it's your first time in a casino, it's best you play roulette. Much safer than the other games. Come with me.' Katya took her arm and led her to the virgin roulette table, saying, 'Roulette's my favourite. And I'm very lucky. I always put my chips on the three same numbers.'

Svetlana nervously twisted her gold ring, uncertain, disbelieving. 'Every time? Isn't that very risky?'

'Not as risky as trying different numbers each time you play.' Katya spotted an empty chair between two punters who were busy laying their bets and guided Svetlana towards it. Katya pointed to the croupier spinning the wheel. 'Ask him which is riskier. He knows.'

Svetlana laughed. 'Now that I don't believe.' She settled herself in the free chair between the two absorbed punters.

Katya gestured to the croupier saying, 'This lady wishes to buy some chips.'

Svetlana looked uncertain. 'I don't have any cash I'm afraid. Will a card do?'

The croupier nodded gravely. 'Of course.'

She handed him a MasterCard. 'A hundred thousand dollars, please.'

He took out a roll of thousand dollar chips.

Svetlana held up her hand. 'No, I can't cope with all those. Have you anything larger?'

The croupier counted out twenty $5000 dollar chips, raised his eyebrows at Katya and gave her a nod of approval.

Svetlana looked up at Katya and said softly, 'Which numbers should I choose?'

Katya leaned over her shoulder and whispered into her ear before moving away towards the bar.

A man was sitting there by himself—short, bald and wearing a very tight-fitting Ted Baker tuxedo, perfectly creased trousers and long pointed black suede shoes. He looked as if he was fighting off middle age—a perfect target to exploit at the tables.

She sat down next to him and ordered a Yorsh.

'What's that?' the man asked her.

'Beer and vodka mix,' she replied. 'Would you like to try one?'

He nodded. 'I'm Helmut—Helmut Klein—from Munich,' he

added, in case she thought he took her for a pick-up. Her accent told him she was Russian and Russians could be very feisty if they felt insulted.

Katya ordered another Yorsh and settled down to the tricky task of getting him to the tables—without him seriously thinking that more was on offer.

After a few minutes of discussing the strength of Yorsh and explaining her system to him, Katya suddenly saw Svetlana coming towards her. She looked close to tears and Katya realised it had taken the croupier no time at all to scoop all her chips off the table.

Katya got in her greeting first. 'Hello. I hope you have won. Now, I want you to meet Helmut Klein. He's new here from Munich and wants to join the fun at your table.'

Helmet held out his hand which Svetlana absently took. She let it go saying, 'It was no fun, I can tell you.' She took a shuddering breath, 'I've lost it all.'

Katya looked puzzled. 'But you have only just started. What happened?'

'I did as you said,' she replied. 'I put it on the three numbers you gave me—none of them came up.'

'You put it *all* in one go on those numbers?'

'Yes. Did I do something wrong?'

Katya gave her a sympathetic look. 'Oh! That's not the way to do it at all. Sit down and have a drink.' She stopped—pretended to think. 'No, no. I have a much better idea. I've been telling Helmut exactly how to play my system and he will show you.' She took Svetlana's arm with one hand and Helmut's with the other.

They arrived at the table and Katya looked at the croupier. 'This lady would like some more chips.' She turned to Svetlana. 'The same amount?' she questioned.

Svetlana shook her head. 'No, Katya, I don't want to play anymore.'

'Don't worry.' Katya smiled at her. 'Helmut will show you what to do and you'll get it all back plus more. Believe me.'

Helmut wasn't going to pass up this opportunity. Svetlana was vulnerable and, in his experience, vulnerable women were manipulable. He ushered her into a seat, saying, 'Katya's right you know. She's got a good system. I've never heard of it before, so it must be good.' He sat down beside Svetlana. 'But, for a start, you don't put all your chips on in one play. A system is a game of patience. So, let's see, what have you got there?' He looked at her chips. 'Perfect. $5000 on 4,7 and 10. I will do the same.' He looked admiringly at her and just before the croupier spun the wheel said, 'Let's order some champagne.'

Katya left them with their heads together. They'd probably find solace together, happy at first as they both won and then, later, commiserating over their losses.

Morosov was watching the screen in his apartment sitting room as Katya moved
out of the range of the ceiling monitor. He took a sip from his glass of vodka and turned to Yuri. 'She's good. She's already got us back her fifty thousand and made us fifty. Those two she hustled will be good for another hundred and fifty at least this evening. It might be useful to keep her for a few more days—at least until word of her useless system gets around.'

Katya felt pleased with herself. She felt sure Morosov would have monitored her on his screen and would have seen what had just gone on. She'd bought some time. Not much, but if she proved to be a valuable asset—and she'd already made him a good profit—he might keep her in the job. There was still so much she needed to find out for G8 to complete her op.

Taban's voice came from behind her, gravelly, low, almost

hissing, 'What the hell do you think you are doing you bitch? You poached my mark. I had him lined up and you took him away.'

Katya turned around–she could almost touch Taban's venom–but she welcomed the threat. If Morosov was watching–and she was sure he was–she could now do some heavy damage. She ratcheted up Tabans fury. 'If he'd been interested, you'd have landed him. Fuck you, Taban. Morosov runs this show, not you. You try and get me in trouble and I'll go straight to him.'

Morosov had swung back to look at the screen. The monitor was directly above Katya and her words cut into him. They confirmed what he'd been worried about for some time but couldn't prove. Taban was muscling in on his territory. Her job was to supervise the gaming floor, not run the show. She needed to learn that.

As Katya walked away from Taban she knew that horrendous woman would be out for blood. That meant she had a few days at most in which to complete her operation to find out what was going on here. She was now skating on the thinnest of ice.

So far, she had learned that Morosov was the day-to-day manager of the casino but who were the real owners? Taban seemed to be more than just a hostess–her dominance over Eu Meh was evidence of that. But what was her *real* job? Was there some significance in her being Mongolian and Eu Meh coming from China? And what about the other Chinese women at the casino? That seemed unusual. Kropse was a small town, unlikely to be on the Chinese tourist map. Was there some casino link with China? She recalled Morosov being nudged to shut up when he'd started to say something beginning "Da–" What had he said? Something about selling her body. *"You wouldn't last a month here, less in Da–"* Those were his words, cut short by Taban. Could that be the China link? China was famous for its criminal gangs, the *Triads*, *Tongs*–running prostitution–and gambling, come to that. Could Morosov have been about to name somewhere in China? Some link to a *Triad*?

She went over to the bar. Ordered a Yorsh. Sat down in one of the chairs. She ran her hand through her hair as she continued to run over her thoughts . . .

The Chinese women had all lost a huge amount of cash very fast. That was a classic moneylaundering ploy in a casino. Was cash being brought in from a Chinese *Tong* to be laundered here? She turned her mind back to the lip movement Morosov had made when he'd said "Da– ". Could that be the island of Dao? It had been a Portuguese Colony and the KGB would have been active there creating contacts with the criminal fraternity to help their attempts to subvert Portugal. The KGB owners of the casino in Kropse would have maintained those links and the new owners could have taken them on. Dao had recently become part of China, so keeping the link with the gangs would be logical. But Kropse and Dao were seven thousand kilometres apart. How could a moneylaundering or prostitution link be sustained across such a distance? By boat? The marina? Possible, but Dao would be nearly a month away from Kropse by sea. By air then? Kropse airport was small but big enough for medium haul jets . . .

'Katya. Lost in thought?'

With a start, she looked up. Yuri was standing in front of her. 'Hello, Yuri. Yes, I was wondering how the couple I set up at roulette were doing.'

'Losing very well. You did a good job–come out to dinner with me?'

His invitation was totally unexpected. But he was a source of information and she knew she couldn't pass up the opportunity of getting close to him. She thought rapidly. The marina might hold some clue to what was going on. If she could get into it . . . 'Only if we have dinner at the marina. I feel like sea air,' she told him.

'It's a deal. We'll meet at the marina entrance, in an hour.'

TWENTY-TWO

Katya had seen the marina from the sea when she'd sailed there as a child and teenager and again recently, when sailing with Yuri, but had never visited it. Now she was here, she was going to take every advantage to find out whether Yuri's strong hint that it was a *mafiya* hideout was true. What were his words– "*You can't run away from them. Ever.*" So, when Yuri met her at the marina clubhouse entrance and proposed that he take her on a tour of the place she was genuinely delighted.

Yuri had been thinking about his conjecture that the old KGB officers, who'd started the casino and sold it, now wanted it back– perhaps supported by a group of their grown-up children, and, unaccountably, the idea had taken hold in his mind. Katya, nosing around for information, was one of the group, he was sure of it.

In his book, the best way to get information was to give some first. 'You know the KGB built this place as a military base,' he remarked as they walked over a metal grid bridge which separated the dock from the main buildings.

Katya had spent days here with her father learning to sail. She'd hated his teaching methods, setting her off in the sailboat and telling her, in that cold, controlling voice of his that she'd learn better alone than with him aboard. She'd nearly died, alone at sea on many occasions when the sudden storms brewed up and, as she'd fought to survive, she'd despised him for his brutality.

She didn't hesitate to answer Yuri's question. 'Of course,' she replied, calmly. 'I expect my father operated from here when he took me sailing. Why, was your father KGB too?'

'No. He was an accountant. We lived here in Kropse and when the casino was built the owners employed him as a cashier. I followed in his footsteps when I was eighteen as an accountant.'

She was interested in the extent of his father's nepotism. It might show how influential the father was–or Yuri was, for that matter. 'That's young to have finished your accountancy exams.'

'As my father told me, you don't need exams to run a casino's books.' He pointed to a three-storey grey building. 'That's the clubhouse.'

Katya looked up at the concrete slab in front of her. She knew immediately that her fiction that her father had operated from here would easily be believed. The whole cement- clad exterior shouted Soviet Military HQ. She followed Yuri through the plate glass front door. Once inside, she found the décor was no different–dull grey walls and unpolished concrete floors. They stood or lay in unrelieved gloom which never altered as Yuri guided her onto stairways and long passages interspersed with grey painted doors. Yuri explained them as they passed by–reception rooms, bedrooms, bathrooms, kitchenettes, offices.

Offices in a marina? Katya became alert. The KGB had presumably used them when it had been a military base but why were they kept after the KGB had been disbanded and it had been turned into a sailing club? And why kept for members of the club? Obviously, they would be there for the administrators and workers, but these offices were linked to the members' suites. She started to take more notice. Where there was an office there was a name plate fixed to the door. Nikolaev. Abdulov. Belov. Vasiliev. Were these the names of the *mafiya* people? Surely they wouldn't blatantly advertise themselves like that.

Yuri disturbed her thoughts. 'You're very quiet, Katya.'

She saw an opening to learn something about the casino owners. 'I was thinking that this is very grand. Every member has an office–are they all casino directors?' She used the word '*directors*' to imply some respectability to the job.

'Not all. Some are sailing members.'

They came to the end of a passageway and Kirill turned to go down a staircase.

But Katya had seen that there was a glass door leading out onto a balcony. 'I'd love to go out and see the view,' she said, hoping to find out more about the marina layout.

'OK.' Yuri answered, happy to take her outside.

She watched as he opened the door. No key, she noted. The view from the balcony was spectacular, stretching out beyond the sailboats towards the narrow marina entrance, then on to the sea which was beginning to darken in the evening clouds now the sun was setting. The beauty of the reds and yellows streaking across the sky reminded Katya of her mother. Grace and art were her life. Katya absently fingered the gold chain around her neck, remembering the only gift from a mother who had remained a distant refugee from the violence of her father. Distant from her as well. Leaving her only a fleeting memory of a beautiful woman seeking solace in her ballet and its glittering world.

Yuri took her hand in his. 'Stunning, isn't it. But you must have seen this before when you sailed here.'

She came back to reality, took her hand away–she wanted his mind on her questions. 'Yes, from the beach or from our *dacha*, but it's strange to think that my father must have seen this particular view. How did you know he was here?'

Yuri lied. 'He was one of the original investors in the casino.' He knew he was fishing but he was now determined to find out if his hunch about Katya fronting some sort of KGB takeover of the casino was right.

Katya was pretty sure her father had been nothing of the sort. He was a rarity in the KGB in that his only interest lay in single-mindedly protecting communism. But she chose to go along with Yuri–it could lead to some information about the present owner.

'I always told my father he'd pulled out of his casino investment too soon.' She lied. 'He could have made a lot more money if he'd stayed. The current owners are making it now, I suppose–Morosov and . . .' She let the sentence drift away.

Yuri turned and walked back towards the stairway. He was elated. Her obvious attempt to find out who the owners were added to his suspicions that she was part of a group of KGB offspring plotting to get back what they'd lost. But how was he going to use that information to put a stop to their plans? Morosov hadn't believed him when he'd first raised the idea. He'd accepted this woman as a punter who'd gyped him out of fifty thousand dollars. Yuri could see exactly what would happen if he went back to Morosov and told him that Katya was part of a conspiracy–Morosov would tell him to stick to his cashier post and not meddle.

Yuri looked down the stairs. One push and she wouldn't survive the fall. But her death wouldn't stop them. He needed to frighten off the whole of the group. One way would be to reveal to Katya the strength of the *mafiya* behind the casino. But that was a secret he'd sworn never to reveal. He walked down the stairway.

Katya followed him, fixing in her mind on the door marked fire escape that led from the balcony down to the wharf.

He pushed open a double door leading into the restaurant.

Katya saw it was as drab as the rest of the building. Brown tables, brown chairs and harsh strip lighting dominated the room. The atmosphere was gloomy–with the same air of tension which seemed to spread throughout the whole place. Only two other couples were there. Neither of them recognised Yuri - They must be sailing members, not *mafiya*, she thought.

Yuri noticed the disbelieving look on her face that he'd brought her here. He laughed. 'The food's good. Come on, sit here by the window.' He moved towards one of the tables.

Katya followed him, sat down and looked out through the large glass pane. The sun had set and the darkness was punctuated by lights on tall posts that surrounded the dock. The beam of a harbour light caught the white crests of lazy waves as they curled in to hit against the marina wall. She heard no noise as they did so and she assumed they had no power in them, probably slack tide. She remembered being sent out to sail alone on nights like this– and on nights when the wind was shrieking across the steep whitecaps.

'Thinking of your father?' Yuri gestured towards the window.

'Yes. It would have been nice if he could have been here.' Katya told the lie easily.

The waiter came with hors d'ouevres–caviar and a sour cream dip. Another waiter put down a decanter of vodka with two glasses.

Katya waved away her glass. 'No. Just bring me a Yorsh, please.' She looked down at the hors d'oeuvres. 'But I love this *Zakuski*.'

Yuri dipped his spoon into the caviar. 'Did you really come here for a holiday or did you come to remember him?'

Katya dropped sour cream on her spoonful of caviar and took her time savouring the flavour. His had been a direct question but she wasn't sure what was behind it. Was he seeking to remind her that she hadn't disclosed where her father had hidden his money? She avoided the question and put one of her own.

'I was trying to remember the name of the person he told me they'd sold out to. I would like to meet him. At least, I suppose it was a him, my father and the old KGB would never have sold out to a woman–they despised them.'

Yuri swallowed a shot of vodka, plunged in. 'Why? Are you interested in getting back the casino?'

Katya couldn't believe what Yuri was saying–Did he really think she was interested in buying into the casino? Quickly, she probed.

'Yuri, your boss tried to kill me because he doesn't believe I have enough money to pay off fifty thousand dollars, so why do you think I'm interested in getting back the Sea Dragon?'

Yuri was now obsessed, believing that everything she said confirmed his idea she was fronting a conspiracy. 'I think you want to get back what your father sold. More than that, I think there's a group of you, now grown-up KGB children, who want that– And you're fronting them.'

Katya was stunned. The whole idea was bizarre, incredible. But if Yuri believed it she wasn't going to stop him.

'Does that mean Morosov isn't your boss?' she questioned. 'I obviously need to know the real owner if we actually are interested.'

Yuri kicked himself for having gone too far. 'That's not something I can discuss.'

A waiter took away the plates of the first course and came back with a dish of whole baked black seabass together with two bowls of salad and one of braised cabbage and potatoes which he put down in front of them.

Katya took her time serving herself and then sat back, saying, 'You know Yuri, you're being very mysterious. Why so evasive? After all, if I'm going to make an offer on behalf of the group I need to find out who owns the casino. If it's not Morosov, I'll make it to the person my father dealt with. I've only got to go back through my father's records.'

Yuri poured out a glass of vodka and drank it quickly, as if to give himself courage. 'Alright, I agree. Morosov can sometimes let his violence get the better of him. I can put your offer forward.'

'But not to Morosov?'

'No.'

Katya took some of the fish away from the bone and ate it, making Yuri wait before continuing with her lie. 'Then if my offer is to be made to whoever my father dealt with, I need to know who it is. I'll only deal with him–or her. Morosov's not to know.'

Yuri began to wonder whether it might be more profitable to go along with Katya rather than fight her. 'What's in it for me?'

Katya felt a surge of anticipation. She was on the edge of recruiting her first informer. Once Yuri was hooked he was hers. She committed G8's budget. 'Five percent.'

'Ten.'

'No way. You'll also get a percentage from whoever sells.' She coolly picked up her mug of Yorsh and drank from it.

He still couldn't trust her. There was something about her coolness that made him uneasy. Then he remembered her out in that squall in the boat, totally calm, relishing the danger. If he didn't close the deal now she was the sort of person who would shut him out. He tried one more time to increase his cut.

'The reason I'm reluctant to tell you the name is that the person will not sell. I'm sure they will resent very much any approach on those lines.' He paused for effect. 'The fact is, it is dangerous for me to make any approach to this person.'

Katya shrugged. She knew instinctively that he was hooked and if she was to run him as her informer he must know who was boss. First rule in the training manual.

'OK. Yuri. Forget it.'

He had no doubt she meant it. After a short silence as he struggled with himself, he said slowly, 'The name you want is Belov.'

Katya immediately saw in her mind's eye the door in the upstairs passage with the name on it, "Belov."

Yuri was speaking again.

Katya hardly heard him. She was mentally looking at her

options. She had sufficient faith in her powers of manipulation to be able to persuade this Belov that her group could make a cash offer for an interest in his casino. In turn that would almost certainly tempt him to reveal something about the moneylaundering side if only to raise the price. Then she'd try and get sufficient information out of him to allow G8 to terminate his operations. Suddenly she saw a huge hole in her plan. Real money in a real offshore account would be needed for Belov to check and be convinced she had the funds. She couldn't see John Hammond or Lev (and certainly not Walt) giving her the back up or the money. So the plan was a nonstarter. Having thought that through she began to think it wasn't a good idea to have persuaded Yuri that there actually was this mythical group of ex-KGB children she was fronting. The dreadful feeling of having made yet another mistake drove her on to rapidly work out her alternatives.

Using Yuri as an informer was the first option. She could pump him for information about Belov. Then she imagined Lev speaking to her. "Don't get overconfident. You think you've turned Yuri, but have you? Is *he* playing *you*?" It was a good question, she told herself. Reluctantly she abandoned the idea and considered the alternative that had lurked in her subconscious, Belov had an office. It would probably have a computer or laptop or documents in it that might contain useful information. The best plan now was for her to break into it and find out. But before that she must know whether Belov was living there.

She realised she hadn't heard a word Yuri had said to her. 'Sorry, Yuri, what were you saying?'

'Where were you?'

'I was working out when I could see this Belov without Morosov knowing about it.'

Yuri nodded his head, a positive gesture. 'But Belov's away until tomorrow afternoon.'

Katya saw her chance to get into Belov's office later that evening and, if lucky, she would find there all the information she needed. She would have escaped from Kropse by the time Belov returned and would be back in G8HQ with all the evidence the DG, Walt and Lev had asked her for. She fought down her excitement as she looked at Yuri and said casually, 'Then I'll see him when he's back. Can you fix it?'

'First, I'll have to tell Belov where you bank your money.'

Katya laughed. 'You must think I'm an idiot, Yuri. Belov's *mafiya* isn't he?' She waited for Yuri's betrayal.

He shook his head. 'You know I can't say that word.'

'Well, by saying that you have said it. So, what happens the moment he knows where my money's stashed?'

Yuri shifted in his seat, his eyes sliding away from hers.

'Exactly. So don't fool with me. Just make a time for the meet.' She abruptly got up from the table.

Yuri looked up, surprised. 'Where are you going?'

'Back to my *dacha.*'

He stood up. 'I'll get the car.'

She turned towards the door. 'No need. The walk will be nice.'

He grinned. 'You're right. No car then.'

Katya stopped. Saw the waiters hovering, one of them waiting to present the bill. She raised her voice so they could all hear her, 'Yuri, there's no way you're rolling around on the beach with me tonight. Just pay the bill and I'll see you tomorrow.'

He gaped at her, then recovered. 'Forget my setting up any meeting.'

She paused by the door and looked at him over her shoulder. 'Five per cent of nothing then–thanks for dinner.'

He watched as the door opened and her shape hazed to nothing as she walked away over the metal grid.

TWENTY-THREE

It was 2 a.m. the same night when Katya left the *dacha*. She slowly made her way back to the marina clubhouse. There was no moon, no stars; the sky was an inky black. Cloud scudded low over the sea, driven by a brisk wind.

She was dressed in a black tracksuit, black running shoes and a black beret which she'd pulled down over her hair. The only other things she had on her were a small torch and a set of skeleton keys. She'd taken those from a hidden pocket in her Attaché case which she kept in her bedroom cupboard. She had no gun, no weapon.

She crept along the beach, cautiously, pausing every few metres to look and

listen–straining her eyes and ears for any sign of human presence. Viktor had warned her when she was a young teenager that the shore was an ideal place to land illicit cargo, and the smugglers had no compunction about killing anyone who got in their way. They would come from the sea he'd said. So she watched out for them.

The *dachas* that loomed in ghostly shapes along the road slightly above her held no worries. In fact, they were a help, they had no lights shining through their windows. She was glad of the darkness, but not surprised. The people who lived in them or rented them were there to spend their days on the beach or out at sea, fishing. They were tired at the end of the day. Even those who went out for an evening were back by midnight to be ready for more outdoor enjoyment the next day.

Suddenly, there was movement to her right. She stopped, slowly knelt down, focusing on the area. She saw the shape of a small fishing boat on the beach and someone on the ground alongside it. She dropped onto her stomach and gradually inched forward. The shape became two people. Engrossed. She slowly slid backwards, then stole past them, randomly thinking they'd be more comfortable in the boat.

The episode heightened her senses even more. But apart from the sudden sharp sound of a lone dog barking in the far distance– an eerie moment–and the loud, low-pitched hoot of a Scop's owl which she knew hovered along the shore line, there were no more alarms.

She reached the entrance to the marina. There were no lights on except the tall marina lamps and the harbour light which swept over the water. Carefully she searched the whole area, picking out the slap of rigging against masts–identifying shapes to determine whether they were human or otherwise. The sound of the wind whining through the rigging made it impossible for her to hear anything. Katya had a sinking feeling that getting into this clubhouse was much harder than she had anticipated. She searched for a place in shadow where she could climb up from the beach onto the dock. Creeping nearer the dock wall, she saw a ladder made up of iron rungs which were rusted. They were of no use to the crew of any boat because there was no water there and the sea wasn't tidal. She assumed they'd been put there long ago by the KGB to allow discreet access to the beach for military operations.

She climbed the rungs and crawled over the lip of the dock to the shelter of a small rib with an outboard engine. She waited beside the rib to see if she'd been discovered. Nothing moved. She blinked her eyes to clear her vision and looked around at the balconies on the first floor where Belov's suite was. She was in luck; immediately spotted the balcony where Yuri had taken her hand and tried to make a pass at her. The fire escape was next to it.

She got up on one knee, looked around. All clear. She sprinted to the bottom of the fire escape. It took her only a few seconds to run silently up the steps and stop by the wall next to the door leading to the passageway inside. She waited to let her breathing ease then leaned forward and looked through the door's glass window.

The passage beyond was clear. Her next move was crucial. If the door was alarmed she was in trouble. She looked back, checked her escape was clear; grasped the door-handle, pushed it down, swung through the door as it opened inwards. Easing around it, she closed it behind her with a click. She stood–waiting. The silence was uncanny. No wind, no rigging clanging. She could hear her own breathing.

Crouching, she edged along the passage to Belov's office door. She took the skeleton keys out of one of her tracksuit pockets. Gently inserted one of the keys in the lock– followed the instructions of her locksmith trainers and heard the clicks as the tumblers dropped. She opened the door, slithered through the narrow gap and shut it behind her. She stood there, holding her breath. Nothing. No sound, no movement.

She took the torch from the other pocket in her tracksuit, made sure the tape around the plastic lens was in place and gave out only a narrow beam of light. She cast it around the room. The office was quite small. On the far wall was a filing cabinet next to a French window. A simple desk and chair faced the wall on her left and, on her right, was an internal door–presumably leading to the suite. It was shut.

Katya immediately walked to the French windows and opened the double doors which led onto the balcony. The drop below the railings to the dock was about ten feet but it was a feasible escape route if someone came in unexpectedly. She walked over to the filing cabinet and put her skeleton keys in her right hand while pointing the torch at the lock with her left. She saw that it was a cam lock. She'd been expecting something much stronger and sophisticated. This would be easy. She leant over and inserted the lockpick.

The sudden blow on the back of Katya's neck sent her sprawling. Her head hit the cabinet–she started to black out. She felt a foot smash into her kidneys, rolling her over onto her back. Above her she saw Taban bent over her, her face screwed with effort as her hand shaped to deliver the fatal neck chop.

Desperate, Katya threw up her arm, grabbed Taban's wrist, held on, rolled right

over; heard the crack as Taban's elbow shattered. Taban's scream galvanised Katya to get up, kick her in the soft stomach and keep kicking. Taban fell away. She struggled to her feet, charged forward, her uninjured hand ready with another strike. Katya grabbed her arm; pivoted; hurled her through the open windows. Taban went clear over the balcony rail. There was no sound except for a dull thud as her body hit the dock.

Katya didn't rush to the balcony to check what had happened. Time was vital. She had to get into Belov's filing cabinet and Taban's scream as her elbow splintered must have been heard. People would come running.

She headed towards the cabinet, realised her hands were empty–no torch, no lockpick. She'd dropped them in the fight. Frantically she got on her knees, searching, feeling around with her hands. Her nerves tightening with every second she spent. Taban might at this moment be getting up, screaming for help having survived the fall. Someone may have found her. Katya gritted her teeth, forcing herself to breathe slowly–to search systematically. Her fingers brushed against something metal, cold–the torch. Praying it wasn't broken, she pushed the switch forward. A dim streak of light puddled on the floor. Slowly, fighting the urge to speed up the motion, her ears straining for the sound of people running along the passageway outside, she swung the light across the carpet. Something glinted under the desk–the lockpick. She grabbed it. As she pointed the torch beam towards the cabinet she noticed the interior door to the suite was open. That was how Taban had come in so silently to attack her. It took precious seconds to close it–precious seconds to curse herself for not locking it immediately she'd seen it.

She slid the lockpick easily into the cabinet keyhole. A couple of smooth twists and the cabinet. . . She heard the sound of loud, urgent voices, of feet racing along the passage.

Without hesitating she withdrew the lockpick, switched off the torch, put them both in her pocket as she ran to the French windows, climbed the balcony rail, slid over, dropped to the dock. She stayed a moment–searched the area for movement. None, certainly not from Taban. Her blood had spilled across the dock leaving her lifeless.

Katya had left open the French windows–a red herring to suggest Taban had fallen or jumped. Now she heard shouts and fists banging on Belov's door.

She slid across the dock to the iron ladder. Looked down at the beach below. A figure was running along it, fast, heading towards the bottom of the ladder, head down, arms pumping. Katya was caught between this person and the people she could hear shouting upstairs. There was no way out. Her heart jumped. Automatically, she scrabbled back from the ladder. Her foot caught in a chunk of metal. She looked behind. The rib was there and her foot was caught under the outboard propeller. Frantic, she pulled it free, feeling the skin rip; rolled behind the boat–the dock railing behind her. She put her mouth in the crook of her elbow trying to quieten the sound of her breathing.

She heard the repeated clang as feet hastily mounted the iron ladder. They clattered across the dock. She rolled beneath the dock railing. Hung onto it; dropped straight down onto the sand. The breath driven out of her. She heard a yell. Taban discovered. Then a crash—Belov's door forced.

She got to her feet, bent double and ran. Wincing in pain as the injury on her ankle cut into her.

TWENTY-FOUR

Katya reached the *dacha,* removed her shoes outside the front door, brushed away the sand and crept up to her bedroom with them. She pulled off her tracksuit and beret in the shower, washed the sand from them down the drain. Then she retraced her steps and made sure no sand was left anywhere. Ludmilla would spot it for sure.

She finally collapsed into bed, exhausted. No training exercise had prepared her for the extreme tension of an actual operation. The physical effort required came naturally, but the mental stresses she'd gone through drained her energy. Now she was in bed, safe—or so she hoped–she needed sleep. But her mind refused, insisting on roving around what had been, a shambles. The only success she'd had the whole evening had been learning that Belov was the owner of the casino, probably the head of the *mafiya* who ran it. That and a half promise from Yuri that she may be able to meet him. But even that was a false hope because in reality she had nothing to trade with him and she'd planned to avoid the meet with Belov by getting the information she needed out of his office. None of which she had. She tried to comfort herself that she'd turned Yuri, but decided she shouldn't kid herself. Yuri was out for himself. Which wasn't comforting when questions were asked about what he or she had been doing at the marina shortly before Taban had been found.

So, she had a name, Belov, but she knew that was of no real

help to G8. She had no other useful information about him. They wouldn't understand why she'd failed to check the door Taban used to get into the office and attack her. Also, she couldn't truthfully tell them she had recruited an informer. If she returned to Basingstoke she'd be an empty-handed failure and would be classed as unfit for operations. She wasn't prepared to live like that. So, going back to the casino, trying to salvage something out of her failure, was her only alternative. The thought drove sleep even further away. What if she'd been spotted at the marina or arriving at the *dacha*? It was almost dawn before she finally slept.

The next morning it was Ludmilla singing to herself in the kitchen that awoke Katya. The sun was already streaming in through the bedroom window. She looked at her watch. It was past 10 o'clock. She was about to jump out of bed when she remembered her injured ankle. She put her foot on the floor and gently leaned on it. There was no pain, but the skin was scraped and noticeably so. She'd have to cover it up somehow.

As she had expected, Katya found Ludmilla full of news about Taban's death. What was unexpected was Ludmilla's delight that "*that bitch*" as she called her had at last met with her just deserts. A gentle enquiry from Katya prompted Ludmilla to tell her that she had worked as a cleaner at the casino for twelve years until Taban had arrived. They were match and oil–Taban was Mongolian and Ludmilla was Caucasian, born in the mountains. Ludmilla had lasted three weeks before Taban had got rid of her.

'They say she jumped,' Ludmilla concluded, after giving Katya a lurid description of the body.

'Jumped? But why?'

'They say she and Belov were having an affair and he was cheating on her with another woman.'

Katya saw a chance. If Ludmilla had been at the casino twelve years she must know its secrets. 'But Belov owns the casino, why would he want a cow like Taban for a lover?'

'It happens,' was all Ludmilla said.

'Does he often change women?' Katya seeking a weakness she could exploit.

'Why? You looking for a job?' Ludmilla cackled with laughter. Then stopped abruptly. 'Don't get near him. He's poison. That's all I'm going to say.'

The look on her face told Katya she'd get nothing more out of her. But she kept the thought that, another time, Ludmilla might be approached from a different angle. One thing Katya didn't believe though was that the talk of Taban's apparent suicide was any more than prurient gossip. Enquiries would be made by Belov and Morosov. And she had to be prepared for them. She spent the day on the beach and at the dacha, thinking things through.

Early in the evening Katya took a taxi to the casino, making sure she wore her black trousers so as to cover the injury to her ankle. She teamed them with a loose-fitting red silk blouse and black ballerina flats. As she sat in the back seat, half an eye on the mix of French renaissance buildings that made up some of the town, her brain was analysing why she was going there.

Katya turned her mind to what she had planned to do once back in the casino. If Yuri could arrange a meeting with Belov she would have a spring board from which to gather some information about the *mafiya*. She knew the risk was enormous. Even if he agreed to see her, she had the problem of convincing him she was interested in investing in the casino. And of persuading him that the whereabouts of the purchase money was to remain a secret until the deal was done. As she thought about it, the whole idea seemed incredible. But as Lev had once said the more fantastic the tale the more believable it was if money lay at the heart of it. And, however much Yuri's interest in her was sexual, he believed fervently that she was a KGB backed advance guard–that a pot of money was to be made. Her objective was to get information and the best way to do that was to negotiate.

The taxi stopped outside the Sea Dragon. Katya drew in a breath. She must prepare herself to be surprised, even upset, at the inevitable news of Taban's death.

She practised on Luka and Anatoly. They seemed suitably impressed with her shock at their solemnly told story of death on the dock. She was immediately interested in their rhetorical questions which were both "*Why did she do it?*" rather than "*What happened?*" The implication was that Taban had done away with herself. Katya probed but was met with a wall of silence.

She was surprised that Yuri wasn't there when she walked onto the gaming floor. She picked up a buzz of curiosity and gossip about Taban's death. Was it suicide? An accident? Murder? Had she been drinking heavily? Was she pushed? Why? Who by? Questions were being thrown around the casino in a low hum. Katya joined in with casual questions as she tried to gauge the extent to which the death was felt to be suspicious. So far no-one had mentioned that anything unusual had been seen there at the time. But two or three people had heard that she and Yuri had been there for dinner and asked her about that. Had she seen anything? Heard anything? She had feigned ignorance but felt herself tightening inside. One mistake, one slip giving a fact that wasn't public knowledge would see her in front of Morosov.

She suddenly realised she might appear to be too inquisitive. Morosov may well be surveilling her through the ceiling cameras. She needed to be active, to do her job of steering the punters to the tables. She looked around. Waiters were busy discreetly handing out drinks and canapes; there were people standing around watching the punters; a few 'guests' were at the bar. A young couple, smartly dressed, crossed the room but they looked too at home around the tables to fall for her *"system"* ploy. She spied an older man with silver hair wearing a beautifully tailored dinner jacket and trousers, weaving slightly unsteadily towards the bar.

As she walked towards him she was intercepted by Euh Meh. She looked frightened and Katya remembered how Taban had scared her in the slot machine section. She could only be there to tell her about Taban's death.

Eu Meh beckoned her to lean down and listen while she whispered a message, 'Morosov wants to see you.' That was all.

'What about?' Katya said softly.

Eu Meh shook her head. Fear widened her eyes–she wasn't about to tell. She hurried away.

It was no use following her and trying to get her to talk. She would cause a scene. One which Morosov would see on his screen. Katya knew that would serve no purpose. Morosov knew about Taban. If someone had seen the fight at the marina or watched Katya escape he would make it impossible for her to leave the casino. She was dead as of this moment.

TWENTY-FIVE

Katya didn't waste time thinking about what awaited her in Morosov's office. Instead she mentally prepared herself. With every step she took on the staircase to it, she imagined herself on her boat in a storm. She was in her element there. The bigger the wave, the stronger became her will to surmount it. The fiercer the wind the wilier she became to conquer it. If the sea couldn't frighten her, defeat her, nor could Morosov. She must be strong. Turn every accusation into an absurdity.

She arrived at Morosov's door. Instead of knocking, she walked straight in; saw Morosov bent over his computer. 'Eu Meh gave me your message,' she said baldly.

He looked straight at her. 'What happened to Taban?'

Katya mentally saw a wave rearing up, ready to break over the bow of her boat. She automatically steered into it. 'I heard she committed suicide. It's terrible news.'

'I asked you what happened, not what you've been told. You were there. So tell me,' he rapped out the words.

She imagined she heard his voice as a fierce wind. 'I don't understand. Yuri and I had dinner. I left–what more can I say?' She'd nearly said "*I left at about 10*" which would have been fatal as she wouldn't necessarily have known the time of Taban's death.

His eyes flickered and she knew he'd spotted her hesitation. She waited as he made her sweat.

'Why did you hesitate about the time you left?'

In a flash she saw herself adjust the tiller to steer past a rock.

'What? Oh, I see–no I wasn't going to mention the time, that was irrelevant. I was going to say I left because Yuri was chancing his luck with me and I wasn't interested. But I didn't want to discuss our personal lives.'

'I think Taban was killed. I already know you were out there alone and you had no love for her, did you?'

In Katya's mind's eye, she watched the storm break. 'Kill Taban? That's ridiculous. OK she wanted me dead, but I have bigger objectives than wanting her out of the way. You know it too.' She nodded towards the metal noose dangling from the ceiling. 'Otherwise why didn't you use that on me when she told you to?' She paused. 'Because you know I've got cash hidden away, isn't it?'

'You are a clever woman, Katya Petrovna. I've watched you at work on the punters. Manipulation, deception–you're good. Too good to be a low-life immigration clerk in St Petersburg. So, you can either tell me what you did to Taban and why or–I'll ask Luka to join us.'

Katya could almost feel the wind tearing at the sails. She had to reef, reduce the focus on her. She had to bring Yuri into play. But that meant introducing her phoney KGB story–and Belov. And she didn't want Morosov to be a part of that. She needed to outflank him, deal with Belov direct. 'Tell me where she was found?' Katya asked.

Morosov was shifted off balance by the question. He'd expected her to bluff about her whereabouts not ask about Taban's. 'You know very well. On the dock below the balcony next to the fire escape.'

'Balcony? No-one's mentioned that to me before.' She abandoned Luka and Anatoly. 'Luka and Anatoly told me she'd committed suicide. Well, if she was found below a balcony, then that seems to make sense.'

Morosov sat back in his chair–drummed his fingers on the

desk, deep in thought. He was sure she'd had something to do with Taban's death–she obviously hated Taban and had left Yuri after a good reconnoitre of the clubhouse. She was calculating enough to commit murder and Yuri was convinced she was involved with her father's old KGB officers. It was a typically professional kill and, also typically, he wasn't getting anywhere with her. She was as slippery as an eel. He could ask Luka to join them but the problem with Luka was he enjoyed killing and he might go too far before she talked. Abruptly, Morosov leaned over his computer and spoke into it. 'Yuri. Come into my office.'

On a few occasions Katya had faced death at sea. She knew this was one of those occasions. She'd left Yuri frustrated and furious he'd betrayed Belov's name to her. He would now be desperate to avoid the taint of corruption by accepting a bribe to bypass Morosov and get her a meeting with Belov. He would sink her to save himself.

She watched Yuri creep around the door as he entered the room. His eyes looked everywhere except at her. She knew she was right. Remembered his cowardice during the squall. 'Been telling lies again, Yuri?' She taunted him.

Instead of denying it to her he denied it to Morosov. 'I told you the truth. Don't believe her.'

'What truth did you tell him, Yuri? That you'd get me a meeting with Belov behind this man's back.' She gestured to Morosov.

Yuri opened his mouth to protest.

Katya went on, remorselessly. 'You saw Taban after I left the restuarant, didn't you? You needed her help to get to Belov–she was his mistress. She turned you down didn't she.'

Yuri yelled with rage–slashed his hand across her face. 'You bitch, that's– '

He was cut off as Katya slammed her fist into his stomach. He doubled up, retching, struggling for breath.

Katya spat on him. Turned to Morosov who sat there, mesmerised. 'You think Taban was murdered? Then here's your murderer. This bastard was going to sell you out and Taban either told him to go to hell or wanted too large a cut. So he got rid of her.'

Morosov stirred. Rubbed his eyes with both hands as if this would help him understand what was going on. He leaned his elbows on the desk, moved his hands to the sides of his face and rested his head on them–looked up at Katya. 'And you were going to sell me out as well. How does all this help you?'

Katya drove on–started to explain. He held his hand up to her, stopping the flow of her words–his face a vicious mask. 'Get out onto the gaming floor and do your work. Don't think you can leave. I'll see you later–here. First I need to deal with this.' He pointed at Yuri, not bothering to hide the contempt in his voice.

TWENTY-SIX

Katya held her head up high as she left Morosov and went down the stairs to the gaming floor. Too many people—certainly the casino staff—knew that a summons to Morosov's office heralded bad news. She also knew she must appear unruffled, in charge. Otherwise the staff would have no doubt she'd been in trouble—that it was advisable for them to keep their distance from her. She also knew that whatever was happening right now in Morosov's office he would have half an eye on the video screen—watching her.

The question uppermost in her mind was how to capitalise on the accusation of murder she'd made against Yuri. She wasn't convinced that Morosov had believed her. Yuri had told her he'd worked at the casino since he was eighteen. That was a lot of years of working his way into Morosov's confidence. Not an ideal background against which she could hang the charge that he'd killed another employee favoured by Morosov. When Morosov had threatened *"to deal with"* Yuri, he could have been bluffing. Even now they could be planning her death.

Rapidly, she ran through her mind the employees she knew whom she might convince of Yuri's guilt. Not the croupiers, their only interest was in taking their cut. The bartender had obviously been warned against her. Eu Meh was too young, too scared, and had no influence. Xiao Cheng, the Chinese woman with the diamond necklace? Katya had listed her as dangerous. She was sure she was involved in the moneylaundering side of the casino. Who else? Anatoly was a front man, a gatherer of gossip about the punters, nothing else. That left Luka, the bouncer, the killer. She was about to dismiss him as well when she thought of his accent. It was from the rough side of Moscow, like hers when she chose to put it on. They might be street bred but that wasn't necessarily a recommendation to get close to him. Then she remembered the large $100 tip she'd given him. And his attempts to be friendly– holding the umbrella over her, sympathising after her massive loss at roulette. Was he friendly because of their common background or did he just want her? Was he a possible source of information; there was only one way to find out.

As she arrived at the casino front entrance Luka saw her coming. He quickly caught her wrist to prevent her going down the steps–he'd obviously received orders from Morosov to stop her leaving.

'Don't worry, Luka, I've just come out for some fresh air.' She surreptitiously looked under her brows for where the surveillance cameras were; spotted the overhead one which was directed at the space between the steps and the front door. She moved to it and waited there. She looked down at the street. The night air was cold– under the street light she saw a young couple stop, hesitate–then start up the casino steps. Half way up they stopped, turned and went back down to the street. Holding hands and laughing they walked away– otherwise the street was empty of people.

Katya shivered suddenly. Looked at Luka. 'A slow night?'

He pursed his lips, shrugged.

'You liked Taban didn't you?' She tossed out the question.

'She was alright.' In fact, Luka knew she was more than alright. She'd been an early and enthusiastic conquest of his before time had blown out the flame. They'd remained on friendly terms but no more. Taban had sought more useful relationships.

'You know Yuri killed her?' Katya spoke loudly, not so much

for Luka's benefit but for Morosov's, if he was watching her on his screen.

Luka's reaction was all that Katya could have hoped for. He raised an angry voice, 'That bastard? Killed her? I don't believe it–no, I do believe it, but would he have had the guts?'

'Taban found out he was trying to sell out the casino–sell you out, sell you all out,' Katya spoke quickly, but clearly enough for her words to reach the hidden mic.

Luka thought this over. Puzzling over what she meant but not wanting to question her. Not wanting to show his ignorance of casino politics.

Katya smiled inwardly. Lev had told her how to carry out conversations like this. When to push. When to shut up. She waited as Luka's need to know overcame his reluctance to ask.

His words came in a rush, 'How do you know all this?'

'He told me. You know I had dinner with him last night?'

He nodded eagerly.

Katya knew he was now so keen to have the story he'd believe anything. 'Luka, you're from Moscow, aren't you? Like me? Lived on the streets during the bad times. . .' She let the thought gel in his mind. 'So, if I tell you something secret, you'll keep it to yourself, won't you. We understand each– '

Anatoly burst out of the front door.

'Katya Petrovna. You're wanted.' He held the door open.

TWENTY-SEVEN

Katya felt the odd sensation that she was floating. There was a buzzing sound–then a roaring noise. She was suspended in a giant beehive. Hanging. An image of Morosov, her eardrums exploding. She tore at the wire noose with her fingers.

She heard someone's voice. Words with no meaning. Her nails dug into her skin as she scrabbled to find the metal.

The person spoke again, the speech clearer. 'You're awake, then.' The meaning was unintelligible to her. Of course, she was 'awake. She was fighting for her life–life being choked out of her.

She felt someone shaking her. Heard more words booming out of a tunnel. 'Wake up. Come on. Wake up.' How could she? Death wasn't being awake. Death was Morosov and the noose.

She gasped as she felt a deluge of cold water dashed into her face. She was breathing. Why? She was dying. She heard a voice . . .

'Don't try and pretend you're asleep. You want some more water?'

It sounded like Yuri. She was confused. Yes, that was surely Yuri talking. Why? He was dead, wasn't he? She'd made sure of that, made sure Morosov knew that Yuri had killed Taban. Instinctively, she whispered, 'But you're dead.'

'Your mistake,' came the voice.

Her mind fought its way out of the fog, telling her Yuri was right. Otherwise, why would he be there. But where? Where was she? Why was she lying down? What was the noise in her ears? She opened her eyes, blinked in the strong light. Her eyes moved away from it, focussed on a curved blue ceiling just above her. The ceiling had lights let into it and below them the walls were painted a darker blue. She found she was lying on a long leather seat the same colour as the walls. Opposite her, sitting in a large leather chair, was Yuri. He was unharmed. Dressed in a yellow patterned shirt and cream coloured chinos. He was looking relaxed. There was no sign of Morosov. She used her fingers to feel around her neck –no noose–it was wet and water dripped there from her hair.

'Sit up. You and me are going to talk.' Yuri's eyes fixed on hers.

Katya was fully awake now. She obeyed him, sat up, swung her legs over the edge of the seat and found the floor with her feet. She looked around. Suddenly understood the strange noise, the feeling of floating. She wasn't in a beehive, she was in an aircraft. A private aircraft. The size and luxury furnishings told her it was probably a Gulfstream. . . Automatically, she reached for the technical details stored in her memory. They were long range aircraft–flew at 40,000 feet and were fully pressurised. Therefore, it was unlikely Yuri was going to open a door and drop her out of it. And even more unlikely because Morosov hadn't taken the opportunity to kill her in the casino. But what had happened? Her last memory was of Luka, or was it Anatoly, telling her she was wanted by Morosov? Why was she in this aircraft? Going where?

She bit back a sudden rush of fear–fought to keep the tremor out of her voice by mumbling, as if still drugged, as she said, 'What happened? Why am I here?'

'I ask the questions.' Yuri leaned forward, tapped his fingers on her knee. 'Understand.'

He was in control. This was his aircraft. He was obviously supported by Morosov. Katya knew that this was not the time to fight him. She had no idea what had happened between leaving

Luka and now. She must have been drugged. But how? Drink? Injection? Had they given it to her to question her? Had she told them about G8? Had they found her burner in the *dacha*? She must stay calm, play for time, find out–give away as little as she could. A simple reply was enough. 'Yes,' she muttered, subserviently.

'Why did you kill Taban?' The question came like a pistol shot.

She shook her head. Left the negative gesture as her reply.

'One of your KGB mob, then?'

Katya didn't grasp what he was talking about. What KGB mob? Was this some devious way of getting at her connection with G8? Had she talked about them? She decided to give a little information to see where it led. 'If you think I'm part of some KGB gang because my father bought into the casino then you must realise that when they find out how you've treated me you'll be finished.'

Yuri took his hand away from her leg. 'You don't understand, do you? They aren't going to find out. Where you're going and what you'll be forced to do you won't survive a month. No-one will know who you are or care. You'll be used up.'

Yuri spoke almost casually, as if talking about a day at the office. His face betrayed no emotion. Nor would it. He'd been terrified when Katya had done a convincing job telling Morosov that he'd killed Taban. Morosov had been inclined to believe her. It was only the long association he'd had with him and his plausible suggestion that Katya was a KGB front that had persuaded Morosov otherwise. Even so, he'd told him that he, Yuri, was to be her executioner. He was to take her to their casino in Dao and make sure she didn't come back. He could hear Morosov's harshly spoken words ringing in his ears and he certainly wasn't going to disobey him.

Katya watched his face working. There was hate there but also–or did she imagine it–resentment? Of course, he was obediently doing Morosov's work. But she knew he wasn't cut out for the harsh reality of *mafiya* enforcement. That was why he blustered and threatened. She summoned her courage–laughed at him. 'Yuri, you're just a cashier, a bean counter who can't even sail a boat through a squall. So where are the guts you're going to need to get rid of me?'

The aircraft's engine note altered.

'We're landing.' Yuri stood up, leant over her, put his hands on her knees, slid them up her trousers.

She lashed out with her leg–caught him in the crotch. He screamed, doubled up, falling to the floor. She smashed her foot into his face. Blood spurted from his nose. She hit harder with her other foot. His head jerked back–his body twitching as he passed out.

The aircraft lurched as it touched down. She looked around frantically to see if any of the crew would come running. No one did. She knew private aircraft had a limited take-off weight–perhaps there was no spare capacity for anyone other than the flight crew.

Wasting no further time, she climbed over Yuri's body and rushed towards the rear searching for an emergency exit. The area was filled with a galley and a small bar. There was no emergency exit there. She squeezed past the bar and saw the lavatory sign. She seemed to be at a dead end. But there had to be a rear access for baggage. Was that through the lavatory?

She felt the aircraft slow right down. It must have taxied to its apron. She had to hurry. She pushed into the lavatory. Inside there was another door. She went through it into another space in the fuselage. Large bales wrapped in black plastic lined each side of it. She looked past them and saw an external door–access for the baggage handlers. She started towards it. Stopped. Felt one of the bales. It seemed to contain paper of some sort. She dug her nail into it, working her finger through the tough fabric. It suddenly cut through. She ripped the plastic apart. A bundle fell out, hit the floor and spilt the contents. Katya found herself looking at a flood of $100 bills. She counted six bales–made a rapid calculation. There must be a fortune there.

The aircraft brakes squealed. They must be almost at the ramp. She grabbed a handful of notes, stuffed them into the pocket of her trousers; lunged for the baggage door. Wrenched it open. A blast of humid heat met her at the same time as the scream of the engines just above her head. It was dark outside–difficult to see where the ground was. Runway lights lit the tarmac. Immediately, she jumped the six feet to the ground. Rolled over. Lay still.

She watched as the Gulfstream taxied away to the stand about fifty yards away, in front of the terminal. The blast of its engines swept over her. She waited until it eased off. Looked up and around. Searched for an exit. Saw a baggage trolley disappearing into a tunnel. Crouching low she dashed towards it.

Breathing heavily, she leant against the wall of the tunnel, getting her bearings. Was she to risk going along it and meeting baggage handlers or was it better to double back and head for the runway?

She heard the rumble of a trolley approaching. Spun around and sprinted back to the tarmac. She cursed the brightness of the red silk blouse she had put on to go to the casino. How long ago had that been? A runway light picked her out, casting her shadow across the grass alongside the taxiway. She heard a shout. Dived to the ground, rolled, kept rolling until she was in shadow, picked herself up and raced away into the darkness. Ahead of her in the distance she saw the main runway, bathed in the landing lights of an incoming aircraft. Suddenly knew she was forgetting her training–was blindly reacting instead of planning. She dropped to the ground and forced herself to think.

Carefully, she studied the airport layout. She saw a shimmer of water in front of her. It stretched to the runway. She felt trapped. There was no way out in that direction, the landing strip was in the middle of water. It must have been built on reclaimed land.

She turned around. In front of her was the terminal. Aircraft were parked on a large tarmac apron in front of it. Mobile boarding stairs led up to them for passengers to embark or disembark. An aircraft was taxiing in to join them. She waited until the aircraft stopped, then, keeping as low as she could she zigzagged to arrive beside its undercarriage. She knelt in the shadow. Watched the steps being moved to the passenger exit. Heard the door above her being opened and the footsteps of passengers coming down the steps. It was the moment of highest risk. She crept up to the side of them. Then stood up and stole forward to join an elderly, white haired woman who'd just stepped onto the tarmac.

The woman looked startled. 'Are you alright, dear, you look lost?'

Katya patted her arm. 'Sorry I troubled you', she said.

She followed the passengers into the terminal. Once there she faced another dilemma. She had no idea whether the passengers had arrived on an international or local flight. She had no passport. What made it worse was that Yuri must have been discovered by now. The crew would be searching for her. Or would they keep her disappearance quiet to avoid awkward questions about why she had fled—and why Yuri had a broken nose? She realised she'd asked herself the question only out of optimism. She'd wasted time. How was she going to get out of the terminal? Thinking more clearly now, she decided she must get rid of her red blouse. It was too distinctive to give her a chance of going unnoticed.

She followed the crowd until she came to the Duty-Free area

before reaching the immigration hall. It was large and brightly lit with colourful advertisements for alcohol, sweet goods, clothes and shoes. Once there, she hung around the till pretending to study the magazines on the rack beside it. Three or four people paid for their purchases and then she got lucky. A well-set man, wearing a Panama hat and dressed in a charcoal-coloured lightweight suit came to pay. He must have spotted something in a far aisle because he rushed over towards it, leaving his passport and boarding card on the counter.

Katya seized her opportunity, sidled up to the cashier; pointed to the magazine rack. 'I can't see Vogue there. Do you have it?'

The cashier, a heavy middle-aged Chinese woman with dark hair wrapped around a large tortoiseshell comb, leant sideways to look at the rack. Quickly, Katya deftly separated the boarding card from the passport and slid it into her pocket. 'Never mind,' she said. 'I'll get it in town.'

Without looking back, or at the man, she quietly slid away to the clothes and shoes area. There she worked fast. Picked out a neutral-coloured linen jacket and put it on over her red blouse. She heard a commotion by the cashier's desk, didn't look there–concentrated on trying on a pair of black trainers.

'Ma'am. Ma'am.' The cashier was calling to her. 'Did you see this gentleman's boarding card?'

Katya looked at her, blankly. Turned her mouth down, shook her head.

'Come on, you must have seen it.' The man gestured angrily at her.

'Are you accusing me of taking it?' She raised her voice to attract attention; to make him embarrassed.

The man ignored the other shoppers gawping at him. 'No, but you were there, you must have seen who did. It didn't just vanish,' he said angrily.

Katya knew she had two options. Burst into tears or become righteously aggressive. Bursting into tears would bring sympathisers, even security. This had to be dealt with quickly and finally. She marched towards him, hobbling with one trainer on and her other shoe off. 'You, pompous shit. You lose your boarding card so you can't get your girlfriend her perfume and you blame me. Perhaps you want to explain that to security–or, better, your wife.'

There was dead silence. The shoppers open-mouthed waiting for the explosion.

He snatched up his passport. 'Sorry. Sorry,' he muttered, and almost ran out of the area.

'Good for you,' shouted the cashier, giving Katya a beaming, thumbs up. 'Pity you're not around to sort out the other bastards like him.'

Katya smiled and shrugged one shoulder.

She tried on another pair of trainers. Satisfied she then picked up a typically touristy white cotton sun-hat; then a black holdall with a shoulder strap.

She walked around the area and approached the cashier from the rear–put the hat, trainers and boarding card on the counter and followed the card with two hundred of the dollars she'd taken on the plane, saying, 'I don't know how you cope with these men. All men are . . .'

'Bastards,' the cashier supplied.

'True. These and this jacket, please.' Katya undid the price tag from the jacket button and handed it to the cashier with a smile. 'You don't mind if I wear the jacket, do you?'

'A pleasure, ma'am. Shall I put the trainers and sun-hat in the bag?' she asked, as she did so. 'That comes to one hundred and forty-two dollars.' She waited while Katya paid, then handed her some notes. 'Your change in yuan.'

Katya took the money, nodded goodbye and left. She stopped

at the first restroom she came to and went in. Put on the trainers and the sun-hat. The outfit she now had on made her black evening trousers look like normal day wear. She was no longer a refugee from a casino—just a normal tourist.

She left the restroom, by-passed the baggage area and headed for the exit, eyes down as if lost in thought—expecting every moment for airport security to shut down the terminal until Yuri's attacker had been found.

'Hello.' She felt a hand on her shoulder.

Katya prepared to fight; to run.

A woman's voice—she was speaking again. 'Don't you remember me?'

Katya turned and looked at her—it was the elderly, white-haired woman who'd got off the plane. 'Oh yes. I'm sorry. I was lost wasn't I.'

'You still look lost,' laughed the woman. 'Eyes down, meandering around not sure of where you're going.' She paused. 'I'm right aren't I?' The accent was Portuguese.

Katya hesitated. This woman sounded as if she could be helpful. But would she be nosy? Ask too many questions? On the other hand, she presented a possible way of escaping the airport—and Yuri. Katya took the plunge. 'Well, you're right. I was impulsive and brought myself here because I wanted to see the place.'

The thought came to her abruptly, where was she? She'd been too scared and busy to notice and Yuri hadn't told her. The people in the terminal were of mixed nationalities so they gave her no clue as to what country she was in. Suddenly she recalled the Duty-Free shop sign had said "*Dao*". Who had said something about Dao? Hadn't it been Morosov?

The truth hit her. Morosov hadn't believed her story that Yuri had killed Taban. So he was getting rid of her. What had Yuri said? *"You'll survive a month if you're lucky."* What was in Dao that made him say that? god, that could only mean–she heard the woman talking.

'So, you haven't anywhere to stay by the sound of it.'

'Well, I was going to ask the bus driver.'

'My dear girl, if you ask a bus driver that question here you could wind up anywhere. I'm Inez Cruz by the way and I run a small travel agency in Grand Canal Shoppes. I'll be pleased to recommend just the sort of place you will like to stay in.'

Katya looked at her. This woman could offer her a way out but was that safer than going alone? The woman was well-dressed in a smart cream trouser suit and had friendly brown, almond-shaped eyes; quite an angular jawline–probably a perfectionist Katya thought–but she seemed charming and ordinary. Katya took her chance. 'Thanks, that is very kind of you.'

'Come on then. My car is waiting.'

Once again Katya felt the rush of hot humid air as she left the terminal. She looked around. Almost immediately a bronze S-Type Jaguar with twin headlights drew up.

'Here we are, dear.' Inez Cruz stopped, a look of dismay on her face. 'I never asked your name. How silly of me.'

'Katya–Katya Lebadev,' replied Katya as she took a random surname.

'Jump in, then, Katya.' Inez held the door open.

TWENTY-EIGHT

Katya was exhausted. She sat back in the soft leather rear seat of the Jaguar and tried to switch off. On the way to the Grand Canal Shoppes, Inez Cruz pointed out various notable buildings and chattered on about Dao's Portuguese history and its takeover by China four years previously. Katya nodded or made suitably encouraging replies as she looked out of the window watching the old colonial Portuguese buildings. Their dilapidated shuttered windows and balustrades were interspersed among run-down concrete structures with square windows. They reminded her of pictures she'd seen of Macau, another Portuguese territory taken over by the Chinese.

One thing that Inez said did alarm Katya–Dao was a small island which meant her chances of escape were going to be very limited. She knew she should take notice of where she was going but the streets were narrow and twisty making it difficult to remember the route. Bright overhead electric signs in Chinese characters advertised shops either side of the road. There were few people around. The whole place gave her an uneasy feeling, as if the end of its colonial history had left it without a future. This place was surely used up. The thought was immediately followed by a question. What on earth was so interesting to Belov that he had connections here?

She was jolted into the answer as the Jaguar turned a sharp corner into a sight straight out of pictures she had seen of Venice. Except these buildings were brand new. The architecture was pure gothic–there was even a canal with gondolas on it. Modern shops blazed with lights which shone onto luxury clothes, jewellery, furniture. A large restaurant overlooked a square filled with tables where well-dressed Chinese were dining al fresco. Others strolled around the shops or leaned over balustrades watching the gondolas. Through the car windows she heard the hum of conversation. An exciting sound. This would definitely be the Dao that Belov would be keen to have links with. It may well be a tax haven like Macau. She tried to analyse the notion further, but her mind wouldn't focus. She had reached the point where she desperately needed to sleep. But she knew she had to make a final effort.

'Is this where you have your agency?' she asked Inez.

'Yes. It's very exciting after the rest of the city, isn't it? I was lucky and got in on the ground floor when they started construction in '99 and– ' She broke off. 'Here we are.'

Katya looked out of the window and saw a series of archways. She could see an office with a huge plate-glass window. It fronted an interior bathed in soft lighting glowing on colourful pictures of the world's major cities. Clever not to advertise the sea and beaches, she thought.

Following her gaze Inez read her thoughts. 'Yes, Dao is an island but I advertise the cities. The Chinese want to see them and improve their knowledge of the world's culture. There are currency controls here but they are easing a little.' Katya looked at her, wondering why she had mentioned currency controls. They were hardly relevant to advertising.

'My goodness, you do look all in,' Inez told her. 'Now here's my card. Your hotel is just next door and if you get out, I'll show you. Just give them the card and they'll do you a good rate,' her words came in a rush.

Katya climbed out of the car and looked around for the hotel. She couldn't see it. Suddenly Lev's warning after she'd climbed into his taxi in St Petersburg screamed at her. This woman, Inez Cruz–what did she know about her? Katya recalled her standing at the exit to the terminal. Why was she there? Looking back, Inez must have waited there as she bought the clothes and stuff at the Duty-Free shop. Katya couldn't believe she'd been so stupid as to get in this woman's car without some background conversation– like, were you waiting for me? Actually, I'm not lost. Where is this hotel? How much will it cost?

She felt herself slipping into sleep; tried desperately to shake off the lethargy she felt from the drugs. Oh god she'd made another mistake . . . She decided to run. To escape. She started for the other side of the road.

'No, not that way. Here.' Inez Cruz grabbed her arm and pointed to a door under another arch–her voice sharp.

The driver had got out of the Jaguar. Large, menacing, he stood on the edge of the road; arms folded.

Katya felt drained. In no shape for a fight. She turned, looked through the arch. Above an ornate, stone pillared doorway was a discreet green and red neon sign, the colours of Italy. "*Hotel Dolce. Welcome to Venice*" A boutique hotel. She felt foolish, stupid. Jumping to incoherent conclusions. Fatigue probably. 'Oh, I didn't see the sign. The hotel looks wonderful, thank you so much.'

'It's a pleasure. Don't forget to give them my card.' Inez started to go towards her office. 'My apartment's over the office. So, I'll say goodnight.'

Katya waved her goodbye and pushed open the hotel door. It was surprisingly spacious inside. A wide entrance hall, with washed peach coloured walls and a mosaic

floor–a reception desk to her right. Behind it sat a middle-aged woman with brown

almond– shaped eyes and white hair; like Inez Cruz Katya thought. Related to her? Possibly, she had the look of her.

'Good evening.' Katya introduced herself. 'Katya–' she hesitated, 'Lebadev.' She'd nearly forgotten the new identity she'd given herself. 'Inez Cruz said to give you her card.' She pushed it across the desk.

The receptionist took the card, glanced at it. 'Inez? Yes, of course. Let me see. For you, a discount of twenty-five per cent.' She turned and took a brass key from a rack behind her. 'Room 101, first floor on the corner.' She looked over the counter to the floor by Katya's feet. 'No luggage.' A statement, not a question. She straightened. 'The lift's over there.' She pointed across the hall to an ornate gold painted grille-style door. Dismissed Katya with an abrupt, 'Goodnight.'

Katya nearly reeled as sleep tugged at her–whatever narcotic she'd been given was obviously still in her system. Dimly she wondered why the woman on the hotel desk hadn't asked for a credit card or some sort of deposit.

The decorative grille-style door hid a modern lift which took her to the first floor in seconds. She found Room 101 easily and almost fell through the door. She was aware of a luxuriously appointed room before dragging off her clothes and using the en suite bathroom for a quick shower. She grabbed a silk bathrobe, with a tie belt, off a hook behind the bathroom door, put it on, then collapsed onto the silk-sheeted bed. Falling asleep in an instant.

She slept soundly until she was awoken the next morning by the sound of a key scraping in the door lock. Before she could sit up, the door had opened.

'Good morning. Breakfast?' A young Chinese waitress was saying as she pushed a trolley into the room.

Katya smelt fried rice. She sat up and saw on the trolley a bowl of it alongside a plate of doughnuts, fried buns and–how long ago had she last eaten? She instantly felt ravenous.

After the waitress had left, she fell upon the trolley, poured out some orange juice and drank it before stuffing the doughnuts and fried buns into her mouth–hardly chewing before she swallowed. At last she felt she could eat no more and climbed back into the bed. She had to think.

How long could she stay in this hotel before her money ran out? Her money–she hadn't counted it yet. She reached for her jacket and took out the dollar bills from the pocket. She found they were all $100 bills. Thirty-four of them. More than enough to buy a flight to London. Probably enough to stay in Dao for a few days.

She analysed her options. If she flew home what had she learnt to report to G8? Belov owned the casino in Kropse. There were strong indications that money was laundered through it. There was definitely a link with Dao. But what? She recalled the bales of dollars in the baggage hold of the Gulfstream. Why had they come to Dao? If it *was* a tax haven the money might be laundered through it to businesses in the area. Mainland China, for instance? Also, what was in Dao that was so terrible she would not survive the month? Could she go back to Lev and John and Walt without knowing what the Dao connection with Kropse really meant? On the other hand, if she stayed here how could she find the link? Was it a casino? If so which one? She had no idea. And if she went nosing around, she'd almost certainly be picked up and given back to Morosov or simply left to rot in whatever place Yuri had in mind.

She tossed the dollars in her hands, trying to find a solution. One escaped and fluttered onto the floor. It brought to mind Inez Cruz's remark about currency controls. Currency controls worked both ways. They could limit the amount of cash taken out of China but also the amount brought into China by foreign nationals. She took the idea a step further. Were the dollars on the plane entering China illegally, for some purpose being pursued by Belov? That almost certainly made sense if Dao *was* a tax haven.

Abruptly she made up her mind. She'd stay. Try to find out what was happening in Dao and hopefully that would lead to a better understanding of the link to Belov and Kropse. She saw the local commercial directory next to the phone on the bedside table. She leaned over and picked it up; flicked to "*Casinos*". There wasn't one.

Suddenly a wave of tiredness swept over her. She needed to sleep if she was to think clearly. The directory slipped from her fingers onto the floor.

The next thing she knew or rather heard, was a knock on her door. She wasn't fully awake and didn't respond. The knock became more persistent.

'Alright. I'm coming' she called. She got out of bed, tightened the tie around the bathrobe, went to the door and opened it.

'You took your time.' This was muttered in an English accent by a thin, slightly stooped man, dressed in a tropical suit and an oversized Hawaiian shirt. His small sharp little eyes looking eager as he pushed past her into the bedroom.

'What the hell are you doing,' Katya shouted, holding the door open.

He looked alarmed. Marched back to her, gripped the door and pushed it shut. 'Do you want the whole neighbourhood to hear? Inez Cruz told me this place was private and I paid her extra for that.' He looked her over. 'Well at least you're dressed right.'

Katya didn't need this remark to make her see red. All her earlier instincts that Inez Cruz could be more than she looked came flooding back. This weasel had been set on her by that woman. Katya exploded. Shoved him away, flung the door open, stepped next to it to keep it open. 'Fuck off you bastard, before I call the police.'

'Bloody hell,' he stuttered. 'She told me you were in Room 101, ready for me.' He almost ran into the corridor

'You tell her she was wrong' Katya yelled after him, slamming the door shut. Shaking with rage, knowing her plans were totally overset. She'd have to move out straight away– before the Inez Cruz woman or Yuri's thugs caught up with her.

TWENTY-NINE

Inez had just sat down on the sofa in the sitting room of her apartment. She never tired of the room—white leather sofas and chairs with stark white wood furniture created a startling contrast with the carmine walls shining a deeper red under dim ceiling lighting. She was tired after a day catching up on her work at the travel agency. She called it a travel agency but, apart from wealthy tourists who actually wanted to travel, it was cover for her real income earner—an escort agency.

She'd been born to a Portuguese family descended from the early settlers. But her father didn't have the business sense of his forebears and committed suicide when his trading firm went bust. Her mother followed him shortly after, leaving Inez to fend for herself. She quickly found that her looks earned her good money from her father's business acquaintances. Word spread and the island's night life became her source of clientele. It wasn't long before she found other attractive girls and women in the same predicament and, for a fee, she set them up with men willing to pay top dollar. The money was rolling in but she wanted more and began scouting Dao airport for lone, defenceless young women or girls who arrived alone and had a certain lost look on their faces. She had tried to define it but it was elusive—sometimes evasive, other times needy. Whatever the look was it invariably led her to a woman escaping drudgery at home or a girl needing a roof having left home and was now penniless. Some gentle persuasion soon found them joining the Inez Cruz's "*travel agency*".

She was particularly pleased to have picked up this Katya woman. She'd been convinced Katya hadn't been on the plane she'd travelled in—she'd have noticed the long stunning auburn hair and that expensive red silk top, for sure. Then the surreptitious way she'd inserted herself into the queue departing the aircraft was suspicious. And, later, the woman had tried to cover that red top with the linen jacket and had hidden her hair under the white hat. It was almost laughable. Who was she trying to kid? Inez knew it would be easy to pick her up and put her straight on the game. She was just the sort to sell herself for easy money. It was lucky a regular had been looking for someone just then, but she wondered if she'd charged enough. She'd have to pay $200 of the $700 to Katya. But then this was a try-out. She'd get a thousand dollars for her, next time—she was a stunning girl with her tall, slim figure, her beautiful face with those fine, unusually large violet-blue eyes and that long glossy auburn hair.

The man in the tropical suit was as angry as Katya. He'd paid Inez Cruz $700 for her. $500 for sex and $200 for the complete privacy he needed so his wife wouldn't find out. He'd trusted Inez Cruz and used her services whenever he stopped over in Dao and they'd always been satisfactory. Now this screaming woman had put all that in jeopardy.

Inwardly raging at his humiliation, he took the lift to the ground floor and marched out into the street. Furiously, he punched Inez's number into his cell phone.

Inez's mobile buzzed. She picked it up from the coffee table in front of her; pressed the receive button.

She heard a voice yelling. 'What the hell have you let me in for?'

'Who is this? What are you talking about?' she said, icily.

'That woman in 101 you sent me to. What the fuck are you doing–there's no way she's on the game.'

Inez didn't believe him. 'Don't you try and get your money back. She's looking for work. What did you do to her?'

'Don't go there, Inez. I paid you for privacy and all I got was her yelling and screaming "rape". She bloody threatened me with the police.'

'What do you mean, the police? Don't be absurd,' her voice carried disbelief with every word.

'She told me she'd call the police.'

'Bloody hell,' her voice rose, in alarm. 'You didn't give her my name, did you?'

'Well, of course I did, you stupid bitch. Why wouldn't I when I'd paid you for her.'

Silence.

'I want my money back. I'm coming over.'

'No, you don't. If she gets hold of the police it'll cost me a damn sight more than $700 to get them off my back.'

'Fuck you, Inez Cruz. I'm not losing my money– '

'You come here and that'll be the last thing you do. I mean it. Piss off home to your wife and don't come back.'

She shut off the call; didn't waste time blaming herself. Instead she went back in her mind to when she first saw Katya creeping from behind the plane's undercarriage. Where had she come from? Not the terminal, that was certain. The airfield then? But there was nothing but sea water in that direction. Another aircraft? That was more like it. Hadn't she see one park up just before their own? A private jet. . . Suddenly Inez felt certain.

She pressed the call button on her phone. 'Reception? Tell my bodyguard to go to Room 101 immediately and lock the door. He's to stay outside until I get there.' She rang off, pulled up Contacts on her mobile. Pressed the call button.

'Hello? It's me. Inez.' She waited for the reply, then said, 'Good. I want some information on a private jet that came in yesterday evening.' She paused, listened, before saying, 'Yes. Right away.'

She got up and, holding her phone, walked over to a cocktail cabinet and poured herself a glass of white wine. She sipped the *vinho verde*, savouring its crispness; comfortably calm in a crisis. Her mobile buzzed.

'Yes?' She listened. 'Thank you. Your next visit will be no charge.' She ended the call, put down her glass and walked thoughtfully towards her front door.

THIRTY

Katya didn't wait to shower. She flung on her clothes and trainers, grabbed her holdall. Out of the corner of her eye she saw a hundred-dollar bill lying on the floor by the bed. Her dollars–She'd almost forgotten them. She remembered going to sleep with them on the bed. She couldn't see them there. Had someone come in while she'd slept? Stolen them? Frantically, she scrabbled around the bedclothes. A dollar bill dropped onto the pillow. She found more, counted them, thirty-four. She shoved them in her pocket as she rushed for the door–grabbed the handle, pulled. The door didn't move. She pulled again. The door was stuck–or locked? She tried to open it again. Useless.

Katya swung around, looked at the window, quickly went to it. It was made of one sheet of glass. She could see it was sealed and, from its thickness, toughened. There was no way out there.

She heard the door open. Turned. Inez Cruz stood in the doorway.

Katya felt trapped, dug deep, kept up her anger. 'What the hell d'you think you were doing. That man– '

Inez came into the room. 'That man was a long-time client of mine and you just lost him for me. That's cost me–and I aim to get my money back.'

Katya swung the holdall in her hand–a threatening gesture. 'You get out of my way, Inez Cruz or whoever you are.'

A Chinese man edged in behind Inez. He was built like a sumo wrestler. Katya knew she was no match for him. She let the bag drop. Faced Inez. 'You want money. OK, I'll get it for you but not—'

'You came in on that private jet just before me, didn't you? The Gulfstream?'

'What are you talking about?'

'Don't deny it. I saw you. You came from behind our plane's undercarriage to join our queue. You were running from something. Someone on that Gulfstream.'

Katya showed her contempt. 'You must have drunk too much on the flight. I came off before you and turned the wrong way.' She decided to change tack. This Inez Cruz could be bought off. She was nothing more than a pimp—money would talk. 'Look, we can sort this out. I'm not going on the game for you—that's what you do isn't it? But I can compensate you for that bloody idiot who thought I was. Although I don't know why I'm being so generous, I would have thought you'd want to see the back of him.'

Inez heard her out, the false smile on her lips broadening. 'You have more courage than sense. I don't want your money. I want what the owner of that private jet will pay me for you.' She looked Katya up and down. 'A lot, I think. What did you do so you had to run? I hope you didn't kill him, I want my money.'

'Then you'll get nothing.' Katya said. 'I didn't come from any private plane.' The words sounded hollow even to her.

Inez shrugged. 'We'll see. The Gulfstream's still on the tarmac and I have friends looking for the owner. We'll wait, shall we?' She sat down on the bed.

Katya had another look at the sumo who was standing with his back to the open door, arms folded, and decided to wait as well. Something might turn up to her advantage. Incongruously she hoped it would be Yuri. Once away from Inez Cruz and her sumo, she could take him out and try to escape again. She didn't want to contemplate the future if Inez Cruz was in it. A woman who ran prostitutes in China had an easy way of disposing of their enemies.

They didn't wait long. Inez hadn't spent her sort of life in Dao without having influential businessman at her beck and call.

They heard the lift door open. The sumo turned, moved to make way for someone coming towards him. Katya held her breath, hoping it was Yuri.

It was. He squeezed past the sumo and stood there looking around. His face had livid bruising around his eyes and a strip of white plaster was stuck across his nose. His eyes found Katya.

'So it *is* you, you bitch.' His voice sounded nasal. 'Come here.'

Inez stood up. 'You need to tell me who you are because you owe me a deal of money.'

Yuri ignored her, kept his eyes on Katya. 'I said, come here.'

'Fuck off, Yuri,' she spat the words at him.

He started towards her—was jolted off his feet by the sumo, who held him off the ground.

'I was hoping you'd be sensible,' Inez said, conversationally. She gestured to the sumo. 'Or do you want help with that?'

Yuri shook his head. Inez nodded to the sumo, who dropped him. Yuri fell onto his knees. 'You know Belov's Casino here in town?' he snarled.

She stared at him. '"Yuri?" Of course, that's Russian, isn't it?' She thought for a moment. 'So, you're part of Belov's outfit? Well, that does make a difference.'

'I thought it might,' he replied as he struggled on to one knee. 'So give her to me.'

'No, you've got it wrong. My price has just gone up. If this,' she nodded towards Katya, 'is one of Belov's girl's escaped, he can afford to pay to get her back,'

'Not if I take her instead.'

Yuri struggled to his feet. The sumo stepped towards him. Yuri stepped back, shrugged, took a mobile out of his trouser pocket, speed dialled, spoke into the phone. 'Know anyone called Inez Cruz?' He listened. 'OK.' He shut down the call. 'How much?' This question to Inez.

'Ten thousand–dollars,' she hissed at him through her teeth.

'Three.'

'Seven.'

'Five. No more.'

'Done.'

'Call in tomorrow and go to the casino cashier.'

Katya was trying to take in the startling fact that Belov was able to own a casino in China. G8 intelligence had instilled in her that crime in China was owned and run by the *Triads* and *Tongs*. Belov was Russian and Russian *mafiya*, so how had he managed to bypass the rules of the centuries old gangs that ruled the underworld?

'Right, I've got a score to settle with you, you cow,' Yuri's words brought Katya back to earth. He stood by the door, waiting for her. She made herself reluctantly walk over to him. If he hit her, she'd decided to take it, then take him when they'd left the hotel. He waited for her to go past him into the corridor. She turned to walk to the lift.

There, standing with his broad sloping shoulders against the wall by the lift, his thick brown hair falling over his high cheek-boned face was Kirill. A man she knew. A man she hated.

THIRTY-ONE

K irill thrust himself off the wall, blocking Katya's way. 'Being a fucking nuisance as usual, Katya?'

Katya couldn't believe it. She hadn't seen him for five years, but it was Kirill alright. Over six feet tall; still with the tough and rugged good looks she remembered, and those shrewd eyes, brown with flecks of gold, which looked at one with such contempt. His brooding presence seemed to fill the whole lift lobby. What was he doing here?

Katya had first met Kirill when she'd escaped at night from her home and gone to the streets of Moscow. The drabness of communism had just been kicked out by all the exuberance of the West's excesses. Freedom had become an overnight sensation. The downside was the *mafiya* gangs which sprang up to take control of the businesses–seeing profit in everything. Extortion, blackmail and murder became the methods of choice as their tentacles spread deep into the areas abandoned by the State. Kirill had been in his early twenties at the time and one of their pimps running a string of young girls. She'd seen him at work and knew, even at that young age, that he'd enjoyed it. She'd done her best to stand up to him–not physically, but by using her wits to help the girls escape him. When she'd heard of a girl being groomed by Kirill, she'd warn her, even telling her to stay at home, however awful home was, because a life there was better than being in Kirill's clutches. Kirill had found out and had threatened Katya with retaliation. He'd never carried out this threat–she didn't know why–but when she'd gone to Uni in St Petersburg she was relieved to see the back of him.

Her response was automatic. 'I hoped you'd be dead by now.'

He reached out, grabbed her chin between his fingers; pinched. 'You mind your mouth. You'll be working for me.'

Katya drew her head back, rubbed the bruise on her chin, certain she must show no fear. 'That won't happen, you bastard,' she said, with what she hoped sounded like contempt,

Suddenly she felt a fist smash into her kidneys. Her back arched as she gasped in pain.

Yuri had come up behind her. 'You'll do as you're told, bitch. Now get into the lift.' He shoved her forward.

The lift doors opened and, bent sideways to ease the ache in her back, she limped into it. Yuri and Kirill pushed in beside her, leaving Inez and the sumo standing in the corridor.

The lift stopped on the ground floor. Katya was hustled out through the hotel's front doors and shoved into a waiting car.

She didn't notice much of what happened after that. She concentrated on trying to ease the pain in her back by preparing herself for what was to happen next. Kirill had said she was to work for him. What did that mean? She suddenly realised that she'd been so intent on analysing what she must do to complete her operation that she'd never thought through why she'd been drugged and put on the aircraft to Dao. If she was to be killed why hadn't Morosov simply used the noose in his office? Why had Belov sent her thousands of miles away? Distance–the word took on a significance she'd missed before. Distance also meant dis-association. Morosov must have believed Yuri's certainty that she was bent on taking over the casino? That would certainly explain why Yuri was still alive because when she'd left him with Morosov she'd been convinced he was about to be killed. It would also explain why she'd been sent to this place. Morosov, and probably by now

Belov, believed she was part of a group of grown up children of ex KGB officers who were planning to take over the Sea Dragon. They wouldn't want her death made public–KGB revenge was something to be avoided at all costs. It all made sense to her now. She had been sent here to be quietly liquidated when it suited Belov. It would almost certainly be Kirill who killed her–she'd already decided that Yuri didn't have the stomach for killing.

The plan that now formed in her mind was high risk. But she could see no other way to avoid the end Belov and Morosov had planned for her. She must get alongside Kirill. She must trade her hate for him into acceptance and a working relationship–become useful enough for him to want to keep her around. But his job was pimping and, with it, enforcement–terrorising people, executing them. Could she join him in doing that to people who had caused her no harm? Was she justified in carrying out his instructions only so as to preserve her own life? On the other hand, did she have the wit to outsmart him every step of the way and avoid becoming complicit?

The car stopped. The answer had to wait. She felt a heavy hand landing on her shoulder.

'Get out,' Kirill snapped. He leaned over, threw open the back door.

She climbed out, awkwardly favouring her back and found herself standing on an uneven pavement which fronted a short line of dilapidated buildings. She looked up. They were built of concrete with pillars and beams infilled with aluminium windows. At some time in the past the concrete had been painted in different colours but now the blues and reds and yellows were faded and patched. On the ground floor, she saw rows of metal shutters and above them, thrusting out into the street, were electric advertising signs–the only illumination to be seen. All the windows seemed to be blacked out.

She winced as Kirill pushed her towards one of the shutters. It opened as she approached it. She found herself in a small lobby.

He walked past her to a door set into the wall and pressed an electric buzzer there. The door opened. A deafening noise swamped Katya. Rooting her to the ground.

Kirill seized her wrist and roughly pulled her along with him as they went through it.

Katya didn't resist but looked around to see what this place was. She was staggered at what she saw. She was being dragged through a huge room which must have taken up all the buildings she'd seen in the street. The ceiling was so high above her it probably reached the top of the first floor. Banks of slot machines reflected the harsh glare of overhead spotlights. The punters she could see were Chinese. They were frantically pulling the handles in a manic crash and rattle, unrestrained in their shouts of triumph or disappointment. All of it similar to the slot machine floor of the Sea Dragon. The whole area was a cacophony of sweating action and sound.

Kirill, still holding her wrist, didn't stop until he reached a line of metal-fronted lifts at the rear of the gaming floor. He shoved her into the first lift that arrived. She saw that the bank of buttons showed four floors. Kirill punched the one for the second floor. Katya suddenly noticed that Yuri seemed to be missing. She looked behind her. He wasn't there.

Kirill noticed the movement. He let go of her wrist saying, 'He's gone back to Kropse.'

She didn't believe him. Yuri didn't have the guts to beat her up in revenge for the beating she'd given him, but he would have waited to see Kirill do it. Yuri was probably waiting on the second floor.

Kirill noticed the look on her face—disbelief followed by a flash of fear. He was pleased. As a girl, this woman had given him a hard time in Moscow, outwitting him as he'd pursued girls he wanted to pimp or he'd selected for a beating or worse. He couldn't wait to get her to himself. Revenge would be sweet.

The lift doors opened and Katya found herself nudged forward onto a gaming floor the same size as the one below her. This time, though, the scene did echo that of the gaming floor in the Sea Dragon except that here the décor was oriental. The walls were covered in delicate panel paintings of flowers and birds. The floor was carpeted in deep-pile Chinese carpets, the rich colours–reds, oranges, yellows–in sharp contrast to those on the wall panels. There were a dozen or so gaming tables set up around the room, far enough apart to allow for a free flow of people. The hum of conversation was so low that the click of chips was audible. She noticed the rapt concentration of the punters. Their faces held a curious expression, as if their whole life depended on the turn of a card or the spin of the roulette wheel. This created an atmosphere she hadn't seen in Kropse. There, the gambling was more of a pastime. Here it seemed to be a matter of life or death. They were almost all men. Chinese mostly, dressed in Western-style suits.

Kirill held her waist with his arm, stopped her moving forward. He lent down, put his mouth next to her ear, whispering, 'I brought you here to see the punters. You'll be servicing them.'

Katya thought of a pungent reply but kept silent. This was not the place to have it out with Kirill. She waited for what was to come next.

She found out after a short ride in the lift to the third floor.

The doors opened and they stepped out onto an intimate scene. She was in a circular hall with red wall-hangings and deep red carpeting. Inset into the walls around it were integrated panels. Each had a gold lock and key in the centre. Four men lounged in deep red leather chairs. They were all smoking and the air was heavy. As one, they turned to look at Katya. Two of them immediately rose to their feet, made a small bow to Kirill and spoke in Mandarin or Cantonese, she didn't know which. His reply was brief. His voice harsh, commanding. They scuttled back to their seats.

Kirill was blunt, 'They can't afford you. Anyway, this is just to show you where you'll work. Follow me.' He walked towards one of the panels. Her heart began to pound. She had little hope of fighting off Kirill, he was no Yuri, and these rooms were there for an obvious purpose. Prostitution. She turned swiftly to run to the lift. The doors were closing.

Kirill noticed her movement. 'Don't be stupid,' he said, his lip curling.

He turned the key in one of the gold locks. Numbly she noticed it was Room Number 4. The panel slid away to reveal a windowless room surrounded by mirrored walls. The only furnishings were a king-size bed and a drinks cabinet. An open silver box stood on it, filled with transparent envelopes of coke.

He saw where she was looking. 'Want some?' he jeered as he slid the panel shut behind them.

'I don't do drugs.' She kept her reply short. Tensed for Kirill's next move.

'You will,' he said, matter of factly. 'All the girls do eventually.'

She knew she had to fight him off now or he'd take her, rape her, shove drugs into her. She raised her chin defiantly before saying, 'Morosov said I wouldn't last as a hooker.'

He laughed, an ugly sound. 'He's right. That's why you're in this room. He's making sure you disappear.'

Katya was certain that reminding Kirill of the days in Moscow wasn't a good idea, but it was the only thing she had left to bargain with. She forced her tone to become persuasive. 'Come on, Kirill, you can't treat me like that. Remember our days in Moscow.'

His mouth dropped open in astonishment. 'Moscow? You dare remind me of Moscow?'

She cut him short. 'OK, we weren't on the same side and I gave you a hard time– '

'You can fucking say that again– '

She hardened her voice, 'But that's the point–I *did* give you a hard time.'

He screwed up his nose. 'What d'you mean?'

'You can use me– '

'Shit. I know that– '

'Not like that. I'd fight you– '

The challenging look on his face made her hasten on, 'I've still got friends, remember my father was KGB– '

'Word was you hated him– '

'True but the KGB stay together– '

'The KGB's finished, or didn't you know?' he sneered.

Katya abandoned the threat. She realised too late she would have had a better chance of success if she'd promised him that her KGB friends would buy him off. She might be able to do that later. There was more than one way of offering a bribe.

'Look at this place,' she said. 'The punters here are hooked on gambling. I can help them spend their cash. Increase the profits– increase your take.'

'Forget it. I'm just here as liaison with Kropse. There's nothing else you can do here.' Kirill was dismissive.

She threw out her last hope. 'I was a really successful floor host in the Sea Dragon. Ask Morosov.'

Kirill looked at her intently. She had a point. She'd be dead in a month as a prostitute. If she was a good floor host. . .

She saw him waiver. Took advantage of it and quickly followed up with the bribe. 'Morosov and Belov needn't know.

They think I'll die here in a month. I can work with you, steer the punters to a particular table and we share the profits.'

'Me? Go down that route? Morosov sure as hell will find out or worse, Belov. I'd be dead–or is that what you're hoping for?' Again, she heard the ugly laugh.

She changed tack once more. Held out a greater profit margin. 'I've got a system. The punters love it–well, until they're blown out. I turned in tens of thousands of dollars for Morosov in just two or three days.'

'So what? He knew what you were doing. What you're proposing is different–it's skimming.'

She caught the subtle change in his approach. 'Yes, and I'm damn sure you've got a tame croupier or three. You wouldn't be the same Kirill I knew in Moscow if you hadn't.'

If he hadn't known this woman, he'd have turned her down flat. Raped her and left her to rot. But he did know her. She'd run rings around him in the cellars and back streets of Moscow. She had her father's innate manipulative streak and her mother's charm. She was lethal. Skimming was just the sort of thing she could pull off.

She took advantage of his hesitation, added quickly, 'You won't regret it.'

His greed made up his mind for him. 'I'll try it out. But only for a couple of days. If it doesn't work–' he paused, looked around the room–I'll put you in here to work.'

She felt a rush of relief. But she mustn't show it. 'I'm happy to start on a thirty per cent split for me– '

'You're lucky I'm even thinking of going for this. You get fuck all. . .'

'I'm doing all the work– '

'And I'm taking all the risk. You're dead already, don't forget.' He opened the panel door. 'Stay here while I think about it.'

The panel closed behind him and she heard the key turn in the lock, leaving her alone to think. She had saved herself, but only just. She needed to tempt Kirill with more than the cash from small time skimming. She believed him when he said he'd give her two days. If she was to survive, let alone complete her op, she must somehow lure him into believing there was more reward to be had than that. She had to convince him the KGB were really backing her, waiting to take over the Sea Dragon. Yuri had believed her— so much so she'd been sent here to die so her KGB backers would never know what happened to her. Could she get Kirill to believe her as well? He had just shown he was as greedy as he'd been in Moscow. There was a chance.

She lay on the bed, drew her knees up, hugging herself. But there was no comfort in it. She was staring into an abyss. She didn't think she had long to live.

THIRTY-TWO

John was watching Lev and Walt on the plasma screens during a video meeting in the G8 Conference Room.

Walt, in a voice of barely controlled anger, was sounding off. 'I told you both that Katya was too inexperienced to start on ops. I warned you, yet you went ahead and now she's gone missing.' He opened his mouth to say more. Shut it again. He cherished his reputation for being temperate. He needn't embellish a point he'd made that strongly.

John waited to hear Lev's usual defence of Katya before contributing to the meeting.

Lev was thinking of the phone call he'd had with her. Her desperation at losing a hundred thousand dollars of G8 money; her disbelief that there was no more money; her determination to finish the op even if it meant doing it alone. A phone call he couldn't disclose to Walt or John. If they knew the trouble Katya had made for herself they'd bring her back, and as his protégé that would not only damage her but also damage him. He knew they were quite right in their view that she'd gone AWOL. Therefore, he had to be careful not to appear too blatant in his defence of her, otherwise these two would wonder why.

He chose his words carefully, 'Walt, she's only been gone ten days, eight if you take away her visit back here. What's eating you? We have officers who are out in the field for weeks at a time.'

'But they keep in contact with us,' Walt said, drily. 'We've heard nothing from Katya. She comes here saying she's cracked the whole case, is sent away with a flea in her ear and then. . .' He paused for effect. 'Nothing.'

Lev went on the attack, looking to undermine the strength of Walt's accusation. 'What are you saying, Walt? That she's dead? Taken by the *mafiya*?'

'No, of course not,' Walt said crossly. 'We'd have heard something otherwise. I'm saying she's undisciplined and should be brought back–immediately.'

Lev followed up with the leveller. 'If you're saying she's not in trouble, there's no reason to bring her back. The lease on the dacha has been extended to the end of the month.' He considered whether what he wanted to say next would tip Walt over the edge. Decided it needed saying. He took a cigarette out of the pack in front of him; lit it and spoke through the exhaled cloud of smoke– as if to hide an element of surprise. 'You know, Walt, we in G8 could do with looking at some of the FSB's training methods. We need to give our officers more rope–if they don't make mistakes, how are they going to learn?' He thought of strengthening his argument with a reference to the sadistic training methods of the KGB but decided against it. No good reminding them too often of his background. He sat back, satisfied his point had been well made.

Walt looked shattered. 'You can't seriously– '

John hastily intervened. 'True, Lev. But there's a difference between giving them rope and letting them drift about the ocean at their own pleasure. We'll give her another week and if we still hear nothing we'll then send one of our agents out to find her. All agreed? Good.'

They didn't argue with him. One of the reasons they'd supported him for the job as Director General was his unshakeable ability to cut through the fog and make decisions.

Lev watched his screen go blank. He thought to himself that

a week was a long time for an inexperienced officer to be alone in the field–especially in the dangerous wilderness occupied by the Russian *mafiyas*. At the time of the phone call with Katya he hadn't felt guilty cutting her loose. The FSB was harsher than G8. And the KGB techniques which had been used on Katya by her father were even harsher. She'd survived all three. Moreover, she was Russian. She owned a depth of courage unfathomable by others.

He stubbed his cigarette out, deep in thought. Katya was worth protecting. Sometime in the future she would lead G8, he was sure of it. She had every quality needed. She just needed experience and a helping hand to curb her neck-or-nothing impatience.

He frowned, reached for his mobile. It was time he called her again.

THIRTY-THREE

The first night Katya spent in Room Number 4 had seemed like an unending nightmare. She'd dozed then awoken with a start as a streak of fear had pulsed through her. Fighting it, she'd dozed again, only for the fear to return to be fought once more. Finally, exhausted, she'd fallen into a fitful sleep.

The sudden noise of the door panel opening shocked her awake. She automatically jumped out of bed, preparing herself to fight off Kirill. She almost laughed aloud with relief as she saw a diminutive Chinese girl tripping into the room. She carried an armful of clothes–a large make-up bag hanging from one of her shoulders. The girl gave Katya a quick, polite nod, hurried over to the glass-fronted, built-in cupboard which covered one wall. She opened it and carefully hung up the clothes; put the bag into the en suite bathroom and, before Katya could say anything, she left.

Katya waited to hear the lock turning in the panel before walking over to the cupboard and looking through the clothes. They were all in her size, a riot of colours and silks. Exotic clothes to suit the purpose of this room she thought grimly. She took out the plainest, a pair of dark blue trousers and a long, dark blue, almost black, silk tunic top and put them on the bed before turning and going into the bathroom for a shower. She decided to pull her hair tightly back, wear no make-up and certainly none of the cheap heady perfumes from the bottles in the bathroom.

She had just finished dressing when the lock in the panel turned.

Kirill entered. His presence seemed to dominate the room as he marched in, his shoulders leaning forward. He jerked his head to tell her to follow him.

It was early morning and, as he took her around the inside of the building, she passed men dressed in loose blue coveralls stationed in pairs at strategic spots–staircases, lift entrances. They were all Chinese. Tough looking men, guards. There were more of them at the doors of the main entrance and at the double doors in the basement kitchen for deliveries and garbage disposal. Kirill showed her the electronic locks.

'Don't even think you'll get a key,' he grated.

Katya wondered why the guards were necessary. The punters wouldn't cause the sort of trouble that needed such heavy defences. Was there perhaps some external threat to the casino? If there was, could there be an ally out there? She must find out.

As Kirill went on, he moved the curtains away from some of the windows, showing her they were sealed and telling her they were all the same.

When he took her back to her room she realised that this tour was to tell her she was in a prison with no hope of escape.

He started to leave then turned towards her. 'I've thought about you working as a host on the gaming floor, and I've decided you'll start right away–for three days to see how you get on. If you fail to make a profit you'll be put to work here.'

Left in the locked room, Katya knew it was no idle threat. If she didn't succeed, Room Number 4 would become her execution chamber. But as a host she had a chance.

She hastily changed the tunic she was wearing for one in a striking sapphire blue, let down her hair, brushed it into soft waves and put on some makeup. She looked at the cheap smelling scent–

ignored it–that was a step too far. No way were they or anyone else going to turn her into a prostitute but, she grimly acknowledged, she needed to make herself stand out if she was to become a successful host. She straightened her gold necklace, the only jewellery she'd had on her when she'd been bundled into the Gulfstream with no credit card, no money–nothing except what she'd stood up in. She thanked her lucky stars she'd found that cash in the Gulfstream.

A few minutes later the lock turned again and the panel opened. A tall Chinese woman came in, she had straight black hair and black eyes the colour of charcoal–sad eyes that had seen the worst of the world. She beckoned and wordlessly led Katya down the back corridors and stairs to the casino's gaming floor.

Katya saw Kirill waiting for her by the dimly lit bar. It stretched along one wall and was decorated with red and black lacquer gambling scenes. Glass shelves behind it were filled with bottles of expensive champagne and spirits. She noticed the four barmen were dressed in black trousers with red jackets which matched the lacquer design. They were busily pouring out drinks and chatting in hushed tones to punters sitting on high bar stools.

She walked across the deep-pile, dark blue carpet, ignoring its richness and the exquisite detail of the wall panels and chandeliers. Instead she memorised where the various tables were, how many punters were at each, what ethnicity, sex and age they were. As a host, she needed to know these details.

'Sit down,' Kirill said, peremptorily as she came up to him.

She sat on a bar stool facing the room.

'No. Turn and face the bar.' A command not a request.

She did as she was told. Composed herself to listen to Kirill's instructions.

'How many punters on the floor?' His question ripped out at her.

She was caught by surprise. This wasn't a question she'd expected from someone whose job was liaison between this casino and Kropse.

He noticed her hesitation. 'Don't know do you? That's the first thing a floor host would notice. I'm wasting my time.' He slid off his bar stool.

Katya launched back at him, 'Eight punters. It's early. Two females, at the blackjack table in the corner, both Chinese. Off the peg clothes, I'd say. Chance gamers with the housekeeping money. Not worth my bothering with them. Two Chinese males with them, ditto. At the craps table there's one, possibly African, male, crumpled suit and tie, probably just come down from a night on floor three with some spare cash– '

Kirill steadied himself, putting a hand on the barstool; narrowed his eyes. 'Smart. Who's the mark?'

'The couple on the roulette table. She's dressed in designer clothes, emerald ring, large. His watch is gold, probably Swiss. They seem slightly drunk, probably been out on the town and jumped in here for a spot of extra excitement–might just have got engaged.' Katya smiled inwardly. Her G8 trainer had always been amazed at her powers of observation.

Kirill grimaced. 'Impressive. Well, don't sit here. Go to work.'

She stood up.

He waved a finger at her, lowered his voice, 'Not your system. Don't try and use that. It's too early. I'll let you know when you can play that.'

She shrugged–a sod-you gesture. She wasn't going to let him dominate her now she'd got her own way. But she wasn't about to disobey him either.

She'd been right about the couple and their engagement–and she schmoozed them until they realised they'd burned through three thousand dollars at the roulette table. Katya knew she'd done her job well as she was still their friend when they waved her goodbye.

The croupier was impressed and told Kirill so. He was an old hand who'd seen it all, so Kirill took notice of him and started to take a quiet interest in Katya's work on the floor. He had a scam going with the croupier on Table 3, not large but skimming enough for a small profit. He wondered whether he could use Katya to increase it.

Katya had already seen how much interest Kirill had in her skills as a host and she worked hard. Meeting, greeting, bringing the punters to the tables. The Chinese punters were all polite and bowed their thanks but kept her at a distance. One or two men seemed to have an air of authority. She wondered if they were Belov's link to his casino here.

She summoned her courage and approached one of them. 'Good evening. I'm Katya your floor host. May I show you the bar or, perhaps the blackjack table?'

'Fuck off, Kropse cow,' had been the reply. She was shocked. Not at the language but at the tone of the man's voice. The bile had seemed directed at Kropse rather than her. He obviously knew who she was, so could there be some animosity towards Kropse? But who from? Who were these men? She stored away the thought to be built on.

She'd steered customers, as they were known, to the gaming tables and soothed their problems at the bar but this didn't seem to have turned in much of an extra profit. If she had done well, surely Kirill would have told her, so as to encourage her to keep going. The longer she thought about it the more uneasy she became. Kirill was not the sort of man to make a threat and forget it. She knew the consequences if she didn't make a big enough profit.

Apart from the sheer effort of staying alive she was under

another pressure. She had G8's mission to fulfil. So far, she'd found out nothing about the casino or how the cash in the baggage hold of the Gulfstream was being used. Who were these remote Chinese she felt were seniors in the Chinese community? What was the real relationship between them and Morosov and Belov? She felt a failure but knew that if Kirill noticed any unnatural curiosity in her she would be taken off the gaming floor. And, walking back to her room early each morning after work, she was reminded of the tightrope she was balanced on. The sight of men waiting for the numbered panel doors to open into the bedrooms and the white, scared faces of the young girls forced to greet them was a grim reminder of the fact that there was no safety net for her if she failed.

Convinced she had only days to live, she decided to force the issue. She had nothing to lose. It was towards the end of the third day that Katya spotted a heavily made up woman of uncertain age and nationality. Her black designer dress, showing off very large, expensive diamond jewellery, shrieked money. Katya moved in on her. Speaking English in heavily accented Russian, she talked of gaming and mathematics, gradually conjuring up a cloak of mystery. After a drink at the bar she very quietly and subtly introduced the woman to her system. After another drink, she guided her to a roulette table.

The woman bet throughout most of the night. Punters tried to stop her as she lost and lost. Convinced the system would eventually work, she increased her bets as she tried to recoup her losses. She went down heavily.

Katya didn't wait to the end. She sidled away and went to her room.

She was in bed, tired out and nearly asleep when Kirill burst in.

'What the hell d'you think you're doing?' he shouted at her.

Shock hit her. She couldn't find her voice. Had he come to rape her? Kill her? Or what?

'Did you steer that woman to Table 3?' Kirill demanded to know as he came towards her.

She didn't answer–couldn't answer because she didn't know what the right one was.

Kirill flung up his arms. 'She kept telling everyone that the system you gave her was infallible–mathematically proved by a Russian expert. She just kept betting.'

He started towards her.

She caught her breath. What had happened? Was this the end? Was she looking at death?

Suddenly Kirill stopped by the bed. There was something uniquely attractive about her. She was beautiful–desirable, of course–but there was more. What was it? Her cunning? Possibly. Ruthlessness? Perhaps. But it ran deeper than those assets. Confidence? Far too much. Courage? Courage was no stranger to him. He'd needed every ounce of his to fight off the big rival *mafiya* gangs in Moscow who were always trying to muscle in on his girls. Yes, courage was no stranger to him–and she had it. A common bond? He almost laughed out loud, he'd be wanting her next for real. But the thought had a calming effect on him.

'I came to tell you it worked. It worked so well we need to talk.'

Katya let out a breath. She knew instinctively that now was the time to introduce him to the bigger game– the KGB connection, the lie Yuri believed. But how to do it to win his interest? Telling him outright would only elicit derision.

She decided that sarcasm would be the right weapon at this stage. High risk, of course, because Kirill had a side to him– hidden, but almost tangible to someone like her who'd mingled with the riff raff of Moscow in her formative years. Appearing to be confident, she ran her hand through her hair to tidy it before saying, 'What do you do here Kirill because you sure as hell have no head for business.'

He squared up to her, his face reddening. 'I run–' He stopped, unsure how to go on.

Katya let him slide his brooding eyes over her. The look in them had changed. It was different from lust. She knew he was looking at her with new eyes. She was no longer the street kid giving him a hard time. But it was difficult to know what his new vision of her was going to be. She gave him a helping hand. 'I've shown you how to double the casino profits. If you'd listened to me earlier, you could now be on your way to taking over this place.'

She'd struck a nerve. Kirill had survived threats, a knife in his ribs, a wild drive by shooting that had only just missed him. He'd held out in Moscow until the Kropse *mafiya* had recruited him to run their girls at their casino there–and now he was "liaison" here in Dao. No way was Katya going to dominate him.

'I don't need you. I can run this scam by myself.'

'I'm not talking about a *penny ante* scam on the tables. I've got KGB connections.

'Fuck your– '

'Listen Kirill. Why do you think Belov wants me dead?'

'You owe him a hundred and fifty thousand dollars.'

'So, he has kept you out of the loop.' She loaded the sentence with conspiracy. Treachery in every word.

He bit. 'What d'you mean?'

'You think I'm just a punter, spending my father's legacy and getting out of my depth. Forget it. It's much more complex than that.' She made the lie bigger. . . 'I'm on a reconnoitre for a group of ex-KGB officer's children who are now all grown up and who want to buy back the Sea Dragon.'

'I don't believe it. Those KGB men sold the place years ago. It's *mafiya* now–Belov's.'

'That's what you think. But the fact is there's a new group– the now grown-up children who want to take the casino back. They know about the colossal sums of cash Belov flies out of Kropse to Dao and they want a part of that–want to be able to send *their* cash abroad so it will be laundered and untraceable. But Belov and Morosov got wind of what I was doing and had me sent here.' She rushed out the words before he could stop her.

Kirill thought for a moment. His actual job for the Kropse *mafiya* was an extension of his life in Moscow. He'd got no further than trading girls and women for Belov's casinos in Kropse and Dao. When he'd talked to Katya about being the liaison between the two, he was boasting. In fact, he was finding girls in China to be traded to Belov's casino's in Kropse and Dao. In return, the Sea Dragon's illegally laundered profits were smuggled to Dao from where Belov used the dollars on the black-market to invest in vast, multi-million dollar building projects in China. It was a private circular moneylaundering operation kept well hidden from the Chinese authorities. Kirill hadn't seen a penny of that cash, he was on a salary fixed by Morosov. If Katya was telling the truth, was there something in this for him? Either by warning Belov–fuck Morosov–or by joining her.

He stalled. 'I don't understand.'

'You know as well as I do, Kirill. The KGB never died and its alive now through these sons and daughters. What they want they still get. I may have failed but they'll send someone else and in the end, they'll get the Sea Dragon–and probably Belov as well.'

When Kirill had met Katya in Dao he'd considered her as simply a commodity to be traded for the most profit. He'd learnt that lesson in the orphanages he'd grown up in– being shunted from one to another like some sort of useless baggage; abandoned, neglected, beaten and bullied by the women who ran them. In all of them the girls were traded–every one of them, willing or unwilling. He learned that that was all they were useful for. But as he summed up what he knew about Katya and added that to the coup she had scored with that punter, he realised she was worth more than that. It was a new sensation for him and he was unprepared for it. He began to wonder if there was something in what Katya was saying. But he mustn't appear too eager.

He stood up, summoned his strength to make the first apology he'd ever made in his life. 'OK. You were right about your system making a profit. I want you to continue–for the time being . . . but you will steer the punters to one table only–Table 3.'

He stopped there, tossing up whether to tell her more. That thought made him feel vulnerable and he told himself he must be careful. But if there was money to be made with her KGB friends it would be useful to make her feel closer to him. He decided to tell her what only two other people knew. 'I've got a scam going with Heng, the croupier on the table you steered that woman to– Table 3. He and I share a small percentage of the profits. The other partner is a cashier, Lin. The punters on Table 3 are guided to her desk to exchange cash for chips. Some of the chips she hands over are forgeries. When Table 3's profits are calculated she keeps the value of the forged chips out of the total.'

Katya was shocked. This knowledge meant that apart from the risk to her from Kirill, she was now at risk from these casino employees as well.

Kirill sensed her alarm. 'I know, the scam's high risk, which is why I'm telling you so you'll know to keep your mouth shut. But it's safe. Lin's trusted by Belov and her activities aren't monitored. You can use your system twice a week. That way we won't attract too much attention to that one table.'

Katya knew she'd been fixed with the secret. But, if she was going to be able to tempt Kirill into joining her KGB ploy, she must play for time–there was no going back. Kirill had to think she was on board the whole way.

'What's my percentage?' she asked.

THIRTY-FOUR

A week later the profits for Table 3 were so big that Lin was worried they might attract Belov's interest. An investigation could blow back into the forgery scam. So, Kirill had decided that in future Katya's system could only be used once a week at most. That would be an acceptable period of time in which exceptional profits could be expected to arise without causing comment.

This evening was the occasion when Katya was allowed to trap a new gambler. It was very busy—a Wednesday and the 17th of the month, a doubly lucky day for gamblers born under the star signs of Gemini, Virgo and Aquarius who were freely betting in the certain knowledge that fortune would favour them.

Katya was sitting on a barstool nursing a Yorsh. She was wearing one of the pairs of dark red silk trousers left in her cupboard and one of the dark blue long silk tunics. She'd left her hair loose. She thoughtfully picked up her Yorsh, took a sip, and looked around the punters for a suitable mark when she felt a sharp nudge on her shoulder.

An angry voice said, 'Why aren't you working?'

It was Kirill. He gestured to the barman—a short sharp silent request for vodka. Katya had noticed that he drank to excess. She wondered whether this was just the usual habit of many Russians or whether it hid something deeper in him.

'I'm looking for someone I can take with my system so don't complain,' she replied forcefully.

He tossed back the vodka the barman gave him, fixed his eyes on her, the gold flecks in them darting amongst the background of brown. 'I *am* complaining. You aren't making much profit for us at the moment.'

His words cut into her. Was this his lead into firing her? Or could he be interested in joining with her in a takeover of the Sea Dragon? She covered her fear by striking back. 'Look, Kirill, you were the one to limit me to one scam a week. Steering the punters to Table 3 is all very well but they aren't spending much more than any other gambler at any of the other tables.' She lowered her voice, 'Why are we wasting our time on this chickenfeed when we could be making some real money?'

He was satisfied she'd sensed what he was looking for. He leant towards her. 'You mean that scheme with your KGB friends?'

'I offered Belov a buyout of the Sea Dragon.' She lied. 'He didn't want it. Sent me here to get rid of me. But my friends have a fall-back plan–to remove Belov by force, put in new management.' She waited for Kirill's reaction.

'Who'd be in charge?'

The one word told her all she wanted to know–she'd hooked him.

'I had thought of Yuri. But he's Morosov's man. Now I've met you . . .' She left the temptation as an unspoken gift.

He grasped it with both hands. 'Belov owes me nothing.' He held back for her to spell out the plan.

She knew he was on the edge of becoming her informer. But after the debacle of Yuri she didn't celebrate–gave him his first task to test if she was right. 'Why are all the guards here? What's the threat?'

He looked around to make sure no-one was within earshot. 'Belov owns the casino but there is a Chinese *Tong* in Dao, the *Zhang Tong*.'

'And that's a threat?'

'It's Zhang, the head of the *Zhang Tong* who's the threat. He runs the protection rackets here. Since the Chinese threw the Portuguese administration off the island, he has become stronger–also his *Tong* is the only one on the island. Belov traded on the Soviet links to the Portuguese here but they are no longer reliable. I think Zhang for some time has been looking to take over the Dao casino.'

She nodded slowly, assessing this information, before saying, 'So that's why the guards. But surely with all these guards here the defences are solid, Belov's got nothing to worry about.'

Kirill knew this was a probing question. What she was really asking was how weak were Belov's defences. 'I don't think Zhang has the firepower yet to take on Belov.' There, he'd said it–a hint at his commitment to help her.

He picked up his glass, sipped the top off his vodka, waiting for her reply.

Before she could do so, a large Chinese woman in an electric blue cheongsam leant between them calling for the barman. Kirill jerked his head at him–a signal to get rid of her. She caught it and her eyes went wide as if she recognised Kirill. Her whole demeanour changed abruptly–subservient, almost frightened.

The barman curtly told the woman he'd serve her further down the counter. She hurried away, head down, past Katya to where the barman was waiting.

Katya had recognised her immediately. She was one of the women she'd seen losing thousands of dollars at the Sea Dragon blackjack table. What was she doing here? Why was she frightened of Kirill? Was he something more than simply the liaison agent between here and Kropse?

Abruptly she got off her bar stool, saying, 'I'll talk to you later.'

Not for the first time Kirill felt outplayed by Katya. Another burst of annoyance engulfed him, but this time it was mixed with admiration. He tried to understand his feelings, at the same time pushing them away. Suddenly, an altogether different thought occurred to him. Katya was like a drug to an addict. Utterly dangerous but irresistibly necessary for one's existence. Was he crazy? What on earth was he thinking?

He watched her walk over to a Chinese man who was nervously looking about him, heard her say hello to him, saw her smile and ask, 'What are your lucky numbers? Mine are . . .' The voices faded out of Kirill's hearing as he watched the two of them drift away towards Table 3.

As Katya whispered the practised words into the man's ear, she reflected how well she'd read Kirill. She believed she'd found a vulnerability in him–a kind of admiration for her. Above all, she knew him from the street life in Moscow days. His problem was that he didn't understand women. He thought he could always control them through aggression and fear–couldn't accept that women could be subtle, manipulative. She was both and was certain she could still play him. Importantly, he had a foot in both this and the Kropse camps. She'd also begun to see Kirill for what he was. She'd noticed he spent a lot of time with the girls in the brothel on the third floor–and not just for the obvious reason. There was an authority in his dealings with them. Also, he seemed familiar with the new girls. And that woman at the bar–she knew him, had been frightened of him. Putting this all together told her that Kirill was the same loathsome pimp he'd always been. Except this time, he was working in the major league. Now, he'd had a taste of the sort of money he could get hold of by a well-planned scam. He was as vulnerable as she could wish him to be.

For the first time since she'd arrived in Dao, Katya felt she was making headway. At least for the moment. Now she could start work on finding out about Belov's link between this casino and the Kropse casino by using Kirill as her informer. She felt sure that would lead her inevitably to the scheme behind Belov's moneylaundering and to bringing down the Kropse *mafiya*. And what about this *Tong* leader Zhang? If he was an enemy of Belov, could she use him in any way?

THIRTY-FIVE

Later that night, Katya saw the Chinese woman who'd been so frightened of Kirill. Katya was on her way to her room when the woman came out of Room Number 9, adjusting her cheongsam. Katya put out a hand to stop her going down the stairs.

'I saw you at the bar,' Katya said to her. 'I've also seen you in Kropse so have you moved from there?'

The woman put a finger to her lips, pointed to Katya's room.

Katya took her arm and steered her into Room Number 4, sat her down on the bed.

The woman could hardly wait to talk. Her words a distraught, jumbled outpouring. 'Yes. I've seen you in Kropse too. You're like me, I couldn't pay my gambling debt. I've been sent here from Kropse because I wasn't good as a floor host. Now I'm in these rooms—it's horrible, terrible. There are men every day and I can't get away—' Tears splashed down her face—' But then you know.'

'No. I'm a floor host here.' Katya didn't know how much time she'd have to talk to this woman. What was clear to her was that she was desperate enough to talk. Katya took a gamble.

'I saw you launder at least ten thousand dollars there one night.' She threw out the words, brooking no denial.

'You know about that?' she asked. She stopped crying, twisted her fingers together. 'I couldn't help it. My boss gave me the cash.'

Katya was immediately interested. 'Your boss?' she asked sharply.

'Yes. He's a lawyer—in London. I was his secretary. I'd done it for him a few times before, well, quite a lot of times actually. He said it was only money the tax man wasn't going to get. You know, money from clients who paid him in cash. I think it was also for clients themselves on other occasions.' She tried to give a half smile. 'Nothing really illegal.'

The woman's answer surprised Katya. This was the first hard evidence she'd had of the extent of the Sea Dragon's laundering scam. It extended to the financial centre of London and this poor woman had no idea how serious it was and how her boss had used her so cynically. 'I suppose your boss gave you some extra cash to gamble with?'

'Oh yes. He was very kind, really. But then I got carried away one night and . . . god, it's awful, I lost thousands and he wouldn't settle my debt–Now I just can't get away from–' She started to cry again, the tears flowing freely.

Katya saw she was at the end of her tether, asked her, kindly, 'What's your name?'

The woman wiped her eyes. A hopeful look creeping into them. 'You can help me? My name's Geri. Geri Carter'

'Geri. Understand this. I can't help you. The only person who might is Kirill.' She left the sentence as it was. Blunt and uncompromising. What she had in mind was entirely unlikely to be accomplished, but if it worked and this Geri Carter actually did get out of Dao then G8 could use her as a witness.

Geri burst into racking sobs, her words jerking out in denial. 'But. . . that would mean. . .'

'You have no option, Geri. Do you want the alternative–the men waiting to get into your room? They won't help you.'

Geri gulped, gave her a horrified look, got to her feet. 'You think Kirill might help? Come with me.' She headed out of the door, oblivious to who might see her.

Katya felt she had no option but to follow her.

Geri walked blindly to the flight of narrow backstairs and stumbled down them. Instead of stopping at the entrance to the gaming floor she continued down.

Katya saw an immediate change from the plushness of the upper floors. Here the stairs were filthy, lit by dim naked bulbs hanging from the ceiling. They ended at an opening to a tunnel. The floor was concrete, littered with trodden in foodstuff. Boxes with Chinese characters drawn on them were strewn along the walls in a jumble. The floor surface changed to a filthy carpet. She noticed a chipped door recessed into the concrete tunnel wall. It was splintered–by what, she wondered? Strong kicks? Meaning what? Anger–forced entry?

Geri thrust against it, forcing it open with a crash.

The shock forced Katya to think–to try to plan. But she'd have to wait–to find out what lay behind the door. And, first, she must ignore the horror of this place. She'd seen places like it, in Moscow. The only difference was she went to those voluntarily– as a kid, to listen to music or drink illicitly distilled vodka and beer. Girls did haunt those places, of course, and the street *mafiya* controlled them but there was nothing there to compare with this. Here was hell. Her gut told her that and she must not even begin to think this was Moscow. To do that would be to under-estimate the danger she was in.

Katya saw a dirty linoleum floor, black criss-crosses on dark brown. Why had she taken in that detail? Thin iron posts reached up from it. What were they? To chain people to? She heard a murmur of voices. A shouted command–in Cantonese, Mandarin? The hum lingered. She'd seen the effect of fear in Moscow when the *mafiya* made demands. She relived that now. Those voices belonged to the lost–to those ruled by terror.

Her eyes focussed on smoke blackened walls. Bunk beds lined them to make a dormitory that was so long she couldn't see the end. They were occupied–each one by a girl. Their cheongsams crumpled as if they slept in them.

A face suddenly leaned over her from a top bunk. Chinese–it seemed young. She concentrated on it. Yes, it was young, thirteen, fourteen but deep creases lined eyes that had no light in them. The mouth was taut, as if it had never smiled. She'd seen faces like this on the streets of Russia. The child prostitutes–hawked for a few *kopecks* by scummy pimps loitering in the backstreets. She knew she'd been right. Here was hell.

Katya turned abruptly so she could look around. The girl immediately put her arm up defensively across her face to ward off an expected blow. When it didn't come she slid across to join another girl in the next bunk bed. A hush had fallen and the girls were all sitting up, silent, looking at Katya and Geri with scared, frightened eyes as if expecting trouble.

Geri turned to Katya, opened her mouth to speak but no words came. Her eyes stared blankly as if to shut out the horror. For the first time Katya came to grips with the depravity that was the Belov *mafiya*.

Katya knew she had to take charge of the girls in this room. She had no idea what they might be capable of if they thought she was vulnerable.

She looked around at the girl's faces, seeking one she could question. They all looked away as she tried to meet their eyes, pretending to adjust the cheongsams they wore. All except one; standing by her bunk. She was taller than the rest, dressed in an orange coloured, flower print cheongsam. There were food stains on it and streaks of grease. Her hair had been roughly chopped which gave her an aggressive appearance. She lifted her chin as she held Katya's eyes with her own, dark almost black ones.

'Do you speak English?' Katya called to her.

The girl said nothing, keeping her eyes fixed on Katya.

Katya walked straight up to her. 'I said, do you speak English. Answer me.'

The girl stepped back and swung her fist at Katya's face. Katya moved to one side, avoiding the blow. She raised her hand, a gesture of peace. 'Do you speak English?' she said, quietly.

The girl stared at her, making up her mind about her. 'Yes, yes. A little.' The girl babbled the words. 'Do not hit me, please– *please.*' Katya put an arm around her. 'I'm sorry,' she whispered. Keeping her arm where it was, she looked around the room.

Katya knew she only had a little time for questions. This was a working dormitory. Any minute someone would call for one of the girls to go to work.'

'Who's your pimp.'

The girl screwed up her eyes, trying to understand.

Katya quietly repeated her question. 'Who's your pimp?'

'Kirill,' the word burst out of Geri.

Katya and Geri left the dormitory, Katya closing the door behind them. The journey back up the stairs seemed to her to be another extension of hell. When Geri had spoken Kirill's name, she'd collapsed and Katya had to half carry her up the flights of stairs.

When they reached the third floor two Chinese men were there obviously waiting for the panel doors to open. They hurriedly looked away when they saw Katya's angry face. She took the key from Geri, opened the panel to her room, took her in and laid her on the bed.

She put a hand on Geri's shoulder. 'Forget what I said about Kirill. I'll deal with him.' And, at that moment, although she had no idea how that could be accomplished, she meant it.

Katya left her and went straight back to her own room–sat down on the bed, holding her head in her hands as if to squeeze out the images flashing through her brain.

THIRTY-SIX

Katya didn't see Kirill until the next evening. She was in Room Number 4 and had just finished dressing to go down to the gaming floor when she heard the panel being drawn back. Kirill stood there. For a moment, she panicked that he'd seen her with Geri–was there to challenge her about it.

'We're going out.' A flat statement. He expected no refusal.

The loathing she felt for him almost overpowered her. But the dogged Russian in her saved her. It was the operation that mattered, not her feelings for Kirill. Silently, she followed him out of the room, down in the lift, out of the front door and into the passenger seat of a Volkswagon GTI Coupe waiting at the bottom of the steps. Kirill climbed into the driver's seat; started the engine.

'We're going to dinner. Don't try to get away, I'm armed.'

Katya felt an insane desire to laugh. Dinner and death. It sounded like a bad film.

'Why?' she questioned.

'We need to talk–away from the casino.'

Katya could hardly believe she'd heard correctly. Could this be the breakthrough? Was Kirill offering more than just the casino scam? She banished the image of the girls in a burst of elation. 'I'm happy to talk.'

'You shouldn't be, we've got a problem.'

A tremor went through her. What was he talking about? She'd been working the two tables for eight days now and there had been no inkling that things weren't going well. In fact, two punters had coughed up sixty-three thousand between them. The casino had a healthy profit and the forgeries had brought in about fifteen percent. Big enough to make a decent turn and small enough not to really be noticed. And she was sure Kirill hadn't learned of her visit to the dormitory. Or was she? Had those two men, who'd seen her help Geri to her room, talked? She mustn't show alarm.

'What problem?' she asked, evenly.

'Wait for dinner,' was all he replied.

He didn't talk as he drove and she had a chance to look again at Dao. Like Macau, it had been settled and administered by Portugal until the Chinese had taken over some years previously. Unlike Macau, gambling was prohibited in Dao. This explained how and why Belov's criminal organisation owned the casino. It didn't however explain why the *Zhang Tong* allowed a Russian *mafiya* to run it. A word to the Chinese authorities would have had the place closed down. The idea had swiftly been dumped as she realised that the local authorities would benefit from the profits of the casino. Why close it down? As long as its exterior remained suitably camouflaged the authorities could pretend it didn't exist.

These thoughts passed through her mind as she saw again the narrow streets overshadowed by balconied buildings in need of paint huddled between dingy concrete and glass fronted offices. The lighting was afforded by garish neon signs hanging from overhead wires and advertising products, tailors, nail bars and cafes. The road suddenly opened up into a boulevard running alongside the sea. Here were elegant Portuguese mansions with pillared entrances and manicured lawns. They reeked of money. One of them stood out from the rest. Very modern, obviously architect designed with six tall, slim, pale cream stone columns. Arches between the columns were filled with glass that seemed to shimmer green in the pale light of the street lamps.

Kirill noticed her studying it. He laughed shortly. 'That belongs to Zhang. The man I told you about–runs the protection rackets here.'

'And Zhang wants the casino?'

He wondered what she was getting at. 'Why do you ask?'

'Well, it seemed to me the *Zhang Tong* might be the same as the *mafiyas,* always after extra profit, particularly if it's being made by someone else–you know, like it was in Moscow.'

'Forget the *Zhang Tong,* they're not going to help you get out of here, even if you could contact them.' Kirill, uncompromising.

Katya planted the thought she'd had in mind since Kirill first mentioned Zhang. 'How would Belov get his cash out of Kropse if he didn't have the casino here?'

Kirill suddenly realised what Katya was contemplating. Pitting Zhang against Belov. He couldn't see Zhang winning that contest. His *Tong* was too weak and Belov too well defended. Putting in with Katya's KGB group takeover of Kropse was one thing, trying to do it by forcing Belov out of Dao was another. He immediately dismissed the thought.

Kirill turned the GTI into a gravel driveway, stopped at a pair of steel gates set in a tall chain link fence and got out. Half a dozen guards with pistols in holsters were lounging there. They had the confidence of men who felt invulnerable. Katya made a mental note.

Kirill imperiously beckoned to a young Chinese valet waiting there, tossed him the car keys. Katya quickly got out of the GTI as the youth climbed in the car and, barely waiting for her door to close, drove off at high speed spurting gravel towards Kirill. . . horn blaring.

Kirill walked Katya up to the gate which automatically

opened. Katya found herself inside a large garden. There were no trees, no shrubs or flowers, just green grass, trimmed immaculately and split by a gravel path leading to a long low building. The walls were white painted smooth concrete, interspersed with wide strips of lighting. There were no windows that she could see. The roof was flat. She saw two armed guards standing on it; their guns pointing at them.

Katya suddenly knew she was entering a fortress. She tugged Kirill's arm. 'What is this place,' she asked him. 'I thought you said we were going to dinner.'

'You're meeting someone here,' he told her with finality.

Katya felt terror spill into her. Who was she meeting? Kirill had got her here by subterfuge so it couldn't be a friend. Or could it? Had someone seen her in the casino or by the dormitory and recognised her–asked questions? She had no time to think further, they had arrived at a door, discreetly let into the concrete wall, which opened straight into a large room. A waiter dressed in a brown baggy uniform stood there holding a tray of drinks. '*Baijiu*?' he said as he bowed.

'Nothing for her,' Kirill barked.

The waiter turned immediately, pointed at Katya and said, 'Follow me.'

Katya's heart was pounding as she had no choice but to follow the waiter. The room she was in was crowded with Chinese men and women. As she walked through them she saw the women all wore traditional Chinese dress, expensive Cheongsams in a rainbow of colours, and the men wore brown Mao suits. Whoever they all were, they talked loudly in groups, drinking from the glasses of *Baijiu* they held in their hands. The waiter manoeuvred his way through them until he came to a door in the far wall. He knocked. The door opened and he pushed Katya through it.

Katya hadn't noticed the décor in the room she'd just walked through, but here she couldn't help but notice the silk washed Chinese rugs covering a polished wood plank floor. The walls were draped with silk tapestries, no doubt antique. Black lacquered and ivory inlaid furniture occupied places where they could be appreciated in the soft lighting. Behind a large ebony carved desk sat an overweight man. He could only have been Russian but maybe some Chinese ancestry had crept into his eyes–his thick black hair almost met the deep furrows across his forehead which led to even more heavy lines around his eyes and almost non-existent lips pressed together in a thin slash. The face of a man who'd bludgeoned hardship to find wealth.

He exuded malice.

She could see his eyes were almost shut and that he sat so still she wondered if he was asleep.

She was about to ask him who he was.

His voice startled her, 'Stay where you are.' It was high, thin and piercing. 'Tell me about your system.'

He must be a punter she didn't recognise. She went into defence mode. '4,7,10 in a line. One chip for each number or two chips covering the lines between.'

He half opened his eyes, cruel, deep set and black as night. The high voice ascended another tone. 'It doesn't work,' he said.

She'd guessed right–he was an angry gambler. She'd learned enough to know that gamblers were inherently suckers. They had to believe they could beat the odds. She started to sap his confidence. 'Nonsense– I,' she emphasised the pronoun, 'make money from it.' She followed that up by touching on every gamesters' pride in their ability to beat the odds. 'You don't understand it. That's what it is.'

He moved his heavy body for the first time, leaned over the desk towards her. 'Explain it to me.' His eyes pierced hers.

She hadn't expected him to fight back. She had no

explanation. All she'd done was to fix on three numbers that came up most frequently when dice were rolled. She studied his etched face, he was a survivor, not a mathematician. He wouldn't be able to keep up if she made the explanation complex enough. 'The mathematical– '

She stopped as he leaned back, very slowly; did something behind the desk with his hand. A slim Mac G4 computer rose out of the desk top. 'Yes? You dictate the formula and I'll feed in the data.'

Katya was confounded. There was no way she was going to haze this man. 'Who are you? You've never been at one of my tables.'

'My name is Belov. I think that means something to you.'

Katya knew real terror. Belov. The head of the Kropse *mafiya*. He'd found out about the scam. That was why Kirill wasn't here. Belov was interrogating her first. She stood, frozen, unable to speak, her face chalk white under her golden tan–god, how stupid could she have been to think she could play with this man. Try to con him.

His eyes were wide open now–scouring her face with a hostile stare, his head tilted forward. She knew he was reading her expression, all his years of experience interpreting it.

'Yes.' That hated high-pitched voice. 'It was a mistake to think you could con me. You should always have an explanation for a scam. But then you are young and, I think, inexperienced.'

For a moment, she took his words as a sign of hope. 'Thank you for your advice,' she made her voice sound grateful.

His hand went below the desk and fiddled there. The Mac disappeared into the top of the desk. He sat studying the piece of ebony that had slid over it to make the desk top complete. 'How much are you making?' the words jerked out of his mouth.

She was totally disoriented. One minute he'd been angry,

threatening, the next disclosing who he was and the danger he represented, then he was conciliatory, now accusing. Accusing her of skimming the profit. She must think. Think. Her interrogation training sessions flashed into her mind. Keep focussed on your objective, her trainer, Andrei Savin had said. She firmed up her voice, 'I don't know the figure. That's in your books, but I've been very successful steering marks to the tables. And I've had no complaints.'

'Don't change the subject. I said how much are you making? Tell me.'

As he and Morosov had sent her to the Dao casino to be killed he must know she was imprisoned in the brothel there pending her death sentence. 'I don't make anything,' she said in a flat voice.

'I mean what does Kirill give you?'

There it was, the direct accusation. She mustn't hesitate. She and Kirill must be shown to be enemies—not co-conspirators. 'What about Kirill? He doesn't pay me anything either.' Did this terrifying man know about her and Kirill? 'We knew each other in Moscow. He hates me. He just uses me because I'm a good floor host.'

His thin, cynical mouth worked, making the creases around it deeper. 'That's what my cashier Lin told me.' He sat brooding for a moment. Suddenly made up his mind; brought his pudgy fat hands together. 'You will continue as a floor host. You will use your system sensibly. If you are questioned about it, answer that your numbers are based on the Russian lucky numbers. The Chinese are great believers in luck.'

He gestured to her to go. 'You can go. But don't think for a moment that I can be fooled. I'm watching you and Kirill—and those casino profits.'

THIRTY-SEVEN

When Katya left Belov she found her legs were trembling. It wasn't the surprise of finally meeting Belov face to face or that he was in Dao that had caused the tremors. It was the fear that he suspected her and Kirill of skimming. It didn't need much analysis to realise that it was only a matter of time before his suspicions were confirmed. And, however carefully they played it, their time was limited to a few days at most.

She had to find Kirill.

She moved among the chattering, drinking party goers, thinking how oblivious they were to the drama that had played out in the room she'd just left. Or were they oblivious? Did they know? Were they watching her? If she found Kirill here and went to him would Belov know about it in minutes?

'You're fucked, aren't you, Katya,' the voice, just loud enough to be heard by her, came from behind.

She whirled around, expecting to see Kirill. Yuri stood there, his fist half-raised as if he was about to cheer at her misfortune.

How she hated this man. Even more because he'd led her on to actually think he might become an informer.

She put all the bile she felt into her reply. 'Not after what I've just told Belov about you.'

In a split second his expression altered from triumph to terror. 'What–' His voice shook.

She never heard his question. Kirill came up to them. 'Fuck off, Yuri,' he said, conversationally. He took Katya's arm, held it firmly, and steered her through the crowd towards the front door. 'What does that weasel want?' he asked her.

'The usual,' she replied with an eye to any interested listeners nearby. 'What you're not getting either,' she added.

He pushed her through the front door saying, 'You promised me dinner.' He turned to the car valet who was standing on the driveway. 'My car, the GTI.'

Katya waited, her back to him, discouraging conversation.

The car arrived in a spray of gravel and stopped. The Chinese valet got out, threw the keys to Kirill and opened the passenger door for Katya. She immediately spotted the underlying defiance in the valet's gesture to Kirill–the way he'd spurted gravel when he'd driven away to park the car. It was as if he was telling her he thought Kirill was a bastard. She looked him over. He seemed to be in his early twenties, short in height with pale skin and curly black hair swept back off his forehead. Big, dark eyes gazed admiringly at her, a knowing look on his face. Was he a possible ally if ever she should need him? There was no harm in finding out she told herself. She sent him an intimate smile, her mobile eyebrows slightly raised, slightly questioning.

And she'd been right. He was smart, understood her immediately. 'The name's Ming,' he whispered. 'If you need me let me know.'

She nodded–a slight movement unnoticed by Kirill who was climbing into the driver's seat. For what was developing in her mind as a plan could very well need the services of Ming.

She got into the passenger seat and as the car door shut Kirill accelerated smoothly away. He drove down to the gate which opened automatically–drove through it, then stopped and waited to let traffic go by on the main road.

'We need to talk,' Katya said. 'Not in a restaurant. Down by the beach. Alone.'

She didn't know what was in his mind as he turned onto the beach road and joined the flow of traffic. She sat back in her seat, relaxed, letting the movement suggest she was prepared for a journey out of town to a quiet place. She looked in the passenger rear view mirror to see if anyone was following. She didn't spot anything unusual in the flurry of traffic behind them.

As they made their way along the road, the mansions lining it dwindled in size until they became houses and then shacks and then nothing but scrub and bushes. The road lighting faded with them until it ceased, leaving a deep azure canopy littered with the silver pinpricks of stars.

Kirill suddenly turned the car onto a sand track. Bushes scrubbed the sides of the car until they fell away to reveal a broad sand beach leading to long rolling waves breaking in white foam. The place was deserted.

Kirill stopped, switched off the engine. 'Quiet enough for you?'

In the wing mirror, Katya caught a flash of light from a passing car. It was far enough away to be almost hidden.

She got out, shut the door and waited.

Kirill came up to her. 'What's this all about? It's certainly not about what I want.'

'It's about the girls, you pimp.' She hesitated as he took this in. 'But more important at this moment, it's about Belov.'

He was taken completely off guard. 'Belov? What the hell do you mean, Belov?'

She took off her shoes, left them beside the car, and walked onto the beach. 'He knows about our skimming–that we're using my system to increase the profits.'

'That's ridiculous. Apart from us only Lin and the croupier,

Heng, know anything about it and they're as tight-lipped as oysters. Anyway, Belov's in Kropse.'

She faced him. 'He's here. I've just been with him. He– '

'*Here*? That's impossible. Who told you?'

'He did. He's Russian and he looked like a crumpled cardboard box.'

'My god. That *is* Belov!'

She heard his breathing quicken. 'And if a man like Belov says he knows, then he knows,' she said.

Kirill didn't want to hear this. 'Why are we here then? If he knows, he'd have killed us by now.'

'True. He didn't actually say that, but he gave the strongest hint that he was on to us. He'll have us under a magnifying glass night and day from now on.'

'Then we just stop. Simple. I don't know what you're in such a sweat about.'

Katya gave points to Kirill for speed of thought but he'd just confirmed what she'd always known. She could think more subtly than him. She didn't waste time as he tried to think it through. 'If we stop, we have to withdraw the forged chips and replace them with legitimate ones. I'll bet we don't have that many, so chips will be missing. He'll hunt around the cashiers. Lin is clever but I doubt she knows much about pain–well, the sort of pain Belov can inflict. She'll be screaming the truth in minutes.'

A sudden shaft of light spread across the sea to the beach and lit it up. Moonrise, Katya thought, as if it could help her somehow. 'No, Kirill, we have to keep going until we have a better solution.'

'Get out, you mean?'

'Off this island? Come on, we're Russian, in a crowd of Chinese we'd be picked up in under an hour. I've got a better plan than that.'

Suddenly she swung around, searching the beach behind her.

He took her arm. 'What's wrong?' The words were whispered, urgently.

'I thought I saw a shadow. . . Someone. . .'

'It was only the moon. It just went behind that cloud.' He pointed out to sea.

Without warning, the shadow became a man charging, plunging towards them. He headed straight for Katya, screaming, 'Fucking bitch. Fucking cow.'

Yuri. Face contorted–long knife in his right hand–held back to thrust forward.

Katya went ice cold. Adrenalin surging through her. Combat ready. Time slowing down. Yuri in slow motion. The knife blade trajectory clear in the moonlight. She stepped to one side to avoid him. Yuri sped past out of control. The knife cutting air. Katya turned to meet him as he came back, watched as Kirill kicked him on the turn. Fast. Hard. Doubling him up. A blur of motion. The knife swinging. Downwards. The crunch of a blade meeting bone. Blood spurting. Gouts of blood. Yuri's blood.

Katya swung around to face Yuri's back-up. There was none. The beach was empty, silent save for the crash of the surf hitting the sand.

'Shit. What the hell was that all about.' Kirill, breathing heavily, holding the knife downwards, avoiding the runnel of blood dripping on the sand.

'It was personal,' Katya spoke calmly, breathing normally–a survivor. She gestured to Yuri's body, lying silent in the moonlight. 'Thanks.'

Kirill stood watching her, catching his breath. He knew Yuri had been easy to take. He had had no doubt Katya would have killed him as easily as he had. He'd seen her go passive, icy calm, letting Yuri rush by so she could get into the best defensive position for when he came back. So why, he asked himself, had he put himself in danger to help her? What was it about this woman that intrigued him? A woman whom he had every reason to hate. Who'd simply said thanks when he'd killed for her.

'We'd better get rid of him,' he muttered.

Katya had already planned for Yuri's disposal. 'No. Leave him here. We'll take the knife. . . well, clean it in the sand first.'

Kirill couldn't keep up. 'He'll be found. Belov will be told.'

'And?'

He was silent.

She looked him over. 'Have you got blood on you?'

They searched his clothes and shoes, his face and hands. They washed some blood splatter off his hands in sea water. Otherwise he'd been lucky. There was no blood on him.

Katya stepped back from a final once over of his clothes. 'We go to a busy self- service restaurant in town. Fix a reasonable alibi. Find somewhere to dump the knife. I'd go for a place near the Zhang mansion. The police won't buy that as a clue, but if the *Zhang Tong* are as paranoid as any *Mafiya*, they'll see it as a threat. And that will be helpful for what I want to do next.'

He had no better idea so he followed her along the beach, carrying the knife down by his side. No-one was waiting for them by the car. No-one was about as they left.

The road was free of traffic. Most people were at home or eating a late dinner in the restaurants and café's that served food on the boulevard. When they neared the Zhang mansion, it was only a matter of moments for Kirill to slow down the GTI and for Katya to open her door and slide the knife into an open storm drain alongside the pavement.

They then drove further along the coast and made themselves inconspicuous in the queue lining up for self-service at the restaurant Kirill had chosen. They sat down at one of the scrubbed wooden tables and ate some of the food, then, abruptly, Katya got up– deliberately bumped into the waiter who was clearing the next-door table. She apologised, bowing her regrets and headed for the restroom. She was satisfied the waiter would recognise her if an alibi was ever needed. It was as good an alibi as she could expect.

She turned her mind to Kirill and how she was going to tell him about the plan that had formed in her mind to save themselves from Belov. On the journey from the beach she had puzzled how to present it to him. Her objectives were to get out of Dao before Belov had solid evidence of her skimming; to somehow rescue the helpless girls Kirill was trafficking and to recruit Kirill as an informer. Good luck with that she said to herself, but there was a chance and she must take it if it was at all possible.

She returned to the table and sat down. Kirill was chewing on a mouthful of fish. She closed her chopsticks around a steamed shrimp. 'We need to talk about Belov,' she said.

He wanted to tell her they had to talk about Yuri but he couldn't swallow fast enough.

'Good,' she went on. 'We can't run and we can only stay two or three days at most before he susses us. Agree?'

He nodded. Waiting for whatever ingenious idea she was going to propose next.

'I can work it for us but it will mean you losing your stable of girls.'

He choked on his fish. 'What stable?'

She leaned into his face, furious. Violet-blue eyes blazed into angry brown ones. 'I've seen them Kirill. You told me you were liaison between here and Kropse but you're nothing of the sort. You're still a shitty little pimp.'

His voice was low but his tone was vicious, 'You remember where you are. I can make you join those girls if– '

His threat made her angrier. 'You admit it. I can't believe

you're still in the trade. When we were in Moscow I actually thought you'd get to be better than that. You were above the average *mafiya* thug and had a chance to get a real job. You had no excuse for what you did then, except we were all finding our way. . . trying to look for some sort of decent life. But you haven't tried. Those girls–god, Kirill, how could you?'

He shoved himself away from the table. 'I don't have to take this crap. We're going.'

'Where? We've got a day or so at most before Belov gets the information he wants to have us killed.' She rapped out the words.

'So?' he spat out the word.

She measured him. The man who'd killed Yuri. 'We need to get in contact with Zhang.'

He was stunned into silence.

Katya put it clearly. 'If Zhang kills Belov first, we're safe.'

Kirill opened his mouth to ridicule the idea.

Katya cut across him, 'What do you want out of life, Kirill? Die here when Belov finds out you've been skimming? Or be part of us, part of me and my KGB group, running the Kropse casino without Belov in the picture. It's your choice.'

Her words sliced into him. She was right. His loyalty to Belov wouldn't protect him. In fact, his loyalty to Belov, to the *mafiya,* had blinded him, had led him to take for granted their loyalty to *him*. It didn't exist, it never had. He hated to agree with Katya but it was now clear that he had no option.

'What are you proposing?'

'We–you–have to get in touch with Zhang.'

'Now that is stupid. I'm the enemy.'

Katya knew his reply made sense. Belov was Russian *mafiya,* his presence on the island would make him Zhang's enemy. Kirill would be seen by Zhang as Belov's man. But, that being the case, why did Zhang allow local Chinese to be employed by Belov in the casino? He could easily have terrorised them to stay away. Could that mean the cashier Lin or the croupier Heng had some loyalty to Zhang or, even, were in his pay? Was their loyalty to Belov guaranteed? Only one person could find out.

'You might be the enemy, but what about Lin–or Heng? They might be able to help.'

'And who's going to put that idea them?' Kirill asked, sarcastically.

Katya poured scorn into her reply, 'god, Kirill, still the pushover pimp– '

Fury flashed across his face.

Her next words drove the knife in. 'If you want that job in Kropse you've *got* to get rid of Belov. And you're the only one who can get Lin or Heng on side. If they make contact with Zhang, they can open the door for you to see him.'

THIRTY-EIGHT

Kirill didn't say a word on the journey back to the casino. The contempt Katya had put into her voice had lashed him. It wasn't the fact that she despised him for being a pimp that upset him. It was her assumption that, by now, he could have been something better. He knew she was right. He had the tools life had given him but he hadn't used them. Life had been easy living off the earnings of girls. If they caused trouble they didn't cause it for long. There were always other girls, willing or unwilling.

He remembered thinking how simple it was to believe that that was a good life. But Katya had shown him a better life. Well, not better but richer. He'd seen her mind at work—quick and clever. He'd been like that when they'd first met in Moscow when as a young and very beautiful girl she had been determined to rescue his girls. He'd had a sneaking admiration for her. Perhaps that quickness had been their first point of mutual interest. But he knew he was slower now, his wits duller. He'd become lazy. Worse, he'd abandoned his mind to become a thug—No better than Luka, the bouncer at Kropse, and the other low life *mafiya* gang members. It had taken her to point that finger at him. The only person ever to do it. The others, the *mafiya* gang followers and Morosov, Taban, Belov. . . Belov, that bastard, had simply used him. He cringed inwardly as he thought how they'd manipulated him, had all probably laughed at his laziness and the ease with which they could boss him about.

Slowly, his fury died down and he began to feel a burning anger.

Katya had kept quiet deliberately, pleased with the rage she'd stirred up in him with her display of disgust. After he'd driven a little way she saw him go into himself. Saw an inner struggle, revealed by small signs—a slight tightening of his mouth, a fleeting frown creasing his brow. She'd never thought Kirill a fool and had known him for being quick-thinking and highly dangerous. She'd been genuinely surprised that he had slowed down and was content to use his talents to frighten young vulnerable girls into being his meal ticket. For all his pimping on those streets in Moscow he'd been dynamic, handsome, exciting, a real force. He could have made so much more of his life. So, she waited in silence as his rage dissolved into self-examination. Suddenly she noticed his hands clenching the wheel. A sign that anger was returning. Either he'd come to terms with her contempt or he was feeling some sort of regret. Now was the time to find out.

'I'm right aren't I? You could have done much better for yourself.'

'Fuck off, Katya.'

She noticed he'd added her name. That's at least a step forward, she thought wryly to herself. She took the next step to bring him onside. 'Let me know when you want to become somebody. Personally, I don't intend to wait for Belov to suss me out.'

The rest of the journey was completed in silence. It was so late into the night when they got back that the casino gaming floors were shut. Kirill took her up the stairs to her room. He stood in the doorway.

'Please don't lock me in,' she said firmly as he put his hand on the key to close the panel.

He stared at her, his face inscrutable.

'Where am I going to go?' she added with a shrug.

He slammed the panel shut.

She waited until she heard the lift doors open and shut–tried the handle. The panel opened. The first sign that Kirill might have listened to her. Or was it? She would find out right away. He was either waiting for her to come into the lift lobby or he wasn't.

She stayed there a few moments longer, thinking over exactly what she planned to do.

She changed into an all-black outfit, then slowly edged her way out of the room, her eyes scanning the lobby to the lift. No-one was there. She closed the panel, went straight to the stairs and ran lightly down them–past the gaming floor and into the dirt and stink and darkness of the basement. She hurried to the splintered door that led into the dormitory. Without hesitating, she pushed it open

She heard rustling movements and saw in the dim light figures on the bunk beds pulling sheets over heads. She didn't have time to think about the horror those simple movements conjured up. She went straight to the bunk occupied by the girl she'd questioned when she was there with Geri.

She touched her foot. 'I saw you with Geri, I need to speak to you.'

The girl quickly moved her leg away.

'Please.' Katya spoke only the one word–the word the girl had used to plead with Katya not to hit her when they'd first met.

There was no response. Then, slowly, the girl raised her head.

Katya bowed and smiled at her. 'Thank you.'

The girl crawled along the top bunk bed and looked down at her.

Katya didn't waste time. She pointed to the rear of the dormitory. 'Show me.'

These girls were kept in squalor in this room, yet, when she'd seen them in the panelled rooms on the third floor, they had been clean, tidy and dressed in colourful cheongsams. So where did they get clean and change? She'd never seen them in the staff canteen, so where did they eat? Katya had the vague idea of a plan and the answers to these questions were vital.

'Show me,' she asked again.

The girl slid out of the bunk and slipped to the floor. She beckoned Katya to follow her. As they passed the rows of bunks, the other girls sat up to see what was going on. Katya counted at least thirty-two. She thrust down the rage swelling inside her. She must remain focussed.

The girl walked through a curtained archway that Katya hadn't noticed before. They were in a large hallway. The walls and floor were stained and dust-ridden, as if they had never been cleaned. The girl walked to a door on the left-hand side, opened it. Katya walked through into a large shower room. This in turn led to another room where one wall was lined with clothes rails, along them bright coloured cheongsams were tidily arranged on hangers. A long table occupied another wall. Above it was a mirror and shelves containing makeup.

The fourth wall was bare, save for a metal double door. Katya went straight to it. Tried the handle. The door stayed shut. Locked. But Katya had seen enough. She started to question the girl.

Pointing at the door, she said, 'When is this opened?'

The girl nodded. 'Open for delivery, food for us.'

'Who opens the door?'

'Kirill. He the only one. Delivery only.'

Again, Katya swallowed her disbelief that Kirill was responsible for these girls never seeing the light of day.

She forced herself to smile again at the girl, put her finger to her lips—the gesture for silence.

Once more the girl nodded.

They made their way back to the dormitory where Katya left the girl standing by her bed. But not before she had pointed at all the girls and made the sign of silence. Katya had the information she needed now. But it was a live coal and until it was passed to Zhang it could ignite a fire that would consume her.

THIRTY-NINE

The next day saw Kirill working the gaming floor. He was dwelling on the extreme high risk of what he was about to do. He'd given Lin no reason to trust him. In fact, the reverse. He'd always treated her badly.

It was early and Lin was alone at her cashier's desk idly riffling chips through her hands. Legitimate or forgeries? Kirill walked up to the desk, dropped a 20 yuan note on it. 'Hello Lin. I found this on the floor.' He tapped his finger on the words he'd written across it – "*meet in the store room*"

He strode off to the lift and went to the basement, found the storeroom and waited by the laundry piled up beside a large sink.

Lin arrived almost immediately–bursting through the door in alarm. Kirill pointed to the door. Lin understood, shut it and handed him the 20 Yuan note. Kirill tore the flimsy worn paper into small pieces, lifted the sink plug and fed the bits of paper into the drain. He knew this action would draw Lin further into the conspiracy he was planning. When he'd finished, he replaced the filter, left the water running. He'd planned his opening sentence carefully.

'Belov's onto us–onto you.'

Lin abruptly gripped the sink to steady herself. 'god, he can't be! I've been so careful all these years.' She stopped. 'It's *you*! Your stupid scam.'

'You were happy to go along with it. So don't throw your problems at me.' Kirill, brutal.

'What am I to do?' She sounded desperate.

'You've got one option. Get out.'

There was a silence as Lin took this on board. Kirill waited, letting the alternative sink in.

Lin shook her head. 'No. It's been my whole life. I can't just up and go. He'd never . . .' her voice tailed off.

'Kill you?' Kirill supplied the missing words. 'How can he let you go when the whole casino knows you've been skimming?'

Lin was quick to deny the idea. 'But they don't know.'

'Not yet.' The meaning behind Kirill's words was clear.

Lin's eyes told him that she understood the threat only too well. 'What am I to do?' she pleaded in a whisper, as if the truth could be hidden behind it.

Kirill decided it was time to move on. 'You said your job's been your whole life. Do you want it to continue–if it could, I mean?'

Lin didn't hesitate. 'Well. Of course, but you– '

'There is a way.' Kirill hurried on. 'You've been around a long time, Lin. You must have been approached by people from the *Zhang Tong*–Zhang's always wanted this place . . .' He waited for the denial.

Lin's reply surprised him. 'Yes, of course. But I'm loyal to Belov.'

'How loyal, now Belov's coming for you?'

Lin's eyes widened as the force of this hit her. She'd been approached by the *Zhang Tong* at her home, in the street, in cafés as she ate. Offers of cash were made, then later, a small percentage if she would help arrange for Zhang's take-over of Belov's casino. The offers had never seemed large enough. Now there was an added incentive–no, not added, it had become imperative. 'What do you propose?' Lin asked.

These were the words Kirill had played his hand for. He

hadn't really expected to get this far. How much further would Lin go? 'A way out for you is to help Zhang get rid of Belov, take over the casino. You could ask him for the moon if you did that.'

The moon seemed rather too much for Lin. All she wanted was to stay alive. 'And if I'm found out before the takeover?'

'You'd be no worse off than you are now.' Kirill, brutal again.

Lin played with her fingers, interlacing and untwining them, her dark red nail polish flashing like a warning signal. She pushed herself away from the sink. 'I'll think about it,' she said.

Kirill knew a way of adding pressure without making her lose face. 'It was Katya's idea,' was all he said before walking to the door.

He opened it and looked out. A lone male, one of Belov's guards, was standing with his back to him, talking into his mobile. Kirill nodded towards the stairs. Lin crept out and soundlessly disappeared up them.

FORTY

L ater that evening and dressed in one of the flame-coloured cheongsams, Katya left Room Number 4 to go to the gaming floor. She went straight to the bar and sat on one of the stools. She hadn't had time to order a drink before a smartly dressed Chinese man came up to her and bowed. She recognised him immediately. He was the one who had told her to fuck off when she had approached him a few days earlier. She was surprised at his obvious change of heart.

'*Nushi*,' he started, then stopped as he waited for her to acknowledge this respectful form of address to a woman.

Katya had learnt this social custom and bowed slightly in response, alert now because she knew this man treated the female employees in the casino like dirt.

'Katya—may I call you that?'

She nodded, giving nothing else away but her consent.

'You drink Yorsh, do you not?'

He was buying her a drink? This man had always seemed to her to have an air of authority in the casino—someone who was comfortable giving orders. Someone who was part of Belov's set up? He would never buy a drink for an employee and a female employee at that. What was he up to? 'I'd love one,' she replied. 'Three to one as it's early.'

He ordered for her and added a *Baijiu* for himself. Katya had seen him usually order Black Label whiskey. *Baijiu* was the accepted drink for business discussions. Was there some significance in his change of choice? Was he about to proposition her like most of the male habitués of the place? She took her drink and sipped it without waiting for him to propose a toast.

He looked put out. 'You don't wish to make a toast?'

'I'm an employee. You would lose face if I was to treat you like an equal.'

'That's not really why, is it? You think I want to take you upstairs and you are telling me I can't.'

She felt her heart rate increase. So far Kirill had kept his word. She was a host and that was keeping these vultures away from her. But this was different. This man was powerful enough to swat Kirill like a mosquito. He could get her into Room Number 4 with no difficulty at all. She prepared to fight him. 'You don't look to me like a man who has to pay for a woman.'

She had expected him to react angrily. She was wrong. He burst out laughing. 'I heard you were different. You are quite right, I wouldn't.'

'So why the drink?' she cut in, bolder now.

'I want you to show me this system you keep so secret.'

She cursed herself. For some unknown reason, she hadn't expected this - had been so certain he wanted her she hadn't considered any other reasons for his approach. She realised he was obviously here investigating for Belov and she had been so self-absorbed she'd dismissed the thought. If she gave this man her system he would lose and lose just to find out whether the table profit was actually skimmed. A comparison with his play and losses now with other earlier plays and losses could well reveal a discrepancy in the profit. How was she going to stop him?

He was talking. 'Which table is it you like to use? Three, isn't it? Come on.'

She felt her brain was seized up—couldn't think. But she had to think, otherwise this man who was obviously here to help Belov suss out the scam would. . .

Belov's name suddenly triggered a memory. Something he had said to her during that nerve-racking meeting with him. What was it? Something to do with luck. The Chinese were great believers in luck. That was it . . .

'I'm afraid it's not possible to use my system today,' she said, positively. 'Today's the fourth of the month and I was born on the fourth so the day is doubly unlucky. I wouldn't risk your money for the world–or my reputation either.'

She watched anger chase suspicion across his face.

He had noticed her earlier suspicion of him when he'd first spoken to her. Then he'd seen her look of alarm before she'd told him she was unlucky today. He wondered if this was a clever ploy of hers to avoid taking him to the table. That would make sense if Belov was right about her skimming the profits. He was about to insist she played, but then he considered what the consequences would be for him if she told the other punters her luck was quite out. Belov had told him her system was rubbish and guaranteed to lose. As his losses mounted the other punters would think him a fool that he'd played after she'd warned him against it. He'd lose face and he guarded his position in the casino too closely for that to happen.

His expression altered, he smiled. 'I understand. Not today then–I want to win.' He beckoned the waiter, pointed to the drinks. 'Put these on my tab.' He got off his bar stool and bowed to Katya. 'It has been a pleasure–no, more than that–an interesting experience to meet you, Katya.'

She breathed a sigh of relief as he walked away towards the front door. She'd seen him off.

Suddenly she saw him stop, turn and walk back to her. She caught her breath as he came up to her and said, 'The day after tomorrow is Friday, the 6th of the month. Very lucky for us born under the sign of Libra–I'll see you then.' He bowed slightly and sauntered off.

Katya wrestled with rising panic. She'd saved herself, but she'd only delayed her exposure by a couple of days at most.

Where was Kirill?

FORTY-ONE

Kirill had decided to walk to the casino from his downtown apartment. He needed to think things through.

As he made his way through the streets he found the coolness of the early evening and the slight breeze welcome after the heat of the day. Deep in thought, he didn't take much notice of the people hurrying past him in their brightly coloured clothes laughing and talking as they made their way to the many Dao restaurants and bars. For the first time in his life, he was uncertain of himself. Katya's words *"You're still a shitty little pimp"* kept repeating themselves in his mind. He couldn't believe how deeply they'd dug into him.

He'd known her in the Moscow cellars and on the streets when as teenagers they tore through the good life that the crash of communism had brought them. Western music and local copies of western clothes–he fleetingly remembered the bomber jackets, oversized sunglasses, the baggy jeans. There had been a cacophony of freedom and a fog of what to do with it apart from celebrate. At least that had been his experience.

He had felt Katya was different. He'd heard she was desperately unhappy at home with a KGB father who was a bastard and this could have explained the air of seriousness about her. It was as if she understood what was going on around them and found solace in it rather than just a good time. He'd also found her stunning to look at and vibrant–with that beautiful face and figure and those brilliant and irresistible violet-blue eyes. He'd been tempted to approach her but he'd kept clear because of her father. He wasn't a man to cross.

However, what he remembered most about her was his added frustration caused by the way she'd manoeuvred to rescue girls he was grooming for his trafficking trade. She was five years younger than him, yet she ran rings around him. Perhaps that was the result of the harsh training it was rumoured her father imposed on her. Whatever it was, he'd been relieved in more ways than one when she'd left to go to uni in St Petersburg. He had to admit he'd given her thought during the intervening years but he hadn't been pleased to see her again. The moment he'd seen her in Dao, even though he knew she had only a few days to live, he'd felt that old frustration and the certain knowledge that she would cause trouble at the first opportunity.

And she had. She'd manoeuvred him into letting her go onto the gaming floor and then she'd cooked up this scam that had put his own life at risk. He'd even risked trying to bring Lin into Katya's conspiracy to kill Belov. And Lin had left without committing herself. She could already have told Belov.

Automatically he looked around seeking out potential danger. Someone following him–taking an interest. He was scared but he was also furious. His anger helped him make up his mind. He must do a deal with Belov. He'd trade Katya, Lin and the croupier, Heng, for his own life.

He arrived at the casino and made his way to the gaming floor to see if any of Belov's partners were there. That was when he saw Katya talking to Belov's number one. They were deep in conversation. That could mean only one thing–Katya was definitely saving her own skin. He waited until the man had left.

He then wasted no time in striding up to her; snatched at her arm saying, 'Upstairs. Now.'

Katya started to resist, saw the look on his face, then the interest awakened in the punters who were standing around or making their way to the tables. She capitulated.

Once they'd gone through the panel and into Room Number 4, he hurled her onto the bed. 'You bitch. I should have known it–'

'What the hell are you doing,' Katya screamed.

He jammed his hand across her mouth. 'Telling me you had a plan to get us out, then doing a deal with Belov. I saw you talking to one of Belov's men.'

She tried to speak, but no words came out. She tried to struggle but his other hand tightly gripped hers behind her back. He straddled her, his whole weight pinning her down.

She used her final defensive tactic–one taught her by one of the G8 trainers. She suddenly went limp, eyes closed, making a choking sound through her nose.

'Don't try and fool me!' he yelled into her face.

She didn't respond.

He couldn't kill her, he needed her alive to hand over to Belov. He was about to slap her when he realised both his hands were employed. He decided, if he was quick, he could release her mouth and use that hand to deliver a quick smash across her face.

He lifted his hand. Katya brought her knees up into his back. He arched as pain lashed into his spine. She thrust upwards, toppling him on his side. Her hands were free for a split second before she slammed both of them together on his neck. He collapsed, moaning, clutching his neck.

Quickly she got off the bed and ran to the bathroom, took the belt from her bathrobe. Running back to him, she seized his arms and tied the wrists together behind his back, tugging the knot as tight as she could. She then sat down on the bed to wait.

Kirill lay still for a moment, then struggled upright. He glared at her.

She saw the fury in his eyes; rubbed in her superiority; calmly said, 'You know, we needn't have had all that fuss, Kirill. I was on my way to find you.'

'Like hell you were, you were selling me out to Belov. I saw you.' His voice loud, aggressive.

'That man was testing me. I'd just got rid of him and bought us two days to get out of here.'

All his old resentments came flooding back. 'Like fuck you did.'

'I have two alternatives Kirill. One, to hand you over to Belov with a weeping confession. And I'm prettier than you, so who d'you think he'll believe–you or me? Two, to get both of us out with a chance of saving our lives.' She shrugged. 'It's up to you.'

Kirill knew he had just planned to sell her to Belov and counted on that to save his own skin. Why should Belov treat her any different if *she* went to him on bended knee? He decided to let her talk–wait for her to be off guard. He would then have a chance to take her out.

'I'll listen.' His angry eyes bored into hers as he stood up, his height dominating her.

'You didn't talk to Lin, did you?' Unfazed, she threw the words at him.

'That's where you're wrong. I did. But she didn't commit and I think she's gone to Belov.'

She aimed at his weakest point. 'You would think that. You've been too damn busy with your pimping to think about the possibility of Lin siding with Zhang. Times have changed. The Chinese own the island now and it's only a question of time before Belov is kicked out. And the person who'll do it is Zhang and his

Tong. Lin's not like you. She'd understand that, there's no doubt she'll throw in her lot with him.'

He thrust his face towards her–furious, threatening.

She shoved him back with her foot. A hard-striking blow.

Kirill suddenly knew she was right. He had been riding the crest of a wave, oblivious to the changes taking place. He hated to admit it to her and wondered how he could tell her she was right without appearing submissive.

Katya noticed his hesitation. Recklessly she threw in the rest of her argument. 'Listen to me,' she shouted. 'Lin will be on board and I've got Ming as well.'

He thought for a moment. 'Who's this Ming?'

Katya added fuel to the fire. 'Your problem is you treat everyone like shit, you don't spot their feelings. He was the Chinese valet at Belov's place who brought you your car. He doesn't like you but he likes me. He'll do things for me. I think he wants a change of job.' She paused for effect. 'We can handle that.'

Katya had used the word "we" deliberately and saw the shift in Kirill's eyes as he took on board the conspiratorial meaning of it. His next words confirmed her conclusion that he'd decided to join her.

'What about my croupier, Heng?'

'He'll do whatever's in his best interests and, believe me, if Lin and Ming and you do your jobs, he'll know to put in with us.'

Kirill was silent. He knew she'd thought this through. There was nothing to say. The alternative of going to Belov looked hopeless. He said slowly, 'So–what's your plan?'

Katya had a problem. She'd told Kirill she was sure Lin would go along with ousting Belov, but that wasn't strictly true. He was right, Lin could at this moment be talking to Belov seeking forgiveness.

'I'll tell you when Lin's with us.'

She didn't try to explain the ambiguity in her reply. She was on enough thin ice.

Kirill wasn't fobbed off so easily. He wanted to hear the details of her plan and asked her again. She refused to give them to him and he became angry again. When his bluster didn't change her mind, he became conciliatory, seductive. But she hadn't untied his hands, so she held him off easily. After a few moments, he gave up and, instead, tried to convince her of his admiration of her mind rather than his desire for her body. He found himself stumbling—it wasn't a line he'd taken before with any woman. Gradually he lapsed into a sullen silence.

Katya let him stew until she felt the fight had gone out of him. She then told him that, if she untied him, he could leave and repeated she would explain everything when Lin was with them.

Just as she had guessed, he let her loosen the belt from his hands and quietly departed, leaving her worn out and very soon sound asleep.

FORTY-TWO

Later that night Katya didn't hear the panel open or hear the footsteps approaching her bed. It wasn't until she felt a hand close over her mouth that she woke up with a terrified start.

Her training prevented her from trying to scream. Instead she gathered herself into defence mode. She thought Kirill had returned.

'It's me, Lin.' The female voice startled her. 'Lin. Katya. It's me, Lin.'

Katya brought her hand up and touched Lin's hand. Breathed a sigh of relief as Lin released her—tried to throw off her tiredness. 'What are you doing here? I thought you'd gone to Belov.'

'I went to Zhang.'

The four simple words had Katya sitting bolt upright saying sharply, 'Tell me.' She switched on the bedside light as she waited for the reply.

'I listened to what Kirill said,' Lin answered. 'I don't trust that man so I would have gone to Belov. But Kirill said it was your idea to go to Zhang. You treat me well and I do trust you. So afterwards I spoke to a friend who is a member of *Zhang Tong*. He came to see me tonight and took me to Zhang himself. Zhang wants to see you.'

The flood of words was hardly decipherable as they stumbled out of Lin's mouth in a welter of fear. Katya didn't try to unravel what Lin was saying but, instead, seized on Zhang's invitation. 'When does he want to see me.'

'Now. He's sent a car for us.'

Katya looked at her watch. 2.25 a.m. in the morning. Would she have time to go to Zhang's mansion and get back before the casino employees started stirring for the day's work? She'd have to hurry. 'You'll come with me?'

Lin nodded.

Katya went into the bathroom, splashed water on her face, threw on some cotton trousers and one of the cobalt blue silk tunics, twisted her hair back into a hair clip. There was a long matching scarf in the wardrobe and she took it out on her way back through the room.

They left Room 4, made their way down the staircase and through the girls' dormitory to the rear door. Lin produced a pass key, saying, 'Belov trusts me.'

They went out and Lin closed the door behind them. They made their way down the deserted street. The city and advertising lights were all turned off at midnight so the only light they had came from the half-moon which was casting shadows across the pavement as the night clouds drifted in front of it.

'Those poor girls', Lin muttered to Katya. 'I hate shutting them in.'

'Where else can they go?' Katya felt humiliated at the futility of her reply.

'There's a charity, run by the Portuguese . . .' Lin faltered, as if Katya would have no sympathy for the idea.

'The Chinese won't allow– '

'No. It's been settled between the Portuguese and the Chinese that the Charity is protected by the government.'

Katya turned her mind to her plan. 'Did you ask Zhang whether you could go on working at the casino if he takes it over?' she asked Lin.

'No. He will want to use his own *Tong* members,'

Katya couldn't see Lin's face in the semi-darkness. Was she telling the truth? Now that she was fully awake and had asked herself why Zhang wanted to see her so urgently, Katya had doubts. Had Lin already secured her position as cashier for Zhang; made arrangements to let him take over? Was this walk going to end in disaster? She felt a shiver run through her. Was she going to her death?

Katya probed further. 'The *Tong* members have no experience of a cashier's job.'

'You don't know how the *Tongs* work. They only trust their own.' Lin spoke the words slowly, as if afraid they confirmed that her working life in the casino had ended.

'Then why are you here with me to see Zhang?'

Her reply was simple, 'You told Kirill to tell me Belov was going to kill me. At least this way I stay alive.'

Katya had no reply. Lev had told her during training that these decisions would have to be made. What was worse—criminals getting away with murder and violent crime knowing their cash would be hidden safely through the casino or Lin losing her job as part of a plan to stop it? She heard Lin speaking.

'This is where we are to be picked up.'

Across the street a black Lincoln Town car with blacked-out windows was parked– lights on–engine running. The driver must have seen them because he got out and held the rear door open. They walked over to him and got into the back seat.

He shut the door, climbed into the drivers' seat and drove off. No-one said anything until the car stopped in front of Zhang's mansion.

'We're here,' Lin said in a hollow voice.

Katya felt her stomach churn. She'd now find out exactly what Zhang had in store for her.

The gates to the mansion were guarded by two life-sized

bronze figures of lions–a sign to show Zhang's bravery and power. They were opened by two Chinese men dressed in loose blue clothing. They wordlessly led them along the path to the front door. It was solid teak, weathered to a silvery grey which blended in with the pale cream of the elegant stone columns fronting the building.

The door opened automatically to reveal a large hallway completely empty of furniture. Concealed soft lighting in the ceiling revealed cream marbled walls and floor and nothing else except a door right in front of them. Katya turned to look at the front windows. They weren't there. A marble wall hid them. She suddenly realised that, like the G8 warehouse, the walls were armoured. It would take heavy artillery to blow a hole in them.

Katya turned back as she sensed a sudden rigidity in Lin's body. Zhang had silently come through the door and was studying them. At least, she assumed he was Zhang.

Katya took the initiative. 'Katya Petrovna. Thank you for seeing me.'

Zhang was a young man. Slim, medium height. Dressed formally in a lightweight cream Calvin Klein linen suit offset by a cream silk shirt and a red tie, and, wearing highly polished light-brown leather shoes with red socks.

Red for luck, red for fire, Katya thought as she looked at him. She studied his smooth, lean, rather angular face which was giving nothing away as he took his time in replying. His eyes were unnaturally bright. Drugs? she wondered.

'Thank me only if I've been of assistance', he replied, his voice authoritative, commanding. His accent epitomized Oxford University. 'But you are Russian, so I doubt we'll be able to do business. Like my government, I don't trust Russians.' Before she could reply he'd bowed and said, 'Shall we go outside?'

They followed him into a floodlit courtyard. It was huge–filled with trees–pines, cypresses–and flowers, peonies and orchids. There were archways, pavilions and a tall waterfall was splashing into one of the lotus-filled ponds.

Zhang led them to an open-sided pavilion where he invited them to sit down. Painted red with large, comfortable black and gold chairs, it overlooked the courtyard. A black, highly lacquered table was laid with plates of Portuguese egg tarts. They sat in silence as the waiter hovered with drinks before vanishing silently into the night.

Katya hardly noticed any of it. She was appalled at what Zhang had said about Russians. This was the man she was going to persuade to take over the Dao casino. It suddenly occurred to her that the reason he hadn't done so before was that he was well educated and smart enough to make a shedload of money without it. This was no *mafiya* thug. He was formidable.

She decided to go straight to the point of why she was there. 'Belov's Russian but you *kowtow* to him.'

He bridled at her deliberate use of the Chinese word. 'I don't trust him but he's still protected by Portuguese friends.' He looked at her. 'Which I doubt you are.'

'The Portuguese are no use to me.' She rammed the point home. 'Their power went with your government's takeover of Dao. But that's politics. What I deal in is reality and the reality is you hold the power now.'

Zhang wondered who she really was. He'd wanted Belov's casino ever since the Portuguese authorities were kicked off Dao but Belov was powerful, well protected by the *mafiya* and his villa was bomb proof. So, he had waited until a solid opportunity presented itself. Was this woman that opportunity? She didn't have Portuguese friends who would come to her aid. There were no others on the island to help her—only his *Tong* was capable of the sort of violence required to defeat Belov and he knew that wasn't going to happen yet.

He cut to the chase. 'I'm told you want Belov's casino– '

She didn't wait for him to finish. 'No. *You* want it. I'm just here to help you get it.'

'How?' He shot out the question, his eyes narrowing.

'I've got insiders who can secretly open up both the casino and Belov's villa for your men to attack them.'

His eyes widened slightly in disbelief. She intended that he use his own men to get Belov out. So she *was* unprotected. Or was she? Could she be an agent, setting him up? FSB or, worse, G8? But she was too young and what intelligence agency would put up an inexperienced agent like her against Belov? No, there had to be some other reason behind her offer.

'Why are you doing this?' He rapped out the question, his eyes focussed on her face, watching for any hint of a lie.

When Katya had been walking along the street with Lin and talking about the girls, she'd had a part of her mind on what she would reply to this question. The one thing Zhang would understand would be her fear that Belov was going to kill her. She went for it.

'Belov's going to kill me.'

Zhang stared at her, slowly taking in what she'd said.

Katya thought he hadn't understood–started to repeat her answer.

Zhang held up a hand to stop her. Leaned forwards; said, 'Why does he want to kill you?'

'He's convinced I've been skimming.'

He sat back in his chair. 'That's the only reason I would believe.' He spoke very quietly, as if to himself. 'Yes. The only reason.' He lapsed into silence again but he kept his eyes fixed on hers.

Katya didn't blink. She knew this was make or break. Nothing she could say would alter his process of reasoning. She felt Lin move forward as if to say something–put her hand out to stop her.

'No,' Zhang spoke the word softly. 'Let her speak. Is she part of your plan?'

The spell was broken. Katya didn't wait. 'Yes. Lin here is trusted by Belov. Her job is to open the rear basement doors to the casino and let your men in.'

Zhang shrugged. 'That's all very well but that would mean an assault on only one front which would be far too risky. My men would be outnumbered.'

'I have a man lined up to open the front doors at the same time.' She'd settled Kirill's job whether he liked it or not.

'You've forgotten Belov's villa. He has quite an army there.'

Katya recklessly consigned the car valet Ming to honour his promise to help her. 'That's been arranged as well. A man will be there to guide your men in, and open the front door for them.'

'When?'

'Tomorrow night.'

Zhang looked doubtful. 'That's not much time for me to get organised.'

Katya made her reply blunt and short, 'I haven't got longer than that to live.' Her eyes held his. 'Without me you get nothing.'

He studied her. She was quick, smart, a planner. Was she too good? Was there more to her than escaping a death sentence? On the other hand, if she delivered what she had promised, he'd be rid of Belov and own his casino. And not just the casino–he'd own the island.

'Very well. Tomorrow night.' He looked at his Piaget watch. 'At 2.00 a.m. I'll make my arrangements. You be sure to make yours.'

Katya had one request to make. 'I want Lin to be chief cashier when you take over.'

'You didn't have to ask. I'm a business man, I know where to look for the greatest profit. Lin is my guarantee of that.' He stood up and left the pavilion. One of his servants silently came in, bowed and escorted Katya and Lin back to the car waiting at the entrance gates.

All the way back to the casino Katya remained silent. She was wondering how to get to Ming and persuade him to guide Zhang's men into Belov's villa. All around her was danger–facing her like a hurricane warning with its treacherous wind and lashing rain just waiting to pounce. Would she survive it?

FORTY-THREE

The next morning when Katya went down to the casino she found it busier than usual at that time. She felt edgy. There seemed to be more uniformed and armed guards about. There was no sign of Lin. Had she changed her mind and spoken to Belov? If she had, he would immediately strengthen his defences–ready to counter Zhang and turn the tables on him. Did that explain the presence of the extra men? At the same time, Katya hadn't heard from Kirill–had no idea whether he'd finally decided to back her or not.

She felt alone and exposed. Doubts crowded in on her. She felt totally unequal to the task she'd set herself in that conference room in G8. She'd trusted Lin–but based on what evidence? She'd thought Kirill was on side despite knowing him for a manipulative shit. And she'd bet her life on them. Just as back in Kropse she'd thrown a hundred thousand dollars on three numbers with no sensible reason to do so. For a wild moment, she thought of trying to contact Lev to ask him what she should do. But she knew what he'd say–that she'd been warned and warned about her waywardness, her preference to take things at a gallop instead of slowing down and planning an op meticulously. She cringed as she thought of her father's derision if he could see her. She'd done exactly what he'd done to end his life, trusted the enemy. Fear of failure flooded through her–Walt's conviction that she *wasn't* ready to take on this op; the lukewarm support from G8. She automatically fingered the gold necklace around her neck, a memory of her mother–of the glamorous life she'd led. Now she'd never have a part of that. Why had she submitted to her father and chosen this work when she might have had a life of elegance and colour?

'Katya, snap out of it. I'm talking to you.'

Abruptly, she came out of her trance, hardly believing what she'd heard. It was Kirill's voice.

He was still speaking, almost in a whisper, 'I've managed to get Ming to meet with us. He's in your room.'

She watched him head for the lifts. Pulled herself sharply together. She could still make this right. Energy and confidence surged back through her. She gave Kirill a few minutes head start and then followed. No-one would think it an odd thing for her to do. They all knew what went on–on the third floor.

When Katya walked through the entrance panel of Room 4, Kirill was already sitting on the bed talking to the young valet who parked the cars at the Belov villa.

She bowed to him and smiled into his eyes saying, 'Hello, Ming. How good to see you.'

'This isn't a dinner party, don't waste time,' Kirill said harshly, as he stood up. He looked at Ming. 'Go back into the hall and sit there until I call you.'

Katya closed the panel behind him.

'I saw Zhang last night,' she announced.

'You *what?*' the words exploded out of Kirill.

'Keep quiet.' She lowered her voice. 'I've arranged with Zhang that he's going to take over the casino and Belov's villa tonight in a surprise attack.'

She didn't understand his reaction–somewhere between a half laugh and a snort of derision.

'What?' she demanded.

'Belov left for Kropse this afternoon on the Gulfstream.

Zhang needs to kill him if he's going to keep his casino–he won't be able to do that now, so your deal's off.'

Katya felt as if the floor was heaving under her feet, felt her world shift again. One minute her plans were safe with Kirill's return, the next they were at a dead end with Belov's departure. Desperation gave her mind clarity. Her mission for G8 was to get Belov which she'd hoped would be achieved when Zhang killed him. That wasn't possible now and he'd be well guarded in Kropse. Too well guarded to make any attempt to kill him successful. That meant she'd have to revert to her original op. Find out enough information about Belov and his *mafiya* to bring down him and his moneylaundering operations. Could she use Kirill to do that? She stopped the thought there. She was running on ahead. Lev would tell her to take one thing at a time, don't try to do it all at once. She turned her mind to Zhang. How could she persuade him to go ahead and attack tonight? Kirill was right. Once Zhang knew Belov had left the island and was lurking out there in Kropse, a hovering threat ready to retaliate, he'd back away.

Suddenly she saw the future clearly.

'We don't tell Zhang that Belov's flown,' she said.

Kirill screwed up his face, trying to grasp what she meant.

Katya explained, 'Zhang has made up his mind to take the casino and, I bet, run the island once he's got it. He's hooked. If we don't tell him Belov's gone, he'll attack tonight for sure.' She paused, thinking it through. 'And I guarantee, if he does know about Belov, he won't want us to tell him. Zhang'll lose face if he backs off because he's frightened of retaliation. He'll never do that if he wants to run Dao in future.'

Kirill drew in a breath and expelled it slowly, thinking this woman was extraordinary. Of course, she was right and he hadn't seen it–had almost thrown away his chance to stay alive. Fleetingly, he told himself that he was deeply in her debt. He'd have to work out the consequences of that later. First, he must make sure Zhang was successful.

He went over to the door, opened the panel and called Ming into the room. 'We want you to guide Zhang's men into the villa,' he said without preamble. 'We want the back door opened.'

Katya nodded at Ming. 'Can you do that?' she asked him.

Ming didn't need asking twice. He had his own personal reason for hating Belov and he thought all Russians were bastards. But Katya was different. She treated him as an equal. He thought perhaps she understood the precariousness of life as he lived it under the oppression of a *mafiya* gang-lord. Praying every day that he didn't upset Belov and wind up in a gutter somewhere–dead or alive didn't matter, there was no exit from the backstreets of Dao.

'I can do that,' he said confidently.

'Tell me how you'd let them in.' Katya needed the details.

'The garage for vehicles is underground. It's accessed by key card.'

'You have one?'

'Yes. Belov gave me one so I would be able to park all the cars.'

Katya thought this was odd. Belov had built himself a fortress but handed the garage key card to a twenty-year old valet.

Ming saw the doubt written on her face. He was forced to say what he'd kept back.

'He. . . he is responsible for me–' He lowered his voice. 'He's my father.'

Katya understood. There was no acknowledged paternal relationship but Belov trusted Ming on that basis.

'I hate him,' Ming added the words, cutting them out as if they were in ice. 'There's a tunnel from the garage to the road–his escape route.'

Typical. Just like the *mafiya,* thought Katya, so paranoid about losing their lives, their safety measures often became weapons against them. The tunnels would be perfect for a surprise attack.

'You know what to do then.' She gave him an encouraging smile.

FORTY-FOUR

Zhang's men took less that ten minutes to overpower Belov's unsuspecting casino guards. Just before zero hour Lin and Kirill had unobtrusively unlocked the front and rear doors. As Zhang had predicted, Belov's men had fought strongly against the assault through the rear doors and up the staircase. But, when Zhang's back-up of sixty more heavily armed thugs came pouring in through the front doors, the end came very quickly.

More of Zhang's thugs took a little longer to overpower the guards in Belov's villa. Ming had let them in from the street, but the video cameras in the escape tunnel alerted Belov's guards to make a fight of it. Knives were the order of the day there as bullets flying around in a tunnel tended to ricochet and hit the wrong people. In just twenty minutes, Zhang had taken over Belov's villa as well as the casino. Total control of the island would now be his.

Katya, Kirill and Lin had stayed in Room 4 throughout. Katya had decided that none of the three of them should be involved in the fighting. They could get killed in the crossfire and she needed them alive because this was the moment Katya had been planning for. As she sat listening to the sounds of fierce fighting coming from the casino gaming floor below her she went over the plan. Belov would be desperate after the loss of his Dao casino. There was no way he could take it back. He was now left with nowhere to launder his money to and he would be urgently looking for alternative routes to get his cash out of Russia. She and Kirill would go back to Kropse and offer him their help–a deal with her KGB sons and daughters group to create a new laundering route.

She knew the main problem with that scheme was that she and Kirill were top of Belov's wanted list. Which was why she had made sure that Lin survived. She and Kirill would be the messengers telling Belov what had gone on and they would pin the blame for the Zhang coup firmly on Lin. Katya knew the idea was very high risk but Belov would be searching for a scapegoat and who better than Lin? She was his chief cashier. She was Chinese, not Russian. So Zhang had bought her.

Looking across the room at Lin's tense face she felt a tinge of guilt at throwing her to the wolves like that, but she had Zhang's assurance that Lin would be looked after. In any event, it was the only story Belov would be likely to accept which would save her and Kirill from being killed. And the fact that they had both returned to Kropse as messengers was a strong indication that they were both on Belov's side.

The other problem in Katya's mind was persuading Kirill to go with her. She had reckoned that Belov would be short-handed now that Yuri and Taban were dead. Kirill was the ideal candidate to fill Yuri's position. All he had to do was keep an eye on the cash coming in and going out–She would tell him she could help him with that. Also, Belov would treat Katya with the utmost suspicion as negotiations proceeded with her. He would see no reason to give her the names of his own *mafiya* colleagues. Katya needed those for G8 if they were to be prosecuted. On the other hand, if Belov employed him, Kirill would get to know the names. Now was the perfect time to recruit him as her informer

'How much money could you make running the Kropse casino?' she asked him, almost bursting out in laughter as she saw the look of astonishment on his face.

Kirill looked at her intently, suddenly saw himself for what he could be. Like a conjurer flicking the five of diamonds into the air for it to land on the stage as the ace of spades, Katya had magicked Belov's territory in Dao into Zhang's protection racket, so why not magic him into joining her in running the Sea Dragon? But he knew the idea was preposterous. 'How would I do that?' he asked her.

'I'll tell you how, on the way,' Katya told him.

At Katya's request, Zhang had agreed to put his fleet of Lincoln Town cars at Lin's disposal to transfer Kirill's girls to the safety of the Charity House.

Until he was ushered into one of the cars Kirill hadn't understood that Katya meant that he was to accompany the girls to the Charity House. He was furious. 'Those girls are coming with me,' he shouted at her.

Katya, sitting beside him, kept calm, said quietly, 'I've told you before, Kirill, you're better than that. Why use your talent and abilities ruining the lives of young teenage girls, for sport?'

'It's the way I make money. I've always done it.' Kirill, truculent.

Katya didn't try to talk to him but let him sit in sullen silence as the fleet of Lincoln Town cars wound their way through the backstreets of Dao. Twin girls, aged about fourteen, sitting in the front seat of the car suddenly saw a tenement building they recognised as their home–they burst out shouting that their bastard father had sold them to the twice bastard Kirill. Kirill yelled back at them and the girls fell silent.

'Is this what you're proud of, Kirill?' Katya asked him.

He shrugged.

They drove on in silence, climbing up a forested hill until they came to a two-storied old colonial Portuguese tea estate house, each storey fronted by pillared balconies. The place was vast and at either end two pilastered turrets soared above the red roof line. Gardens spread around all sides, white and pink magnolias and tall palm trees lined the paths and Katya could see that the front lawn spread downhill until it met a sea of magnificent rhododendrons. A number of girls, dressed in modest cheongsams were playing or walking about on the lawns. Kirill looked at them and Katya could almost see his mind calculating which ones would be suitable for his trade.

She spoke sharply, 'We're here to give your girls their lives back not to take more lives away.'

He looked straight ahead, didn't reply.

The car stopped. Katya stayed where she was. The girls in the cars climbed out slowly, silently; scared, looking around, suspicious, not sure what was going to happen to them. Katya let Lin take the group to the front door. Watched as they disappeared inside to start the unending road to recovery–not to a promised land, for that was unreachable, but, she thought, perhaps like her, to achieve something worthwhile and be proud of that. She noticed that Kirill was watching as well.

She opened the car door. 'Walk with me,' she said to him. A command.

She started to go across the lawn towards the rhododendrons, slowly so he could catch up. The girls there respectfully bowed and made way for her. They seemed to sense what Kirill was and edged away.

When he was alongside her she pointed to the house. 'I wanted you to see this place because I know you started in one just like it.'

'Mine was an orphanage. A concrete block with tarmac in front.' Bitter words conjuring an image harsh as the Russian winters.

'And. . . ?' Katya let the word hang for him to define. She needed him to open up. She had to turn him so he rejected his past for something else, something worthwhile, like the girls he'd just let go.

He walked on for a few minutes and she wondered if he had reverted to his sullen mood.

'It was hell.' The words were jerked out of him.

'Not like here then?' Katya, sarcastic.

'Not like here, no.' He relapsed into silence.

They'd reached the line of rhododendrons. They were huge, arching up into the sky like a cathedral. Reds, yellows, purples, pinks, whites, a riot of colour.

'In my place, the girls were put on the streets,' he suddenly said. 'I was trained to pimp for them.' He stopped, as if disbelieving what he'd just said. Then, as if to justify his complicity, he said, 'You remember the chaos of the Afghan war years, no money, the State disintegrating? It was everyone for themselves. Your father was KGB, he had money. I had nothing.' A flat statement.

Katya accepted his excuse without comment. If she judged him now she'd lose him. 'That was then. A time long gone. There's real money to be made now. Why do you think I went to Kropse in the first place?'

He turned to her, derisive. 'To win with your system? You're joking.'

'No. I was sussing it out to buy the casino from Belov.'

'By yourself? That's even more of a joke.'

She explained, 'I've got KGB money behind me. I misread Morosov when I was in Kropse, I thought he'd hold my gambling debt until I got the cash out of our offshore account to pay it off.'

Kirill went into himself, falling behind her on the path as it narrowed to wind through the labyrinth of trees.

She turned around, started to tell him about her scheme for Kropse.

He stopped her. 'Let me think.'

A group of girls came running towards them–laughing as they jumped off the path and danced around the tree trunks to get past. Their laughter faded as they made their way uphill towards the house; their voices a faint echo.

Kirill stared after them. 'It could have been different,' he muttered, watching until they'd gone. 'Yes. I suppose it could be different back in Kropse,' he said, almost to himself. His voice strengthened, he looked at her. 'What do you propose?'

Katya studied him. Had she really done the right thing bringing him here? Was he actually now her informer?

He saw the doubt in her eyes. 'Whatever you think of me, Katya, I've always admired you.' He suppressed a laugh. 'Always a pain in the arse–like bringing me here. But one thing we have in common is we're both survivors. I trust in that. Trust you because of that.'

'Not going back to the girls then?' She'd said it. The test.

'Not if there's a better future.' He half smiled. 'I'm not redeemed but. . .' He looked around, the smile disappearing. 'But . . . this place . . . this place . . .' his voice tailed off.

She was sure now she could take the risk. He'd never know she was G8 or that the KGB group she'd dreamed up was a scam, but he would know she'd be there, steer him, give him a chance of real redemption. She took his arm. 'We're going back to Kropse. We're going in with Belov and then we'll take over the casino and you're going to run it. Become a shareholder.'

'We?'

'My uncle was KGB. He's handling my father's offshore funds. The money he hid away during his life.'

Kirill asked the obvious question. 'What's to make Belov accept your offer? Why should he?'

She let go of his arm. 'Until I found out exactly what Belov gets out of the casino, I was puzzling that question too. When I escaped from Yuri in the Gulfstream I found a load of cash in the baggage hold. I mean bales of hundred dollar bills. Belov was laundering cash to Dao and then into the mainland China property construction market, wasn't he?'

Kirill was set back on his heels. 'You're thinking Belov can't use the route through Dao to invest in China anymore?'

'Yes. Zhang will put a stop to it. And what's more, he'll almost certainly curry favour with the Chinese monetary authorities by warning them about Belov's illegal foreign exchange dealings.'

'So Belov will see our offer to go in with him as a stroke of luck.'

Katya noted the word *"our"*. Her excitement that Kirill was probably on board was increased by his next words.

'I'm good with this. I'll join you. But it's a promise I get a share and run the place?'

'Absolutely.'

As she said the word, Katya wondered where she was going to get the sort of money to put up front to persuade Belov to go along with the deal. And that would be necessary if she was to complete her operation. The problem at that moment was she had no proof he *was* moneylaundering. The bales of money on the Gulfstream would be long gone. Evidence would exist in Kropse of money running through the casino but, again, she had no proof it was illegal. It would take a long investigation to pile up enough evidence to bring a prosecution. So, the shortest route was to persuade Belov to accept some sort of investment to shore up the Kropse casino while it recovered from the disaster in Dao. If she was successful in organising Kirill in some way to manage the casino cash, he would report to her and she would get the evidence she wanted.

Lev may have said there was no more money in the G8 budget, but that had been before she'd destroyed Belov's enterprise in China. Surely Lev would reward her for that when she told him and put up the cash she needed. She had to speak to him. She must get to Kropse, to the *dacha*, to that bag of coffee where she'd hidden her mobile.

FORTY-FIVE

Katya found Zhang only too eager to help with her arrangements to fly herself and Kirill to Kropse. He was only too glad to get rid of all the Russians in Dao. He not only paid for the air tickets but also for the doctored passports. The aliases she and Kirill travelled under would help convince Belov and Morosov that they had been forced to flee from Zhang after his takeover.

For the last time Katya went up to Room Number 4. She changed into the freshly laundered black trousers and red silk blouse she'd been wearing when she'd first arrived and which had been hanging in the back of the wardrobe. Picked up the linen jacket she'd bought at the airport and went towards the door. She paused. Turned. Went back to the wardrobe. Took out one of the pairs of dark blue trousers and a turquoise cheongsam. Put them into her holdall. They could be useful. She went out of the room and closed the panel door.

Before she left the casino, Katya sought out Geri Carter, the woman who'd shown her the girls' cellar prison and the rear doors which opened the way for Zhang's success. Geri couldn't believe it when Katya thanked her and handed her a passport and a one-way air ticket to London–she'd grasped Katya's arm, wildly pumped it up and down–she was free.

As Katya and Kirill boarded the afternoon plane from Dao to Kropse Katya knew that *she* was far from free. Going back to Kropse and meeting Belov and Morosov was the most dangerous thing she'd done so far. But she knew she had no alternative if she was to get the names of all Belov's senior *mafiya* members for her operation to be successful.

Kirill was sure that Belov would never believe they'd had nothing to do with the loss of his stronghold in Dao. Katya briefed him carefully, told him that Belov would have no alternative once he knew of her offer to invest in the Sea Dragon. Greed was king in any *mafiya*–as they both knew only too well from their Moscow years. He hoped she was right.

Hours later the plane landed in Kropse and, leaving the airport in a taxi, they went straight to the Sea Dragon casino. Katya felt the tension rise in Kirill and seep into her. The nearer they got to the Sea Dragon, the more impossible her idea seemed. Why should Belov trust them when the last time she'd seen him he had all but accused them of skimming. She started to feel sick– had a wild idea of jumping out of the cab and running. Anywhere. Just running to get away.

It was too late. The taxi drew up at the bottom of the Sea Dragon's steps.

Luka, in his usual post at the top of the steps, was the first to spot them. Running down the steps, he rushed to Katya, hugged her as she got out of the taxi, his arms reaching right round her. '*Bab-la*,' he repeated over and over again. 'I failed you, I had no idea–' He was almost sobbing.

Katya was aware Luka liked her but this was a display of more than that. She caught the possessive, lover like look in his eyes. She was staggered. There was no way she wanted to encourage that sort of worship. It could be dangerous, out of control. Then she thought rationally–Luka would be ready to help her. She gave him a brief hug; then stood back, gave him a big smile, saying, 'Luka, it's good to see you. Is Morosov around?'

He changed immediately. Alarm flooding through him.

'Don't see him Katya. You must leave. Now. At once. Straight away.' He sounded desperate.

Kirill came around the back of the taxi. 'Leave her alone.' Kirill gestured towards Katya. 'Who do you think you are Luka?' Katya was surprised to hear him sound so angry.

Katya saw Luka clench his fists. The image told her that here was someone who could sort out Kirill if necessary. Jealousy was a lethal weapon if used artfully. She loaded it. 'No, Kirill. Luka is a friend.'

Kirill scowled, pushed past her. 'I'm going to see Morosov,' he said furiously.

Katya touched Luka's arm and followed Kirill up the steps.

There was no great welcome from Anatoly. He was stony-faced, saying just enough to be polite to them without committing himself. If Morosov was observing the encounter on the overhead cameras he would find nothing in the greeting to question Anatoly's loyalty to him.

The slot machine floor didn't seem as busy as usual, the metallic clamour was missing, a muted din in its place. They walked through the punters and Katya immediately noticed the Chinese were missing. She looked out for them on the gaming floor and there were none there either. Katya didn't doubt that Zhang had already stopped the flow of Chinese punters from Dao.

They walked into Morosov's office, Kirill stared at the wire noose hanging from the ceiling. Morosov wasn't there.

Katya took an instant decision. She grabbed his arm. 'Come on, we're not waiting for him to find us here.' She opened the door and pushed Kirill out towards the staircase. Instead of running down the stairs she shoved him upwards.

'What the hell are you doing?' he whispered hoarsely. 'Are you crazy? This goes up to Belov's penthouse.'

She thrust him up the last stair. 'We're going to see him, so keep going.' Without waiting she dragged him to Belov's door and banged her fist on it.

The door opened almost immediately. Belov stood there, stared at her, his heavy-set body rigid with fury–anger written in the deep creases around his black eyes.

'Thank god you're here,' Katya cried, stepping urgently towards him. 'I thought Morosov would kill us.'

'Get out,' Belov roared. 'Those were the orders I gave him.'

Katya stood her ground. 'Then you'll be next,' she uttered the words with total conviction.

Belov opened his mouth to speak. Shut it, his lips compressing into a thin white line of suspicion. He was *mafiya*. More important he was the chief of the Kropse *mafiya*. He'd survived because all his life he'd questioned every event that might affect him. The surprise of Zhang's sudden attack on his property and his casino in Dao and the complete annihilation of his assets in China had devastated him. With Zhang in charge of Dao and hand in glove with the Chinese authorities, those assets were lost forever. And without the Dao casino and his contacts there he'd lost the ability to launder his *mafiya's* illegal cash through China. This had been rubbed in when the Chinese punters in the Sea Dragon had overnight stopped coming. A clear message he was now in danger of losing the Sea Dragon as word spread that he could no longer launder the cash to China. He knew Morosov had been right when he'd told him that his enemies were circling. He had to regain respect–the *mafiya* way.

'The people to kill,' Morosov had said, 'are the people who betrayed you to Zhang– starting with the pimp Kirill and the woman Katya.'

Belov recited the accusation to himself word for word. Yet here were the woman and the pimp at his door–and she was warning him. He'd be a fool not to listen. If they were bluffing, Morosov's noose was always available.

'You'd better come in.' He crossed the room; stood by the window; turned to face them; didn't offer them a seat or a drink. This discussion wouldn't take long.

Kirill was still speechless. His six-foot height, good looks and charm never more ineffectual. Katya plunged in, quickly, urgently, 'We've just escaped from Dao. It was hell. Zhang was hunting us and it was Kirill who got us out.'

'How?' The question short and crucial like a pistol shot.

Katya started to speak–

'Let him answer,' Belov said jerking his head at Kirill.

Kirill was still in shock. How could Belov be a better person to talk to than Morosov? He hardly knew Belov, except to deliver his girls to him.

Belov indifferent, started for the door.

Desperation drove Kirill to talk–taking the line he'd agreed with Katya. 'It was Lin, your cashier. She did a deal with Zhang– let his men into the casino,' his words came in a rush. 'I don't know how Zhang got into your villa. He's made Lin his chief cashier.' He ended lamely.

Belov wasn't satisfied. 'How do you know all this. You got out alive.'

Kirill stared at him, searching for an answer.

'I told Kirill.' Katya, positive. 'Lin told me herself. She said she wanted me and Kirill to tell you–personally.'

Belov's attention was caught. 'What were you to tell me?'

Katya didn't reply, knowing the pause would increase Belov's curiosity. Kirill kept quiet because he had no idea what she was going to say.

'*What were you about to say?*' Belov emphasised each word.

Katya looked straight at him. 'Lin said to tell you you're a bastard and she only wishes you were there so she could watch Zhang kill you.' Without pausing she added, 'She said it was okay though because Morosov would do it for her.'

'I don't believe a word of it.'

Katya saw the look on Belov's face as he said the words and thought Belov did actually believe every word she'd said. He was *mafiya*. Why wouldn't he believe her. She was in his room telling him these things. Where was Morosov?

'Why do you think we're here? Morosov's out to kill us–hide the evidence–blame everyone but himself.' She pushed on, piling lie on lie. 'He and Lin have been linked with Zhang for some time–Lin told me.' She suddenly changed tack to support the lies with a fact, 'You're sending dollars into China through Dao, aren't you? Evading Chinese currency regulations.'

'What the hell–' He fumed.

'Yes. Lin told me. Did you know Morosov was taking ten per cent of that cash and splitting it with Lin and Zhang?'

Wordlessly, Belov went to the drinks cabinet, poured out a vodka and drank it straight. 'Go on,' he muttered.

Katya rubbed salt in the wound with more lies. The more salt, the angrier he'd get and the more he'd believe her. 'Lin told me these things. She was laughing at you, "*the big I am*" she called you. She talked about you puffing yourself up, boasting about your investments in China, when actually everyone was laughing at you because you hadn't the faintest idea that Zhang had been waiting for years for the right opportunity to kick you out.'

'Enough!' The word exploded from him. 'That's enough.'

Katya decided to throw caution to the winds. She had to get rid of Morosov. 'And Morosov, what about him? Taban found out he was creaming cash out of the bales of dollars before they were unloaded in Dao, didn't she Kirill?'

Kirill was about as confused as he could get. But these words galvanised him. 'It's true. Yuri told me–we'd been drinking . . .' He let silence paint the picture.

Belov was shaken yet again. 'Yuri–I haven't heard from him.' His voice cold, suspicious.

Katya and Kirill exchanged glances, each showing they were unwilling to give Belov the news.

Belov saw them–rapped out, 'Tell me–what about Yuri?'

Katya felt Kirill was now in command of himself, nodded for him to give Belov the news.

'He's dead,' Kirill said baldly.

'Dead?' Belov couldn't believe it.

'Zhang's men. . . when they attacked the villa.'

Katya came to the point. 'That's why we're here–with you. Morosov knows we know. And he's going to kill us.'

Belov ran his hand through his shock of black hair as if the gesture would clear his mind. Morosov killed her? Killed Taban? 'It's not possible,' he muttered to himself.

Katya plunged in the dagger words, 'And you'll be next. Lin said so.'

Belov put his empty vodka glass down on the drinks cabinet. Put his hands on the glass top, leaned over them, catching his breath. He saw his face reflected in the glass, his hair askew, lips tucked so far back as to be invisible. He was in shock but he must think. Morosov had been with him ten years. Trusted. As much of a friend as any *mafiya* chief could expect. Belov couldn't believe he'd betrayed him. And what evidence had these two shits given him? The word of Lin. Lin was Chinese and had gone over to Zhang, he believed that. But Morosov? And the woman Katya, what was she doing here? Morosov was sure she was in some KGB group, bent on taking over the casino. She certainly wasn't someone to put one's faith in. Had she invented the story about Morosov to get rid of him? Was she taking advantage of the chaos in Dao to strip out his right-hand man and then move in with her KGB friends? Might she move in anyway now he was at his weakest? For a moment, he thought she might have been behind Zhang's takeover. The thought was dismissed instantly. Her KGB friends would need Dao to launder out their funds. No, Lin was definitely the traitor. But Morosov was not. Katya's accusation fit in too well with her purpose which was to win the Sea Dragon. He would talk to Morosov, watch this woman and definitely watch to see if she had a hold over Kirill. He stood up, faced them.

'Thank you. You can go.'

Katya had no idea what he meant. Did he believe her and Kirill or was there a more sinister meaning behind his words? What she did know was that she had to avoid Morosov at all costs.

FORTY-SIX

Katya left Kirill at the Sea Dragon and took a taxi to her *dacha*. She had to phone Lev.

The front door of the *dacha* was open. Ludmilla must be there she thought and walked in. She called her name. There was no answer. She ran upstairs, searched the bedrooms—no-one there. Her need to speak to Lev was urgent. She went straight to the kitchen cabinet, took out the bag of coffee and put her hand inside it. The mobile wasn't there. Frantically she searched inside the cupboard.

'Is this what you're looking for?'

Katya swung around. She was caught completely by surprise. Ludmilla stood there, holding out the mobile.

'Ludmilla. You startled me.' She looked down at the phone. 'What's that? A mobile?'

'It's yours. I found it in that.' She pointed to the coffee bag.

'I don't have one, you know that.'

'Then you won't mind if I take it up to the Sea Dragon.' Ludmilla started to put it in the pocket of the apron she was wearing.

Katya stiffened; didn't want to harm her. She decided to bluff. 'Go ahead. See if you can get some money for it.'

Ludmilla quietly put the mobile on the counter top. 'Viktor came to visit you. There was no tea left so I gave him a coffee and I found the mobile hidden in the coffee bag. Viktor told me about you. He doesn't know what you're doing at the Sea Dragon but he trusts you.' She paused before saying, 'I do as well. That's why I've kept it for you."

Katya started to speak.

Ludmilla cut across her, 'I don't want to know. Just believe I'll not stop you– whatever you are doing.'

Katya took her arm, squeezed it, had no words to say.

'I'll be off now. There's some food in the fridge.' Ludmilla turned and walked across the room to the front door, calling out over her shoulder, 'I'll be back tomorrow.'

Katya speed dialled Lev's number.

'Yes.'

She sighed with relief as she heard his voice. At the same time, she heard Ludmilla speaking to someone, then the front door shutting.

Kirill came into the sitting room; raised his eyebrows questioningly as he saw the mobile in her hand.

Katya had no doubt if she shut down the call he'd be suspicious. She had to answer Lev. Had to hope he'd be quick enough to understand what had happened. She raised a hand in greeting to Kirill–waved him to one of the sofas. She spoke into the phone. 'Hello Uncle Lev. It's Katya. Have you got a moment?'

There was a pause. Katya willed Lev to speak.

'Yes, hello, Katya. Always good to hear from you.'

His voice sounded warm to her. Or did she catch an undertone of censure? She phrased her next words very carefully.

'We're ready to talk about money.'

She prayed Lev wouldn't ask what money or who "we" meant. She could have said "I want to talk about money" but Kirill would have thought he was being cut out. She tried not to tense.

Lev didn't fail her. He was Russian and used to translating undertones.

'Good. Come to St Petersburg and we can discuss the details. It must be tomorrow as I'm leaving for Moscow.'

'I'll leave tonight. Look forward to seeing you.'

Katya switched off the phone, pocketed it. Looked at Kirill. 'Did you hear that?'

He nodded. He'd heard everything.

She silently thanked Lev for being Lev; protecting her.

She heard Kirill say. 'I'll come too. You'll need some help.'

Katya caught the soft tone in his voice. She was surprised. She'd noticed a change in Kirill's attitude towards her. She'd assumed it was because he'd been impressed with the way she'd handled Zhang and Belov. Then he'd shown to Luka what she could only describe as jealousy and now a genuine desire to shield her. The thought suddenly exposed what she'd repressed that she felt a sympathy for him. An appreciation of what his life had been— of the succession of barriers he'd erected to keep himself safe. Her life had also been one of building walls. It was as if there was a lifeline of understanding that linked them together. She felt unnerved. To even think of Kirill in these terms could lead to feelings she didn't want to contemplate. She pushed them away.

'No, not a good idea,' she said. 'My uncle doesn't know about you and I'll need to explain you to him.' She tried some humour to ease the sudden unexplained tension she felt. 'It won't be easy!' Her eyes quizzed him.

'You're not selling me out?' Kirill questioned.

'Don't be stupid, Kirill.' She softened the rebuke. 'What do you think? No of course not, it's just that you can do more good here. You can drop a hint to Belov that my KGB group of friends would be interested in investing in his casino here. They have moneylaundering outlets that could take Dao's place. I mean China isn't the only country where property investments are

284

propped up by moneylaundering. Get Belov interested. And when I get back we can take things further.'

He came closer to her. 'We make a good team, don't we?'

She looked hesitant.

'Don't we?' he repeated. Then he smiled, took her hand in his and held it tightly.

She refused to acknowledge the electricity which ran between them. She smiled but pulled her hand away saying, 'I'm still finding out Kirill. I'll tell you when I get back.'

FORTY-SEVEN

It was too late to get a flight to London via St Petersburg that evening. Katya caught the first one out of Dao at 8.00 a.m. the following morning.

On arriving in London she'd been to her apartment and had changed outfits and was full of confidence as she walked into the G8 conference room. For the first time in over three weeks she was wearing Prada and her Picasso scent. She felt fresh and energetic. Her auburn hair gleamed and her violet-blue eyes glistened. She couldn't wait to report to John, Lev and Walt.

They were all there. John was standing by the console, his cardigan casually slung over his shoulders–a steady look in his grey eyes. Lev and Walt were pictured on the plasma screen, Walt's face inscrutable, Lev lighting one of his yellow Abdullah cigarettes. She had imagined this scene during her journey and it was exactly as she had predicted. Welcoming home a successful agent. She and John sat on the chairs facing the screen.

'What's this about needing money?' Walt opened the proceedings. He hadn't even said hello.

Katya was thrown. Where were the congratulations for her action in Dao? For getting back to Kropse to continue her op. She struggled to find the words to tell them about it.

'First things first, I think, Walt,' Lev intervened. 'Katya, where have you been all this time?'

Her dismay turned into an angry reply. 'Dao,' she said. 'Where else do you think I've been?'

The effect of this single word was startling.

'Dao?' Walt exploded. 'What the hell were you doing in Dao? You were meant to be in Kropse.'

'How long ago were you in Dao?' John put the enquiry quietly.

'Two days.'

There was a stunned silence.

'You don't mean . . .?' Lev left the sentence unfinished in a cloud of cigarette smoke.

Katya put it all in one sentence–a short report. 'The Kropse *mafiya* had an illegal casino in Dao. I'd been sent there. I contacted the local *Tong* leader Zhang and he took it over.'

'My god, that was *you*.' Walt wasn't asking a question.

'I think you'd better explain, Katya.' Lev's voice had softened–his protégé hadn't let her down after all.

The use of her name reminded her of when Kirill had used it. She wondered why that random thought had seeped into her mind.

'Politely, if you can.' A reminder about her quick temper from John.

She smiled, acknowledging his rebuke.

'It started when I lost all that money playing roulette. I couldn't pay it back so I was put onto the Sea Dragon gaming floor . . .'

They listened in silence as she talked of Belov–of Morosov– of Yuri–of Kirill. She never mentioned her fear of Morosov or the degradation of Room 4. She knew they understood what she'd suffered, mentally noting her strength under pressure, her dogged determination.

After she'd finished, they didn't say anything, grasping what they had just witnessed–the transition of a novice into an agent.

John broke the spell. 'That was remarkable, Katya.' He let the words sink in. 'Yes. Remarkable.'

Lev studied her for a moment before saying, 'True Katya. And very Russian. Let others do the killing for you.'

Walt gave a discreet cough. 'I must point out that in fact all that happened in Dao was the substitution of one moneylaundering outfit for another. You don't think this Zhang will waste a moment before he puts his illegal cash through the place, do you?'

Katya knew this was the time to stand up to him. 'Belov used the Dao casino as a cover to get his cash into the Chinese mainland property market. Russian money into China. Undermining the Russian economy–building his property empire at the same time.'

'And Zhang's moneylaundering is an all Chinese affair–not our business,' Lev said; protecting her again.

'Let's move on.' John focusing the meeting. 'What do you want money for, Katya? You're back in Kropse, Kirill's informing and in a prime position to get the names and background of Belov's *mafiya* and its members.'

'It will take too long. I've bluffed Belov about Dao but I don't think he's believed me that Morosov killed Taban. I'm on borrowed time.'

'So, you need something to be able to get closer to Belov quicker?' Walt putting the problem succinctly.

She wondered if he was being helpful as a means of apologising for his hostility. Decided he was. 'Yes. That's correct,' she said. Neutral words, not sycophantic. She went on, 'I've led Belov to believe I'm part of a young group of KGB offspring that wants to take over the Sea Dragon. Kirill believes it as well. I think I could offer to invest in the Sea Dragon so Belov thinks he's laundering our KGB dollars as well as his out of Russia. I can then track the money he's laundering by using Kirill as my informer.'

'Where to with Dao out of the picture?' Walt, being precise again. 'London?'

Katya stared blankly at him. She hadn't thought of that. Dao was no longer available, so where *would* the dollars go?

John screwed up his eyes, trying to hide an image of more Russian dirty dollars flooding the London property market—worse, the G8 dollars Katya had been given, being laundered there.

It was Lev who put Katya out of her misery. 'Katya, your best asset is thinking on your feet. . . action.' He tapped a new cigarette on the desk top in front of him to emphasise his words. 'To be a rounded agent you need to be able to prepare the groundwork. Walt's right. You haven't thought this scheme through. Do you want to try again?'

'Sounds good to me,' Walt said.

John took the cardigan off his shoulders, laid it on the chair next to him, saying, 'I think you can do it. Take your time.'

Katya felt awful, this was worse than facing Morosov—well, almost. She fingered her necklace, seeking inspiration. A slight feeling of resentment crept into her. This was all the wrong way around. It should be the Directors, with all their experience, telling *her* what to do. She should—suddenly it hit her. It was her proposal to send dollars *out* of the Sea Dragon that was the wrong way around. 'I shouldn't be sending the dollars through the casino, I should be receiving them.'

'What d'you mean, receiving?' John looking for clarification.

'I should set up a casino,' she said, briefly.

Walt looked as though he'd choke. 'Belov's *got* a casino.'

Katya explained; patiently. Reining in her impulse to run on. 'We know Belov can't use Dao to get his cash out of Russia but we could open a phoney casino in some tax haven and offer him that facility instead.'

'He could do that anyway. Why would he use you particularly?' Lev, probing.

'I was reading an article on the plane about online gaming. It's going to be big.' Katya was scrabbling for a handhold. Something was lurking at the back of her mind that she felt offered a way forward but she couldn't put it all together.

'That's interesting.' John intervened. 'You mean offer Belov a link to an online casino?'

'Yes. It would be offshore and that's where he needs to send his cash. But I don't know enough about online gaming yet. It's quite new.'

John leaned forward, spoke into the mic on his console, 'Ask Guy Leeming to come up here.' He leaned back. 'Guy's got the expertise for this. Or his tech team will have.'

They waited in silence until Guy entered.

'You wanted me, John?'

'Katya has a question.'

Guy went to stand by the console, his eyes focussed on Katya, thinking this could be interesting. She seemed to have matured since he'd last seen her. Something about those fascinating violet-blue eyes. They now gave her a shrewder air, less mercurial. He wouldn't chance testing how mercurial she was, though. 'Of course, Katya, go ahead,' he said.

'I'm interested in online gaming. Where is it set up? How does it work?' Katya made the questions short.

'It does what it says on the tin. An online casino only needs a website and a license.'

'What if it's offshore, in a tax haven, say?'

'Depends where. Probably still needs a licence . . . Well, I suppose if it was run off a ship in international waters, it wouldn't. Licensing wouldn't apply.'

'So, I could launder cash through it.'

'Of course. But I don't think that would work with large amounts of cash–'

'Why?' Katya asked.

'Online betting's not like the usual casino where very large cash bets are the norm. Online punters can't use cash so they use credit cards. The problem is that credit cards have a low limit on the amount that can be spent. So, it would take too many bets and far too long to bet the large sums that moneylaundering requires.'

'Oh! Then my idea of an online casino won't work.' Katya put her hands on the console in front of her. A gesture of defeat.

No-one spoke. They were all engaged now, seeking a solution. Top agents thinking laterally.

Guy looked around at them. 'It would help if I knew more about the target. I know it's need to know but on this occasion, I do need to know, if I'm going to be of any help.'

John touched Katya's shoulder. 'Go on.'

She faced Guy. 'The target is Belov. He's a Russian *mafiya* boss who launders money through a casino he runs in Kropse. He's just lost his cash outlet in China where he invested the laundered profits in a property empire. We want to catch him moneylaundering–'*in flagrante*'.'

Guy was thinking how attractive she was. He adjusted his glasses and beamed at her.

Walt raised his eyes to the ceiling.

Guy caught the look, said quickly, 'It's easy really.'

'Tell us.' Walt said, looking at him, making sure his rebuke had got across.

Guy nervously ran his hand through the tight curls on his head and refocussed. 'You could do it through a private offshore bank.'

'How would that work?' John asked; making sure everyone understood.

Guy frowned in concentration. 'The bank would be private and belong to Belov. It would only issue credit cards to punters who are a part of Belov's *mafiya*. They would use them to place bets with the online casino. As it's a private bank it would have no limit on the credit card so the bets could be unlimited.'

'Very neat, but wouldn't the financial tax authorities regulate against that?' Walt asked.

'In some of the tax havens banking secrecy would prevent the regulators finding out. That's if there's regulation there at all.'

'Good. How does the online casino pay the winnings to the punters?'

'Well, it can't be cash, obviously. So, by bank transfer to Belov's bank. He can then use it—fix the *mafiya* to invest in property or anything else that's legitimate business. That completes the moneylaundering cycle.'

'We only need a building for the bank and a ship.' Walt said, drily.

Lev was enthusiastic. 'We can lease them. It will only be for a short time while we trace all Belov's depositors and punters.'

'So what's the right tax haven for us to use?' John asked. 'Any ideas?'

'Can I think about that?' Guy said, his eyes on Katya again. Maybe she'd have dinner with him later. 'Katya, if you come with me we could discuss it,' he said invitingly.

John stood up. 'No. You sort that out, Guy, and let me know.' He turned to Katya. 'You'd better be getting back to Kropse right away. Put the outline of the idea to Belov– capture his interest. I'll arrange for you to be briefed on the detail in a couple of days.'

His words left Katya in no doubt that she'd just been admitted to the dark underworld where life was cheap and courage in constant demand. An Agent. A full member of G8. A thrill of excitement ran right through her.

As she got up to leave she heard Lev say, 'Just one thing before you go, Katya. You frequently mentioned Kirill's name in your report.' Lev stopped so that she understood his words. 'Over-identifying with an informer is dangerous. Don't forget that.'

FORTY-EIGHT

Even though Lev had arranged a quick airport transfer in St Petersburg for the flight to Kropse, darkness had already fallen by the time Katya arrived back at the *dacha*. She was very tired and fumbled trying to put her key into the front door lock, dropping it on the paving. She leaned on the door to bend down. It opened suddenly. She fell heavily across the lintel, completely exposed to an attack. Before she could roll away, strong arms hauled her to her feet and the door was kicked shut.

'Don't hang around outside. You're lucky to be here,' Kirill's voice hissed in her ear.

She struggled out of his arms. 'What the hell are you talking about? Why are you here?'

'Morosov's been looking for you. He's raging mad you took off without telling him. It seems Belov's told him you accused him of killing Taban.'

Katya turned on him, furious. 'So you've been talking to Morosov.'

'You know I wouldn't do that.' He switched on the light. 'Look at me.' He grasped her arms, swung her around to face him, looked deep into her eyes. 'Now tell me I'd do that.'

The look on his softened, smiling face told her that Lev had seen what she had found out too late. She'd let Kirill come too close–wouldn't believe this *mafiya* pimp who dealt in girls like a cattle merchant could have any feelings for a woman. But what shocked her more, as he held her, was the strength of her response.

She wanted to be there. Lev's warning pounded into her, tearing her away from him.

'Of course you'd talk to Morosov if you saw an advantage in it.' She made the words hard, a damning judgement. Saw the hurt in his eyes. Could a man like this really be hurt? Not if she was going to get this op finished. 'Enough of this crap,' she said. 'I've got to see Belov.'

Kirill knew he'd made a mistake. He really had missed her while she was in St Petersburg–disappointed she hadn't trusted him enough to let him join her there when she talked to her uncle. He'd come on to her too fast. There was too much baggage between them, too much mistrust–he should have removed that first.

'Don't believe me then, but you can believe this. You told me to get Belov interested in your uncle's proposal to invest in the Sea Dragon. Well, I thought it might be useful first of all to know more about his *mafiya* members.'

Katya was pleased that she'd got one thing right about Kirill. Since he'd become her informer he'd started to think for himself. 'So what have you found out?' she asked.

'Where the casino books are kept.'

The simple words electrified her. 'Where? When can we get to them?'

'Morosov keeps them in his apartment. He's got this safe hidden behind a Chagall painting.'

Katya was flung from elation to fear. 'Who told you that? Are you sure they won't immediately tell Morosov?'

Kirill sensed her alarm, shook his head. 'It's alright. Your cleaner Ludmilla told me. She used to be one of the cleaners at the Sea Dragon.'

Katya calmed down. She knew Ludmilla was safe, she hated them all at the casino. 'What's the time?' She looked at her watch.

'Half past midnight. Morosov goes to his apartment at 2.00 a.m. when the casino shuts. We'll go in now.'

'You're insane. We'd be spotted within minutes.'

'Not if we go in through the rear entrance. You've got a back-way, haven't you? Where you move your girls in and out?' He flinched. The tone of her last words told him exactly what she thought of this.

'Shit, Katya. We're bound to get caught.'

They looked at each other for a moment, both of them knowing the extreme danger and possibility of death that awaited them. There was a slight hesitation.

Kirill took her hand reassuringly in his. He opened the door and they went out into the darkness.

FORTY-NINE

Kirill led them through the back entrance of the casino. Katya had put on the trousers and cheongsam she'd brought back from Dao and tied her easily recognisable hair back with the claw-style clips she'd worn there. No-one would take any notice of Kirill bringing in one of his girls. The sight was familiar.

They took the stairs to Morosov's apartment and walked in. The door wasn't locked. Who, in their right mind, would enter it without his permission?

Katya went to work quickly–switched on a table lamp, told Kirill to hold it so the light shone on a nearby Chagall painting. She slid her hand around the edge of the frame, found the catch and released it. The painting sprung out from the wall on hinges. No alarm sounded. She got Kirill to shift the light; studied the safe. She almost laughed. It was an old KGB combination lock and handle, probably put in when the old KGB hands set up the casino and built the apartments. She'd practised on these for hours during her early training with the FSB. She rubbed her hands together, warming them. Put her ear against the safe door by the combination dial, started turning the dial.

Kirill suddenly jerked the lamp, turned towards the door listening intently. Katya motioned to him to keep the lamp still. He nodded his head towards the door. They both froze, tuned for any sound. None came.

Katya put her ear against the safe door again, worked the

combination. Her head made a slight movement as if of approval. She went on working. Sweat appeared above her lip. She worked on. Abruptly, she lifted her head, beads of sweat now running down her face. She wiped them off with the sleeve of her cheongsam. Went back to the safe. Turning the dial–listening. A nod of satisfaction. Pulled the handle. The door swung open. Silence. No alarm sounded.

She leant inside. There were stacks of dollars there–of no interest. She pushed a bundle of papers to one side. Carefully noting where they'd been so they could be replaced in exactly the same place. No-one must know she'd been there. The casino book lay on the bottom shelf. She took it to Kirill. Together they opened it.

Names of men and woman were listed on the first page. Katya counted. Six of them, including Belov. That was all. Kirill turned the pages. Each name had a number of pages assigned to it. On each page, there were lines of dollar amounts. Nothing under a hundred thousand dollars. On one page alone, Katya quickly totalled up something near eighty million dollars. The sums were huge.

Here was Belov's *mafiya*. Here was the cash they were generating through crime. Drugs. Prostitution. Extortion. Blackmail. Murder. Rape. Terror. All wrapped up in an accountant's ledger.

Katya memorised the names. *Kim's Game* in a parlour of terror.

She was about to shut the book when Kirill pointed to a name on one of the entries– Taban. It appeared regularly on every page next to a payment of $50,000. In a dozen pages Taban had been paid $600,000. Why?

The apartment door burst open. Morosov stood there, Glock pistol in his hand. He was quite calm.

'You'll come with me.' His voice icy.

Katya suddenly realised why opening the safe had been so

easy. It must have had a silent alarm–almost certainly linked straight to Morosov's office. It was too late to be sorry she hadn't checked.

FIFTY

As they went out of the door of the apartment, Morosov pistol whipped Kirill's cheek. Blood flowed down his chin to spread as a red stain over his shirt. Katya started to help him as he staggered–arched her back as Morosov jammed the Glock into her spine.

'Move,' he shouted.

He didn't say anything else. Kirill knew the way and didn't or couldn't try to escape. There was an inevitability about reaching Belov–and retribution.

Belov's penthouse door was open. Was he expecting them? Had he and Morosov been together when the safe alarm went off? Did it matter, Katya thought, dully. The final act would be the same.

Morosov gave her a shove through the door. She saw Belov standing by the window. How he seemed to like it there, she thought inconsequentially.

'What were you looking for?' His opening salvo was so cold and uncompromising it drove Katya to find a reply. Any reply.

'Proof that Morosov here is cheating you,' she rasped at him– her eyes glacial as they froze into his.

She collapsed to the floor, sobbing with pain, as Morosov slammed the Glock into her ribs.

'Lying bitch.' Spray from his mouth flew across the room.

'It's true.' Kirill forced his lips to move in his broken face and the words were spoken so quietly that Belov looked at him sharply.

Morosov saw Belov's curiosity, brought his attention back to Katya, kicking her hard. As she screamed, Katya clearly heard in her mind Lev's mantra. *"You're Russian, Katya, we get kicked, we kick back, twice as hard."*

She gritted her teeth. 'He killed Taban. You know it,' she gasped.

Belov looked down at her, his expression impassive. 'So you said last time we met but you've no proof.'

Katya winced as a raw nerve ending lanced in her back like a needle.

'You see,' shouted Morosov. 'She hasn't any proof. Just let me finish her off.'

Kirill made another supreme effort. 'Look at the books,' he whispered hoarsely.

Belov didn't understand. 'What? What are you saying?'

Katya half sat, dodged Morosov's foot as he tried to kick her again. 'The books we found in this bastard's apartment. Look at them.'

Belov was thoroughly suspicious now. He wasn't sure whether it was Morosov or Katya he suspected. But something was wrong here. This woman with her KGB contacts would obviously try to look at the books since she had already hinted she could do a deal for the casino. She'd want to find out what moneylaundering the casino was capable of. He'd have done the same thing in her shoes. It was Morosov who'd been careless enough to let her into his safe. On the other hand, why was Katya insisting on blaming Morosov for Taban's death? She didn't need to do that to get a look at the books or conclude a deal. His thoughts were interrupted by Katya.

'Morosov wants the Sea Dragon for himself. Get rid of me and Kirill, and you'll be next.'

'That's what you told me last time but I'm still here.'

'Ask him. Ask him if he wants you to sell an interest to me.'

Morosov was shouting again. 'Don't listen to her. This cow's dangerous I tell you.'

Through a red mist of pain Katya tried to regain the initiative. 'Kirill, go and get the casino book from Morosov's apartment.'

'No.' Morosov's voice rang around the room. 'No. This is ludicrous.' He searched Belov's face with his eyes. 'I've been with you ten years. Are you going to let this fuck get between us?'

Belov went through the options. He could get Morosov to shoot these two and be done with it. That would be easy. But what if Morosov *was* cheating him; had killed Taban. This woman was right. He, Belov, would be next. She'd said it twice now and each time with a certainty.

He walked to an antique desk, opened the front drawer, turned with a Grach 9mm pistol in his hand. He waved it at Kirill. 'Get the book. Don't try anything stupid.'

Kirill left, holding his face. Belov walked around the desk to stand over Katya, pointed the Grach at her. 'I might get rid of you anyway.'

'Let me do it. It'll be a pleasure.' Morosov aimed another kick at her.

Belov stopped him. 'No, this is personal.'

Kirill came back at that moment carrying the ledger. It was closed.

Belov took it. 'Show me.'

Kirill hesitated.

'Well, go on,' Belov's voice was sharp. 'You told me she was telling the truth. Either you've got something to show me or you haven't.' He raised the Grach to point it at Kirill.

Kirill was petrified. 'Ask her, ask her. She spotted it.'

Katya half sat, groaned in pain. Held out her hand. Belov reached down; held the book out to her. Morosov tried to snatch it away.

302

'Leave it,' Belov's frighteningly shrill voice froze him.

Katya took the book. Leafed through the pages. 'Here, look. He and Taban were cheating you,' she said, holding the book out for Belov.

He took it, cast his eyes over the first pages. Shook his head saying, 'There's nothing here.'

'I told you.' Morosov took a step towards him, tried to take the book.

'Look—at the entry listing for Taban—it's why—why he killed her —he wanted—her share,' Katya ground out the words, gasping between each one.

The mention of Taban had Belov opening the book again. He looked closely at a page, abruptly turned it to look at the next. Then, swiftly, he turned page after page stopping only to glance swiftly at each one.

He jerked up the pistol. The thunder of the shot echoed off the windows.

Morosov looked surprised. But only for a second as blood spurted out of his throat in a fountain and he fell to the carpet without a sound.

FIFTY-ONE

Katya had no time to recover from the shock of Morosov's blood spraying over her. Belov now had his pistol trained on her. He shoved the book towards her with his other hand. 'Now you know all my business.'

Her reply was automatic. The standard "*wasn't me*" lie. 'The book's just numbers. How could I find anything about your business there?' she said.

'You found out about Taban.' He kicked Morosov's dead body. 'And this shit.'

She risked getting up. The pistol muzzle followed her. 'I was looking for Taban's name. I was certain she and Morosov were cheating. I didn't need them scamming me.'

He started to speak, then suddenly realised what she had said. '*You* didn't need them cheating. It was *me* they were stealing from. Why would you be involved?'

'I told Yuri all about it.' She waited for this to sink in. Put up another question mark. 'Oh, didn't he tell you? I wonder why.'

Belov threw the book onto a nearby sofa. 'You still haven't answered my question. The casino accounts are in that. You were looking at them when Morosov caught you.'

'I've told you. I looked at the cash entries. Morosov came in and I'd only seen three or four pages with Taban's name on them. Why would I be interested in anything else? I came here on behalf of a group of KGB children with an offer to invest in your moneylaundering process. And all I've had is abuse.' She stopped there, waiting to see if he took the bait.

Belov wasn't prepared for Katya to be so open about her offer. Morosov had told him Katya was hostile. What was she then—friend or foe? He desperately needed a friend. 'What are you offering?' he probed.

'Put that pistol down and we can talk.' Katya rubbed her back by her kidneys. 'Can we sit down? I need a drink and so does Kirill here. You've got a lot to thank us for.'

Belov knew he had two options. Kill these two and face his *mafiya* partners with nothing to offer to replace Dao or listen to Katya's proposal and negotiate. He leaned backwards and put the Grach pistol on the desk, pointed to the sofa where the book lay. He became conciliatory. 'Sit down both of you. What will you drink? Katya?'

'Yorsh, four to one.'

'Vodka,' Kirill said. 'Large.'

'Wait a minute,' Belov said. He pulled a mobile out of his trouser pocket. Speed dialled. 'Luka? Come to my penthouse. Bring a body bag.'

Belov walked over to the drinks cabinet. 'Right, so tell me what this is all about.'

Katya eased her back against the sofa cushions. 'It *was* about my KGB group investing in your casino. We needed another outlet for our profits and we wanted to reach Dao—like you we think the China market is ripe for exploiting. But that option's denied us. So instead of us investing in you, we now propose that you invest in us.'

Belov swung around. '*Me* invest in *you*? That's a joke.'

Katya took the mug he handed her. Waited until Kirill had a glass of vodka in his hand. '*Na Zdorovia*. To our new enterprise.'

She drank deeply and, trying not to think of the excruciating pain in her spine, said, 'A good mix. Just like us.'

Belov felt he was being swept along. He had no idea what this ravishing, dynamic woman was proposing yet he felt compelled to agree. He wished he'd met her years ago. They would have made a formidable team. He tossed back the glass of vodka in his hand. 'Details please.'

'We have an online casino managed offshore– '

He broke in immediately. 'That's no good to me. I can't get my cash out into an online casino.'

Katya drained her mug. Held it out to him. 'Another, please. No wonder you're in the mess you are. You've had your eye off the ball for some time, haven't you? First Morosov cheats you, then Lin helps Zhang snatch your outfit in Dao. I wonder if you're worth dealing with.' As she finished saying the words Katya mentally bit her lip. Would she never learn? Winding him up this badly could put up his guard, she'd lose him.

Belov knew she was right. He'd lain back taking the profits, leading an easy life. But he was paying for it. He'd decided to go along with her proposal and this wasn't the time to teach this smartarse a lesson. He shrugged. Poured out vodka and beer into her mug handed it to her.

This time she sipped it. Put the mug on the coffee table beside the sofa.

'We've got a private bank in a tax haven.' She explained. 'No regulations. Well, there are but the regulators are on side.'

'So, you use unlimited credit cards to bet with?' Once again Belov thought how smart she was–how sophisticated her KGB group must be. The scheme was brilliant. Fool-proof. Except– 'Is there a landing strip at this place?'

'Of course, how do you think we've been getting our cash into the bank? The problem for us is–the bank has only one source of funds and that's us. We need another source and that could be you.'

Belov decided he was onto a winner. His partners wouldn't miss the loss of Dao. This set up was perfect. So perfect that once it was fully operational he would take it over. He tried to sound nonchalant as he said, 'So where is this place?'

'I'll let you know when I'm ready. First, you'll agree to pay us seventeen per cent of your moneylaundered cash as expenses. For that we'll do everything. Aircraft. Bank. Ship– '

'Ship?' Belov burst out.

'Yes. It's in international waters. An online casino ungoverned by the laws of any country.'

'Shit.' Was all Belov could say.

FIFTY-TWO

Katya left Belov to think over her proposal. She judged it was useless to press him further. He was the sort of man she could manipulate but he would resent her trying to bully him. Anyway, she had tucked the five names of Belov's partners firmly into her memory. If he failed to join in her proposal, she could always approach one or more of them. Belov's Dao debacle must have left them uneasy, questioning his judgement. She was sure that If she put her proposal to them, they would jump at the chance of a new way to funnel their ill-gotten gains out of Russia.

She'd already decided to use Kirill to find out more about the five names in the casino book she'd memorised. He travelled in their circles and they almost certainly used the girls he procured for the Sea Dragon. First, though, he needed some medical attention and cleaning up.

She ordered a taxi and took him back to the *dacha* with her.

He was still groggy when they got there. They went inside. She had some difficulty bearing his weight as they climbed the stairs. He muttered his thanks as he clung tightly to her, his arm around her shoulders. She managed to get him to the bathroom where she sat him down on the chair.

'There's a first aid box in the cupboard. Wait there while I get it.'

She let him go and he slumped forward, his head over his knees. Finding the box, she opened it and went about cleaning and dressing the wound on his face. He bore it without a sound and, when she'd finished, he straightened up and took her hand in his. 'So you do care for me,' he murmured.

She tried to pull her hand away but his grasp tightened.

She felt a sudden urge to respond. But Lev's warning flashed into her mind. Kirill was her informer, not her lover. Dismayed, she pulled her hand away. 'I've told you. That's not going to be the way between us.' Immediately she'd said the words, she knew she'd overreacted. She had to keep him interested in her. If he walked away he could endanger her op. Keep him interested–the words sounded hollow to her. Deep down she wanted so much more.

He sensed the conflict in her. 'I'd look after you.' Kirill's smiling eyes looked into hers.

Lev. Lev. You bastard. She had to ignore the look in Kirill's eyes. Hated her snarling words as she said, 'I look after myself. Understand? What use were you with Belov just now? He could have shot me and much you would have cared as long as you saved your own skin. So, don't ever say you'll look after me.'

Kirill winced. He'd been sure she had the same feelings for him as he had for her. Why was she attacking him like this? Did she despise him for being weak–for setting his girls free in Dao? For failing to stand up to Belov? Had she just been testing him? He decided to find out, offered a half apology.

'What went on back there with Belov? I was out of it?'

She lied to him. 'That meeting was the first part of getting you Morosov's job. You know, running the moneylaundering . . . no more pimping . . . it's what you want isn't it?'

He wanted *her* but . . . 'Yes.' There was nothing more to say.

'Good. Now first I have a job for you. Remember that list of names on the first page of Morosov's ledger?'

He nodded uncertainly.

'I want you to tell me who are the most important partners when I mention them. OK?'

'Go on, but I might not know them all. Only the ones who I took the girls and women to.'

The thought that abruptly came into her head was entirely random and Katya didn't really know why she wanted to ask the question. Was it to push him further away from her? To make it easier for her to ask him to go into danger for her?

'Where *are* the girls, Kirill. I mean, I see Eu-Meh and others in the Sea Dragon, but I've never seen where they live?'

At first, he saw her question as an opportunity to redeem himself. She must want to rescue them. But then he realised there was little chance of her doing that, however much he helped her.

'They live all around Kropse.'

'What? Not in the casino?'

'No. it's not like Dao.' He left it at that. He didn't want to be the one to bring the curtain down on a rescue–put more distance between them.

Katya took an instant decision. The idea had been half formed and rescuing the girls and women would jeopardise her plan to shut down Belov for good. She could only hope they'd find their own way to freedom after his *mafiya* was destroyed.

'Right. Now the names in that ledger.' She recited them, word perfect.

He listened. Screwed up his eyes in concentration.

'Leonid Kozlov and Bogdan Gobulev. They are important. There are three others I recognize but I'd go for one of those two.'

'Good. I want you to find out what they do and where they do it. How many men they have, and how much they launder through the Sea Dragon. Ask around. Ask the girls. But be careful, I don't want Belov to hear about it.'

'You want to get me killed.' It was a statement not a question.

She felt herself weaken. Put her hand on his arm. He leant towards her, his face close to hers.

Walt's words fired into her. She's not ready, not ready. But she was ready. She'd been accepted. Was a G8 agent. There was an op to finish. She summoned her courage.

'You're the big *mafiya Vor,* Kirill–crime lord. Prove it and Morosov's job is yours.'

He decided to do it to please her. If he survived, surely she wouldn't continue to resist him but would understand that he wanted her because he loved her?

Katya led him downstairs and out of the front door. She went with him to the waiting taxi. As she watched it being driven away she fought hard not to call him back.

FIFTY-THREE

The next day Kirill decided to find information about Leonid Kozlov. His first port of call was to a man called Fyodor. Fyodor was like a snake, slithering amongst inside stories and shedding them for profit. If anyone could tell him Kozlov's secrets, this man could.

Kirill had taken one of the casino's courtesy four-wheel drive Toyotas—the standard vehicle for driving into the Caucasus mountains, where Fyodor had a cabin. He'd driven out of Kropse onto one of the smooth two-lane highways traversing the foothills. In front of him, in the distance, were lines of purple-hued, rough-hewn pinnacles stretching endlessly either side of the road. Directly behind them, in blinding contrast, were mountain tops, glaring white in the midday sunshine. For Kirill, used to the Moscow area which was flat and featureless, the sight never ceased to amaze him. There, in those mountains, was the place he'd take Katya to. Somewhere clean where the past could be wiped out. He dwelt on the picture—the romance of the soft purple and white colours—until, suddenly, the terrain changed and he turned off onto a track that seemed to lead nowhere. Twin stone-covered ruts, with a rise of tattered grass in between them led around a rocky promontory. To his right and left, windswept fir trees stretched their thinly needled limbs over yellowed scrubby grassland which rose sharply to become bare rock—craggy and unforgiving.

He found he was near the track that led to Fyodor's place and turned his mind to focus on him. Fyodor had been employed at the Sea Dragon checking the slot machines– he'd also worked for Kozlov as a runner, delivering bags of heroin to customers. When Koslov found out he was selling heroin on the side he was going to execute him. But, the story was that Belov found Fyodor useful as a source of information and had him exiled to the cabin where he lived. Fyodor now spent his life on his mobile and laptop, gleaning bits of news here and scandal there, selling it for profit.

Kirill knew it wasn't healthy to be close to those who'd crossed Kozlov and he hadn't been near Fyodor for the three years since his banishment. Added to that Kirill hadn't forgotten Katya's warning that Belov must never find out that she was looking into Kozlov's life. Getting anywhere near Fyodor was a huge risk as Belov would pay handsomely for the story that Kozlov was being investigated. But Kirill couldn't see a better way of finding the information Katya wanted.

He followed the track as it turned sharply. Just beyond the bend was a wooden bridge–rickety rails alongside a slatted floor. Overlooking it, almost out of sight was a large cabin. Pine log walls held up a corrugated tin roof. Flat wooden shutters lay either side of its windows.

Kirill drove over the bridge and up the hillside until he came to the rear of the cabin. He saw a door there, a cow bell hanging on a frayed rope fixed to the roof. He stopped the car, got out. There was no sign of life. The only sound was a slight rustle of the grass under his feet. He hesitated, wondering if Fyodor still lived there. If one of Kozlov's other men occupied the cabin that person could ask awkward questions.

The door suddenly swung open. Framed between the fir-wood posts was a small, pallid man whose face looked as if it had been etched by the axe that cut the wall logs. He was dressed in a brown sweater and a pair of green polyester trousers which were held up by a worn leather belt.

'Hello, Fyodor.' Kirill stayed where he was to test whether he would throw him out

Fyodor looked up at him, his lips tightening. 'I might have guessed *you'd* be back. Must be something you want.' He turned and walked into the cabin, leaving the door open.

Kirill sighed with relief that he was over the first hurdle and followed him into a low-ceilinged room. The gaps between the layers of pine logs had been filled with cement but otherwise the room was the same as the day it had been built eighty years ago. The furniture was sparse, artisan. A large stone fireplace housed a wood fire which crackled in the flames as the fir logs burnt.

Kirill sat down in a wooden chair beside it. 'How are things?' he said.

'Much you care,' Fyodor replied. He went to a shelf alongside the fireplace, took down a bottle of vodka and two glasses, handed one to Kirill; poured a shot into it. He poured one for himself and sat down in a chair the other side of the fire and, without a word, drained the glass.

Kirill did the same; then said, 'How's Kozlov doing now the Dao outlet's been closed?'

Fyodor glared at him. 'You bastard, typical of you to come running to me instead of asking him to his face.'

'Why? You know everything that goes on with him.'

'I left him three years ago and well you know it. Have you been near me since? Like hell you have. Anyway, I haven't seen any of Kozlov's bunch since I was kicked out.'

'I'm here now.' Kirill looked around the room, at the poverty spelled out in the patched carpet, torn curtains, and the chipped crockery on a nearby shelf. There was a heavy safe in one corner. Black. Made of solid iron with a huge steel handle and a double lock. Obviously Fyodor was still in business—just didn't want to show it. 'And I'm here to help you.'

'Huh. To help yourself you mean.'

'No. I'm going to take over the management of the Sea Dragon . . .'

'You *what*?' Fyodor could hardly hide his disbelief.

Kirill went on. 'But I need to know about Kozlov.'

'You're serious, aren't you?' Fyodor's eyes took on a faint, knowing gleam in the firelight. 'How can you help *me*?'

'I can get you back checking the slot machines and a cut of the cash going through the casino books. I'll be in charge of them.'

Silence.

'Do you want it or not?'

Fyodor drew in a breath. 'Kozlov hates my guts. What's to stop him whacking me if he finds out I talked about him?'

'That's why I want to know what he's up to. So I can neutralise him. I've got friends who are investing in the place. Ex-KGB. They don't want trouble from Kozlov. And they'll look after you.'

'That's a promise?'

Kirill nodded. 'So . . .?' he questioned.

Fyodor didn't hesitate. 'Kozlov's still running heroin in from Afghanistan. The war increased his take by a huge amount. The Taliban can't sell it to him fast enough. I hear he's got so much he's finding it difficult to reach enough outlets.'

Kirill looked at the fire. 'So, he's got to launder a lot more cash. . . ' he said slowly.

'You mean he's got trouble now Dao's closed? Well, you're right. He and Belov . . .' He stopped, knowing he'd said too much.' Lifted his shoulders, dismissively.

Kirill stood up. 'OK, if you're going to be like that, I'll go.'

'I'll be dead if Kozlov knows– '

'That's not my problem. Either you want a cut of his take or you don't–and I haven't time to fuck about.'

Fyodor looked around the room. He made a living from trading scraps of information. There was cash in the safe but he was getting older. The titbits that were valuable weren't coming his way any longer. Soon there wouldn't be enough money coming in to put bread on the table. Kirill was offering a lifeline. Dangerous, but better to die by a bullet than starvation. He poured some vodka into his glass, drank it, cleared his throat.

'Last night I was told someone heard Kozlov talking to Belov on his mobile. They were having a row about some proposal to offset the Dao losses . . .'

'Go on.' Kirill took the vodka bottle from Fyodor's hand, drank from it.

'It must have had something to do with you people because the KGB was mentioned. Belov was going to cut your seventeen percent to ten but Koslov told him to pay it - he needed your outlet immediately.' He paused. 'That's it.'

Kirill sensed there was something left unsaid. This information wasn't important enough for Kozlov to ice Fyodor for passing it on.

'Tell me the rest,' he said matter of factly so Fyodor knew he wasn't bluffing.

Fyodor shrugged; resigned. 'After the call ended, Kozlov told someone in the room that he'd do a deal direct with your group for the seventeen–cut out Belov.'

Kirill knew this was gold dust. Katya could now play Belov against Kozlov. He had a sudden thought. 'Why didn't you sell this to Belov?'

Fyodor nearly sniggered. Did Kirill think he was a fool. Of course, he had already sold the information to Belov. On the other hand, Kirill would pay him and pay him well, so he lied to him.

'You got here first,' he said, simply, as he looked down to hide the satisfied look in his eyes.

Kirill now had what he needed. But there was one more question Katya had wanted him to ask. 'How many men has Kozlov got on his payroll now? A lot more since his trade increased?'

'No. It's still about eighteen. The Taliban do most of the opium transport. They get it to Turkmenistan; he flies it from there to here.'

Kirill was satisfied. He got up. Smashed the edge of his hand across Fyodor's neck. He heard the spine crack. Fyodor dropped like a stone. Kirill reached for a poker by the fire, pulled out a burning log into the room. The carpet caught fire immediately.

He left the place and drove away. As he went over the wooden slatted bridge he looked in his mirror. Smoke and flames were already gushing into the sky.

He'd obeyed Katya's instruction. He'd got the information they needed and Fyodor wouldn't be talking about his visit to Belov.

FIFTY-FOUR

The following morning, Katya went downstairs and enjoyed the breakfast Ludmilla had prepared for her. Afterwards she'd gone upstairs to have a shower and to change into dark blue sweatpants and a white T-shirt, catching her hair back in a scrunchie and putting on her Prada sunglasses.

She then went for a walk along the seashore. She wanted to clear her mind. The softness of the sand under her bare feet seemed to match her mood. The warmth of the sun added to her contentment. Even the sea was gently lapping the shore; no sign of its power. She needed to understand why Kirill had assumed such importance in her life.

What was it about him that had suddenly attracted her so deeply? Surely it couldn't be the superficial change in his attitude to the girls he kept. He'd always had girls for as long as she'd known him and she hated him for it. Why did she love him now? Love. She stopped in her tracks. How did that word creep into her mind?

She forced herself to think back. Back to those days in Moscow when she was a teenager escaping the horror that was her father and searching for the elegance of her mother. There was excitement in the cellars jammed with young people like her, screaming to the western music in a long shout of freedom. But freedom that came at a price. The cheap *mafiya* hoodlums haunting the streets, lurking there to grab a few *kopeks* or, worse, herself. Kirill was one of them, the one she'd chosen to challenge, to deny him the girls he traded. She remembered the battle as exhilarating.

Learning to win so as to infuriate him. Yet he'd never retaliated. He'd never set the *mafiya* thugs onto her. Come to think of it, none of them had ever attacked her. At the time, she'd reckoned it was her reputation for being street wise, a fighter, keeping them at bay. Now, reflecting in depth on that period, was it Kirill who had protected her all along? Had she subconsciously accepted that, refusing to take it out and look at it? Refusing to believe she'd actually been in love with him all the time but only now, in the closeness of their being together, understood the truth?

She suddenly smelled tobacco smoke. Abdullah Turkish. It couldn't be–she turned abruptly–there was Lev.

He was walking towards her with his usual swaying stride; one that could cover miles and not tire a person–dressed casually in lightweight trousers and a dark blue long-sleeved, open necked shirt; wearing large, dark tinted sunglasses and a Panama hat he presented the essence of old Russian money–better known as KGB plunder.

'Hello, Lev,' she said evenly, as if meeting him by chance on a beach, two thousand miles from G8HQ was an everyday event.

'Hello, Katya. I thought I'd find you not far from the sea. How are you? Everything going well?'

Of course, he would have known she would be here, he knew her love of the sea. 'All good Lev. How was your journey?'

He took off his hat, smoothed down his hair. 'Lousy. I hate flying–I can't smoke.' He broke off. Pointed down the beach to the marina. 'My god, the marina. That brings back memories of the old KGB–the exercises we had there. Is that where you . . .?'

Katya turned her eyes to where he was pointing. Stiffened. Taban. Her first kill. . .

'Come on,' Lev said briskly, 'can't stand here gossiping. We need to talk. How's Kirill?'

The speed of his question almost caught her by surprise. She recovered quickly and said, 'Under control. He's doing some work for me at the moment.'

He'd caught the hesitation, decided to let her know he had. 'Very good. You took my advice about not getting too close to informants.' A compliment.

She ignored him. A duel with Lev on the subject of Kirill would end only one way—with her in tatters.

He looked around. The beach was deserted. The only sounds the cries of the gulls and the lap of rippling waves. So different to the tension of the Tac Room back at G8HQ when Guy and his IT team had been wrestling with the difficulties their objective kept throwing up. He smiled inwardly. The solution had been blindingly simple. Getting Belov and his *mafiya* partners to go along with it was a different matter, but that would-be Katya's business. First, he must outline how the operation would pan out.

'Here's as good a place as any to tell you what we've planned. We've found an island in the China Sea which is a tax haven and ideal for our purpose. We've leased a building there to be our bank. We've also leased a ship which we will moor offshore to be our online casino.' He paused while she digested this. 'Now, the end game—the end game is to get Belov and his partners onto the ship all together so we can arrest them.'

Katya's immediate thought was how could they be lured there.

Lev answered her unspoken question. 'Your job—our job—is to convince Belov that our new online casino can launder all their cash in the shortest possible time. That it's much more efficient than a normal casino. If we can do that we can offer to take them to the ship and show them how it all works.'

This time Katya did have a question. 'Won't it require incredibly complex software? I mean online gambling normally gives the punters a spread of games; poker, roulette that sort of thing. To run that amount of cash–millions of dollars–through the casino that fast will take a huge number of bets, wins and losses. They won't be convinced the software can do that.'

'Guy came up with the answer. We use only one form of bet–sports betting. There are sports games going on all over the world. Professional, amateur, for kids. Huge sums are bet on the results. The software for that is simple,'

'Too simple for Belov to believe it'll work?' She had to be sure she could convince Belov.

Lev bent down and picked a pebble off the beach; sent it skimming across the water. 'How does that work? That pebble skim,' he asked her.

'Spin, speed– '

'No. It was a rhetorical question. The point is that when it happens one doesn't enquire into the technicalities of why.' He sent another pebble across the water. 'One just enjoys the result.'

She realised what he was saying. 'Of course. Belov's partners bet in pairs. One for one team one for the other. It doesn't matter who wins, they're guaranteed to collect the win money. That's all that matters. They don't need to know any more.'

Lev nodded. 'Belov's greedy. If he thinks he can moneylaunder a lot more cash than he ever has before, he'll want to see how it works. He'll come to the ship alright.'

Katya looked doubtful again. 'And bring his partners with him? Do you think we'll succeed in getting them all to come?'

'We've got to arrest the whole lot at the same time. And that means getting them together on the ship. Your job. Work on Belov.'

Doubt gathered even more in Katya's mind. She'd left it too late to find out much about Belov's partners. How was she going to persuade them?

Lev started walking quicker. 'Now we have to talk to Belov,

convince him we have a brilliant idea. We need to get hold of him immediately.'

Katya joined him by his side. 'I have to wait at the *dacha* for Kirill to report back first. I'm hoping he'll have some useful *intel* for us on one of Belov's most influential partners. If Belov's difficult, we'll be in trouble. I need something to undermine him.'

FIFTY-FIVE

L udmilla was cleaning the *dacha* when Katya and Lev arrived. She was naturally suspicious of this hardened man with his grey hair and a cigarette clamped between his lips. He had *mafiya* written all over him. Yet when he greeted her she noticed the humour lurking behind his eyes. The only thing behind the eyes of the *mafiya* she'd seen at the Sea Dragon had been stark cruelty. Where had he come from? Was this the person Katya went to see in St Petersburg? She caught the look he gave Katya when she introduced him simply as Lev Leviatski. Fond? No, more like caring. So not a lover. A friend? A relative? She was glad. Viktor was Katya's friend as well but he clearly wasn't in the same league as this Lev Leviatski. There was a doggedness about him, a survivor.

She made them tea, spooning two heaped spoons of jam into Katya's mug. She was looking tired, needed building up. She watched them sit opposite each other on the sofas, looking as though they wanted to talk but couldn't because of her presence.

She understood their need for privacy; went and put on her coat and hat saying, 'Right. I'm off now, Katya.'

'Thanks, Ludmilla. See you tomorrow.'

As Ludmilla closed the front door behind her, Lev wondered whether Katya would ever see her again. If the operation was successful, Katya would be back in Basingstoke. If not. . .

Katya stood up saying, 'Make yourself at home Lev, help yourself to more tea, there are some sushki in the cupboard if you'd like some. I won't be a minute I'll just go upstairs and freshen up.'

He watched her walk up the stairs; his thoughts turning to this remarkable woman he'd known since she'd been born. He'd known her mother, too. Vital, wedded to art and beauty–glamour. But courageous enough to leave an abusive husband. He'd been surprised that Katya had followed her father into the world of intelligence. He was sure she leant more towards her mother's personality. But, then, he'd known the father. True KGB, dedicated to propping up the crumbling empire of the Soviet Union. Determined his daughter would carry on his crusade. Perhaps the courage of both parents was the strongest gene in Katya. She'd certainly shown it in this operation. He hadn't probed about her experiences in Kropse and Dao but he had no doubt they had tested her to the edge of endurance. Yes, he was sure this was her driver in the work she did for G8. Looking back, he knew it was his driver, too. It had taken all his courage to conspire to topple the corrupt, uncaring regime that had become his homeland. But was courage alone enough to keep Katya in G8? Of course, she had the other tools–she could manipulate, deceive, think rapidly, but she also had to be hard. Was she hard enough? Would the side of her mother suddenly touch her, propel her into a world where darkness and danger weren't the norm? Could Kirill be the catalyst for that? Might G8 lose her to him?

He became aware Katya had returned and was talking to him. 'Sorry, I was thinking,' he said apologetically.

'Something you need to tell me about the op?'

'No. I was thinking about your mother.' A half-truth.

Katya had often wondered about Lev's relationship to her mother, his protection of her.

'Were you in love with my mother?' she asked suddenly.

Hastily, she went on. 'Not that I'd mind if you were, knowing what my father was like.'

They were interrupted by the front door bell ringing. Katya went to open it.

Kirill was there. He came in, caught hold of Katya's arms, pulled her towards him. 'Katya, I've been . . .'

Lev coughed.

'Who's this?' Kirill's voice alarmed, suspicious.

Lev looked Kirill over closely, judging him as only one Russian can judge another– automatic distrust. 'Katya has told you about me. I am Lev, her uncle.' He didn't get up or hold out his hand.

Kirill gave him a brief bow. Looked at Katya, his eyes full of concern. 'I'm glad you've arrived. I've been worried about you.'

She coloured slightly. 'I'm fine, Kirill. Come and sit down, tell us what's happened.'

Lev saw her blush; the glance they exchanged. He knew love when he saw it. He also knew Kirill for an unrepentant bastard.

'Yes.' Lev pointed to the empty space on the sofa he was sitting on. 'Come and give us your report.'

FIFTY-SIX

When Kirill left Katya and Lev at the *dacha* he drove straight to the Sea Dragon. Katya had asked him to set up a meeting with Belov to discuss the alliance between Lev and her KGB friends, and Belov's *mafiya*.

He climbed the steps into the casino, head bent down in concentration as he worked out how he would approach Belov to give him the news. He mustn't appear to be too eager, Katya had said. But he mustn't be subservient, either. Kirill was worried. He thought that balance would be difficult to achieve since he had never been anything else but humble in Belov's presence.

Luka suddenly came out from behind one of the pillars at the top of the steps. 'You fucking leave Katya alone, you sod.' His words echoed off the front of the building.

Kirill wasn't prepared for him. Reacted to a threat in the only way he knew how. Lashed out with his foot, smashing into Luka's crotch. Luka doubled up. Kirill raised his hand to deliver the fatal blow. Stopped. Luka didn't need to die–he just needed to understand who Katya belonged to. He bent, hauled the man to his feet. Slapped his face–hard. 'Leave her alone. Understand?' He thrust Luka away and walked through the front door.

Anatoly was there, his mouth open, dazed by what he'd witnessed. Luka was the casino's protector. He was now on his knees, gasping. The order of things had changed. First Morosov, now Luka.

'Good evening, Kirill,' he said. 'No need for ID, I expect you wish to see– '

Kirill didn't let him finish. He must announce himself to Belov. Luka had inadvertently given him the authority to do that. Violence ruled in any *mafiya*.

He marched straight past the slot machines, across the gaming floor to the lifts. The punters took care not to catch his eye. A man to avoid they'd decided.

The lift rose swiftly. Kirill stepped out into the hallway, made his way to Belov's penthouse.

He knocked on the door.

'Come in.' Belov's voice barked the words.

FIFTY-SEVEN

Kirill had successfully set up the meeting with Belov and later that day he, Lev and Katya were in Belov's penthouse. Belov didn't know who impressed him more–the charismatic Katya–or the man she introduced to him as her uncle, Lev Leviatski.

He'd met them prepared to be dominant, dismissive of them. He'd then heard their proposition and knew it had been prepared meticulously. It was certainly believable that this man Lev was an ex-KGB officer. Once he'd understood it, the simplicity of the scheme was staggering. He wondered why he'd never thought of an online casino himself. Morosov should have found out about them. Good that idiot was out of his life. These people would make an excellent fit with his partners.

'You haven't told me where the bank or ship are,' he said, probing.

Lev settled back in his chair, leaving Katya to answer the question. He looked out of the window at the squally sky. Dark clouds were racing by, a storm was coming–there would be one in here too if they weren't careful.

Katya stretched. The last half hour had been demanding. Belov had understood how the bank would be involved–*mafiyas* knew all about tax havens–but she'd had to spell out how an online casino worked.

'You'll appreciate we won't release details of the whereabouts of the ship or bank for the moment,' she replied. 'First of all, we want to know whether you approve the moneylaundering process.'

'I think we could. But I need to know where the cash is being flown to. Is it within the Gulfstream's range? How difficult will it be to get the cash on board through the airport authorities? Are some of them your people or are they being bought? What banking regulations are there? Would the finance authorities interfere or are they onside? I can't possibly accept your proposal without knowing these things.'

Lev decided to play the KGB card. 'We're ex KGB. What do you think we are? Some cowboy-outfit? We've run this operation for two years. Of course, everyone's been bought. The place we're in needs our bank. We pay huge fees to the Government, plus cash sweeteners to the administrators.'

Belov found himself apologising. 'I'm sorry. The KGB was disbanded years ago. I thought you'd have lost your influence.'

Lev shrugged. 'The problem with you *mafiyas* is that you're so confident you're running Russia you can't see what's right in front of you. The KGB may have been abolished but its officers still run the oligarchs and between them they run Russia. It's just easier for us to let you think you do.'

There was a pause as Belov studied his thick fingers, running a hand over them.

He raised his head. 'We can't pay seventeen per cent for laundering our cash. It's far too much. Ten.'

Katya gestured to Kirill. 'You can answer that, Kirill.'

Kirill looked directly at Belov. 'Your partner, Kozlov, is prepared to pay seventeen.'

Belov was stunned. How the hell did they know this? It must be a bluff. 'I don't know what gives you that idea. Me and Kozlov are agreed on ten per cent.'

Katya shook her head. 'Don't try and bluff. Kirill's information is rock solid.'

Belov could read faces. One of the attributes of a leader. Kirill's told him he had a snitch in Kozlov's drugs cartel. Of course–Fyodor. It could only have been Fyodor.

'Split the difference,' Belov said. 'Keep me happy.' It was worth a try.

'Keep Kozlov happy you mean.' Lev, straight to the point. 'Well, we want to start off on the right foot. Agreed. Any more business?'

Belov saw his control slipping away. It was time to be assertive. 'Before I agree this plan I'll want to see the online casino in operation. I want to go the bank and to the ship.'

Lev stood up. 'Of course. Make your Gulfstream available for take-off tomorrow morning. Katya will give you the details.' He held out his hand to Belov. 'Right, I must go. I need to make arrangements with the bank and ship. See you tomorrow.'

Belov stared after him as he closed the door. How had the KGB lost the Cold War with people like that in charge?

Katya broke into his thoughts. 'We want you and your partners on board the Gulfstream at 5.00 a.m. sharp– '

Belov immediately objected. 'All of us? I can't do that. I've got to get them here
first–'

'I have strict instructions. You must all come. All six of you. We don't want disputes raised later on by people who haven't checked out both the bank and the ship. All in or none in. Take it or leave it.'

Belov shook his head. 'No. It's not possible. They know nothing about this.'

'Kozlov knows,' she interjected. 'He's already tried to shaft you. D'you really want to leave him behind with the others– scheming behind your back?'

Belov was silent. A thunderous expression on his face.

'It's up to you.' She waited a moment then headed for the door. 'Come on, Kirill. We're wasting our time here.'

Kirill followed her. She stopped in front of Belov.

'Alright.' Belov almost shouted the word through gritted teeth. 'Alright. I'll bring all of us.'

She took his hand. 'Good. 5.00 a.m. tomorrow morning.' She took her hand away. 'Oh yes. And no cash on this trip. It's only purpose is to show you how the process works on the ground. See you in the morning.'

After they had gone Belov sat down, searching his memory. Something was out of place. He squeezed his eyes shut, racked his brains. What was it? Abruptly it came to him. His eyes opened wide. She'd mentioned five partners. She'd lied here in his penthouse when she said she hadn't read through the ledger. Which meant deception came naturally to her. What else was she lying about, he wondered. His lips tightened.

FIFTY-EIGHT

After they left Belov, Kirill insisted on going with Katya to the *dacha*. She knew full well the danger of her agreeing to that. There was work to do, finalising the details of Belov's arrest on board the ship, and Kirill wasn't part of that. He must never know she was G8 or that Belov and his *mafiya* was a target. But, at this moment, she was thoroughly confused. Her feelings for Kirill were in direct conflict with her duty to G8. She was sure now that she loved him, knew she wanted a future with him. She had sensed that he had given out signals that he felt the same, but he hadn't offered her a future to take the place of G8. She feared his interest in her might be to seduce her simply to satisfy his ego. So she let him come with her so she could find out.

When they arrived at the *dacha* they went into the sitting room. Katya didn't offer him alcohol. For this conversation, she wanted him stone cold sober–easier to deal with, to spot any lies. A cold assessment by one Russian of another. Her love of G8 against her love for him was so finely balanced and so important that it had to be tested, ruthlessly.

'Sit down, Kirill. I want to talk.'

He came towards her. She stepped back and pointed to the sofa opposite her, across the coffee table. She had to have distance.

He sat down and looked at her, a question in his eyes.

She found it difficult to begin. Did she tell him outright how she felt? Would that drive him to lie about his true feelings if his only objective was to get her into bed?

He saw her hesitation; took the lead. 'I was driving into the mountains, yesterday. . .' he paused. Was it only yesterday he was killing the old man and torching his cabin— something he'd never tell Katya? He went on, 'and thought they were just the place for us to start our lives together. . .' He stopped, unable to find any other words to tell her how he felt.

The simplicity of what he said almost made her cry. He could have said anything else, flowery phrases, protestations of undying love but these words and no others told her that he'd shown her the man he truly was. No longer the young boy who'd been dumped in an orphanage, learning brutality, abuse; forced on him over the years as tools of survival. He wouldn't need those tools when he was with her. They could find a life together. Russia was now a place for the young like them, the bright, the determined.

She got up and went over to him. Wordlessly put her arms around him and gave him her lips. She felt the fire of his response and knew she hadn't been wrong.

A loud voice suddenly resonated into the room.

'Oh! Sorry. The door was open so I came in.'

Katya pushed Kirill away, her face flushed. Viktor stood there.

She recovered quickly. 'Viktor! Come in.'

He looked awkward. He'd heard about the man who was with Katya. Bad things. That was why he'd come—to break them up. This man wasn't for his *Malyshka*. 'I just came up for a cup of tea. Would you have time, Katya?' he asked.

Viktor was her oldest friend, she couldn't just get rid of him. Besides she now had the answer about Kirill that she wanted. That he loved and wanted her too. She could take time to give Viktor some tea. Then she really must think about the pitfalls she must beware of when she was travelling with six *mafiya* partners on the Gulfstream—persuading them onto the ship.

'Wait a second, Viktor.' She walked towards the front door. Kirill followed her and they went out onto the veranda, leaving Viktor in the sitting room. A soft darkness was falling as Katya took Kirill's arm. 'I'll see you in the morning by the Gulfstream,' she said quietly.

He thought her violet-blue eyes looked even more beautiful than ever as she smiled at him.

'But I want to stay here, Katya. Surely– '

She had to lie to him. Hopefully for the last time. 'First, we must make sure we set up your job at the casino. That means making Belov and his partners happy with the online casino arrangements.' She emphasised her deceit by looking firmly into his eyes. 'You know that,' she said urgently. Then she told him the truth, 'Afterwards we've got all our lives together.'

At that he moved towards her, took her in his arms, kissed her–he started to protest again as she broke away. 'No. I mean it,' Katya said. 'I'll meet you at the aircraft.' She lowered her voice, 'Don't forget to make sure no cash is put aboard.'

With an effort, he released her; turned and reluctantly left.

She watched him go, then went back inside the *dacha*, closing the door behind her.

'Let's get your tea, Viktor,' she said smiling at him.

He bowed his head so he wouldn't show the anxiety he felt for her, said conversationally, 'The man who has just left, you know him well.' A statement, not a question.

She wouldn't lie to him, but she wanted to keep her secret to herself. 'Yes.' She walked to the kitchen. Changed the subject. 'Cherry jam?' she suggested.

The doorbell rang.

Under her breath Katya swore. She'd told Kirill to stay away. It had been difficult enough to control herself and make him go. How could she do it again? 'Viktor, see to it will you. Tell whoever it is to go away.' She half hoped Kirill would pay no attention; that he would stay.

'Viktor? Where have you sprung from?'

It was Lev.

They came to the kitchen together. Lev was beaming. 'I haven't seen Viktor since the old days. Thought he was at the bottom of the sea.'

'Viktor's looked after me,' Katya smiled.

Lev put his hand on Viktor's shoulder. 'Well, I'm afraid I must ask you to leave us, old friend. I'm leaving this evening and must talk to Katya about her father's estate before I go.'

Viktor remembered Lev as KGB and as Katya's protector. Rumour was that Katya had had trouble up at the Sea Dragon. And now Lev was here. Something was going on and it was about more than her father's estate. His worried eyes looked at her as he said, 'I'll be going then. Good to see you, Lev–I'll see you tomorrow, Katya?'

Katya went to the door with him. 'Yes, see you tomorrow, Viktor. Sorry about the tea,'

She shut the door behind her, turned towards Lev. 'I thought you'd left.'

'No. Sit down, I haven't long before my flight leaves.' He sat on a sofa, leaned forward towards her as she took a seat opposite him.

'I've finished the arrangements for tomorrow,' he said. 'Belov's Gulfstream will fly you all to Jiao Island which is between China and Taiwan. It's an eight-hour flight so at the limit of the aircrafts range. I've arranged plenty of champagne and food and your job is to make sure everyone is comfortable– '

She made a face.

'Don't think it will be easy. These people are dangerous, they're in the dark and they'll ask questions. One false step and they'll be onto you like rats. You must put them in the right mood to travel straight on to the ship. Incidentally, the ships name is *Igra*.'

'Where will we meet?'

'At the airfield on Jiao. I'll take you straight to the ship's launch and we'll go on from there.'

'Will they be arrested as soon as we arrive on the *Igra*?'

'No. I want evidence of their betting, so they are clearly caught moneylaundering. I don't want us involved in the actual arrest. It could get messy and we won't be armed.'

'So how will the arrests be made?'

'They have to log on to the casino website. Once they've done that they'll be given the opportunity to lay bets. They'll be immersed in that and we can slip away onto the launch and back to shore. I've got an armed G8 team ready to then take the launch back to the *Igra* and arrest them.'

'It all sounds very simple,' she said uncertainly.

He looked at his watch. Stood up. 'It will be if they've been lulled by you on the aircraft. I must go.'

After he'd left she kicked off her shoes and poured herself a Yorsh. The danger she was heading into was worse than anything which had come before. She was glad Kirill would be there.

FIFTY-NINE

Katya left the *dacha* first thing the next morning. She'd decided to wear a pair of crisp black cotton trousers, one of her designer red T-shirts, and a pair of black ballet flats. She made sure she was wearing her gold necklace and couldn't resist a spray of her Picasso scent. If Lev wanted her to get her passengers in a good mood; a hint of scent would go a long way to help. She went out onto the veranda, going over the plan in her head as she waited for the taxi to take her to the airport

It soon arrived and, as she climbed in holding a small overnight bag, Katya felt a tinge of excitement. Not sure if she was pleased that her op was going to schedule or cautious that something would go wrong. At the moment, though, the sun was coming up over the mountains, the sea looked warm and inviting and she'd found love with Kirill. . .

When she arrived at the airport she saw the Gulfstream was parked at the end of the runway, engines running, ready for take-off. There were people climbing out of two Bentley Continental GT coupe's parked alongside it. One of them was carrying two large suitcases. All thoughts of Kirill were pushed aside. She jumped out of the taxi and strode towards them. Large suitcases could mean they were full of dollar bills. A shoebox of $100 bills could carry $100,000. If Belov managed to get suitcases of cash into the Gulfstream baggage area, he would want to deposit it in the bank when they got to Jiao Island. That meant the partners would split up when they got to the island and would be more difficult to keep track of – this could ruin the plan to get them all onto the *Igra* together to be arrested.

She saw Belov coming down the aircraft steps. Better to have a row now in front of his partners so everyone knew the rules.

She pointed to the suitcases; called to him. 'You haven't been putting cash on board, have you?'

'The answer is no!'

She turned to the man with the cases. 'Open these up. I want to make sure.'

The man glowered at her, looked at Belov.

'Open them up,' Belov ordered.

The cases had clothes in them. No dollars. No weapons.

Belov breathed a silent sigh of relief. He hadn't been so sure his partners were all up for this trip. He looked at Katya. 'I don't need to take cash. I want to see how much you have in this mysterious bank of yours before I commit.'

He waited for her reply. None came. 'Where is this bank? Surely you can tell me now.' He sounded aggressive.

'When we're airborne,' she said firmly. Then, looking around she asked, 'Are they all here?'

'Yes, all except Kozlov. He's missing.'

Katya tried not to look anxious. She decided it would be better to let him retain his authority over his partners. They would stay together that way–lemmings to the cliff. 'If he doesn't arrive'– she looked at her watch– 'in the next four minutes the deal's off. As I said all in or none in–and we've got a schedule to keep.'

Kirill came out of the aircraft. His eyes lit up when he saw her. She slightly shook her head at him, careful not to be seen by Belov. A display of affection at this point would make her appear weak. She wanted Belov off balance and under her control.

A car drew up, another Bentley Continental GT coupe–tyres screeching as it came to a sharp stop. Out stepped Kozlov. Katya looked at him. He was typically Russian with his round face, broad nose and dark hair. There was also a swagger about him, a sure bully. As he walked past Belov towards the steps that led up to the passenger doorway he said curtly, 'I'm not convinced this is the way forward.' He glared at Kirill. 'I don't trust him. Or you,' he said, pointing at Katya. 'I know nothing about any of you,' he snarled.

He turned to Belov. 'Have my suitcases been taken out of my car and put in the hold?'

Belov didn't answer; started up the boarding stairs.

Katya knew that if Kozlov got away with bringing any cash in his suitcases she'd have no chance of controlling him—or any of them for that matter.

Ignoring Kozlov, she said loudly to Belov. 'If this man has one dollar loaded on the aircraft the deal's off.' She decided to made it plainer—he was dealing with a KGB group, not a bunch of amateurs. 'If we can't trust you to work with us, we'll find someone else to partner with.'

'Fuck you,' shouted Kozlov. 'I need to know whether this thing works from beginning to end. I need cash to do that.'

'He's got a point— 'Belov started to say.

Katya walked straight up to him, brushed her hair away from her eyes, jammed her face almost into his. She said fiercely, but not so loud Kozlov could hear. 'Are you going to let this shit try and stitch you up again? If Lev and I hadn't protected your interests, Kozlov would have done a deal direct with us—cut you out.'

She saw the indecision on his face, before he said curtly, 'Leave it, Kozlov. It's part of the deal.'

Swearing and fuming, Kozlov marched up the steps, pushed past them and boarded the plane.

Belov thrust his face even closer to Katya's. 'If any part of what you've told me turns out to be a con, you'll be the first to go.' He turned and climbed the aircraft steps.

Kirill and Katya followed. The steps were pulled up. The door shut. The pilot started taxiing the plane down the runway.

Belov and his partners were all settled in their white leather seats. Kozlov loudly complaining to one of them that he wished he had never agreed to this ridiculous plan. He'd find another way to launder his money, he grumbled. Two others were quietly talking, their heads close together. One sat back and closed his eyes. No one was paying any attention to Koslov. Except Katya. Was Kozlov going to ruin the whole plan? She would let him fume and then try and win him round. The crew mic was next to the bar and she picked it out of its cradle.

'Your attention please,' she announced. 'Your destination is Jiao, an island in the China Sea between China and Taiwan. It's a disputed territory between them but as it's so small it's been allowed to self-administer. It's a tax haven and we've had a bank there for two years. We fly our cash in to the airstrip and deliver it direct to the bank. The authorities are taken care of so we have no trouble. We also have a small tramp steamer, the *Igra*, which is anchored in international waters outside the territorial limits of Jiao. This houses our online casino. It is therefore wholly unregulated. That is all for the moment. I will explain once we are on board the *Igra* how our online gambling works and how it will be useful to you. In the meantime, the bar is open and champagne is on ice. There will be oysters and chilled lobster served for lunch. Thank you.'

Katya found the flight exhausting. First of all, Kozlov collared her and subjected her to close cross-questioning. Where was she from? Who were her associates? What ranks in the KGB had the parents of this group held? What were their sources of income? Where was their cash flown from? She gritted her teeth and smiled and misled and deceived and manipulated. It was endless. Until Belov came up. He had seen them with their heads together, Katya animatedly answering Kozlov's questions. Both of them getting closer. He had to break them up. He asked her to join him at the bar. And the questions started all over again. . . only broken off when she toured around Belov's partners and filled their glasses with champagne or vodka or both.

She couldn't find comfort with Kirill. Koslov had made it plain he didn't trust him. The last thing she wanted to do was to have them at each other's throats. So she left Kirill alone.

On and on it went—one partner after the other, making sure no-one had an advantage or was more informed than the other. The drink helped. By the time the engine note changed signalling their descent into Jiao, Belov and all his partners had subsided in their seats—peacefully asleep.

There was a window beside the bar and Katya looked out. In front of her and below was a long, low lying island. It lay in a brilliant turquoise lagoon surrounded by a reef where waves created a white necklace. Beyond the reef, as far as she could see, the water was deep purple. The China Sea, sleepy at the moment as the sun was starting to set. She had half expected that Jiao would look like this. What surprised her was the greenery she could see covering the whole place, save where white sand beaches edged the lagoon. She could just see the palm trees gently swaying in the evening breeze. The only thing that would grow in such conditions would be copra. She supposed the old Portuguese traders had planted it a hundred years ago. It explained why such a desolate place was inhabited.

Dusk was settling by the time they landed and left the Gulfstream. The small airfield terminal boasted a single room lit by strips of neon in the ceiling. Their light shone on Lev as he moved forward to greet the party. No-one else was there. No customs officers, no immigration personnel. Bribed by Lev, as Katya knew, to stay away from this important new source of revenue for the island and its administrators.

Belov went ahead of his partners to greet Lev. 'Thank you for laying on such a smooth flight.'

'It's good to see you.' Lev warmly greeted them. 'We'll go straight to the launch which will take us to the casino ship, the *Igra*. The launch is very comfortable–a bar on board and some light eats which I expect you'd like after such a long flight.'

'Aren't we going to the bank first?' Kozlov still unconvinced he should have come, his voice challenging, truculent.

'And we've booked the best hotel in town for you to stay at tonight,' Lev continued.

'What about the bank? I want to see all this cash you say you've got.' Kozlov wasn't going to let go.

'Of course. If you want to spend all night counting it.' Lev shrugged. 'You tell him Katya.'

'As you've probably guessed *Igra* means "game". And the game you will be playing when you are on board is online betting on sports team games. We are giving you credit cards loaded with one hundred and fifty thousand dollars each for you to play with.' She explained how the bets would be made, how it didn't matter whether they won or lost.

Lev finished it up. 'This evening without ever moving from the ship you will have laundered close on a million dollars. Of course, if you'd prefer to sit all night in the bank– '

He broke off as Belov pushed past him. 'Where's the transport to this ship?'

Kozlov moved away, his face red with anger. He knew he'd have to resign himself to see this thing through. There just might be a benefit for him. . .

The dock was a short walk from the airfield. The lighting was poor but through the twilight Katya saw what looked like a new concrete wharf reaching out into the sea for about a hundred meters. Long enough for a small trading vessel she thought. Moored there was a motor launch–sleek enough to impress. She estimated it to be about forty feet long. Big enough to give plenty of room and comfort to the group. She smiled inwardly. Lev must have persuaded John to let him have a hefty budget for this op. She wondered what the *Igra* would be like.

Lev was speaking, 'Please–all of you go on board. We use this launch to provision *Igra*, there are plenty of supplies on board, so help yourselves.'

They climbed down the gangway. Belov leading the way, Kozlov reluctantly following him. The other partners went where Belov led and were anticipating huge gains from this venture. The cash from their rackets–arms sales, narcotics trafficking, murder for hire, extortion, blackmail, prostitution, fraud had been piling up. They were just happy that they now had an alternative to the Dao casino for laundering it.

The captain started the twin engines, set the course on the satnav and guided the launch away from the wharf and out into the lagoon. The narrow cut in the reef caused angry protests as the partners shouted it was too dangerous to go through.

Katya moved into the wheelhouse, smiled at the uniformed Captain and took the wheel. She was a far better skipper than him, deftly catching the drifts and currents as she accelerated into the open sea.

Kozlov eyed her from the open door. There was more to this woman that he would like to learn about. She and he could make a good fit. His eyes smirked as he looked at her. It was time he had a new mistress.

The sea finally became smooth and Katya left the wheel in the Captain's hands. She made her way to the saloon to make sure the partners were finding the bar well stocked and had everything they needed.

They'd been at sea for about an hour when she first saw the pinpricks of the Igra's lights. As the launch got closer she made out the superstructure. About fifty meters long, she reckoned–a stretched cabin aft with large windows adjoining a high bridge. There was another cabin forward which had a line of portholes. The classic image of a converted deep-sea trawler. Above the bridge was an array of satellite dishes. There was a boarding platform on the Igra's starboard side. She started to corral Belov and the partners towards the launch door.

Kozlov immediately objected. 'Where's my money, the hundred and fifty grand you promised? I'm not going anywhere until I've got it.'

Kaya felt her heart race. If he was given the credit card before he boarded the Igra, he could raise yet another objection, stall, even demand to be returned to the shore. He was dominating, could influence the others to join him.

'Well, what are you waiting for?' Kozlov demanded.

SIXTY

I t was Belov who saved the situation. He knew that Kozlov didn't care whether he was given the money then or later. In Belov's mind, what Kozlov was doing was making a bid for leadership. That wasn't going to happen. Hardly waiting for the launch to stop at the *Igra's* boarding platform, he jumped onto it. 'Are you coming or aren't you, Kozlov,' he shouted.

They all followed his lead and clambered onto the platform.

Koslov immediately saved face. He criticised the state of the ship's rusted hull.

'How long's this tub of a ship going to last,' he complained.

Katya answered him coldly. 'The ship's been anchored here at sea for six months. Of course she's rusted. Her only job is to carry the *comms* equipment for the casino.'

Kozlov grunted–reluctantly accepting she knew about the sea – she'd navigated through that dangerous reef.

In fact, Katya was well aware the trawler was on its last sea legs and chartered only for the duration of this op.

Kozlov climbed onto the platform with the others. Lev then took them onto the deck and to the saloon which was in the stern. It occupied the width of the ship. G8 had made some improvements there so as to impress the partners. The deck was plushly carpeted. Dark green leather club chairs were set in a semi-circle facing a large plasma screen attached to the stern bulkhead. A well-stocked bar was in one corner. The large windows had all been blacked out.

Kozlov was immediately suspicious. Blacked out rooms spelled trouble–torture or worse–always blood.

Noticing Kozlov's suspicion, Lev pointed out the plasma screen which displayed a number of pictures. Light from the windows would make it difficult to see them he explained. Kozlov watched. A number of team games were being played in a number of different countries–football, cricket, rugby, tennis.

'What are those?' Kozlov asked.

'You are in the heart of our online casino. Those are the teams that you can bet on– to win or to lose, and a number of other bets as well, like the score.'

'Where are the croupiers?' Kozlov demanded, suspicious again.

Lev waved his cigarette at him. 'There are none. Think of the savings you're already making.'

'That's no answer.' Kozlov fronting up. 'Who operates this online business–where are they?'

'It's here.' Lev indicated the screens. 'Well the computers and online software are in the engineering compartment to keep them cool. But it's all automated and what you see here is all you need to make a bet and pass your cash through this casino into the bank. And, of course, you can bet from any corner of the world.'

He looked around. 'Kirill?' He gestured to a cupboard next to the bar. 'If you will hand the contents to our colleagues here.' He used the word colleagues deliberately. It drew them in. They were already part of the scam.

Kirill walked over to the cupboard; opened it. There were six laptops stacked inside. He took them out and handed them to Belov and the other partners. They immediately started to open them. Katya saw their attention was on the laptops, caught Kirill's eye, impulsively smiled at him. A message painting their future together.

Lev went behind one of the chairs put his hand on the arm of it. 'Now if you gentlemen would like to sit down and switch on your laptops. . .'

Mesmerised, they did as he asked.

'You will find they are fired up. Please go to the search engine and open *Igra* Online Services.'

He waited in the silence. Six of the worst, most violent and degraded international criminals were acting like children finding their first app.

'Good. Now the site tells you to enter a twenty-character password. I suggest you make it as complex as possible. Once you have created it you can use it immediately to access the gambling site. The plasma screens you see here tell you which team games you may bet on. You will bet on both teams to win.'

'What with?' Belov, greedy as usual.

Lev put a hand in his pocket. 'I promised you a hundred and fifty thousand dollars each to bet with. Here it is.' He gave each partner a bank card.

Kozlov looked at his. 'Bank of Jiao.' He read out.

'Yes,' agreed Lev. 'Our bank. Your bank. Now, if you follow the instructions on the site you may begin your evening of online gambling. Enjoy.'

One of them called Kirill over to help him work out what to do.

Lev moved away from the chair towards the door. Carefully jerked his head at Katya. The partners were all engrossed in studying their laptops, working out their passwords. Quietly he opened the door, pushed her through.

He followed her immediately. 'Quick,' he whispered.

Katya raced down a narrow passageway leading towards the bow of the ship. She came to a hatch in the starboard side. A man stood there in the shadows, a length of rope in his hand. She didn't recognise him. She stopped abruptly, turned in alarm to Lev.

'G8,' he growled under his breath. 'Move out through the hatch.'

She looked through the opening. There was a ladder there. It led down to the launch.

'Go on,' urged the G8 agent. 'Quick.'

She climbed down the ladder and jumped silently onto the deck of the launch. Lev and the agent followed, the latter still holding the rope.

The launch engines spluttered into life. Katya nearly fell as the throttle was pushed forward by the skipper and he turned the vessel tightly to speed away from the *Igra*.

Katya found Lev holding her steady. 'Well done, Katya. Very well done. If you hadn't smoothed the way we might not have got them.'

His words galvanised her. She looked around. There were other people on the launch. She saw Ami and Guy. The two others she didn't recognise.

Lev noticed her surprise. 'The G8 team. I thought you'd like to see Ami. . . and Guy who did all the tech work.'

'But where's Kirill?' She suddenly panicked as she realised she hadn't seen him leave the saloon.

'He can't be with us, Katya. You know that. He's an informer, he doesn't know we're G8. He must stay on the ship.' Lev spoke quietly.

'You mean he'll be arrested?'

He was silent.

'I don't want him arrested. He helped us.' Katya put out her hand, pleading. 'Please Lev.' She'd been about to say Kirill meant everything to her but she saw Lev's disapproving look and broke off.

'Come with me.' Lev turned and walked to the stern of the launch.

She followed him feeling confused–not knowing what was going on.

He stopped in the open stern area. The wind whipping his grey hair. He opened his packet of Abdullahs and took one out. He didn't speak until he had lit it with his lighter, shielding the flame with his hand.

'There isn't going to be any arrest,' he said.

She felt relief sweep over her. 'Thanks Lev. Thank you. I knew you'd make it all right.'

He studied her. 'I don't mean that.'

She didn't understand.

'What–he said slowly–What do you think will happen to those men we've just left in the *Igra's* saloon?'

She was bewildered by the question. 'They'll be prosecuted, won't they? Sent down for long prison terms.'

He pointed towards the *Igra*. 'That ship is in international waters. Who's going to prosecute them?'

She searched for an answer.

Lev went on, '*Igra* is registered in Jaio. They would be prosecuted there. How long do you think they will be on the island before they bribe their way out?'

She was stunned. 'Then what has all this been about?'

'The completion of your operation.' He took out a mobile phone from his inside jacket pocket. Pressed the send button.

The night sky lit up in a blinding flash that seared Katya's eyes. Hardly had it dimmed when the deafening thunder of the explosion burst into her ears.

She watched in horror as the *Igra* appeared through the smoke-filled sky in two flaming halves–upended. For a brief moment, the two halves stood there before they slowly sank–

disappearing under the waves into the cold dark ocean in a welter of spewing foam. The fires went out. A moment later the launch rocked crazily as a wave of water hit it. Then there was silence.

EPILOGUE

Katya opened the door to the Tac Room. She heard the hum of secret conversations and saw the coloured lines of vital information crisscross the giant plasma screens. This was where it had all begun–the nervousness when called to the Directors Conference Room– the thrill when chosen for her first op–the failure of her first mission to Kropse–the degradation in Dao . . .

Kirill.

Her love for him.

Her life with him obliterated.

She would never know whether he would have been faithful to her image of him. But she desperately wished she'd been given the chance to find out. Anything was better than the bleakness he'd left in her conscience. The realisation that in those last drowning seconds he must have known she'd betrayed him, leaving her with the painful shadow of loss, of guilt.

She felt someone join her. It was John. She was glad he was there and that she didn't have to make that dark journey to the conference room to confront him–them.

'What we–I–did was wrong,' she told him.

'Lev told me he'd explained that to you,' he replied, evenly.

'I'm Russian. Of course I understand why Belov and his *mafiya* had to die. It was only right. But Kirill . . . ' She stopped. It was too difficult to go on.

'Kirill was an informer. Part of them, not you.' Katya turned. It was Lev who'd come up–spoken the words she couldn't say.

He put his hand on hers. 'Look around you, Katya. You have proved you are part of us. Part of the G8 family. This is your future.'

Whatever that future held, for the moment her tears blurred it.

KATYA
DAVID BICKFORD

A couple of years have passed since the Libyan dictator, Gadaffi, was savagely murdered. The half billion dollars he embezzled from the Libyan people for his personal gain was stolen by a depravemoneylaunderer known only as Cartwright. Now, a rumour has reached Katya Petrovna, deputy director of the G8 intelligence agency, that Cartwright has been spotted at a luxury hotel development on the coast of Morocco.

Following the tip off Katya and her team head to the Sahara where her life dissolves into a terrifying nightmare as she discovers Cartwright is as violent and treacherous as he is corrupt.

Dredging up every art of manipulation and deception learned from her early life on the streets of Moscow and a dozen G8 operations, she stumbles blindly into

Cartwright's dark world of moneylaunderers, prostitution racketeers and terrorists.

As the screw turns Katya plunges deeper into danger. The pressure to find the money and return it to the Libyan people intensifies. Long buried conflicts from her past begin to surface. Is there a way she can escape to a life of freedom or should she overcome the whisperings and complete the deadly mission.

Whatever Katya has in mind. Cartwright has other thoughts.

ONE

The InterContinental Hotel in Gibraltar was not designed to create a meltdown. The architects had positioned it on a cliff overlooking the spectacular seascape of the Bay of Gibraltar. All the rooms glowed with soft colours and lighting and they induced a state of tranquility in everyone who stayed there. Everyone, that is, apart from Katya Petrovna. She was impatiently pacing her room, clutching her mobile to her ear, listening to John Hammond the Director General of the G8 Intelligence Agency being unhelpful. He was insisting on sending her on an operation for which, as his Chief of Operations, she knew she was underprepared. The target was hidden and dangerous.

Trying once more to make him see sense, she deployed sarcasm as her weapon of choice. 'Yes, John, I understand you've planned this op but I haven't. Look, we're chasing this man Ronald Cartwright for half a billion dollars, so tell me, why can't G8 simply fork out the cost of a drone to suss out if he actually *is* in this place in Morocco? Why some elaborate deception op when he probably isn't there at all?'

She listened to his reply, restlessly shifting her mobile from one hand to the other as she gazed out of the huge window at the sun rising over the sea. She'd just arrived from Tunis where she'd spent three weeks with her team trying to track down Cartwright and the cash he'd stolen. There was no sign of him which wasn't surprising as the man who'd been Gadaffi's moneylaunderer would surely know his way around North Africa – that is if he was still alive which, in her mind was questionable. Now John was shunting her off again, this time to some new hotel development in Sidi Ifni. Why? Because a rumour suggested Cartwright was financing it and might be there, inspecting his investment. 'This is yet another rumour, John, just the same as the one that sent me to Tunis. And that's not all - over the last six months some word on the street or other has sent me chasing off to Hong Kong, Singapore, Abu Dhabi and now Tunis without a single sighting of him. What's different about this Sidi Ifni tipoff.'

She shook her head, impatient as John argued some more – found another persuasive reason not to go. 'You agreed my team would have R and R here after that wild goose chase in Tunis. They deserve it.' She thought about that as John sent another blast down the WiFi. She'd so far been given no idea of what to expect when she got to Morocco. She was in the dark as to whether Cartwright would be protected by minders. Half a billion dollars would pay for a lot of heavies.

She interrupted him. 'How do I know Cartwright won't have protection when we get to Morocco? He ran with terrorists when he was alongside Gadaffi - you know that, and I've got to prioritise the safety of my team.'

Her mouth hardened as he, in turn, interrupted her. Waiting for her at the airport was a chartered helicopter he had arranged for her to fly to Morocco. He had also assembled her team and told her they would be waiting in the chopper. John had clearly made up his mind, and there was no budging him – if he said she had to go into this operation blind, she would simply have to go.

'God, you remind me of my father – bullying, arrogant – '

His retort incensed her even more.

'You might think there's a difference between a KGB colonel and the G8 DG but I – 'she got no further. John had cut the call.

Quickly, she took out her flight bag and threw in a change of clothing - khaki loose pants, loose button-down shirt, jacket, cap, sun cream. Clothes for Sidi Ifni and the desert heat.

On her way through the foyer she asked the concierge to make sure her room was kept for her. She felt she might be back.

Making her way to the hotel car park she climbed into the hired Mercedes and drove down Harbourview road towards the airport. Inwardly seething at John's high- handed management, she was glad she'd got in that jibe about the KGB. Not that there was really any comparison between John and her brutal father but as John's Operational Chief she wasn't about to let him think he could always walk over her.

Usually, the traffic threading down the steep roads to the air terminal was light. Not this time, though. She was stuck in a queue of stationary cars and trucks, the drivers variously hooting their horns or leaning out to shout curses.

She switched on the radio and used the time to think about Cartwright. He had started his working life as an accountant in London, soon finding he had a talent for shifting dirty money through the shady world of tax havens. Some years ago, word had reached G8 that he'd been picked up by Gadaffi's regime in Libya to work for the corrupt dictator. His job had been to hide Gadaffi's mountains of illegal oil revenues. Cartwright had hidden this revenue for him through crooked financiers in offshore centres. The job had lasted until Gadaffi was slaughtered by a mob of angry Libyans. Cartwright didn't hang around for the same fate. He'd left Libya in a hurry, rumoured to have with him Gadaffi's personal fortune - half a billion dollars in cash which he'd loaded into shoeboxes and put in a convoy of eight Toyota Landcruisers. The convoy had then disappeared into the desert. The new Libyan Government unsurprisingly wanted their cash back and had asked G8 to trace the money and recover it. So far, the cash hadn't turned up and no trace of it had been found in any of the international tax havens. Was it still in the shoe boxes or had Cartwright actually succeeded in laundering it into accounts across the world?

The world of Libyan politics was like an ill-lit mine shaft, shadowy and dangerous. So far, she thought sardonically, she hadn't even seen either Cartwright's shadow or any danger. But John was convinced he was out there somewhere and if he'd survived Gadaffi's regime, he was, without doubt, dangerous.

These thoughts were suddenly cut short as the tall lorry she was following abruptly turned down a side road. She saw a sign immediately in front of her pointing to the airport. Instantly, she swung the Mercedes to the right directly in front of a truck loaded with vegetables. She ignored the driver's loud horn blast, skimmed past its front fender and accelerated into the sharp turn and into the airport's short-term car park. Unruffled, she slid to a halt in one of the parking bays.

Katya dumped the car there and, with no time to display a ticket, grabbed her flight bag from the back seat, glanced at her watch and started to run towards the towering glass facade of the main terminal. Almost immediately she stopped. A person running drew attention, and drawing attention was simply bad practice for any intelligence agent. She forced herself to walk, falling into her customary long, swinging stride as she quickly threaded her way through the parked cars and made her way towards the terminal's main entrance.

Without stopping she edged past a family of tourists struggling with outsize suitcases and, wielding her flight bag like a shield, she rammed her way through a group of students into the terminal. She shivered suddenly as the cold air from the freezing air-conditioning cut through her. Ignoring the commercial passengers queueing in front of the public check-in desks, she strode purposefully to the special check-in area for air charter helicopter crews and passengers. She went up to the Immigration desk and thrust her passport across the tall counter towards the officer sitting on a high chair behind it.

'Quickly, please, I'm in a hurry,' she announced.

Without looking up, the officer put out his hand and took her passport. He adjusted his round, steel-rimmed spectacles, and then very deliberately and painstakingly leafed backwards and forwards through the visas stamped in it before going back to the first page. Katya watched him slowly moving his thin lips as he read every line. She fumed. How long did it take to read the words written there? Katya Petrovna, born Moscow, passport issued Moscow, Russia, the date... Just her luck to meet with a bored, by-the-book bureaucrat when she was in a hurry. She narrowed her eyes, noticing the grubby collar on his uniform and the hazy smell of alcohol on his breath. Angrily she tapped her fingers on the counter to try to get his attention. He deliberately ignored her, shuffling his right hand sideways along his desk until it found an 'I Love Gibraltar' mug. His fingers curled around the handle. She realized he wasn't simply doing his job, he was being awkward and difficult on purpose—for some reason. But what? Her passport was in order, nothing was suspicious. Suddenly she remembered the words of Andrei Savin her training officer at the Russian Federal Security Service in St Petersburg - "Never, never push an official if you're in a hurry"

Resentment burned inside her. She leaned over the desk pushing her face close to his. 'You see that chopper?' She pointed to the Augusta AW 101 helicopter sitting on the apron outside, its rotor blades slapping the air, ready for the urgent departure John had ordered. 'The take-off slot is in exactly four minutes and I'm the pilot.'

He looked up, seeing her for the first time, taking in the deep violet-blue eyes, and the long waves of auburn hair, and he immediately regretted not looking up sooner. A suggestive smile flickered across his face but it came too late. She had already snatched back her passport, and moved to the automatic glass door that led out onto the helicopter apron. In seconds, she was gone.

She sprinted across the helipad towards the chopper. A furnace of searing heat rose from the concrete, mingling with the heady kerosene fumes from the Augusta's exhaust. She was now close enough to the chopper's open pilot's door for the backwash from the five spinning blades to whip her hair across her eyes, stinging them. She blinked and, brushing the strands out of her eyes, saw her co-pilot, Cato, frantically beckoning to her, mouthing 'two minutes' and holding up two fingers.

Typical of his humour to laugh at her discomfort, she thought. She hefted her bag through the doorway and laughingly mouthed at him, 'Back at you.' Then pulled herself up into the cockpit and climbed into the pilot's seat.

She turned to him and shouted, 'Thanks for warming her up.'

Cato, a tall, well-built West Indian simply nodded his head, a short braid of black hair falling over his aviator sunglasses.

Turning sideways, Katya pulled at the open door and slammed it shut. Immediately, the noise of the blades was diminished.

She studied the instrument panel: navigation compass, digital map, altimeter, auxiliary tank fuel gauge. She looked at Cato. 'All preflight checks done? Navigation fed in?'

His sunglasses glinted as he nodded again and handed her a headset.

She put it over her hair, adjusted the microphone and glanced over her shoulder at the two agents sitting in silence in the seats behind her. Oleg, a tall, blonde Ukrainian with whom she'd done more missions than she could remember, and Yas, a tiny, raven-haired Iranian, known for being taciturn but fast on her feet. She knew them both intimately. They were both in their 30s, and, like Cato, dressed for this op as tourists, in tee shirts, chinos, trainers. They had no tattoos, no designer sunglasses, no rings, no jewellery—nothing that might make them memorable or mark them out in a crowd to identify them. John had chosen them well.

She saw them both give her an expectant look - their eyes reflecting alertness and restless energy, qualities which marked out the true intelligence officer. They were waiting for her to deliver the mission briefing, but she hadn't time and wasn't ready yet. She would have to make them wait in patience - the most difficult skill for any agent to learn.

A voice in the control tower came through her headset demanding her departure.

She ignored it and took an extra ten seconds to care for her team. 'Good to see you,' she said to them. 'Sorry you're straight on to the next op without any rest. Way it is, I'm afraid. Seat belts all on?' She paused. 'Good, next stop Morocco.'

She murmured into the microphone, glancing up at the control tower as if she could see the air traffic controller listening to her, and then, with a skilled, gentle movement, she opened the throttle, pulled up the collective and lifted the eleven tons of machinery off the pad in a slow, climbing arc.

A COLD WINTER
DAVID BICKFORD

Lev Leviatski, Soviet Political Adviser in Cold War Berlin is on the brink of treason. The young, enlightened Russian patriot is appalled by the news that Soviet troops are secretly massing on the Afghan border. He sees the pending invasion as a hole which will swallow the Soviet Union and destroy the Russia he loves and for which his parents died in the battle for Leningrad.

He tries to tell the Soviet command to pull back from the brink but the KGB, which he hates, silence him. So, secretly, he plans to create a major crisis in Berlin to alert the world to what is happening. The risks are enormous both for Lev and the wife and son he adores. And the risks increase as every move he makes is countered by the American Political Adviser, Mike Peterson, - a man who's determined that the Soviet Union must be smashed in the mountains of Afghanistan, so he can rescue the East German girl he loves.

As Lev plots and counterplots, he descends into a savage battle for supremacy over Peterson, ruthlessly shattering the lives of innocent Berliners to gain any advantage. A fight which flashes into such intensity, he forgets that, in the dangerous labyrinth of the underworld of the East West undeclared war, the KGB is silently waiting.

Will Lev be able to expose the truth and prevent an impending invasion? Or will he meet his downfall at the hands of his fiercest rivals? Find out in this electrifying tale of espionage, power, loyalty and love.

ACKNOWLEDGEMENTS

My heartfelt thanks for all the hard work, dedication, and support the whole team has provided throughout the journey of bringing this book to market. It has been an incredible experience to work with such a talented and committed team, and I am deeply grateful for your contributions.

My publishers Pj and JD at Coinkydink are outstanding, and all my thanks go to them for making this such an exciting journey.

So many thanks to Sue Poulsen, a special editor.

Photographer: Adam Whitehead - @adamwhiteheadphotography

Stylist: Natasha Royt - @natasharoyt

Jacket Designer: James Macey - **blacksheep-uk.com**

Interior Jacket: Lorna Reid

Web Design & Hosting: Ryan Hawkes - **pretzelfilms.com**

Press & Marketing: Hannah Ashcroft

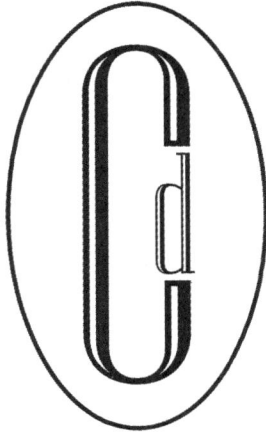

www.coinkydink.co.uk

FOR EXCLUSIVE CONTENT AND MORE INFORMATION ON DAVID, VISIT

www.davidbickford.co.uk